Or,

The Antediluvians

A Novel

K Hank Jost

i

This is a work of fiction. Names, characters, places, and incidents are the product of the author's imagination, and should not be confused with your idea of reality.

Published in the United States and Canada by Whisk(e)y Tit: www.whiskeytit.com. If you wish to use or reproduce all or part of this book for any means, please let the author and publisher know. You're pretty much required to, legally.

ISBN 978-1-952600-38-8

Cover design and original illustrations by Justine-Juliette.

Editing and oversight by Stefan O. Rak.

MADSTONE

...Winds or storms in particular arise when God moves further away from the earth. In the circumstances contrary to the Order of the World which have now arisen this relation has changed– and I wish to mention this at the outset–the weather is now to a certain extent dependent on my actions and thoughts; as soon as I indulge in thinking nothing, or in other words stop an activity which proves the existence of the human mind such as playing chess in the garden the winds arise at once. [...] The reason for this is simply that as soon as I indulge in thinking nothing God, presuming that I am demented, thinks he can withdraw from me...

-Judge Daniel Paul Schreber, 1842-1911

March

I.

Cracking across the cheeks, saccharine, innocuous, hollow, and baring teeth that would sooner cut out their tongue than stoop to honesty; at the bell, a smile:

"Welcome, y'all! Come on in, get dry. Come on, come on. Don't be shy." Cashier waddles out from behind the register. Churned lumpen by life, everything sour squeezed out of her. Reaches first for the child jumping squelchy-shoed on the doormat, soft-yeared Naseer, wrist held tight by his mother, Angela. Sets then to loosing the jacket from his shoulders. "Don't want you dripping all over the candy, now do we, sweetheart?"

Angela descends to assist. Dress forcing knees together, pumps peeling away as the angles change. Sloughs sleeves to release. "Sorry about all this," she says, "it was cats and dogs earlier and we just—"

The afternoon: Unseasonably frigid and wet, overcast in the sweated dregs of a cold front fallen from somewhere inconceivably northern. The threat of more icy fists, splash over splatter, has sent the whole Cobbles shopping for shelter.

"Not to worry, dear! Not to worry! Weather this time the year is strange. Hard to pin." Cashier stands again, folding the shoulders of Naseer's little suit-coat. "Y'all sure do look nice though. Lord in heaven, you'd think it was already Easter!" Arms out to the two men. Naseer's father, Jawad, unshoulders his houndstooth and folds it once before handing it over. His elder brother, Rohaan, digs out a several-times folded slip of paper from an inner pocket before letting his oversized navy-blue jacket off. Drops the slip into his shirt's breast pocket. A palm pat assures it secure.

Cashier presses the jackets to her chest, a show at ignoring their soaking into her t-shirt. Bends at the waist, looks behind the counter for somewhere to place them: "Don't usually get many customers this time the year, especially when it's like this outside. Where is it y'all're visiting from?"

Rohaan grins. With as much molasses as he can muster: "Born and raised, sugar. Born and raised right here. Madiston-made."

She's found a milk crate up under the counter. Flips it to receive, drops in the mess of cloth. Head rises then, cocks curious, "That so?"

"Oh, yes'm, you betcha–" Rohaan starts but, finger through belt loop, a jerk from behind flattens his hackles.

"Reckon, reckon we've got all kinds out here these days." Again: Smiles. Cheeks high and tight, smushing her eyes. "Country is indeed a melting pot. Just melting and melting and melting." Button on the register. A lever. Another bell, sharp and hard. The machine's drawer shoots open. A ream of ones. Licks her thumb.

Rohaan blindly bats his brother's finger off his belt. Glances over his shoulder: Family standing there with the weight of the day dragging their foreheads to hang off their chins. Angela's got the squirming child sat in the crook of her arm. Kicking shoes muddy the midsection of her dress. Rohaan's lips thin. Teeth take their tongue. Hands slip fisted away into their pockets.

Jawad, nodding toward the pastel aisles and variform displays, toward the plastic metropolis of dead sugar: "Shall we?"

–A real question there. Unusual. Nothing of the foreman. Supposed to fall out as lawful writ recited from memory, but that was, well, would wager perhaps that the brevity or ambivalence of the whole affair had gotten to him. Duress. Professionalism. Dispassion. Apathy. Doctors and nurses are the worst about it, can't expect much more from a lawyer. Make a fella feel small, though. The slow sifting through files, knowing Dad's just another name smashed between manilla leaves. The attempts made at small talk. Client. Representation. Easy to get put-off. Understandable. Executor. Deceased. The deceased. Dad. Even *your father* drawn out once or twice, doesn't feel quite right. Just say his name. Something bubbling inside, stomach flip that portends of outburst. Understand that desire to shout, moreover that feeling like you can't, because that's what's really the worst. Who cares about want? Want all the time always constantly, only becomes unbearable when it's made clear that the desire can't be sated. Shaking there on the floor years ago begging that poor woman, what was her name? Spent forever in detox and group and can't remember her name, but remember that cold No sir, Mister Al-Zahrani. No sir, Mister Rohaan, I can't give you anything right now. You'll just have to ride it out like everyone else. I know. I know. But, I know, you can call me whatever dirty words you like, but I know. Just have a glass of water here. Look, here's some ice, just say his name at the very least, say it somewhere other than in the will. A will was written so a will had to be read. Could have been easier though, cut out all the fanfare. Hand it over and everyone can go. The leftovers of a life barely lived. Honestly. Few assets other than liquidity. House a lease, so that's a bust. That ancient and failed attempt at a sedan only good for parts, so split the piddle with Jawad but, no land or heirlooms or secrets or anything like that. Should have just done at the start what it was all building to from the get, skip the legal poetry and slide over the checks. $12,757.43 each. Half to Jawad and half to the failson, combine them and there's the real value of Dad's life.

Slow in the motion at the end of it, rust on the gears as Jawad rose from his seat. Shook hands. Thank-yous. His half of a split soul in his billfold. Clear on his face that the numbers were what truly rang the knell. Week-and-a-half of contacting relatives and making funeral arrangements kept it all at a distance. Hadn't been there when Dad's body died, only heard it through a cellphone speaker, delivered tinny, distant, and rehearsed as the evening news. Didn't see, didn't see the whole thing. Didn't hold his purpling finger as the I.V. dripped clockwork gobs of thick liquid bliss. Didn't count the breadth of the valleys between his heart's waning preponderances. Hadn't said, as everything came to a halt, "See, Papa, it's good stuff. It's really good stuff, isn't it?" No. Jawad hadn't cried those hot and quiet tears, a brief sun-shower, just enough to knock the building boil from the air–

"Yeah, yeah. Let's get after it." Rohaan takes the first steps further onto the sales floor, but the moment Naseer's feet find flat they leave him in the dust. Zooming past and into the cloying thick of it.

"You keep an eye on that one, Albert!" Cashier shouts across the store to a man behind a low wall-and-plexiglass-pane partition, set about operating an unburdened taffy-pulling machine. Centerpiece of the establishment. Whirrs and jangling, chains clanking. Empty arms. An arcane juggling routine.

Albert looks up bewildered behind a set of arboreal brows and, catching sight of the child, chuckles from a mouth sparsely poplared with teeth of caramelized driftwood. Flips the machine off and hollers at Angela, tailing Naseer best her heels'll allow: "That'n yours, sweetheart?"

"Yessir." She says catching him up by his armpits before he can get his grubby hands in the bulk bins, "Sorry to let him loose like this. I just–"

"Nah, nah, now. Don't you worry a bit about it. Scoop him up and bring him on up here. I'll show him something neat. Show him a real-life dinosaur."

Dough too sticky to yet knead by hand, Naseer gives no credence to Angela's manipulations until she hisses at him, "Sit still, Na-nah. Still. Let's go talk to the nice man." Marches him then over to the partition, lifting him so that he can see over the smudged clarity.

"Watch out now!" Albert says. Hands gloved in thick rubber grab and dig into either side of a massive, melty log of cooling sugar. Albert wrestles the lazy gator and throws it atop the taffy-puller's arms. Looks over at the confounded child, "Ready, boy?"

Naseer is mute. The molten, glassy slab slumps toward ribbon.

Angela, singsong: "Want him to make the candy, Na-nah?"

Naseer smiles from the other side of comprehension and nods, "Yeah, candy. Candy, candy, can–!"

Flip of the switch and the machine jumps to life. Naseer tiptoes and shimmies startled along the wall's edge at the suddening.

"What, what is it, Mama?"

"I don't know, honey," hands pressing to his swelly baby belly to hold him steady. "Why don't you ask the nice man?"

Summoned by the whispers, Albert moves away from the machine. Brows bolt up to flash glaucously silver eyes. "What do you think of her there, Captain?" Thumb shot back in the direction of the continuous ordeal: Taffy lightening in color with every stretch. Deep red rising dawn to pink.

Mouth agape. Glistening threat of drool at the corners. Naseer looks away and up to this strange man. One word, one question: "Candy?"

"Oh! Oh yes, indeed! Got a smart one here, don't you ma'am?" Decades-dulled teeth. Smiles brown down to the child. "Good old-fashioned, true-blue, honest-to-goodness, saltwater taffy. Nothing in this world better."

"Salt, salty candy?"

"No, no, no. Nothing of the kind." Back over to the machine to guide a wayward lump into the fray. "See, it's, well, what's your name, son?"

Naseer looks up at his mother, a quizzical furl twisting his forehead.

"Go ahead, tell the nice man your name."

"My, my name is–"

"Naseer," Angela slides in, "his name is Naseer. Isn't that right, Na-nah?"

"Oh, well I'll have to agree with you there, Captain. It is certainly indeed quite *nice in here.*"

No laughter finds the occasion fit. Sound of machinery.

"Well," Albert picks up the routine again, "how old, how old you reckon Miss Sue here is? How old, Mister Nice-N-Here, how old you reckon old Sue here is?"

Chews on his lip. Eyes looking for distraction or exit, but then grins and: "A one-hundred!" A burble of belly laughs follow the exclamation. Settles into another outburst: "A one-hundred and a million of years old!"

"Oh! Hey there, almost! Closer the first time, Mister Nice Guy. Here," plucks a blue plug swirled with an orange stripe from a barrel of surplus taffy, "that's for good guesswork. Go far in life you can manage to guess right most of the time! But, yessir, old Sue here is darn near a hundred whole years old. Ninety-seven come July, I reckon." Angela takes the candy from Naseer's clumsy hands and sets to unwrapping it for him. "See, my daddy, Papa Brown, built this here machine with his bare hands. Can you believe it? With his own two hands. Whole thing hisself with all the machine learning he'd learned in the army. Yessir, and ma'am, come home from the Big War and was gonna open hisself a candy store. Said seeing what it was he'd saw'd make any man appreciative of the sweeter things in life–"

Pleasant autumn sets about his eyes as Rohaan reads the labels of the sweets on display and listens in on the familiar beginnings of the confectioner's story–Hasn't changed a lick, has it? Same fella? No real way to know, but the story remains. Untouched or altered, surviving since fieldtrips. Studied the 'colonial period' every year it seemed. End of the eighth day to somewhere around the second time the world fought itself, birthed all the fixins that this place and people still decorate themselves with. Bus down to the Cobbles along the Bay and get a taste of history. Carriage ride along the water. Po' boy lunch. Authentic. Real stuff recreated over upon over. Story always starts with the patriarch, the Big Dad, round-bellied and good-natured, slow of heart but stuck around longer than anybody'd given him hope of. Krauts didn't kill him, so what the hell else was gonna try? Built the machine like he'd just said, own bare hands. Sometimes even invented it himself, out of thin air and good cheer. Brief explanation of the nature of the machine, right? Gotta pull the taffy to get it aerated so that it, that's why it's all fluffy. But it's never actually fluffy, just sticky and sweet and, yeah, yeah, all the different flavors all taste the same basically as well, just nothing but corn sugar and a suggestion. 'But,' inevitably through the chews of a window-toothed smartass, 'why saltwater when it ain' even salty tasting? Is there saltwater in it or anything like that or what?' And the answer is always 'No, not at all! Nothing of the kind!' but that gets the next movement of the tale rolling, the part about the storm. Big Dad. Big War. Big Storm. Bible shit. Sounds like when you boil it down, like the parts the counselors didn't ever read from when they get started in on the actual program, the pieces without forgiveness, where God acts like a god. In brief: Big storm comes through, floods everything, whole town, whole street, everything. Courthouse, library, factory. Symphony orchestra paddling out of the concert hall using the cellos and basses and kettledrums as rafts. Old fisherman in the middle of it catches something big, tries reeling it in but just drags his boat over the open water, fights the fish for days before the ebb reveals the hook was snagged on the church spire, water rose *that* high. Caught Christ with a dime-store jig! Big Dad. Big War. Big Storm. Water comes back down, and everyone's got to piece what's left of their lives together. All Papa Brown's got is the candy store. Nothing left but the machine and a few barrels of taffy soaked soggy with the sea. Well, Papa Brown, ever the wit, gets set to selling. Put food on the table, sell what you can, call it famous saltwater taffy before anybody knows about it, authentic famous original saltwater taffy and, lo and fucking behold it all, not a person in town or county's got a complaint about the salty flavor! Everyone, in fact, loves it! Papa Brown sells it all. Machine, Sue, well, Sue survived but she's just got a bit of a purr now, bit of a shake, so let that, down to the children gathered, so let that be a lesson in perseverance and since everyone loved it so much Papa Brown kept the name saltwater taffy in the happily-ever-afters, all the way to this day, and well, why then, why then don't y'all put salt in it no more? Why then, why then does every tourist trap candy store up along the Atlantic make the same claim? Everyone's got a Big Dad and Big War and Big Storm—

Rohaan's hand rises to press again his breast pocket as Old Albert wraps up his spiel and relieves the sugary mass from its contrapted contortions. The check is still there, crinkling lightly beneath the dress-shirt's thin fabric. Eyes scan the store for Jawad, but he's nowhere to be seen. Angela's got the child now picking wax-paper wrapped plugs of taffy from the bulk bins, reverent now that there's a myth above it all. Rohaan peeks outside and finds Jawad half-a-block's length down the Cobbles. Leaned against a wall. Facing the Bay. Smoking away.

"Thought you'd quit," he says on his approach.

"Same." Winks an eye as an acrid curl climbs his cheek. Produces the pack from his slacks' pocket, "Need?"

"Angela won't say anything?"

"Given the circumstances, reckon we'll all tread lightly for a bit. Keep the pet peeves in their kennels..."

—Sure, sure. Know what this is though. This gesture. Code for 'don't leave me alone.' Not an invitation for conversation but a plea for silent accompaniment, for someone to keep an eye on you so that you'll not disappear—"Ah, alright. Just this once. For Dad, in memory..."

Jawad's face remains stony as Rohaan flicks the flame for his first cigarette in years.

Rain's stopped. Sky's leaden matte is beginning to crack. White sunlight cleaving tracts in the clouds. Canyons of mercy blue. Almost light enough now. A few people have returned to walk over the Cobbles, no longer holed-up in kitschy shoppes. Collapsing their umbrellas as a petrichor sweetened gust gives the all-clear. Horse-and-buggy drivers lined along the brick seawall set to defrocking their steeds of their big rain-slickers. Threatening a nice day after all this bone-chilling, miserable drizzle.

Rohaan finishes his cigarette woozy-headed, lead-lunged, and slug-blooded; looks out toward the Bay for something kind to focus on until the nausea fades. Figure along the stone wall: Grey hoodie, leaning on its elbows. Holds a palm out to check for undetected rain. Flicks the hood off. Stringy brown hair falls over a sallow, unshaven face. Scritchy reddish tufts burnish the cherubic softness of his cheeks. Rohaan turns away from the young man's potential line of sight–Hate seeing co-workers in the real world–From the hoodie's front pocket, the young man produces his own pack of cigarettes. Flips the lid and counts–Four and a lucky–Sucks his teeth–Thought for sure there were more. Gotta cut down. Can't just throw around money springing for smokes. Have one now, cool. One now and then not another until back at home. Not another until Jess, until it's all straightened-out in here, up top, in the mind. Took the walk. Stretched the legs. Got the blood moving. Just gotta get back now–

She'd been reading on the porch, frying the resin out of last night's cashed bowl:

"There's still some of that stuff Obbie gave us," said as the boot's laces crossed through their eyes, "In the desk drawer. No need to smoke resin."

"I know, Bucky. But that stuff's for special occasions."

"Gotcha," shook his feet to make sure they were on right and tight. "Well, alright, babe. I'm gonna take a walk, get my head on like it's–"

"Supposed to rain any minute now, B." She was sat on a rattan lawn chair, sweater stretched over knees at her chest. Bundled and comfy.

"Yeah, yeah," kicked a snubbed butt off the porch, "I'll be back soon. Just gotta get some juices flowing before I start in." Stepped then onto the first stair down.

"The stuff is looking great by the way..."

"What's that?" Turned back around.

"The paintings. They're looking really great. Really coming along." Smiled.

Buck smiled back and popped a cigarette twixt his lips, "Thanks, babe... I'll be back in a bit and we can make lunch, alright? Love you, Jess."

"You too, B. Have a nice–"

Waited to get out of the neighborhood, to where the live oaks make way for the Murphy side of Harris Park's vast expanse, to where the Jefferson Street Housing Project, the brick-and-brooding *Jaspers*, leans cathedralic over the east, tearing toward the sky in a tumbling promise, before pulling out his phone, connecting his earbuds, and opening the web-browser.

First time through the video: A minor eternity. Dismal conditions of the sidewalk on North Murphy caught him dragging his feet more than once. Phone screen up only inches from his face. Hyper compressed sops and moans crackling in his ears, speakers on their last leg. Took note of everything he could see in the room she was in, every possible identifying feature. Eyes darted over the writhing pearly expanse of her increasingly naked and splayed body, coming to rests in the scene's periphery. Edge of the mattress. Leg of the desk or chair. Windowsill. Plastic water bottle stuffed with dryer sheets and grimy black cotton balls–Boilerplate amateur pornography. Lighting, angle, grain, all unsavory and plainly unerotic. Known the whole of her for long enough that nothing on this screen could possibly offer a surprise–Thumb dragged the node of the progress bar back to the start before it faded to black–The room itself looks foul. That how it really is? That dirty? Faking the throes or not, room looks godawful. Carpet that sticky? Bed that sunken? Air all dusty and, is her skin really that thin, cheeks that caved?–

His head came up as the rain came down. Looked around for an awning through the grey sheets and–Goddammit–8th and Smith bus stop shelter. Had walked all the way to within two blocks of the Museum on his day off. Jogged over to the little glass enclosure, postered-up with service-change notices as incomprehensible as they were inconvenient. Sat on the bench as the world around him was swallowed up in curtains of frigid shower. Thumbed again the node, back to the start–Saw fit to blindfold herself. Rather full scope of the rest of her though. Christ, *she* even looks dirty writhing around in all that filth–

Once the rain had settled, he rose to walk again. His feet carried him toward the water, to the Cobbles. Hadn't been there all winter–Maybe even since moving into town tail-end of last summer–

After a drag, Buck turns back to face the Bay. Leans his elbows on top of the wall. Water frothing greenly below. Mind so cluttered it may as well be empty. In the distance a cloud bank splits and drops ladders to illuminate Riley Island's rising from the horizon. Lazily breaching leviathan. The Ferry cuts wakes across the water on its way to Riley's bayside docks. No tourists are yet packed onto the deck, just a few eternally sunburnt surf-fishers who know that the fish bite best after a downpour. Again, Buck's phone rises from his pocket. Thumb runs the progress bar back to the start.

&&&

–Clockwork cliché. Again every time the same as the last. Same as the same is the same as. Endless variation reduced to a singular variant, and that's what they repeat. Say it just like the plaque on the wall. **'Guests Get All The Glory'** then some faltering verbatim. The Belchard family history woven out from worn yarn. Ignore the fibers' fray. Threadbare is the term for the tale, told fit to clothe the Emperor. Gonna tell it like that, may as well just read directly from the plaque, make no pretentions toward extemporizing, toward expertise. Beat the drum despite the broken skin.

"Now children," every time bending slightly at the waist as if in their ivory they tower so terribly, "this gallery is a very special place for the Museum and our community. Everything on display here once belonged the Belchard family, who I'm sure you're all quite familiar with." Docent's eyes then'll rise to make contact with the teacher's or chaperone's or group leader's or whatever whoever it may be to confirm that the children are familiar with at the very least the generalities of the Madiston Mythos. Then it's, "Now so let's direct our attention back to me and let's all do what we talked about before we started in on our tour, let's all get our imagination engaged..." It's good advice, honestly. Really have to imagine, damn near hallucinate, to see this display as anything other than what it is.

"So let's all now, everyone now, let's all close our eyes and, yes even you Miss," then a name already forgotten, "let's all close our eyes and gentlemen, all the boys, let's imagine ourselves in some suits, some just perfectly dashing suits with some, maybe some ruffles in the front and on the collar and big brassy buttons, maybe a cane and now, now the little ladies, all the girls now let's put on in our mind just the most lavishly beautiful gowns we can possibly imagine, spray ourselves with expensive perfume and burden our delicate necks and wrists with just the most divinely ostentatious jewelry, and let's all smile big for our debut among this teeming throng Eugenia has gathered for us in her mansion's ballroom and, and, yes, and, on the count of three, on the count of three we'll all, direct your gaze upward, eyes still shut, but be ready and look up and on the count of three we'll all open our eyes and witness for ourselves the–"

Centerpiece of the whole exhibit: the Grand Chandelier. Hanging above everything, rendering it kitsch and trifle. Blooming out in all its crystal from a gold ceiling rose. Same as, the very same, yes indeed, hers in fact, yes, Eugenia Belchard's Grand Chandelier! "One of the late nineteenth century's masterworks of craftsmanship. Yes, we're all very lucky to witness its shimmering glory," though, and they always skip it, excuse being that the information is on the plaque should anyone be interested enough to pry further, that what hangs above everyone now is at best seventy percent original, at best but the plaque doesn't say that exactly either, says more that this now above everyone *is* seventy percent of the original, which is very different from the truth indeed. The truth contains that *at best,* or more accurately *at most,* remove the quality from quantity and recollect honestly that it's written somewhere and read at some point that *the most it can now possibly be is* seventy percent as it was but is much more likely, probably, even not accounting, mind, for the alterations the Preparators had to make in seventy-four, year of the tiger, ox, or rabbit can't ever remember which of those but definitely Christmas of, Christmas season moreover, of nineteen seventy-four, fourteen or fifteen then, Christmas season of nineteen seventy-four and they had to bore a bunch of holes in it, through the metal arms to run wires through to hook the lights up to so that it can glow like it does now. Incandescent. But, not accounting for that, most of the crystal shards are certainly replacements and, read somewhere at some point, diagrams even so maybe at the College, maybe in one of Uncle Reggie's local history folders that he'd had bound when he was doing that project about local history or maybe just loose papers on his desk, either way point is that the Belchard Estate, northeast along Salt Creek just far enough away, was bequeathed to the city long before the city decided to do anything with it so all this shit now here on display sat in the mansion abandoned and falling apart and even that the Chandelier itself had fallen from the ceiling and, remember the diagrams from the manufacturer, dated 1889 so plaque's got that wrong as well, ten years, 1899 make it read like it's some sort of millennium piece or something but, manufactured say in 1889 but shipped and mounted there for the millennium ball up at the mansion on the estate, either way best to be clear on the details because the thing was absolutely massive so no way that even this monstrosity up here now is seventy percent, at best it's "a crystalline testament to the wealth and opportunity the Belchard family afforded to late-reconstruction-era Madiston."

Ladle it thick there. Rich mother sauce of *noblesse oblige*. Grow out from the Chandelier's cherished complexities a convenient abridgement of Madiston's history: Small fishing village to modest port city to its final fabulous moment just before the present where culture flourished and the arts were alive and well and this Museum really meant something. Link it all back to Belchard's Draught Fine Brown Ale, frosty mug of the Ol' Buford, still drunk to this day by all locals in libational obligation even though for decades now it's been brewed in giant vats near the Great Lakes and bottled in climes where English isn't even a second language.

Docent's spiel wraps up with an encouragement for the little public-school chickadees to take some time and explore all that this grand marble and dark oak hall has to offer. Glass enclosed displays of tintypes and cutlery, porcelain and lace, inkwells and feather-pens, all authentically *Belchard*. Items not yet alien enough to be artifacts. Opulence fit to break the imagined cotillion to shambles. Say then, with a smile and wink at the Docents: "And if y'all've got any questions, children, feel free to run 'em by me! I'm all ears and answers!"

A harmless jab scrambling the distinction between Educational Staff and the lowly Attendants. Never fails to ruffle their feathers and purse their lips. Can't do anything about it. Only have to worry four days out the week and kids usually lack to gumption to talk to strangers anyway. A few of the Docents even have good enough humor to play along and say in charming condescension, "Of course children, ask our Mister Carl here anything you like. He's certainly full of stories to tell." The children meander then, lost in their imagined pomposity, sent back to earth by smudged glass cases keeping it all out of reach and drifting further out into the voidful realm of disinterest. Problem there. Hard to know something without touching it, hard to believe in stories whose secrets are hidden.

Walk by where they're clumping. Bunched-up around the tintype and photograph display. Portraits of each Belchard up to the final greatest-granddaughter in sixty-eight. Family tree. Interest waning from the children's faces. They'll soon waddle away, go look at the bejeweled utensils or mindlessly walk along the wall waiting for an adult to give them the gathering call. Then one says, now, pressing his finger to the glass in the way specifically prohibited, pointing at the branch that blooms into a portrait of Mister Buford Belchard himself: "That's the man my Daddy drinks."

Swoop in there: "I see your father is a man of discerning tastes."

"My Daddy is a—"

Descend all popping-kneed and, "Do you know who that man is?"

Always the same. Little boy's face scrunches up at the rise of a question he'd not thought to ask, moreover that he'd considered answerable. "That's the man on my Daddy's bottles that he drinks. My Daddy drinks beer at night and that man is on his face, that man's face is on the bottle of it."

"Ah, very good. But, do you know, do you know why that man is on that bottle? Do you know who that man is?"

"No, is he—?"

"Let's wait now, wait now, let's not go about guessing so quickly now. Let's think about it a little bit, let's think it over before we–" The other children in the clutch begin to slink away. All the same, he'll tell them all about it on the bus ride back to the school. "Why do you think that man is on the bottle?"

"Is it cuz he–?"

"Don't guess now, son. C'mon. No guessing. Let's do the work. If we don't know, let's make some observations and work out from there. How's that sound?"

Catch his feet then turning toward where the rest of his group has gone. Best pose a question to engage the inquiry, none of this doddling.

"Go on, let's look at him. What can you say about him from this picture?"

Boy looks back up and, "Is he angry?"

"Well, what do you think? Does he look angry?"

"Uh-huh..."

"Great. Why do think he would be angry?"

"I don't know–"

"Well! Let's do the workings out then. What else can we maybe say about his picture?"

"Is it–?"

"Well, first off, it's rather old isn't it?" May have to just help the child along here. Not going to get anywhere. Best way to teach something as inscrutable as deductive reasoning is sometimes just to do it, can't explain it outside of itself maybe. May have to just: "It is. Don't see pictures like this very much anymore, do we? Almost never unless we're here in the Museum looking at them behind glass like this, right? Right. So, very old then, picture is quite very old. Back then, though, if it's as old as we right now think it is, back then being in a picture was, having your picture taken moreover, was very expensive to do, so what can we maybe assume about this man here if we know that then?"

"Is he, maybe he is rich?"

"Right! Exactly. Probably has a lot of money! So, now this, now this next part I'm going to have to guide you through because you might be a little young to know all of this yet, but here's a big secret. If he's rich that means he's probably very important as well, because, even though you'll hear the opposite as you grow-up never forget this, it's impossible to be rich and of no importance and it's pointless to be important if you can't be rich off of it. Now so, he's very important because he's very rich, very important also because we remember him, he's in a museum and your father drinks the beer he's on. Right. So, why. So, how and why could a man so rich to have his picture taken and so important to be on beer bottles even though his picture is very old and important enough to be in a museum, how can and why does he look so immiserated in this picture?"

"Is he sick, maybe?"

"Holy cow!" Shoot up again. Knees back all fire and crack. Hands on hips and a grin, "That, son, is as good a deduction as any and a kinder guess than most." Rub the child's head on the way back to crouching, "But, sadly, we're a tad bit off in our conclusion. See, I think it *was* a sickness that took him in the end, but still that's almost everyone that's ever been has that story, something with his liver if I remember correctly, so no, see, see, it's got more to do with how long it took to take a photograph back then, couldn't be expected to smile all the way through so you'd have to–"

A piercing whistle cuts through the Ballroom's marble echo. Docent calling all the children back to gather and move on. Always just before the root of the thing can even be dug up, never enough time to tell the children the whole of it. Have to know the myth in full before the facts can be found out of it. Got to meet the man before knowing why Daddy drinks him–

&&&

She steps away from the car. Derek leans across the empty passenger seat and commands through the open window: "Hey, you're gonna be alright. Okay?"

Stops cold on the muddy lawn. Crosses her arms. "Promise me." Smirks.

"I can't make the promise if you're the one keeping it."–He's a good man. Know that. Know it breaks his heart leaving like this–

"Fine. Then, *I* promise."

"Promise what?" Car jerks forward a touch as he leans further across the center console, foot lifting a moment's breadth off the brake.

"Promise I'll be alright."

"That's right."

"Right."

"So, Tuesday?" asked like every Friday night the past six months.

"Actually, Monday next week."

Cocks his head. Puppy registering its name, "Monday?"

"Yeah, there's that meeting in the morning. They want everyone there. I don't know why they don't just send an email or whatever but Miss Shareese said it's mandatory so–"

"No problem. Monday it is."

"Bright and early."

"Yes ma'am."

–Urge is always strongest in this brief leaving silence. 'Love you' rests right there on the teeth. The need for a morning smoke. Tempting and easy, but perhaps maybe even bettered by the delay. A waste of words better spent when the water's a bit higher. Safe enough to assume though, calm the heart and dry the palms, safe enough definitely to assume that he wants to say it, that he believes it himself. So just, be fine, be content and even happy in the silence, the lull, the soft void around the topic of love, of plans, of the future. These miles feel further than they are, especially when both parties are working so much of the week and only one's got something to run away from–

Car pulls away and drives a touch up the dead-end stretch. Rolls into a neighbor's driveway and backs out to turn around. Pulls past her and the house again and Derek blats the horn. She nearly leaves her skin. Before she can turn round to raspberry him down, Derek's rocketing away, tires kicking up clumps of wet gravel. He's not got far to go, but it's a ways enough away to guarantee her totally alone.

Taillights swallowed by night and Aura turns to the house. Windows dark save for the widest ones on the far side, glowing a pale blue–Never stop flickering. Never ever stop flickering. Curtains there cover whatever it is that Mother is watching but do nothing to shut out the flicker. Speaker woofing even audible out here in the yard and, no way in hell the neighbors don't notice, don't see and hear it. Volume only ever cut when Mama's comatose and wouldn't wake for a second coming or when blinding migraine tears have carved enough snotty glisten to get her to concede, pleading past the pain at the foot of her recliner. No doubt neighbors have a nickname for the house. Lived here for years, this decidedly *sub*-urban development on the outskirts of Cortland County's inland border. Flat and sandy namelessness distinguished by post office and post office alone, devoid of any life more ambitious than crabgrass, air repugnantly redolent with the fumes of the nearby rendering plant. Never once spoke with any of the neighbors, only things evidencing life are the lights on in their houses and the routine disappearance and reappearance of minivans and pox-painted sedans in the driveways–

Aura digs in her uniform jacket's pockets for the cigarette she'd bummed from Derek as they pulled up–Have the last one before heading to bedlam–Perches the butt in the corner of her mouth. Searches then for the lighter. Comes up empty-handed–Goddammit, could have sworn it was, maybe fell out in the car. Certainly had it at the bar. Bummed it out to Buck and Jess a few times. Nice seeing her tonight. Been a minute. Less and less of her lately. Must've taken winter pretty hard. Understandable. First year on the coast, not used to the unwavering inclemency. No one ever talks about that. Endless days raining sideways, wind sending everything up. Everything always stays wet all year. Never think about that when someone says the word 'coast' or 'ocean,' mental image is always just sunshine and breeze. Get that for maybe three weeks in the summer before the storms start up. Then the autumn lag. Air settles and smells like memories, sun sinks in the middle of the day one day and it's just cold and wet until it's hot and wet again. Good to see her though. Good to see Buck seeing her. Arm around her waist the whole time. Eyes darting around before kissing her cheek. Thinks no one sees. Started to feel guilty having Derek around. David and Derek kicking in the door of St. Never's, buying a round, laughing loud, smelling like sweat and grease and smoke and hadn't even given him the chance to take a shower tonight, just one more drink or two, another smoke with Buck and Jess making googly eyes at each other and then off to his place north side of Salt Creek, off to bed, one last roll around before the weekend and Mama–

No dice. No spark.

Checks her phone for the time–Christ, how long in the sheets? Best hope she's already asleep. Maybe a lighter somewhere in the kitchen–

Aura pockets the cigarette and walks the squishy length of the lawn to the front door. Every step the sound of the television in the living room grows. Incessant infomercial driving through the walls and out into the world.

Certainly early, but not a bit bright. Whatever sleety system it was that rolled through this weekend has now decided to roost before again taking flight. Still coming down. His shoes haven't dried since getting caught in it three days ago—Best weather for hangovers. Beats the hell out of being rot-gutted in the hot mug of summer. Every sip, dog's hair or holy water, just pours right back out. Skinned in cheesecloth—

Buck closes his eyes and faces the steely sky. Cold rain runs rill over the hill of his nose and cheeks, pools in the pucker of his lips. A dribble or two on the tongue to wash his teeth of their scuzz. Takes a sopping seat under the bus shelter. Southbound D. Murphy and Harris Park. Smoke curls lazy from the end of his morning's first and rolls dice in his belly, frustrates further the fists behind his brows. Across the street, the northbound shelter, a figure is laid up on the bench despite the dolphin-toothed hostility. Its head hangs from the bench's edge, like to fall off its shoulders—Fella's either blissed beyond retrieval or deader than a forgotten story. Either way, reckon nothing to be done. Heard that the city's tried everything shy of corralling and shipping them all westward like they say's been done up in Cortland County, up around the beaches. Harris Park and its junkies, inseparable. Immune in their inebriation to any natural discomforts or municipally applied deterrents. Warms the heart a bit even to see one that's sought shelter from the rain, maybe a step in the right direction. Past few wet and windy days and they all still, see them regardless, all still pace in the park all the same, one end to the other, heads hanging about their chests, feet dragging trenches in the mustered mud, swaying and swaying until they find somewhere to collapse. Same as the same is the same as.

None such thing as a deal too sweet. Assured her of that last summer. Settled into that sagging bungalow in its sump. Ignored the park and its hoi-ing polloi. Got off at this very bus stop, swamp-assed and sweating all face melting. Known then what's known now maybe, maybe would have just caught the southbound back to the Depot. Known then what's known now maybe, known how the busses run like they barely do, known what that clutch of brown-brick towers on the park's far side was, known just how dark it gets when the power doesn't get paid. Known then what's known now maybe would have just eaten the ticket back to Cackalacky. But Jess'd grinned when she saw the house, said it was like a witch's house, said maybe we could start a coven or, then, maybe a cult and finally there was a mattress in the bedroom by the end of September and it was like it was all actually meant to be for a little while–

&&&

"Do you have a phone charger?" Passenger door open and car's boyish smell spills strong into the rain-crisp air, "And a lighter?"

"Good morning to you too, sweetheart. Lovely weather we're having..."

Aura slides into the car, cigarette already hanging from her lips. Hair frizzed, mushed flat on one side. "Lighter?"

"Yeah, yeah, babe, yeah." Digs into his jeans. "Here."

Bent cigarette lit to dull the air. Aura leans her head against the window. Eyes squeezed shut.

"You alright, hon?" Pulls the car away from the curb and whips around out of a neighboring drive. "You don't look so–" Sweatshirt and sweatpants, grimy sneakers. Pale. One hand pressing the cig to her lips. The other held tight across her stomach.

"Phone charger?"

"Uhm, no, actually. I think I left it at the, Aura, are you alright?"

"Yeah, yeah. Just didn't sleep much and, need some coffee is all."

"Want to me stop on the way into–?"

"What time is it?"

"Early. Early, early."

"It'll be fine. I'll get some once we're in town. I'm just going to take a–" Unrolls the window. Flicks the remaining smolder into the drizzle. "Just let me take a nap and I'll be alright. I'll be fine. Wake me when–"

&&&

"We're all just going to have to cooperate. Simple as that. No way around it." Mister Bennie, Assistant Director of Madiston Municipal Art Museum, lets the silence hang precious and available for ruinous rebuttal by any and all other parties present. His hands bring plumb and flush a stack of papers, black with numbers and final words. Plumb and flush. Placid and implacable.

The quiet thickens between the meeting's members: Miss Shareese and Mister Rohaan, Co-Exhibition Floor Managers and Heads of Attendant Staff, and the three lemon-faced Docents, a silent chorus. Adjournment has again been reached with nothing as yet being solved or soothed.

–Silence here's an invitation. Know that, played this game long enough. Ten years now as intercessor between waged and salaried offices, learnt a thing or two. It's a trap, a big old hole in the ground covered over with grass, a way to even the playing field so they can kick everyone in the head, stupefy into submission. 'Any questions' question isn't nothing more than an opportunity for someone else to take up the mantel of 'bad guy.' It's bait. Leave it empty and, though power remains unchallenged, every saint keeps their halo, so–Miss Shareese breaks the mounting muffle: "Reckon you can just go ahead and leave it to us, Mister Bennie. We'll take care of it all on our end. Nothing you need worry over. Right, Mister Rohaan?"

"Huh?" For most of the meeting now he's had his phone between the spread of his legs, flipping through sketchy online white-page listings, nodding and mumbling agreements to echo whatever it was it sounded like Miss Shareese was assenting to. "Uhm, yeah. That's right, Shah. Of course–"

"You just let us handle it, Benjamin. We'll figure our way around it on our end. Never you worry." And she rises. Gathers her clipboard up under her jacket's arm and says with granite authority, "C'mon Roh."

"Thank you all. We'll talk soon." Door shuts just shy of slamming. Bennie back down to feigning with the forms, flush and plumb. "Is, is there anything else I can do for you, ladies?"

Docents haven't budged from their places against the blindered office window–They don't fit here. This isn't their place. These gummy-painted cinderblock walls, heavy Babel of filing cabinets. This water-stained, drop-ceilinged, mini-fridge hell. So delicately manicured and maintained in their matching cardigans and straight-banged chop jobs. Stand there like they're better than this, like it's this place's fault they married up instead of fucking down and missed their shot at 'the scene,' but, but it's this place, this office and others like it, the *work*, the mind meltingly dull work that gets done here that's the only reason their expertise in art history or whathaveyou has any sway whatsoever so there's no fucking excuse, not a goddamned one for, uncross your fucking arms you ungrateful fucking, not a single fucking excuse for them all to line-up like this just to dish out the fucking silent treatment!–

"We're going to have to meet somewhere halfway on this. This is a massive shift in priority and puts the Museum in a tough spot, but it's the only move forward," flush and plumb. Flush and plumb the dwindling grant funding. Flush and plumb the lack of local interest. Flush and plumb the nosedive in attendance. Flush and plumb the massive undisplayed collection. Flush and plumb the shot at being something really and truly special. "This is a big shift, ladies. But, and I need you all to remember this as gospel, this is *not* a coup d'état. Compromise is still key–"

"Shah! Look here at this one," Rohaan thrusts the phone in her face as they walk down the hall toward the break room. The Attendant staff has been requested to gather early for a briefing regarding changes that are to be made.

Snatches the phone and stops her walk. Clatters nails across the screen. Scrolls through the listing: Studio, 1 bath, kitchenette, fifth-floor walk-up.

"Hard pressed to find something that cheap south of 8th, you know?" Hand up under hers to catch the phone should it drop.

"They're going to want a list, Roh." A flick of finger rolls the webpage back to the top. A constellation of fuzzy mobile phone photos. Poor lighting. "They're going to want a list by the end of the day."

–Not every demand can be met. Unreasonable to think that everything should be under one's control. Have to negotiate and take others into consideration. Know what can be budged on, that's the key.

Know what can be budged and fudged and hold at the chest everything that can't be let go of. Make the demand though, make the demand plainly and clearly. Don't just stand there with arms crossed and mouths twisted all sour and expect your mind to be fucking read! Can understand it at home, prenatal depression is a bitch and the third trimester is no joke, but shouldn't have to deal with the same sort of nonsense here—So: "Ladies, if there is nothing else, you may see yourselves out. I've got to catch up on some emails and—"

"No, no, Shah, I've thought through all of that already. I've got some references lined up and all. Former counselors and psych guys, maybe throw in one or two of the guys I bunked with, the ones that stayed clean anyway. My record's cleaner and clearer than it's ever been. Never late on rent at the Jaspers and, well, everything else is so far back that it shouldn't—" Stops her scrolling with his own finger. "See that? See that? The view is wild! Downtown, the Bay, catch the sunrise every morning. The whole Fire District below—"

"Don't call it that, Roh—"

"Fine, sorry. South Murphy. New City, whatever. Clubs and restaurants and, anyway, yeah, I've got this locked, Shah. Credit is more or less solid and finally have enough to put down whatever they'll need. History may even work in my favor—"

"Roh. They're going to want *a list*. A list of who we're going to let go." Excitement melts from his face, all the bounce deflating and revealing the forty-some-odd year-old sack beneath. "We've got to make the decisions before they do. Better do the dirty work ourselves so we know exactly what mess is getting made. End of the day." Hands the phone back. "Careful with those gas burners, though. Make sure they don't leak."

&&&

Sleep flies from her, leaving its worst in the wake. Bluebottles fleeing dogshit.

"Hey, hey, hey, it's okay!" Derek's hand on her shoulder, "Jesus, babe."

"Oh, fuck me," Aura holds her stomach and collapses inward in the car seat. "I was just starting to dream."

"Sorry, hon." Leans over to kiss her cheek.

"Christ, it's bright."

"What do you mean?" Looks out the windshield at the lead grey sky.

Mutters something before saying, "Nothing, never mind. Can I bum a few—?"

"Sure, sure, here, just take this pack. I'll grab some more at the gas station."

"Thanks," peers inside squinting. Three left. Mumbles: "Are we there yet?"

"Uhm, yeah, we're here. Just pulled into the parking—"

"Oh no-o-o-o..." Crumples again. Cheeks redden. Fists sheaves of hair.

– Never know exactly what's the best strategy here, situations like this. Need to learn because it's always some variation of this that starts off the week. Pick her up from her mother's shithole, guess some of the stink and rot clings to her soul and, don't want to come off as paternalistic or patronizing. She can get toothy if she feels like she's been cornered. How many nights talking through the bathroom door because she's just tanked enough to lock herself in and scream about how everyone is trying to trap her all the time. Gets like this and there's only one thing to do, though. Hold her tight and tell her it's going to be fine while all this works through her system. Never certain if it's worth the possible bite or if it's all just bark and, Christ, she's had longer to sleep now than she would have. Salt Creek Bridge iced-over and some sucker smashed into the median, morning rush hour traffic jam shit, so she's had her sleep, *she's* not the one running late–

"Want me to take you to my place? I can try and call in to work, tell them I'm going to be later than–"

"What time is it?"

"Almost–"

Aura looks at the digital dash clock. "Oh, shit..."

"Look, babe, I can take you to mine but you've got to make a decision. Jawad's been chopping balls off these past few weeks, so I need to–"

"Fuck, fuck, fuck." Heel of her hand to her left eye.

"Aura, are you alright? Is it–?"

"Just need some coffee is all. Shit. I gotta get inside, babe. I gotta–" Quickly kisses him and opens the door.

"Alright, alright, babe. I'll see you tonight, pick you up from–"

"Uh-huh, uh-huh, okay, okay." Again, hand to her eye. Shuts the door behind her.

Car fishtails as Derek pulls out of the parking lot.

Squinting against everything, she makes her way across the greasy, glistening blacktop. Head ducked for rain. Museum side entrance. At the door she rummages through her purse for her employee keycard. Out spills everything. Balled-up receipts. Lipstick tubes. Coins. Perfume bottle. Tampons. Debit card. Keycard. Refrigerator magnet framing Mama and Papa all newly-wed. At the last item, a memory:

"Nah, nah, Public Library is all the way southside. Don't want to go all the way down there." Lifted the pint to her lips to think a minute. Buck smirking, lips shiny with whiskey. "I'm at the College Library every day during my break. Plus, Public Library'd want an address and like probably give me a bunch of shit for living up in Cortland County and like, don't want to fuck with that."

"Doubt the College would give you a card, though."

"Yeah, probably, but maybe I could–"

"Do you even like reading?"

"Dunno, been a long time since I, wait? Why? You think I'm not the type of person who like likes to read and shit?"

"Woah, woah, alright Aura. Jesus, relax."

"Never really tried to, you know? I don't know, I'm over there all the time, maybe they'd let me–"

"Just steal one."

"What? How?"

"I don't know. All those security shits they've got, like the sensors, it's all magnets so like maybe magnets?" Drained the last bit of whiskey then from his rocks glass. "You'na smoke?"

"Nah, let me finish my beer."

"Fine, fine," leaned across the bar and hollered, "Craig! Craig! Lemme get one more, another one more shot again."

Smirks now a bit at the way the memory rose up blissy through the watery shimmer in her peripherals. Bends to gather everything. Tummy flips. Zips the purse and swipes the keycard through the slot on the lock console. Where there ought to be a strobe of green inviting the rapid-fire *onefoursixtwo* to complete the entrance ritual, there is only a dull buzz and flash of red–Goddammit–Tries again. Same as the same is the same as. Reflexively puts a cigarette in her mouth, lights it, and pulls out her phone–Goddammit. Dead. Of course. Blasted white noise into her earbuds all night trying to drown out Mama's television. Died sometime in the morning. Sudden silence in lieu of an alarm–

Leans against the doorframe. Deep drag. Closes her eyes against the rising ache.

"Good morning, good morning, good morning!"

Eyes open and an automatic grin as Mister Carl emerges from the rain's chiffon. Waddling off the pavement, onto the grass beside the concrete path, paying mind to neither squelch nor sop. "Morning, Uncle C."

Stops just short of the doorway's recessed edge and runs his palm over the short-crop of his hair, pulling water as from a sponge, "Certainly is a Monday, ain't it sweetheart? Like just made to wash away Sunday. After every Sabbath, a new beginning. The Lord doth find himself yet again hovering over the face of the waters, a week's work washed away! Every night a flood and so on and so the God of Abraham is made a Sisyphus! His world an ouroboros! And He commits again and again the very mortal sin of Onan and on and on! Must rest every seven days! Pulled His pud raw and tunneled His carpals–" Eyes brighten at the cigarette between her fingers. "Say, sugar, you got a spare?"

"Uhm yeah, Unc, but we'd better get in. We're going to be late–" Pounding rises about her temples, queasy shake in the foundation. "I just need someone to let me in, my keycard is fucked."

"Oh, ain't likely they'll say nothing we don't already know. Here, give us a smoke for the morning. I'll get you back tomorrow!"

"Alright, alright. It's no problem." Aura's cigarette catches a raindrop while she searches for the near-empty pack. "Would you mind just swiping me in? I don't want to be–"

"Sure thing, baby." Swipes his card. Fudges the code. Swipes his card. Fudges the code. Misses the track, re-swipes, and lands the dismount. Buzz. Click. *Aw-pray voo, Muh-dam Mwah Zhel!*"

Chilled air pours from the open doorway and Aura slips in. Wet shoulders set to shiver. Door about to shut behind her and, "Hey, Uncle C. Gotta buzz me in here as well." Points to the console above the handle for the questionably apostrophized **Employee's Only** stairwell entrance.

A flutter in the hall's dull light and Mister Carl's keycard hits her in the chest. Clatters to the floor.

"Thanks..."

"Hey," leaning in, smoke curling fine into the hallway, "does it seem dark in here?"

&&&

Drips from uniform cuff and hem pool, puddle, and now begin to run. A previously invisible topography in the breakroom's linoleum. Mud from shoes settles silty and marks dark the finer flows, ponds then into basins beneath the Lifer's table, in the shadows of the vending machines. Tributaries trickling from under Buck's own shoes. All toward the door, gathering to glisten around the sweep and sill, climbing up the jamb until it will, *must*, spill over. Break the levee. Flood into the hallway.

"Fucking mess, isnt' it?" Aura plops down in the seat next to Buck. Arms crossed, shivering in her heavy, wet sweater.

"Certainly one to talk. Gonna catch pneumonia, girl."

"Fucking freezing. I was fucking locked out and–"

"Locked out? Should've called me, I'd have–"

"Phone's dead." Kicks off her shoes and sloughs her socks. While massaging her feet, she motions with her head to the drip machine between the limey sink and ancient microwave. "Did you see that coffee go on?"

"I don't know. Can't remember. Hangover's killing me. Had my head down since I got here."

"Alright, well, I'm gonna risk it." As she stands, she presses again the heel of her hand to her left eye. "You need?"

"Sure. Sure, why not. Down with the ship."

A thumbs-up and two paper cups. Checks the pot's temperature with her knuckles before pouring a sludgy dram for each of them.

Back at the table, she holds the cup with two hands and hangs her face over the rising steam. Eyes closed. Brow scrunched.

"You alright, Aura?"

Her eyelids squeeze tighter. The space around collapsing stars. Lips twist to bare her teeth.

"Are you, is one starting?" Leans in to ask quietly. She nods and the seal of her eyes begin to glisten. "Alright, here. Put your, put your head down." Spreads his hand out over the back of her head, fingertips swirling smooth circles on her crown as her face meets the table. "Just relax. It's alright." Shoulders begin to hitch, marking out the rhythm of swallowed, inaudible sobs.

"Am I given to understand and believe that not a one of you thought to check the weather before coming in today?" Buck looks toward the door as Miss Shareese's booming heralds her entrance. She sidesteps over the puddles as she makes her way to the countertop. There she leans back, shelves her bottom and crosses her arms. "I'll be sure to leave an apology for our Custodial Staff. Maybe we can all take them into consideration moving forward. Everything we do has consequences. Isn't that right, Mister Rohaan?"

He's leaning in the doorway, looking down the basement hallway, chewing on a thumbnail.

Clears her throat and: "Isn't. That. Right. Mister. Roh. Haan."

"Huh?" Scans the faces in the crowded breakroom and grins, "Yes, ma'am, sure is." Eyes back down the hall.

"Thank you. Now, reckon we can move on," raises her clipboard, collecting herself on the yellow pad page, marked with the beginning of the heinous list that will occupy her much of the day. Breathes deep and takes account of everyone present. The Lifers are at their usual table, wrapped-up in something other than paying attention; everyone else is huddled hodgepodge, dripping on the already moisture warped laminate tabletops; those who don't usually work Mondays are line-up along the back wall having been deprived of their seats by the people who are scheduled for the floor today, leaning on the cinders or against the metal cabinets filled with who knows what. The only unusual presence is the three Docents. Vultures on a power line watching the life of some tire-smeared jackrabbit wane. "Alright. Good. All present except for–"

"There he is! We've been waiting for you, Mister Carl!" Rohaan croons from the doorway, "So kind of you to join us!"

Stops in his puddling tracks, center of the hallway, and lifts his jacket's flaps. Curtsies, "Why than you kindly, Sultan."

Cords in Mister Rohaan's neck stretch, "Please, please, join us."

Mister Carl in the doorway, all eyes on him now: "Well everyone, I'm sure you're wondering why I've gathered you here today." Looks up at Miss Shareese with a wry smile. Wipes his hair and throws another cupful splashing to the ground.

"Good morning, Mister Carl. Go ahead and find a seat. We haven't got all day."

–Unusual. Just as unusual as the Ballroom's archways being closed, oak doors locked. No light shining down the west hall–"Alright Shah, but you gotta promise me once we're done here you'll let me untie that knot that's got your face all buckled. Alright?"

Thins her lips and does her best to the keep the salty glimmer from gathering. Looking at him standing there not knowing a damned thing. Away and, "Now that we're all here, let's go ahead and get to it. There are going to be some, Aura? Aura, please lift your head up off the table. I need everybody's undivided attention..."

III.

Keyboard cracks off the desk. Bennie wakes with a snorting start—Fuck. Third time in what? Two weeks? Third time in two weeks. Getting to a point now where it doesn't even, can't even feel it. No dreams. Just nothing and—Gasps. Heart kicking a thick parade. Gunky lips and mouth-breather tongue fuzz. Wipes the boogers from his eyes—Gonna knock the whole computer off one day, just wait, it'll happen. One day. A storm of sparks and glass and plastic smoke and well, then they might actually listen! Then they, then they might actually listen and come down and replace the damned thing. Or, or, or they'll, fucking Christ, they'll *crunch* some *numbers* and find that, oh, lookie here, it's been shown, we ran the tabulations and it was revealed that, see, lookie here, it's actually cheaper to communicate by carrier pigeon so yes, just stay cooped-up down there going clucking cuckoo and wait for us to get in touch—

Down on his knees. Picks the keyboard up. Fingers tingling—Must have laid funny. It's like goddamn time travel, just w*hoosh* and sudden groggy now—Up again, straightens the monitor. Plastic-hulled antediluvian hulk. Flashes the missive that must have sent him sleeping. From the Director of Museum Operations:

> Benjamin,
> You and Curatorial have made it abundantly clear that I am missing something, but the numbers, as we all know, don't lie. As per my last email, we are still patiently awaiting expenditure estimates from you and Putsch's team. Second-Floor rotations are one thing, but this still seems like a stretch. I've had Accounting crunch the numbers we have available to us and, again as per my last, we've found—

—Nothing that you weren't sufficiently warned of before committing to the Ballroom's decommissioning. Can't pull out now. Can't cover your ass before it's been bared. *Crunch the numbers.* Hand-wringing nonsense. The classical managerial maxim. The unfettered honesty of mathematics. The numbers don't lie. The holy *a priori*. This is of course, only need to take a breath-brief glance at history, this is, of course, why empires fall the way they do. Get caught up in the numbers. More and more and more gross accumulation. Basic stuff. Moreover, it's the stuff that this institution is built as a bolster *against*. Can't fall into the same traps here. Can't let the priests get into our ears, speaking of holy numerals, whispering divine decree, telling the poor tyrant at the top, so stratospherically lonely, telling the poor bastard that it's because he's directly descended from, literally though, *fallen* from, just short of grace, descended from the fulfilling heights of the gods, of the immutable sums of all things, right, descended from, fallen, below, that this isn't the top and that the top is and will forever be out of his material reach. But, we now, we the priests, the keepers of the numerical books, Accounting, the direct line to the Almighty Absolute, we know all things past and present and future so give it all over to us so that we may give it all over to God and then the whole thing'll start to crumble because the guy in charge forgets that he's still ultimately the *guy*, the man, the human, the monkey, in charge and that his concerns ought to be those not of holy sums and differences but of feeble human grievances and, Christ, c'mon, c'mon, eyes already burning at the screen–

Slaps himself to shake off the sleep. Checks his phone. Flashes a chyron reading 5 NEW MESSAGES from HEIDI<3. No missed calls– So everything's fine. A real problem she would have rang. No emergency. No broken water. Just probably the usual when-will-you-be-homes, so– Checks the time–Fucking Christ, 7:30? Been closed hour-and-a-half now– Sand raw in his eyes, Bennie places the phone down and stands. Stretches to touch his toes. Hops and flaps in something approximating a jumping jack. Calisthenics in a dungeon–Torture. No wonder can't focus or stay awake. Everything in this little office is just taupe and manilla and eggshell and olive and drab, drab, drab, all fatigue...

Can't just follow the footsteps marked-out by the numbers. Get exhausted and go bleary-eyed. Blinded by looking too close and, well, this an art museum after all. Gotta take a *step back* from the painting to get the whole picture. Mussing about with pencil-pushing accountants when you're designated as non-profit and supported by the municipality's money is like fretting over the brushstrokes in a splatter painting. Not only does it not matter, but it turns out there aren't any brushstrokes at all, just dribbles dribbled blindly from high-up and far-away. Want some numbers? Some real numbers? Market is cornered. Madiston Municipal Art Museum is the only such institution within a hundred miles. *Carte blanche*, baby. College across the street and all the funding the State is ever going to give enough of a shit to dole out. So, won't get anywhere counting the salt in our shakers if we don't season what we're serving. Taxpayer-funded. Practicality isn't the M.O. Wanna talk fiscal responsibility? Burn the motherfucker down. Want some more numbers? Our fire insurance is aces. Understand now, understand the impulse to run this into the ground like a business. Worked long enough in plastics manufacturing, top of the field and bottom rung, so if you all want to talk numbers, especially in worlds where money just falls into your lap, then look no further. Came in clutch with this whole Putsch arrangement, no one else was gonna get him on board for less than we did. Used ZyraCom for all his projects back in the day. He was in the Rolodex you all paid for. So, look, the numbers look like they do for very good reasons, everyone's seen them. Granted it looks bad to pay a team of Preparators to basically reconstruct the second floor every three or four months, permanent exhibitions look better on paper, but what's not being accounted for, guaranteed what's not being accounted for is—

Air's stifling in the hallway as well. Fluorescent tubes flickering in their casings. Buzzing. Everyone's gone. Bennie's stomach does a backflip and growls—Should eat before home. Lord knows she'll be fit to bite your head off. Break room's got vending machines. Better than nothing.

But, again, all of this has been planned for. Don't know how many times it has to be said. Been a week, guys. One fucking week. Already knew that attendance was going to drop. But attendance was already dropp*ing,* understand? Soon that gallery was just going to be absolutely empty. Everyone knew it was coming. This shift has been on the docket for years, maybe even since before, so, look, it was under the auspices of rebranding that you all even, Jesus, you all even said it! Said it a thousand times! *Antebellum Kitsch*! Wanted to distance yourselves from the rampant scourge of Antebellum Kitsch and now you're going let some crunched numbers convince you that, never mind, look, you wanna watch money disappear? You wanna see what happens when the city council votes on budget shit to redirect their funding to fixing the roads or cleaning up the parks or fortifying the flood response systems? You want to be out of a fucking job then go ahead and tell Curatorial that you know, you really appreciate their getting all those collectors to loan out pieces for the second floor and, look, no one here is a critic, no one here knows what the fuck all anything about art is, but it's plain enough to see that this institution is operating above its pay grade on that second floor and that it's only because of that second floor that someone like Dermot Putsch even looked at us at all. That's private donor shit up there, showcase material. *That's* money! *That's* holy fucking numbers! No one fucking likes it, sure, fine, whatever, it doesn't matter! We. Are. Tax. Payer. Funded. We have no allegiances to any market except, yes, the *prestige* market. Cultural capital! Only thing that this piddling little city has going for it is that we're not a fucking cultural wasteland like Cortland County. Only thing that gets people coming here is that we're batting in a higher league because of the College and this Museum and whatever's left of whatever it was that the Belchard's were supposed to have built. Fuck, Riley Island is *protected land!!* Sea turtles and birds and fish and shit! Cortland hasn't seen endemic animal life since the goddamn Mesozoic! All this numbers shit misses the point. Can't believe you fuckers would–

"Excuse me?" Entering the breakroom Bennie'd rounded immediately toward the vending machine. Lightheadedness blooming behind his brow. "What did you say to me?"

Turns, "Oh! I'm sorry, I didn't see you. Was I–?"

"Yeah, you were." Big man in coveralls. A knit cap. Pouring a whole pot of coffee into a metal thermos. Custodian.

"Shit. Talking to myself, I guess. Sorry."

The man smiles beneath a bushing beard. Shakes some sugar packets to punctuate. "If that's how you talk to yourself, you ought not be apologizing to *me*, son..."

&&&

–A week or so feels long enough. Let the rubble settle. The air clear. Seems fair. All these apologies are useless if they fall on deaf ears. So–

Door opens at knuckles' knock. Warmth springing behind his toothy smile: "Shah! Hey, sis! Come on in! Come in, come in, come in!" And he bends to pick up the bags she's brought with her. A peek inside at the stacked Tupperware. A deep inhale of the smell that's managed to seep through the seal. "Oh, Shah, what's all this? You didn't—"

"Sorry for not giving you a ring or anything earlier, Carl. Just thought I'd bring you some things before I went over to Winnie's."—Worried sick, as well. No knowing what someone does when their world disappears. But, best left unsaid, better unthought—

"No, no, Shah. No apologies necessary!" Pushes the door back with his bottom as to let her in, "How, how is the little Winston these days?"

"Oh, he's fine, sweetheart. Nothing but a worry for his poor mother, she's down at the hospital as I'm sure you know as I've told you and all but, yes, the child is just fine, just—"

—Heavens to Betsy, what is this?—Unlike she's ever seen it before. Past fifteen years of her friendship with Carl, ever since he'd moved into Jefferson Street Housing, never once has she seen his apartment in a state other than absolute disarray. Here and now, though: The few pieces of furniture Carl possesses are pushed and lined-up against the far wall of his meager living room. Where the floor should open into void it is instead piled with towering monuments constructed from the books that are usually strewn about. Shot angels. Reference tomes stacked and topping a series of thin folios. Volumes threatening to slip out. Towers twisting and keening—Certainly expected some sort of adverse reaction to being fired last Monday, but in no way expected it to be so—

"Shah-Baby, you didn't have to bring all of this!" At the card table where the kitchenette gives way to a mockingly small dining space, "I mean, this is just too much, hon. Macaroni. Chicken. Cornbread. Potatoes and gravy. Don't tell me you went and made all this yourself just to—"

"Just want to make sure you're taken care of is all, Uncle C."—Best to keep the tone delicate. Seems probably very possibly quite easy to go and spook him back into the frenzy that must have rendered all this. Mouth zipped and uncritical. Common courtesy. Broke the heart anyway seeing them so ill-taken care of like he'd had them, so this is at the very least an improvement, right? No longer are they all bent and broken-spined.

Splayed and creased and hell, look there, in the kitchenette, dishes ain' even piled up in the sink. No more mud it looks like on the carpet so, sniff-sniff, and none of that mannish, smoky, diarrheal sourness that used to hang around in the air, clouding everything up as pine pollen. Just, organized in his own way is all, right? All the aberrations have been subdued so, yes, just go on and go help him with food and–

"Really, Shah, this is too much."

"Nonsense, least I could," helps unpack the bags. Setting out the full spread. Almost too many containers for the small card table. Sentinels of text looming behind them in the dark. "This, uhm, the place looks fantastic by the way, sugar. Glad to, glad to see you took some of this time to get a little organized."

"Sure thing, yeah, thanks. It was uhm," turns away from the food toward the grove of books foresting in the waning daylight. "Just kind of hit me, I reckon. Too old now. Too old now to sit in filth and well, I'm home now as well, all the time, no more, uhm, well you know so, but yeah. The world just kind of piles up around you. Boxes you in with yourself, and I–"

"Mm-hmmm. It certainly can if you aren't careful. That is true."

"Yeah. You know, you only see the worst of yourself in a smudged mirror. Grey and grimy and gross and, you know it's your own blood you spit when you don't brush your teeth often enough, and all that dirt and stink that follows you like evil in a dark forest, and you've just got to–"

"Mm-hmmm. Certainly can if you aren't too careful about it. You want some soda or sweet tea, sugar?"–Cut him off before he gets philosophical. Only so long before he starts in with *'well, such-and-such once wrote that yada-yada-yada'* or *'that's the truly fascinating thing about etc. and so-on-and-so-forth'* or *'perhaps we should ask a question of the question itself'*–Hands him a plate piled high. Something to plug up the dam.

Carl shovels in a mouthful of macaroni and brown gravy, steps from the linoleum onto the living room's carpet, and speaks through the chewing slop: "You know, I still don't know if I've got it quite organized like it ought to be."

–Best leave the gap there silent, don't pry any further than he's already got it opened. Know what this is, seen it before in everybody else. Sun before the storm sort of thing, yes ma'am. Dawn of a nervous breakdown. Expectant mother cleaning the house every day over and over. Expectant father talking more and more about what it means to be a man. An attempt to control the environment always ultimately results in the realization that the environment is anything but controllable, always disaster–

"I suppose, hmm... I suppose I just want to be sure that it's like, I don't know, the way that *he* had them all, you know? Available and ready for reference. Loaded in the chamber, hammer cocked, ready to fire-off tome after tome after tome–"

–Can't recall feeling any overwhelming sense of order or anything like that at all in his office. More or less similar to this, so maybe he's got a point, but seems like it was all just stacks and piles and, sure, a long low shelf, but even that had been in disarray. Willy-nilly–

"A library," Carl'd said on the Museum's steps that autumn evening over a decade ago–*Over a decade?* Well, had to have been, but Lord, how time flies–Under the orange sky steadily bronzing gold. Said: "A library, Shah. Imagine that."

Squinting and twisting her nose all puggy as he lit up a cigarette, she said "That so?" pillowy with permissiveness, countermelodied with an implicit 'go on, I'm listening'–Had been more or less silent for days by that point, remember that. Didn't even say that his Uncle had died until just before. Held it so close to his chest and around his heart... Heavens, imagine the ache. Docents were sure happy. Remember that, remember hearing them in halls chattering among themselves that maybe the fool had finally run afoul enough to shut up. Cruel, cruel, cruel. Couldn't see the pain in his eyes, talk all day over and over about the emotions of dry ink and oil, of dead men and mysterious strangers, but can't see it in front of them, can't see anything real in the eyes of a person, an actual real solid mourning human being–Nodded silent permission for the dam to blow, bit her cheek against the urge to chime in and divert the inevitable flow–Didn't give the details of whatever accident it was that took him. Could see that he couldn't bear them and that's, well, some of us just aren't made for it is all. Safe to say, safe to remember the funeral. Less closed-casket, more bolted, riveted, and welded-shut–

Carl's lyrical meandering that day on the steps ended with him looking long across the street to the concrete brutality of the College's campus, "Gave me a number to call. Said to call and ask to be let into his office to get his books. I don't think I've been in there since, God, must've been fourteen or fifteen, teenager. No, once more after that, reckon maybe. That last real big storm."

A few days later they were let in by a noodle-armed, crater-faced TA. Carl's shoulders were high and tense moving through the doorway. A vicar at the altar. Eyes around, remembering it all. Bent at the hips to examine the low and long bookshelf until, finally, he achily took to prayerful knees. Silent.

Silence, Shareese leaned against the office's doorframe. Eyes welling-up to burn and glisten. Stopped short of sniffling. Interruption tantamount to blasphemy. Almost leapt into the air when their host intoned, meatless and pigeon-chested: "I, I have it from the Department that the University will be willing to buy a good portion of this collection for the Library. So, uhm, whatever you don't take, I suppose let me know and I'll get in touch with someone to get the wheels turning on compensation and–"

–Remember grabbing at the get what was remembered. Knees popping and sizzling under age yet unreckoned. Titles materialized shiningly from the wall of spines. Remember the pictures mostly, wasn't keen on reading in those days, wasn't ever able to pay attention long enough, so remember mostly the volumes heavy on art and light on history. Uncle Reggie was, at the time, when, what would the circumstances have even been that summer? Can't remember that for the life of, can't recall where Dad had gone and of course Mom was working always, cleaning houses and all and all that and, Dad was, Dad was around but, but just maybe it was Reggie then, maybe, was there a pretense like that? Reg needed an assistant, someone to keep things organized or, no, nothing like that because he had it all organized in his own way. Right. His own personal chaos. What was it he said? To study the city, our city, Madiston, some big preservation project, think it may have been even what brought the Chandelier to the Museum. Funny how life does that sometimes, but said, he said that to study the world you've got build for yourself a city and then all the big stacks of books in the office, the piles of papers, the, yes, a paper polis, every word a person in the world of their own sentence, every paragraph a family history, every photograph a landmark, every citation a memory, all woven together and piled and stacked and ordered into a pristine ineffability, an analog for existence as a whole maybe if things actually worked that way, who knows, but remember grabbing at the get for what was remembered—

Off the shelves and into, at first, neat piles. Higher and higher until they start falling over. Carl looked then back up to the doorway where Shareese stood glassy-cheeked. The shine there brought up his own salt and, just as chin and cheek set to trembling, he said, "I want to keep them all..."

She came down then, to her own knees, and took him up in her arms. There they cried together. Cried themselves into borrowing a friend's car. Cried themselves into packing it with boxes and boxes of Uncle Reggie's books. Cried themselves into hefting those boxes onto the Jasper's elevators. And cried themselves, as the cardboard gave way, to unceremoniously dumping them onto Carl's living room floor, where they laid in occasionally disturbed chaos until a few days ago when Carl set once again about stacking.

—Reached first for the ones remembered. Dug them out of the mess and brushed off their jackets. Stacked them neatly. Center of the room and then another stack next to it of ones that seemed interesting. Another tower of purely technical texts, the obscurities published in the single editions by university presses. Then classics, a lot of classics and so that made a pile and then it was, then there was the—

"Got them organized any which way, Unc?" Shareese chirps as Carl sets his half-empty plate down on the carpet. Steps toward the booking bosk.

"I do," a dismissive tone, "or, I'm maybe trying to, I guess."

"How's that then? How've you got them organized?"

"Well it's, uhm..."—Difficult to explain and what's the point? Can feel it, Shah. Not as foolish as you seem to think, can feel your eyes and your mind and your worry and your love and thank you, honestly thank you, but–

"Want any more food, Unc? Any more of these potatoes or, I've got some pecan pie as well so if you–"

"Sure, sure, yeah, just–"

"Some tea, hon?"

"Sure, sure." –Straighten this tower and maybe, yes, Wittgenstein rides the line, not quite philosophy in the same way that, but still, technical text or at a certain point the distinctions disappear. Read and know enough and–"See, Shah, the trouble is that to get the whole scope of it all, I've got to really read it all, you know? And, you know, it's a question not necessarily of where to start but where to go. Can find yourself reading in circles, you know? The Greeks lead to more Greeks. Can bounce between Plato and Aristotle until you're dead. Economics, right? Try to, try to understand economics and the minute you hit Marx you're knee-deep in Hegel and then all of a sudden you're reading Nietzsche and Freud and the all that Frankfurter nonsense which just brings you back to Marx which just sends you back to Hegel and now you aren't even thinking about economics or any of that or the Bible, right? Try the Bible and suddenly you're trying to learn Hebrew or Latin or, God forbid, reading the Greeks again, and then it's the same death spiral of Plato and Aristotle. Try to avoid it though, try to avoid it and read from your interests, right? Try to maybe want to read some more maybe like science stuff, and then you're suddenly reading mathematics and the philosophy of mathematics and then, guess what? Plato. Aristotle. So push out and, that's not even taking *Literature* into account, in which case you're back to the Bible then Shakespeare then Ovid then Homer then, push out and you want to read something outside of all that like the Gita or I Ching or whathaveyou, but those are just different circles to get caught in and the circles are always, always it seems, going to catch you so, what I mean is that there are, seem to be anyway, the fundamental texts that no one can ever escape, and you'll always come back to them, so no matter where you start the stack, no matter what book you open first you'll end up just back at–"

"Here you go sugar, don't get all riled-up just yet now." Stepping onto the carpet, holding out another paper plate mountained with food.

Carl lunges and, "Hey, hey, hey, watch out!" the plate tumbles from her loose grip, spattering on the carpet.

"Carl! Now, heavens, now what was all that?" Lowers herself to tend to the mess.

"You were, you were," he's down now, "you almost were going to spill it on–" And holds up an impossibly thick volume bound in void white cloth. Title etched in deep bronze: *Thermopoetics of Plasticity: The World as Human Byproduct.* The attribution: *Essays by Dermot Putsch.*

"Oh, hon, I'm sorry. I didn't see it there all by its lonesome," scooping the plops back onto the plate with her bare hands. "What is it, sugar?"

"First," Carl sits back cross-legged and opens the book on his lap. "This is first on the list. I think it might–"

"Oh, well then, I, uhm, I'm very sorry, Unc. I didn't mean to–" The height of her apology is interrupted by her phone buzzing in her cardigan pocket. Reflexes produce it without her exact consent. Incoming call: Tash Jones. "Winnie's mother is calling. Gimme one second..." Tinny voice in a huff. Nodding on Shah's end and then: "Alright, hon. You're lucky I'm just across the Park tonight. I'll be right over, don't you worry. Just make sure he's got a fresh diaper on when I get there. Don't want to start up the evening with the little one in any more tears than Mama leaving already brings up..."

&&&

"Another, y'all?" Craig's sausage-fingered, freckle-frosted, ginger-fried hand slaps the bar top between them. "Give you one more for happy hour."

Buck turns to Aura. Eyes heavy, boozy lead in their lashes, "Another?"

Aura checks her phone. Blue light raising her features from one chiaroscuro to another. Firelight to moonlight. "Uhm yeah. Derek says he's on his way so–"

"Another!" Back to Craig. Raises his lip-and-thumb smudged mug. "A Buford for old Buck and a–?"

"Gin and tonic, same as–"

"Gin and tonic for the lady, barkeep. Make it snappy!"

Craig takes the glasses away. Thumb and forefinger. Rolls his eyes. "Frosty and a G&T for the lady."

"Right!"

"Right…"

–Mug gone and nothing more for an anchor. Just the stool and native gumption. Ship-rocking. Whole world beneath behind. Harder on the liquor than usual lately. Keep the acrid sour from curdling the soul. Tamp it down, keep it from burning the throat. Off the tongue where it might say something without preparing an argument–

"Water?"

"Huh?"

"Water." Craig confirms and delivers two vessels to Buck before shoveling the ice for Aura's highball.

Two hands. Baby grabbing for its bottle. Buck gets the broad girth of the mug in his grasp and brings the foamy bitter to his lips.

"Thanks, Craig. Appreciate it," Aura says. Mimes then the flourish of a signature in the air.

Craig nods and makes his way to the register.

"Buck, here. Have some water–"

"Yeah, yeah, yeah, right…" Glass in hand, spills a splash over the rim. Chugs it all down. Burps. "Happy now?"

"The fuck's up your butt?"

"Nothing!" Crumbles to grumbles.

"Is Jess coming tonight or–?"

"No. Filming…"

"Oh, well that's good, I guess. Right? Good that she's busy with her work and all and, tell her I miss her though. Been too long. Tell her we need to have a girl's night soon or something like that." Squeeze of lime into the fizz. "How's her project coming?"

"Oh, it's coming. I can tell you that, that much…"

"You know, Buck, you're a real bummer when you get like this."

"What? What the, what? I'm just tired and fucking like–"

"No need to take it out on me, though." Hand on his shoulder and, the precarity of his perch immediately renders the tender touch cadaverous. "Alright, alright, sit up now you–"

Buck rises and reaches for his water. Finds the empty pint. "God, goddammit, Craig!" A mutter takes flight and soars to shout, "Craig! Craig! Let me get another–"

"Be patient, Buck!" Craig barks, "I'll get to you when I get to you!"

"Here, here, here," Aura stands and leans over the bar, stool as modest boost. Grabs the soda gun from its holster. Fills the pint. "Settle now, settle..."

Slugs the water down. Shoulders drop in slumping pacification. Thousand-yard stare once it's empty again.

Aura rifles through her purse. "Here, I've got something, here, maybe this will take your mind off whatever it is that's bugging you so bad." Drops a small book bound in green cloth onto the bar-top.

Buck leans over it. Squints. Gives in and covers his left eye with his hand. "Shakespeare is garbage."

"Oh, fuck you, B. That's not the point. Don't you remember? Here, look," flips the book over and opens it from the back. "Here." Points to the little manilla pouch holding a ruled piece of cardstock stamped with check-out/return dates. Inked across the pouch itself are the words: **Property of S.B.C.U. Library [Madiston Campus].**

Buck's free eye widens as the revelation sinks into his brain's pickled stew. A grin: "Ha, no way. Haha, Aura, that's so fucking, I can't believe you like–"

"Honestly can't believe it worked at all, honestly. Just literally rubbed a fridge magnet over the little strip inside and walked-out with it. Fucked up my keycard for work but whatever, I can't believe it actually–"

Book in his hands now. "Haha, no way. I can't, that's so, holy, ah-haha, goddamn girl–"

"Shakespeare inn't so bad now, is it?" Plucks the volume from his clumsy wet hands–Still a library book and, don't know, despite the thievery, doesn't feel right to fuck it up. Planning on, gonna return it one day, after it's finished–

"No, no, babe. Shakespeare is still lame." Covers his mouth to hide a burp that gurgles like it's got company, "but, uhm, sorry, but still pretty badass. Fucking cool. Just like, fucking took it, just straight-up stole fucking Shakespeare from the fucking–" Falls into a giggle fit.

As Buck is swallowed into a busted- gut, sinking further below the surface, into the undertow of deep and necessary catharsis, Aura takes a moment to open the book the right way round and have an honest look at it–Just kinda snagged it off the shelves. No time to really browse. Sweaty hands and pits from the get. So aware suddenly of the dark navy polyester jacket, white button-down baggy around the waist, black pants a size too big swallowing shoes, suddenly so aware of how all that must look there in the Library. Though, calm now, everyone's faces were sunk into their own books, no one notices what they don't notice. Mid-terms or finals or something? No way to know without knowing. Should have gone maybe, should have gone to more school after school instead of, well, would know then, right? Would know what this time the year is in terms of the school term or whatever, maybe still could. Could one day get around to it maybe. Get out of these rags, a bit of makeup, hair washed and done up, eat some fruit or something and maybe then could pass as someone who didn't miss their chance. Only five or six years out anyway, the age people usually go *back*, whether to button-up the holes they'd left in their life or to add another chunk of hope to their future or, not the age when people go for the first time, don't reckon. Don't think that's how it works. Probably need to go to a junior college or technical school or something like, something with more immediate applications than proving that hey, yeah, no, extraneous circumstances, things completely outside of, yeah, Dad shoved-off and Mama lost her goddamn marbles and, no, no, no, solid enough GPA at graduation, don't remember a damned thing though, nothing to write home about in either direction. Know people with degrees that did worse. Haven't had time to apply. Hell of a prom night though! No, no extracurriculars, but there weren't any really to be had out up there inland edge of Cortland County. Kinda dead. Took some kind of exam though. Just like all those baby-faced students today, clustered around tables, books butterflied open before them, papers spread about. Went upstairs to where the more serious students have their own little boxes and just kinda grabbed the first thing in sight. Never been a big reader but definitely fallen in love with the Library itself. It's quiet. Went there on a lunch break one day, hungover and needing like a coffee or something and was just kinda struck dumb by how mute it was. Kept going over there, eventually started looking at the stacks, flipping through the pages, heart in throat. What if someone sees, a student librarian or something, what if they–

Flipping through the time-yellowed pages now, smell of mellow vanilla decay, soundtracked by Buck's laughter–May have maybe missed the mark with this selection–A square of text hovering over a field hued the color of kidney-failure, topped with a number–A roman numeral, no less. Had a few drinks granted, but skimming these lines there doesn't seem to be anything of any meaning in any of it. Bits of it *sound* nice and sweet on the teeth, tongue ticking through, but it's all just rhythmic nonsense. Don't recognize half the words and some of them are even spelled wrong–Flips back to the front–This the same Shakespeare ignored in high school? Supposed greatest of all the greats? Can't even make a line without misspelling something?–Title page is clear: **The Sonnets of Shakespeare,** *including A Lover's Complaint*–Here's a complaint, Bill, learn to spell for the love of God–Blank pages and then a dense tract of prose. In plain English above the inky cascade: **Introduction to a New Edition: <u>On Presenting Shakespeare's Poetry in Shakespeare's English</u>** *by* **Dr. Reginald Lloyd.**

"Oh God, I need to get some air." Buck rises. Wipes the shine from his joy-rouged cheeks. "Goddammit that's funny. Aura, you're a badass. True facts. No doubt. The baddest of the bad. Just fucking–" Doubles over again, "Stealing from the library!" Aura ducks down a tad at the approbation. Slips the book back into her purse. No more than two blocks away from the campus and St. Never's is one of the few bars within a walkable radius. Though it's the height of a weeknight, there's bound to be students about, if not faculty.

Buck plugs a butt between his lips as they fall from their grin. "Care to join?"

"No. I'm good for now. Go ahead." As Buck turns, Aura again produces the volume. Rubs her eyes in the dull light to smear the liquor away and opens it to the introduction.

Outside the drizzle has returned. The bracing chill from last weekend has yet to leave the air. Faces the building's wall and lights the cigarette with the roof overhang as shelter–Just can't get comfortable. Haven't once had a day where everything was just alright. Maybe a few, but never a series of them, not as long as, that's not how this was supposed to go. Sure, could have and should have in retrospect expected things to be hard. Being an artist or whatever isn't supposed to be easy or everyone would be trying to do it. But, fuck, hungry and wet and tired and now just fucking drunk all the time–Smoke kicks rocks in his belly and the ashy desert of his tongue floods with a sour, tannic gunk. Flow of spit and mucus that can only mean one thing.

Buck launches himself off the wall to the other side of the sidewalk, where some straggling, lenient sapling is planted in a mercifully unpaved patch. Proceeds to paint the soil puce with foamy jets from his giggle-shook belly.

–This how it's going to be now? This the life? Given up everything, all the easy allotted to everyone else, just to end up standing out here again, vomiting cheap beer to help the tree grow? This the horse to bet on? Can't even go home. Gotta stay away while she does her filming. No, no, no, that's not exactly it. She's said plenty of times now that she's got no problem with, says the mic on the phone isn't strong enough to pick up any moving about so, can do whatever it is that, can read, cook, clean, paint... Well there's no fucking way any of that could get done knowing she's in the other room, no doubt *hearing* it all, shoving shit up inside herself and making kissy faces to everyone and well, shit, the museum doesn't pay enough and now hours are cut and this whole thing seems to be easy money so maybe, maybe need to take a long hard look in the mirror and ask, just pose the fucking question, just honestly, with a straight face, stripped of romance, without poetry or ambition, with all the emptiness musterable, and just ask, just ask how much should be given up for the sake of being a, God, God, just get it all out, just pour it all out and stand up straight and act like nothing has happened and then finally look in the mirror and ask–

"Woah, woah, is that old Buck?" Hand falls like a brick on his back, striking hollow and inserting a gasp into the purge's flow. Sudden dot in a dash-heavy morse code. "Little hard on the sauce, homie?" Hand grabs the back of his neck. Smell of sweat. "Go on now, get it all out. That's the way now. Come on, come on." Two voices of similar pitch fall then into laughter. Good-natured chuckles, not an ounce of ill-will in them.

Flow subsides and gives rise to a series of rib-rattling belches. Buck straightens-up. Runs the sleeve of his uniform jacket over his flotsam-flecked lips. "How you boys doing?" Searches his pockets for smokes.

"Not bad, Bucko. Not too bad." Both of them, Derek and David. Towering figures with that former-athlete build. Cheesing their faces off. Can smell it on them. Sharp in the drizzle, that blissy pissful edge of stem-and-seed weed. Dogshit stuff.

"Y'all sure seem like it." Finds the pack. Plucks and plugs.

"Shee-it, took it to the face, baby–"

"*To the face, bay-bee!!!*" David chimes as echo. The meathead mimic routine. Say it until it loses meaning.

"To the fucking face!"

"Face, baby, face!" A Basset's deep, howly growl...

"Glad y'all're feeling good..."

"Where's my woman?" Derek barks and snarls, holding his hands out front of him miming a bruising grope.

"She's inside, D." –Christ, this one's settling like castor as well. Can't imagine there's more in there left to stir up–

Derek spins on his heels and all but kicks the door down. David jukes as if to follow but turns instead to Buck. "You got a spare, brother?"

"Uhm," flips the top of his pack to reveal the leafy dark of his lucky, "sure thing, Dave... Here." Thrusts the pack forward.

"Oh fuck man, if it's your last one, I don't want to–"

"Nah, nah, take it. No problem..." –Never going to understand why, why always the need to kowtow to these sorts, these barrel-chested, brainless oafs–

"Alright man, if you insist."

"Yeah, yeah." —Not like they've ever done anything. These guys in particular, anyway. Always been nice. Laughed together. Shared rounds. Had conversations, though the deeper they get the more their contributions reduce to sparse *yeahs* and *sure thing, no totallys*. They're good guys all around, no doubt. Honest. Work hard on the shipyards. Earned their right to think as little as possible sort of thing–

Only the sound of the rain piddling on the sidewalk as they smoke.

Cherries having eaten their way nearly to the filter, David speaks up: "I don't know if she's told you yet, but Jess hit me up a few days ago..."

IV.

Naked and sweating. On the bursting verge. Headache and garbled guts–
Once upon a time it would just get slept through. Coming back to the self
is the hardest part. Haven't yet slept. Or, maybe a shallow, dreamless,
restless slumber. Time travel to now where it's all ache and only ache.
Slimy withering. Fruit left out in the heat, bursting through the easy
slough of sun-leathered skin–

Dawn's creeping across the ceiling's popcorn stomp. Puffy spatters
casting long shadows, scars of a night's bruise. Orange out from the blue.
Yellow to drive it pink. Mountains over river valleys and flood plains of
dusky mauve, dustier every moment the shadows shorten. Room
spinning. Never completing a rotation. Sublating always back to its
original. Reconstructing itself. Every turn stronger a wall and firmer a
floor–Coming back to the world or is the world coming back to, ugh,
Christ, reality somewhere in the rub–Ceiling patterns congeal into the
faces of family–There's Jawad and Angela and little laughing Naseer.
Father's unburied lipless scowl...

"C'mon Mister. That's it. Just one step at a time there." Remember
that, certainly remember that. "Fine, fine, hold onto me if you need to.
Five floors is a motherfucker, ain't it?" Voice from a shouldery man.

Toes dragged over the lips of each step. A strand of mucus dribbling.
Spider-silk in the duff. All but dropped there where the welcome mat
ought to be.

Remember maybe something like: "Nice meeting you, Mister. Hope to
see you more often. Congratulations on the new apartment. Welcome to
the neighborhood," or some other facile collection of phrases poured
between exhausted huffs and, fuck, fuck, fuck–

Rohaan rockets from the couch. Only piece of furniture the former
tenant'd left behind. Sweat breaking like cold steel. Slides on his knees,
squeaking across the bathroom tile, and plunges his face into the toilet
bowl–Like when the City used to knock the lugs from the hydrants after a
heavy rain to wash the murk from the main, rust from the line. Steam
from backs. Break the fever. Playing with Jawad and the neighborhood

kids. Cool in the hard water. Crystal scream beating bellies burnt cherry. There it is–Thick and enmeshed with itself. Every gnawed bit a memory rinsed from his mind. Boogers of shrimp and fry fluff. Leaves of lettuce toothed translucent. Cuspid-cubed carrot and flecks of flecked stuff. All held together by an unidentifiable orange meal and mash...

"Oh, oh, big spender!" The Bartender'd said yesterday. Broad and generous in the middle. Kind-eyed. Doughy smile. "Welcome to the neighborhood indeed, my friend!" Took the menu away. Left behind a tall glass of water, a sweating bottle of Buford, and a rocks glass filled within a finger of the rim with something heinous and expensive poured from a dusty-necked bottle.

Drank a solid three-quarters of the water before he even got started in on the Buford. Warmed itself to a plaqued slurry by then. A different bitterness than the one he recalled. Used to drink them like *they* were water. The whiskey sat even worse. Spread over his tongue with a raw burn. Rubbing alcohol in an open wound–Goddammit, just drink it! No reason shouldn't be able to! A fucking adult, just–

"You still, uhm, eyeing that promotion you were talking about?" Jawad had asked last week once they'd gotten settled at their table. Angela busied herself with situating Naseer in a booster seat, stringing a bib across his chest. They'd only made it another block or so down the Cobbles before the sky heaved once more and forced them again to seek shelter.

"What promotion was that, Jawad?" Cigarette a few minutes before hadn't settled well–Reckon the body starts to recognize poison as poison when it's not constantly being poisoned–Leg wouldn't stop shaking once they'd sat down. Old nag creeping inside his mind, suggestion of one more, a stick of fresh air, set things right, despite the nauseous evidence to the contrary.

"Gosh, Roh. I don't know. You were talking about it maybe a few months ago. Something about–" Server then brought the drinks: Iced tea for Angela, cola for Rohaan, milk for the child, and a frosty-shouldered bottle of Belchard's for Jawad.

She hovered then. Waiting for their lunch orders. The kitsch of whole place leaning in with her: Driftwood facsimile tabletops, anchors hung over the bar, fiberglass fish, and picaninny postcards. Menu declared the establishment the Runaway Tavern & Fish Fry. A block of text down the menu's middle, surrounded by a search party of entrees, appeteasers, and drinks specials, running copy telling the tale tall as can be of the fugitives kept behind bars in the building's basement way back in the 18somethingandsomethings. Further how their ghosts still haunt the premises after dark, how a ghost's favorite refreshment isn't the slurped souls of the living, but instead a quickly quaffed bottle of Belchard's Brown Ale and a double shot of rye whiskey.

"Said something about moving up into management, I think." Jawad circled back after the orders were taken. Lifted the bottle to his lips. Crustaceans of ice scuttled over the scowling face on the label.

"Oh, that. Yeah. That's what I'm doing now. So, I guess, yeah–" Could smell the beer. Yeasty musk. Tar on his tongue.

"Congrats then, Roh! Why didn't you tell me? What's the raise? What's the bump?"

–Can't celebrate. So much digging to get out of that place. Never once heard it said straightaway but, can't celebrate. Once in the pit it's just, no rope, no ladder, can't just climb back out. Anyone that says otherwise is lying and *that's* the truth. Anyone that really wants to help'll just drop a shovel down into the hole because, can't celebrate, have to dig to get out, have to dig to the other side of the world and come out there. Only way out is further down. Have to dig through Hell itself and then keep going and because they don't say when it's done and there might not be daylight on the other side and now there's a hole straight through the world and it can't be filled again otherwise there'd be more digging to do and, and, and, can always fall back in, get confused, climb back out the wrong side again, into the night, blind and tired and thirsty–

"Oh, it wasn't much, Jawad. Just enough. Helped a bit, I guess." Watched then as Jawad's thumb ran over the bottle's label. Tintype-styled portrait coming away from the glue in neat, watery, paper pills. Read the brand's slogan at the bottom of the label: ***'As Good As It Gets!'*** "It was like ten. Just over ten..." Hand rose then to pat his shirt pocket. Soft crinkle of the check's crease.

"Oh wow! Just over ten dollars? Shit, looks like lunch is on you then!" Slapped him on the shoulder. "Didn't know you was a high-roller like that! Ten an hour over minimum? What's that put you at? Near twenty an hour now?"

"No, Jawad, no. You misunderstand." –Jawad, you misunderstand. You misunderstand–

&&&

Scotch-taped onto the inside cover: A folded piece of plain white, flawlessly inked by hammer and ribbon:

Dear Reggie,
Apologies upfront for the presentation, but I can't for the life of me bring myself to spill ink over the pages of a bound book, even one that I wrote. I'd sooner burn the Bible cover to cover than underline a clause of smut-slathered, pulpen trash.

Anyway, Reginald, my friend, I hope this volume finds you well and in as perfect a condition as possible. I hope you'll find the formatting of our good-spirited dustup toward the end (best for last, as they say) to be more suited to the length of each line than that typographical catastrophe committed by the dunderheads at Diremption Quarterly. Never until piecing this volume together was I able to go back and read through our little exchange, so never have I been able, until now, to tease apart the debate enough to have anything of substance left to say. Perhaps that is why I have been out of touch for so long. At any rate, I hope you can accept this apology for my silence. Let it be known that the echoes of our conversation still ring about in my head and, as I'm sure you'll be unsurprised to know, I now have quite a few rebuttals to offer; but, that's a different missive altogether...

Also, I've just this week received a copy of the edition of the Bard's sonnets for which you penned the foreword. A splendid setting no doubt. I found the argument you presented there much more compelling than I'd expected, so praise where it is due and all.

Give me a call soon. Or I'll call you. Or perhaps we can continue to titillate ourselves with silence.

All the best and burn the rest. Merry X-Mas.
–Dermot Putsch. '94

Then signed at the bottom in a flourish of permanent marker, ink now running rainbow around the edges–How many times typed-through to get it so perfect? Not a letter out of place, slip, or doubled stroke, no dry spots on the ribbons or, wonder if this is one of the 'Big Wigs' Uncle Reggie used to talk about. Say things like, 'Only a few Big Wigs left in the world,' all that summer, sifting through papers and preparing for something to do with the Belchards. Sat there in the perfect quiet of that office, flipping through the more picturesque texts of his library. Hold up a page then and ask him of the glossy print of some masterpiece in a museum somewhere further away than across the street, 'Reg, this one of the Big Wigs?' Eyes would rise from the papers in front of him, fingers always stained from his habit of thumbing the ballpoint's tip while he read, and the reply would be something like 'Perhaps' or 'Minor figure, but worth investigating' or 'Certainly is' followed up with a lecturesome rant longer than reckon his classes during the semesters could have been, or, or, or when too many questions had cropped up all he'd offer was a terse 'There's a reason it's in a book and a reason why the book is on my shelf.'

That's the one that stuck. That jab was said just enough times that summer to stick. Taffy to teeth. Seed in fresh-wet-soil. *There's a reason it's in a book.* No volume that got noticed could ever again go unthumbed, rarely returned then to the shelf from which it was plucked. All it takes is a convincing cover and an impassioned blurb and well, *There's a reason* enough. Liberate it. Set it free. Take it home. Even before Reg passed, this apartment was a lepidopterarium for wayward texts. Reg's library only brought the monarchs and goliaths.

Too many to read, though. That's always been the problem. Everyone who loves books says it, but it's true. There are too many. Best to learn to ignore titles and chapters and page numbers. Bindings are a false boundary. Literature is rhizomatic. Covers are membranes more permeable than they think they are. Skip and skim and bounce around. Start reading on a good sentence and then stop once the prose falters. Run the rapids until the river dries. Outside of a few maybe cornerstone texts and all it doesn't really matter where whatever's been read gets read, insights all smash together and authors don't really probably exist–

Carl turns past the title page and:

Table of Contents:

–This one, though? The whole thing. Page for page, top to bottom. Get all the way to Uncle Reggie's actual words. Must've been in his thirties at the time of the interview, doing all that preservation research for the city but, whole life in academia and never published anything except that foreword to the Sonnets, which is excellent, but still, no treatise or anything, no manifesto or essay collection. The man was a teacher and that's maybe what was so, anyway, it's time that's always stood in the way. Always had work. Always tired when there wasn't any work. Never able to focus during days off because the next workday hovers humid, choking every breath and bringing up bile with every little hiccoughed hope. No. No job now though. Got that problem solved. Just flat-out fired after all those, who cares, nothing but time, nothing but time now so, some severance and some time before it all just, finally get to sit down and get to do some real reading and–

Outside the day is cracking open. Winter's severed tail finally settling out of its icy flail. All the blue flows through. Only clouds those steely puff balls. Not yet fallen enough to pour themselves out. Trees across on the other side of Harris Park, along Murphy Street, are starting to green. Not a drop of yellow among the leaves. Emerald unfurling. Even the Park's grass is attempting verdant shoots. Rain last week's got cursed ground convinced of its gold. The junkies are pacing and gathering around the parched fountain at the Park's center. Weathered winter coats thrown into greasy piles in the shade. All barefoot and in their skivvies. Sweat shellacked long-johns–That nice out? Early in the season but weather's been strange enough this year. Wouldn't be surprised.

No use wondering though. Throw on some shoes and go see for, seize the day. Be too hot to move before too long so take a shot and get out in the niceness while it's fresh. Air all crisp, not yet bitter and thick with pollen. Doesn't seem right to let it go to waste–

The book is just barely open, not yet even cracked to its meat–A few pages. Get invested, get something to chew on and then, then, then go out with something to think about! That's how it's done!–

Turns from the contents to find the first essay:

A Job Well Done:
L'Esprit de L'Escalier

I: Heresy as Orthodoxy

All gods[1] are born, even more so than humans, already dying. The classic revelation in this vein is of course Nietzsche the Virgin-King's late 19th-

---

1 Best to get some definitional concerns out of the way up front. For the purposes of this essay and all other essays moving forward, the only exception being the 7th section titled **Adamah to Adam/Adam to Atom**, the term 'god' will stand in for *any* bit of 'non-material' that is principally a product of the relations between people, whether personified deity or general notion, some emergent *other* whose existence is wholly dependent upon our unified, though not necessarily conscious, reinforcement of its being. See: Yahweh's fears over Babel. In short, the model we are reaching for here is that of a continually developing and collapsing pantheon of *concepts*. Hopefully, the finer points of this model will be duly unpacked over the course of our time together. Onward...

century declaration of the Murder of the Almighty. As dramatic and satisfying as that in its poetry may be, it fails, as all poetry does, to capture the true essence of the state of affairs it aims to illuminate. Perhaps then, something like 'All gods are born to be killed' would do as a possible rephrase? Might seem radical, but therein is developed an adversarial relationship between Us and our gods while simultaneously leaving Us blameless for their existence in the first place; in doing so we negated the truest portion of *Der tolle Mensch's* millennial insight, that We are in some way responsible for the God which has been killed having been killable in the first place, that the relationship in truth is *authorial*. No, it seems apparent to this writer that we do not give birth to our gods with the intent to kill them, and that the continual tragedy of their dying (dropping like flies these days) is the source of a deep trauma in the human spirit across all boundaries cultural and material. Dear reader, it is increasingly obvious to me that We give birth to our gods only *after they have already started to die!*

To posit the existence of a god is in essence to make the case for its preservation in the face of its increasingly obvious non-existence. At the risk here of giving bloody birth to a new god (which will need to have its infant neck broken and soul poured soupy from its fontanelle within the next few pages if We are to move through this morass unscathed), I will attempt to state here a General Theory for The Formation of The Divine:

&&&

Blue-Ridge Sinai Hybridized Honeydew Kush. Purple at the puckers. Inviting, yellow filaments out the flowers. Glitzy, glassy shards of resin and, between the buds themselves, gobs of orange-gold sticky sap. Goopy jewels. Growing and alive in the light like it wasn't ever cut from the stalk. Ickier and ickier every day they've had it shoved away in a prescription bottle under junk mail and passports and a facsimile of the lease in the bedroom's desk. Pop the lid and go straight to the Moon just looking at it– Obbie'd said grinder's useless, break it up by hand. Roll it up with some cherry cavendish, spliffs are gonna be the way to go. No blunts. No bongs. No pipes or anything. No ripping. Puff shit. Roll it up with the leaf. Make it last. Burns mad slow. Modern moonshiner bootleg shit, artisan for your ass—

It's got his arms floating out to his sides as he sits on the floor, laid back against the mattress and box spring. Lids shut and Buck has fallen—A mile or two behind the eyes. Well past the cold and dark parts of the mind. All the walls slick with mother's milk. Drip, drip, drops from stalactite father-figures saltily onto the cave floor—Legs out in front of him, toes antipodal to the center of his being—Crashed violetly all the way down to this warm womby place, Delphic spring of pre-lingual association along the ego's screaming edge, to toddle around the soft world of a baby-brain. Klutzy pudged hands reach for something sweet to teethe—

Eyes open now. The triptych set against the wall. Three canvases no bigger than his chest, gobbed and gloopy with greens and blacks and purples and smears of white run to grey in an orange fray. Three portraits of the same mind mediated by actions of that very mind's body. Devoid of tonguable language. Three unscramblable images, missives, messages, prophecies from a ways away from the drippy place he now rests, from the world he fell from. Through a pinhole, way up in the dark, the best parts of what he is when the light is bright and his belly is hungry—Mouth dry, could really go for something sweet—Where this whole he's fallen into is covered over with words and worry. He smiles here, counts them: one, two, three paintings along the carpet of this sinking swampy house, with no money and almost out of everything else. His hand floats down to the tray by his side, made from a flattened Belchard's can, bent into a boat. Plucks the still rolling but roachy spliff from its place over the ashes. Up to his lips and another resinous crackle fills his lungs like liquid lead.

A knock and something from another plane—Rogue planet, maybe— Opens the door—Universe suddenly filled with another living thing, another mind. In orbit now, out there where the light comes from and, a collision, two galaxies tangling their starry arms. Pinprick of light goes dark as—Buck's nose is filled with the smell of coffee and tobacco and alien fruits and—Gravitational center meeting in quiet cataclysmic joy— Smoke and cream and sugar on her lips, her tongue a tender hook behind his teeth, pulling him closer even though they can't possibly be any closer.

A nip at his earlobe and the spliff is snubbed. Hands on her body, warm through the sweater. His sweater on her body. Hand high along bare thigh. Legs wrapping. Her waist, pelvis like a belly, little line of fine hairs, tract darker and darker toward her warm skin, cold in the room, and everything stands. She smiles as they kiss. Her kiss is smiling as it kisses. He smiles as they kiss and there's sugar and cream on their lips and it's sweet and warm though everything is standing against the cold air and the sweater, his sweater, her body, his sweater on her body has left her against his chest, flannel shirt unbuttoned and her breasts, his chest, press again. Roll onto the hard carpet. Hand holding the back of her head. Cradling through the black of her hair. Giggle and grinds. Cotton against denim. Tighter and tighter. Warmer and–Climbing back up the walls of that womby pit. Look down now from the height of eyes, over the lips of their lids. A thing of beauty rent open beneath. Smiling teeth with that heart stopping gap from behind lips that taste like smoke and coffee and cream and sugar and her hand, thumb tracing the peak of cheek where the skin softens to blink–

Buck smiles, holding himself up as her legs wrap: "Hi, Jess..."

Pulling him down with a pinch of his chin, "Morning, hon."

&&&

Eyes open to queasy silence. Pried from velvet sleep by the cruelty of late-morning sun, she rolls away, drawing Derek's threadbare sheets over her face. Squeezes her eyes shut again. A vise gnawing at her temples, muddy boots in her belly. She smiles into the pain. A grin of booze-fouled teeth against the sweat stained pillow. Most people here would utter the day's first helpless groan of hungover malaise. But for Aura to wake like this, immediately identifying the pain as that of a hangover and not the true honest hell of a migraine, keeps the panic out of her chest. A hangover has cures, or at the very least things that can be done to settle the symptoms. Hot shower and an icy facewash. Salty sports drinks. Take-out Chinese. Tylenol and Pepto. A good fuck to get the blood moving. A hangover comes *tsk-tsking* with lessons. A punishment at the fore and self-flagellant pleasure at the end. A day hungover is truly nothing more than a day spent *getting better*, a dreamy convalescence. It is the defeat of terror and fear, the crushing of a nightmare. Not so with a migraine–No one's ever earned a migraine...

Still though, must stay still to ward off a coup from the inside–She reaches her arm back to pull Derek over–Hold tight and together so everything doesn't just give in and liquify–But where he ought to be, there is nothing. A slightly warm void of fabric. She grabs his pillow and brings it over to her chest. Lifts her legs. Curls into a tight ball. Aberrant pearl.

Tries for sleep, but the day has made itself known. The dark of her eyelids oranges purple. There's the groan she initially smiled against. Now aware of her body, the fermenting mush of her mind begins to spin. A tissue-pinched cockroach dropped oozing into toilet water. Clambering against the impossible smoothness of the porcelain bowl. The flipside of the feverish pleasure of a day spent hungover is, of course, that there is initially something from which to heal. The concrete security of dreamless sleep gives way to the immensity of a black-out's void. The *scaries*. That indiscrete terror of having lived without having really been there, a selfless being wearing one's drunken face as a mask, joy at one's own absence–Christ, drove home last night. Had to have, but can't really say because there's not a memory one past when? How many drinks then? Nobody thought to call a cab, can guarantee that. Derek wouldn't have taken one anyway. Probably not totally blotto, but certainly absolutely not in any condition to fucking drive and how many more times reckon that bridge can be crossed before finally the car just crashes through the railing? Washed out to sea, thrown useless into the ocean by an untroubled Salt Creek. These the odds? This the bet? Stake it all on what? An escape from her? Jesus fucking–

Eyes open now and no chance of them closing. On the nightstand the time flashes from the digital clockface. 10:47am. Too early. Next to the clock is the green spine of the Sonnets. Being used as a coaster for a sweating glass of water and small bottle of Tylenol–Derek's a nice guy, a good man even–

She sits up. A march tempo set in her temples. Reaches the miles-long stretch between the bed and the nightstand. Glass at her gunky lips. Room temperature. A slime almost. Spilling over her cheeks. She breathes wheezy through smoke-choked nostrils. Everything an emergency. Little animal inside taking control. Screeching rodent. Heart humming. Eyes dart to the wall where the alarm clock suckles from an outlet along the baseboard. Phone usually plugged in there as well, charging through the night. Nothing now, though. Kicks the sheets from her legs and hangs her feet off the bed. Slight chill in the air reassures her skin to its body, gooseflesh telling her she's alive and really here. Aura stands. Stretches. A headrush frazzles her peripherals and a clot of last night descends her inner thigh.

Clothes lie in catastrophic clumps all about the floor. A telltale trail leading from the door to the center of the bedroom–Looks like it was fun. Wish there was something to remember–A soreness in her throat, hot sting on her ass, sucking sop between her legs, all portending of a particularly athletic session–Worrisome there that there's no memory. Recollections of sex have been hazy of late. Love unspoken and now, this uptick in boozing. Feels hollow like faith. Same sort of resentments maybe. Don't make more of it than need be. Wish for protraction and foreplay and tenderness and, not to curdle it all cheesy, but maybe poetry might be baseless. Derek's never been soft of touch. Never violent. But brutish and simple and earnest and well, just want to remember it is all. What, what even, what fucking day is it? It's been fade-to-black every evening for who knows how long now, and–

Upends her work pants from the pile of socks and underwear. A downpour of change and keys. Pen, lint, and a receipt. Plunk of phone and cable. Picks the phone up. Presses thumb to screen. Nothing. Clicks the center button. Nada. Flips the little switch on the side. Fuck all–Goddammit–dead.

&&&

"Yep. Way I reckon it, you gotta rise with the sun. Best policy to have." Plastic spoon scrapes the bottom of a yogurt cup. Digging in the corners for slivers of macerated cherry. "Want a chance of chasing the day down to its end, you've got to catch her where she begins..."

His feet are propped on the edge of the table. Chair's precarity squealing on its back two legs–wonder if that little-fella-low-center-of-gravity works to his benefit leaning back like that or, if maybe, just jerked the table ever so slightly from beneath his hooked ankles, if he'd fall backward and at least be good for a laugh–

"Yes ma'am, yes ma'am. Overmuch rest'll make you lazy, sluggish, and impotent, intellectually impotent, I should say," legs come down without any comedy, and now it's elbows on the table. Limp wrists suspending the gutted, brown husk of his lunch sack. Tiny white hands. Mice scrounging around inside for something else to munch on.

–Little rodent of a man. Go back to your brood, hole up in your hovel. No idea what's wormed its way up his ass for him to be taking his lunch in the breakroom with the underlings, but someone is going to have to tell him that his pale, puckered face and leering, beady eyes are making everyone nervous–

"Maybe it's just how I was brought up, you know Shah?"–Getting fresh there, Bennie. Dropping that Miss and clipping the name friendly. Watch it– "Maybe, well, maybe I was just brought up to have some sort of drive, you know? Maybe my father kicked it into me enough, encouraged the right sort of behavior and all that. Never got to sleep in much on the weekends either. Had a job in high school, not like these–" Bites her cheek at whatever it is that Bennie's thinking about pouring forth next– Can't be good. Mischaracterization of the spoiled state of modern children or something about adults working jobs that teenagers ought to have, whatever poison it may be, whatever south suburb, polo-shirt, brunch-munching bullshit he's getting ready to spill–"Anyway, reckon what I mean is," –All this *reckon* this and *reckon* that all of a sudden, like he's lived here all his life. Lord, still the soul. Not keen to listen to much more of this here–"I mean, well, how much of your childhood do you remember, Shah? Does any of it," motions with his hands. Condescendingly didactic: "Does any of it, uhm, *stand out*, I guess?"

Her eyes fall back to the sandwich in her hand. White bread, mustard, and ham. Collects herself. As her eyes rise again and his cockscomb falls, she catches sight of a tight-cheeked and doe-eyed plea scurry across his face–Amazing how all these boys are brung up the same way. Taught to swallow it all down and hide it under their voices, stomp out every quiver and shake and break. Can't hide it from someone who knows, though. Sometimes think maybe they know they're known, can feel themselves being seen through, feel the softness of their puffed chests under a steady gaze. Had enough of them ask similar questions in the past, showing up on the doorstep holding a swaddled baby like it isn't theirs, saying something about the child's Mama had to work and I'm still working nights ma'am and I didn't know what to do but bring it here to you, I don't know what to do and, but they're all younger, kids themselves, all *their* fear comes from not yet having had the chance to grow up, being thrust into a life they were still hoping they hadn't asked for. Try hard enough and that jaw can be set firm again. Can humble the man out of a boy not yet grown. That boy's close enough to the bottom that he'll talk to the preacher if he's told to, he'll find God just to forget he's alone, but this man here, this Mister Guy-In-Charge Boss-Man Bennie, this is a different story: What's just flashed across his face is the dust cloud of some internal war he's raging, realizing himself as he really is and, well, cross hearts and all that, Lord knows so there isn't any use in hiding it, but don't particularly wish to spend a lunch break helping this, pardon, simpering, little whathaveyou unpack his inability to man up despite his hardware. Still haven't quite got around to forgiving him yet, adding the old fellas to the list a what, just a few or just over a week ago? Lifers and all that, working here in their twilight since the severances and pensions from the bottling plant packing-up and shipping-off didn't amount to anything but pocket change. Can take Carl being axed. That was the compromise, give in on Carl and throw in the two new hires as well if the Museum can maintain the older fellas what can't pay for their medicine anyhow. Cut hours if you have to, but keep them on the payroll at the very least. Seemed good enough, middle-of-the-road, two new hires and one troublesome goof. Deal with Carl's fallout as a friend and favor and all that, but the Lifers were a step too far. Would rather just not speak to him if there's no immediate need for it. Not until the head has cooled and an honest prayer's been said. But he's come in hot this afternoon, jabbering away from the moment he stepped into the breakroom, before even unrolling the cinch in his brown paper bag. Talking full bore. All there is to do now is chew as fast as possible–

The look that had flashed is back, taking his face fully. Eyes watering at his screed's buried plea going unanswered. Shah swallows and says as if she'd let her mind wander: "What was it you asked, Mister Bennie?"

"Oh, just," straightens up in his chair, sets his shoulders back, laces his fingers together on the tabletop–It's always the same. Subconscious screams for help and then acts all surprised to have it recognized. Postures as if it's being attacked– "I was just wondering how much of your childhood you recall..."

Shareese smiles and nods, "Oh, sometimes I remember a lot of it. Sometimes whole stretches get crammed into one day, though. Summers off from school, no difference one day to the next or, hell, one *summer* to the next. Remember my late teens very well. Feel like they never stopped some days, until you wake up with back pain, of course, but, you know what I mean?"

Face scrunching as he tucks a pecan into his cheeks, "Sure, maybe." A pause to swallow. "I don't know if–"

–Walls already going up that quick, huh? Put in a position of actually having to engage, get your soul a little naked, be more explicit in your questions, can't just keen away about nothing, and you want to shut it all down? Nuh-uh, not today. Sucked up and spoiled the lunch break, nuh-uh, no you don't–"Anyway, Bennie, how's the lovely Professor doing?"–Secret weapon: call his wife by her title. No man likes that his wife's got a title–

"Oh, she's, well, she's as well as can be, I reckon."

"Must be getting close to due, correct?"

"Yeah... Sometime in the, uhm, in the next two weeks, if I remember correctly–"

"Exciting news, Bennie. Gonna be a father soon!"

"Certainly, feels sooner than I'd–"

"Bet she's ready to drop it. Fit to burst." A bite of her sandwich, appetite returning to the fore. "Last I saw of her she was, what? Late last summer? So, what, end of the first trimester?" Pregnancy high and new and lunar, shining through the hole fashionably cut in the midsection of her black one-piece bathing suit. From up and behind them, a voice tinged by the dainty roundness of a vague Europe: "Is this where they have the girls at?"

Shah turned around, holding her hand flat across her brow to shoo the sun away, "Yes ma'am. I reckon it is." Scooched her beach chair over a touch, to within a few inches of where the new-hire girl, Aura, had been sat quiet on her towel. "Feel free to join, not a one of us's ever been known to bite."

The woman smiled flatly. "Maybe for a little bit I will. I am here only to pick my husband up." Though nothing about her appearance hinted at her being in any sort of rush. Chic bathing suit, woven wide-brimmed hat, gem-inlaid sunglasses.

"Oh? And which one is that, sugar?" Shareese asked, readjusting the beach umbrella so that the full trio could have some shade.

Still standing, the woman gazed out toward the ocean. Pursed her lips and pressed her knuckles to the center of their glossy pucker. "He's... Where is–" Dropped her sunglasses down the bridge of her nose, perching them on the crux of the button. "Oh, he's..." with an air of disappointment, "he's the very red one." Pointed a sorcerously manicured finger out toward the clutch of boys and men busying themselves with a football in the climbing surf. Mister Bennie's slope-shouldered and soft-stomached form bounded about, shining sun-fried.

"Oh! Is that so?" And Shah turned toward Aura, whose gaze was still locked with the eastern horizon. "Honey, this is Mister Bennie's wife! Isn't that just–"

Aura turned then and looked up past Shareese to where the classically cut figure of this new woman shunned the glare shadowy. Said something close enough to "Hello" to be heard as such and then shut up again, tendons rolling along her jaw. Turned back the way she was initially facing. Her gaze fell. Eyes clenched shut. Aura'd been up on the sandy heights of the beach since about an hour after they'd all arrived on Riley Island, whole staff taking the ferry from the Cobbles altogether that afternoon. A sort of team-building day for the slew of new hires. Alone in the sun.

Seeing that Aura had no intention of yet cracking open to pearl, Shareese refocused her attention on this new woman–Against all odds not only Mister Bennie's wife but also seemingly the mother of his expected child–As she set about spreading her beach towel over the sand. "Here, here, let me help you with that–"

"No, no, no need. No such thing. I won't be allowing myself any amount of helplessness until I'm so big that I–"

"Alright, sugar, not a problem. You just let me know what you, *if* you need anything, I mean. Love to lend a hand is all."

"That is indeed kind of you. What are you called?"

"Shareese, sugar. And you are?"

"Heidi." Laid out on the towel she began digging in her tote bag. Shifting papers and a tangled phone charger.

"Well it is a pleasure-and-a-half, I've got to say. I hadn't known that our Mister Bennie was expecting a child–" Slapped her hand over her mouth. Sudden shame of breaching etiquette. No way to know whether this Heidi was the sort that found it embarrassing to be pregnant and seem it at the same time.

"I can understand." Smiled a genuine row of perfectly crooked teeth, cheeks bunching peachy. "Hard to imagine he has it in him."

Shareese snorted. Redoubled covering her mouth.

"I cannot blame you, though. I cannot blame you for thinking that at all. I cannot because I know very much that he does not–"

Whatever sort of giggle-fit that was then climbing up Shareese's throat stopped its ascent. She looked over at Heidi with raised eyebrows.

"Oh, nothing quite like shame in it, Miss Sherry!" Placed a hand on her thigh. "Very modern, you know. Frozen egg and a donor, not his fault, nothing to be done about it. Just a workaround. Has a perfectly clean driver's license, so he drove me to the clinic. So... Close enough."

All said completely flat, without so much as a sheen of ironic glee or sardonic needling. The frozen egg bit had Shareese immediately squinting sideways, investigating the lack of lines around Heidi's eyes and the corners of her mouth–Old enough to need to revert to a frozen stock or?–"Well, that's just as well then." All she could think to say.

"No need to do things in an old-fashioned way anymore, you know, Miss Sherry?" Grinned again that iridescently dull smile.

"Oh, I suppose, honey. Nothing wrong, I don't think, with old-fashioned if it works, though."

"Sure, of course, but, I mean, take it coming from me," placed her hands like parentheses over the bashful burgeoning of her belly, "old-fashioned is working less and less more and more, you know?"

"Oh, I reckon I can't say much either way." Water bottle. A modest sip. More to let the conversation settle out of these increasingly fraught waters than on account of thirst. "Are you, are you thirsty, sugar? I've got a few more of these here in the cooler here." Leans to lift the lid.

"Oh, no, no, not at all necessary, Miss Sherry. I am prepared." From her tote: A bulbous, dark-green glass bottle. The cap came off with a viper's hiss and a vesuvian eruption of bubbles. Frothy neck to her lips and a few hefty swigs.

It's not until Heidi screwed the cap back and looked over that Shareese noticed her own mouth was agape in a silent gasp.

"Oh, goodness, Miss Sherry, no! It's just *mineralvann*–mineral water, I mean." Placed her hand then back on her belly. Hen's feather on an egg. "It's good, even. Don't worry, Miss Sherry, it's good for the baby. Lots of–"

"I see... I didn't mean anything by it, Missus–" neck hot all of a sudden.

"Americans." Cracked the cap again. "Pardon me, not you, but Americans in general. American mothers. They are so bad that they can't imagine anyone else being any more prepared or better at it than they are. Lack awareness..."

Shareese's shoulders tightened, and she bit the inside of her cheeks. Pressed her tongue to the roof of her mouth and inhaled deep through her nose. A lungful and composure regained. Shareese opened her mouth to speak, to find yet again calmer seas to sail.

"She's actually, now that you mention it Shah, she's been asking about you recently." Packing his garbage into the empty sack. "Says you two had one time, must've been the beach day last year I guess, don't know of any other time you two might have met, but anyway, she says that you two had an interesting conversation on the subject of parenting or something and that you mentioned you did a lot of babysitting. I guess we were talking about what happens when she's back to teaching and I'm working and all that and she said that she remembered you did that and all, babysitting and stuff and, well, if you're available..." Eyes lock.

"Oh. Sure. I don't see why not. If I'm available, of course." Turns her sandwich to take a bite out of the side that's still got crust. "All very exciting stuff, Mister Bennie. Do you know, I mean you must, whether you're having a boy or a girl?"

"A son. A boy. She's going to name him Anders, she says." Tone deflating a puff with every syllable. Not against his will, but wholly without it. Zips up a plastic bag full of refuse and drops it into the brown sack. Crumples and launches it all toward the garbage can near the door. Misses by a mile. "Shit." Rises. Phone from his pocket to feign checking the time. Last night's messages, several again from HEIDI<3. "Anyway, Shah. I ought to get back to it. Sorry to cut it short. Good talk and, uhm, I'll keep you updated..."

–And it's back into the dark of the office. Door closed behind you and, there was a time, there was a time from the beginning to maybe four or so years ago maybe when that door'd be open all day, people invited in as you caught them walking down the hall, long chats with new hires and, hell, you knew everybody's name. All long past, though. Instructed from on high to assert this office in all four of its walls. Director wants you cut off from everything so that you can see it for all it really is and that's just fine, makes sense, but hell, left the private sector for a reason. Wanted to do things with people, for people, around people, but suppose the same rules apply. Impartiality, raw data, that's what decisions are made of and you want to make the decisions that keep everyone and everything as stable as possible then you've got to maybe get as far away from people as you can. That's the only way to do it, suppose, and you've just got to maybe live with the looks and sneers and snarls that come along with it.

Management will always be situated at the end of long leers and side-eyed glances of derision. Worked it long enough to know. Now, though, with the Ballroom closing for this lark of an idea, which, mind, the whole staff is in full support of and get that in writing if you can, but it's still basic best-practice to call a Hail Mary a Hail Mary, audible or otherwise... Who knows how many years this place has left? It's a different world though, that's what's not being completely understood maybe. Can't just, you know, can't just cut things off at the pass, can't just do like you did over at Zyracom and increase sick days to stave off a strike. You know? This is a different world, this is a cultural institution, funded by the people for the benefit of the people, for the benefit of the municipality moreover, you know? Can't grow too complacent in your faux-ivory sheen.

But hell, none of your business really, is it? Been made very clear that your job is to sit down at this desk for at least eight hours a day, to act as a node in the line of communication. Close the door and foster a humming quiet, answer emails at a steady pace but with language imprecise enough to create the illusion to all lording parties above that the middle tier hovering over the workaday is being very, very, very deliberate in its responses, that everything is being considered with its due weight, and that yes, it will all get done when the time is right so let's not go about making rash decisions that could have deep effects on the lives of those we hold contracts of employment with... Let's not forget our duty to the citizenry of Madiston and, honestly, the surrounding towns and counties, the state even. The citizenry of the state, moreover. Public servitude and all that. We at Madiston MAM must work diligently to maintain our status as not only a cultural touchstone of the region, but also as an educational center and community forum of sorts, divorced as much as possible from the cynical marketplaces that have sprouted up along this coast, commodifying history and culture and reifying it all as—

A cramp bites at his knuckles and, pressing thumb to palm, Bennie reads back over the response he's typed in reply to today's official banality. A click and drag to highlight the whole thing and a backspace to send it away. Begins again. Reads over the message from the Director. Eyes move across the screen and again that weighty shroud starts to settle cloudy over his mind. Maybe it's lunch on his stomach. A few moments to digest. Fatigue coming on strong, Bennie stands up and stretches. Slaps himself across the face and runs in place—C'mon, c'mon, don't you dare. Get home late again and there'll be hell to pay with her being so close—

In the corner, near the door, is the sign that Curatorial dropped off a few days ago—There's something! An errand! Get the blood flowing. Take the sign upstairs and put it in the foyer, in front of the big doors to the Ballroom. Put it there so it can announce officially to everyone what all this constant construction racket has been. All this hammering and sawing and screeching, thuds and shatters, all day every day for the next few months only and then, yeah, run it upstairs, say hello to the Attendants one-by-one maybe, check in on everybody, make yourself known, let them all know that Mister Bennie's got it under control and that everything will be better than normal soon enough! Yeah, run the sign upstairs so that the first thing every visitor sees is: ***Coming Soon: Dermot Putsch...***

&&&

–Just barely holding on at this point. Sort of next morning that eclipses the night before. Gotta laugh at it, though. What you'll end up doing anyways, you know? Can't let the irresponsibility of it all weigh too heavy on your mind. Odds are there are people making worse decisions, trying their luck at the end of their rope. You remember the bridge well enough, a straight shot, no ice, back to normal, no need to panic over something you survived. Remember most of the night, so couldn't have actually been all that plastered in the end after all. Remember how she'd jumped on you the moment y'all got in, pulling on your shirt and getting your belt buckle in her hands like some steer's harness and, looked so pleased with it all once it was done. Y'all laying there, nary a sheet on the bed. Straight fucked them right off. Sweat-shined and breathing ragged and then, shit, she fell right to sleep, just wrapped up under your arm, nuzzled her fuck-flushing cheeks against your chest and well, couldn't wake her up then, now could you? Gonna be hell to pay in the morning, knew that. Had sobered up enough to know that there's no chance in hell you were driving all the way to the inland edge and back and well, couldn't just wake her up, hadn't seen her so relaxed in who knows how long. Goddamn a Saturday and goddamn her fucking mother. Should have got her out of bed this morning, should have woken her up and taken her home, but again, just looking at her all bundled there in the sheets, sleeping deep and couldn't bring yourself to–

A sound rises as Derek approaches the apartment. Pathetic mewl of a stir-crazy cat opens its throat into more human registers. The thinness of this complex's walls. Had gotten used to the source of the sounds getting lost in their soup, all white noise. But, as far as he knew none of his neighbors had a cat. No pets allowed sort of thing. Digging for his keys in his sweatpants' pocket, he'd be damned if the hollering wasn't coming from inside his own apartment.

Keys stubbornly eluding his fingertips, Derek sets down the rustle of plastic and paper bags he's had disarrayed about his arms. French fries spill like matchsticks from the maw of one of the grease-spotted sacks. A girthy bottled sports drink rolls across the breezeway's concrete, coming to a stop against the fence. Keys clenched and choked out of their jangle, Derek opens the door. Fullness of the screaming pours forth: tatter-lunged, mucous, hollow-throated, the horror of someone finding themselves as something totally alone...

Leaves the bags on the walkway. Into the apartment. Her cries fill the space humid. Rubs his eyes and takes a deep breath as he stands at the closed bedroom door. So immediate and real and solid and heavy that it's impossible to imagine it being any worse on the other side. As he wraps his hand around the door's knob Derek notices a tremor in his arm, sourced up by his shoulder and running tendons to cords all the way to his fingertips. Knuckle-numb tingle–Anger. Pissed-off as a motherfucker. Been through this sort of episode more than once. Anytime y'all've not been in a sober enough state to get her back to her mother's house Friday night, this is what the Saturday morning's been like. Just about can't take it anymore, can't stand to watch someone, her, Aura, *your* someone, get her strings pulled like this. Nope, no more. Put a foot down, pump the fucking brakes on this daytime talk show, trailer-trash bullshit–

"Hey! Hey! Hey! Aura, I'm here now. Aura, I'm here." Scoops her up naked and sweating into his arms, presses her whimpering face to his chest. Her phone is on the floor, screen displaying the ticking time of a call with **MOM**. Can hear the tinny hiss of shouting on the other end. Lifts her and takes her back to the bed. "I got you, girlie. I got you."

Aura's eyes stare blankly up at him as he brushes the hair sticking to her forehead away. Thumbs the salty glisten off her cheeks. "I, I've got to go, go home. I've got to go–"

"No, no," he says. "You don't have to go. You're staying here. You're not going anywhere. Aura, I–"

&&&

"Goddamn, I love you." Rolls over to again clink the bar through her nipple across his teeth. "Don't, uhm, don't have any cameras hidden, do you?"

"Oh, would you hush, Buck." Presses his face to her chest.

Sound of lungs filling beneath her ribs. A sigh's sustain. "You wanna go again?" Warm and wet, a handful of curl and flesh. A searching finger finds a searing pearl...

Digging into his hair, lifting his face again to hers. "You think you can?" Smiles into a kiss.

Bites her lip and slips a knuckle further. "I mean, probably not," he says, "but if you can..."

"No, no, just come here,"–So sweet when he's like this, like all the gunk's been scooped out. All the bitter broody bullshit leaves him, relaxed and limp and cuddly. Arms turn into noodles and get grabby. Falls asleep ninety percent of the time, just fucked tender. Melts. That was part of the initial surprise with him, someone so toothsome, so ready at all times to gnash out and bite, can turn into something malleable and weak and just plain soft. Though that's part of the fear, right? That the fire was never really burning? That it's all bluster and bull until he gets you, then it's chocolate left out in the sun. Oozing and sticky and cloying and– "You think they're done?"

Buck's eyes open. A little worm of annoyance squirming between his brows, "Huh? Do I what?"

Still got his hands between her legs. A twitch makes her kick. "Christ, B." Lifts his wrist and splays the hand over her belly. "The paintings, do you think they're done? Finished?" Motions with her chin.

72

"Oh," his eyes close again, "maybe. Hard to say."

"What do you mean?" Shifts her shoulders as to ready and lift herself upright again, off the cold floor. Concrete through the carpet.

"No, no, no. Not yet, Jess. Wait." Wraps his arms further around her middle as she rises. "C'mon, a few more minutes here."

"I've got to get ready, B."

"Make them wait." Dives grinning into the ticklish region where her belly softens.

"No, no! Stop! St-stop!"

"C'mon, Jess! Nap with me or–!"

She yips and bolts upright. "I've got to be on when my profile says I'm going to be on. Otherwise–" Looks down the length of her own body. An examination. Unnecessary prods and pulls and pinches. Finds some faint and fresh vampiric mark on her hip where Buck bit her a moment ago, mutters: "Gonna have to cover that." Looks down at him as he lazes his hand out toward where his shirt was thrown. "It's just like a real job, B. I've got to clock in at the right time, you know?"

"I show up late for work all the time, Jess. No one gives a shit–"

Bites her tongue and turns away. Dirty towel from the pile near the closet. Runs it quickly between her legs, through the spreading sop–Some fights aren't worth having. Some things aren't worth explaining. Not worth getting riled up for. Hard to mount a defense, anyhow you know? So much work to plunge into the finer details of how it all works, and furthermore why it need work like this in the first place. Better to do what needs be done and nudge him along with kindness and love and all that good stuff that promises are made of–Opens the closet door and slips in, pushing a rake of hangers along the rack toward the back to reveal the thinner row of things made from lace and leather. It's all snaps and buckles. Sheer fabric–Eroticism lies in impracticality–

"What time is it, Buck?" She says over her shoulder. Always a rush to get ready, especially when he's in the room–Feels wrong to demand certain privacies in such a small place. Not a rush because of the schedule necessarily, that's still ultimately your call. Just good business to be consistent. But, in a rush because there's always the fear that he'll see–

"I don't know. Phone is in my pants and my pants are too far away…"

–See what it's all started to look like. Doesn't watch anymore, not since the beginning. Hasn't in a few weeks, at least, so far as you know. Put on a happy face for a bit initially, said stuff about how it was kinky and like rad that you'd found a way around like the system and all that. Hasn't stood in the way of any of the things you've told him had to be done. The streaming and, recently, adding a partner. Didn't bat an eye when you told him that the solo shit wasn't going to cut it anymore, that uploaded content was going to have to push further, that the law of demand still does, and always will, dictate the nature of the supply–

When she steps out of the closet Buck is still laid out on the carpet. He's got his flannel back on, barely buttoned, but he's completely bottomless. Cock flummoxed flaccid and dripping. Some sick bird. "Hey, c'mon now," she says sweet, "get dressed so I can–"

Buck looks up, eyes scanning the form towering over him. "Is that it?"

Jess again examines her length, this time outfitted in a frumpy cable-knit, turtleneck and checkered skirt, "Gotta start somewhere." –It's about the contrast between what you see and what you get. Sweater comes off and it's suddenly studded leather and growling machinery. It's a whole thing–Buck looks away and over to the paintings, "You really dig them?"

–So now he wants to talk–"Yeah babe, I do. I think they're really good. You should go talk to the lady that runs that coffee shop near the College. I've seen stuff much worse on the walls in there, priced at like–"

"Yeah, maybe. I don't know. It's hard to tell." Standing now. Chicken-legged.

"Hell, B. If you want, *I'll* go talk to them. Gas you up and then–"

"Maybe a few more passes. There's some extra layers that could be added and–"

–Could talk about this any time, literally any time. Any other time. There's a schedule to keep and you don't have the luxury of playing muse for him right now just–"Well, give it a think then, Bucky. Let me know if you want me to take them over. Could price them pretty generously, I bet and, but, I need to get started, so…"

"Oh shit, sure, sure," scurries for his jeans and slips them on commando. Pats his pockets for keys, wallet, lighter, smokes and goes in to kiss her. "Good luck, I'll just be–"

"Only an hour, B. Love you."

"You too, Jess." And closes the door behind him.

House is cold. Last summer the draftiness seemed like a perk, like free A/C or something, but once the wet of winter came the air got still and frigid and, even with spring breaking through today, stubborn. Makes his way to the porch to catch what of the sun manages to trickle through the trees that canopy their little sump of a neighborhood. Takes a seat on the moldy outdoor couch and lights up. Closes his eyes. Kush subsiding, birds singing, breeze rustling new leaves. A car trundles down Murphy Street. Through the wall and blindered window behind him he hears, muffled: "Hey there, boys and girls and everybody in between. Miss Lady Jay here, live and living..."

&&&

–You can't let a day like this go to waste. Would just be criminal. Sure Putsch would agree. Strip back enough of that fibrous pretension, those five-dollar words and self-conscious desire to be heard, and you'll find like always just another sensualist, just another man among men who's forgotten they'd forgone the pleasure of a nice breeze. Every one of them is the same as the same is the same as.

No, read just enough to get it burbling in your brain. Can't rush these things, might dilute the understanding. Sometimes you've got just go back to where you missed the shift, find the spot that everything suddenly started to sound like gibberish, right after the whole General Theory for the Generation of Divinity or whatever he'd called it. Just a mess of footnotes referencing texts everyone should have read but no one ever has. Even experts in whatever their field find the more litigious and Levitican portions of their canon to be less than enthralling. Seems though that it's those sort of places that Putsch seems to think the truth dwells but, never mind, never mind, no use now, don't clear it away but let it settle. Sometimes you can't just go back and reread until you

75

understand, sometimes you've just got to dog-ear the page and close the book. Sometimes it's the longer books that want to be read in shorter stints and, yeah, you've just got to dog-ear or bookmark or lay it page down on the table or whatever and come back to it later once the dust has settled and maybe, sometimes, it suddenly gets clear again until its murk gets kicked up by something new. Sometimes, though, sometimes you've just got to muscle through the confusion, you know? Like with long poems or something sometimes you've got to just stop asking questions and imagine as close as you can what the poet is asking you to imagine and then and only then like do you really get it. Sometimes the best way to read is to just watch and listen. Let yourself be taken away from where you're sat to where the poet or writer or whatever is already going—

The breeze off the water cuts salt-edged and fishy through the thick musk of fryer grease and suntan lotion. Hadn't realized how far he'd walked until he took a lean against the low wall, until he took a deep breath. A dull ache set about his legs then. Hardly recognized the place, the Cobbles or—What was it that archway'd said?—Historic Colonial Madiston.

No longer just the Cobbles, not since the last really big storm. All this around him now is new, new to him anyway—Been nearly maybe even, holy shit, yeah, been over thirty-some-odd years then. You were still a teenager, what just eighteen, seventeen maybe, right?

Reggie'd pulled up in his little car, just a few days after, just as it all started drying up. That muggy period of time where branches and leaves were still scattered over the streets, where everything looks like its sinking. But, Reggie'd pulled up and asked Pops and Mom whether you were around and you were because, shit, where else was there to be? Had been out of school already just long enough to never go back, working then in the bottling plant, right? Short stint there before it all shut down and, well, wasn't that storm that finally shut it down was it? No, later, in the nineties probably but, that one couldn't have been particularly large just, guess sometimes stuff just gets hit right the wrong way round. Goddamn, hard to remember and keep all this straight. Start thinking about your life and you can only realize this far down the line that it ain' just a life anymore but a history. Makes you feel old, doesn't it? Somehow at the same time bigger and smaller than you actually really are. Was that storm, the big one in what '76 or '78? Whatever, *that* one that moved y'all to the Jaspers, water damage in the house so bad that, well, shit, was really the last really big storm so, yeah, Reggie'd pulled up and asked whether you were around because he needed maybe some extra hands to go and see to what had maybe happened to the College during the surge.

"Water'd come up that high?" Pops asked.

"Sure did, hard to believe, but sure did." So that's where y'all went. To go check on the College, save what you could of the library. Miracle there being, because there's always a miracle in times like that, right? Always a statue of Jesus left over after the church burns down and all that, but the miracle there was that the whole wing of the building, the hall or whatever, that his office sat within was completely unscathed. His library totally fine. Layout of the campus, suppose, diverted the flow or something so, just like with all miracles, less miraculous when you know the melting point of gold or bronze or stone or whathaveyou. Rest of the campus though, some of it anyway, absolutely trashed. Hired out some architect to come and build new stuff where the old stuff stood, all those brutalist protrusions, like some sort of ancient and nameless deity is constantly rising up through the ground to reclaim the realm.

Drove around then after confirming that the library was safe and fine and dry. Roads all closed. Shops and houses slowly growing out from the stubborn ebb of glass-faced floodwater. Made to meander by orange plastic and sandbag barricades, incomprehensible signage, detours into ravaged wastes and a precarious stretch of road cut through a muddy sump threatening to renege on the remittance of its flow. Brought y'all then down what was left of the Cobbles. Sure rebuilt though, didn't they?–

No longer just the Cobbles. Now a 'Historic District,' protected and maintained. Built up to the memory of what had been there before. Concrete grout work in between the stones that make up the namesake give it away, though. Look close enough and there's a discretely repeated pattern. Planned, pastiche, kitsch. Every storefront slapped with the designation of *Authentic* or *Old-Fashioned*. Air smells of vegetable oil. Ocean only on the breeze. Runaway Tavern offers Seven Kickin' Kreole

Dipping Sauces. Four horse-drawn carriages. Banner along the back: **9pm-Midnite, Magnolia Cemetery Ghost Tours, Ghastly Ghouls of the Old South–1 (912) 689-6783 For Booking.**

–"No kidding," Uncle Reggie'd said, looking out over the water. Pointed out to an area where the bay was still as the sea over a sandbar. Glassy and surrounded by breaks, "You remember what used to be there?"

You didn't. Never very much made it out this way even then, only on school field trips every now and again, been out of school for some time by then so, no, you didn't remember what used to be there before it was just still brown water.

"Used to, uhm, goddamn. Used to be a whole Cemetery out there. Like on a sort of grassy sort of peninsula, remember it?"

You didn't.

"I'd heard, but I didn't believe it. Guess it's hard to know just how bad the storm is when you're in it, all becomes sort of white noise maybe. Damn. Yeah..."

You'd had to have disagreed there. If it had been anyone but Reggie maybe you'd have made it known, but the storm never once became something so benign as *white noise* around y'all's house. Howling and trees all falling and, hell, everything up in the air as sky came down.

"Certainly humbling."

Storm had left so much behind, but all of it was torn to bits. Unassemblable back into its original. Hadn't known the Cobbles before you wouldn't have been able to surmise its existence by the wreckage. Washed away is too weak a sentiment, erased too clean. Looking at it then it was obvious that something had been there before the deluge come up, but it didn't feel like it could have been stores and bars and businesses and people.

Reggie'd said then that someone told him that coffins had been actually washing ashore down the Gulf. Taken by the current–

Carl looks now in the direction his Uncle had pointed thirty-some-odd-something years ago. The water now breaks at the edges of a seawall, lifting mounded, grassy land up above the Bay's waterline. Fenced-in and populated by obelisks and crosses and mausoleums. Markers for the memories of washed-away graves.

&&&

—Clothing yourself in last night's sweat-stiffened garments is bad enough, but goddamn salt and vinegar in the wound when the previous night's clothes are also your work uniform—

The landlord had contacted Rohaan in the middle of the day, after a week and a half of cat-and-mouse, phone-tag nonsense. Texted him saying that he had time that afternoon and that the place was going to go quickly, so if he wanted a shot at it he'd better make time to—Didn't even wait for the bus. Popped into Mister Bennie's office and laid it all out for him, ladling the time sensitivity on as thick as possible. The look on Mister Bennie's face. Foolish for even thinking you need ask for permission to leave early. Bennie couldn't care less. Looked as though he'd just woken up from a deathly sleep, nodded slowly and even yawned—

Rohaan hoofed it down 8th, sweating through his uniform's polyester despite the edge on the breeze. A deep pleasure at turning left instead of right at the intersection with Murphy Street. In that moment, knees already barking out squeaking pain, it was all finally behind him. A foregone conclusion—Wasn't going to let this get away, not after everything you've done, not after the lows you've licked and highs you've missed—Turned out, though, that there was no fight to be had:

The landlord, a margarine sort of man, met Rohaan on the street out front of the building, shook his hand, gestured toward the bar that made up the building's ground floor and said something along the lines of "nothing to worry about there, never had a problem." Then took him upstairs. Asked very few questions—No opportunity to spin the yarn you'd rehearsed on the way over—Briefest tour of the apartment, hastily executed, the landlord said: "That's about the long and short of it. If you're interested. First and last plus half for security. Swap you keys for a check and—"

Heart sank there. Rohaan patted his pockets. Entered the dragon's lair without a sword—Left your fucking checkbook at, checkbook is a misnomer, checks moreover. Never had a book per se, never had consistent cause to be writing vouchers. Just a few in the kitchenette drawer and–

"Can I give you cash?" A real show out of searching his pockets. "I don't believe it, but I've left my checkbook at my old place."–Oh, that felt sweet. *Your old place.* No more Jaspers–

"Sure, here, let's go down then. I reckon there's an ATM in the bar."

Legs shaking the whole way back down. It all felt too easy–Last time anything was this easy you'd woken up nearly a decade later in an unfurnished room, bunking with some scabby-wristed amphetamine freak –The landlord lead on the descent, lumbering and huffing and moving slow as cirrhosis. Rohaan did his best not to follow too closely behind, to keep the excitement of his breath off his new landlord's neck. Swallowed his tongue at the impulse to hurry him along, instead opting for a weaseling, "Thanks for taking the time today. I really appreciate it."

Landlord grumbled: "No problem."

They were greeted hardily by the bartender as they entered the dank, tiki-flavored place. "Howdy, howdy, and what brings you in to see us lowly tenants?" Polishing a metal straw.

Landlord did little in the way of greeting, on either front of acceptance or extension: "You all got a cash machine, right?"

"ATM's in the corner there."

Rohaan plugged his debit card into the slot. PIN number and some time while the screen flickered. Did the math for how much he was to withdraw. Made him queasy. His father's liquidity had hit his checking account like water poured into an already hot pan, popping and gasping into steam as overdraft fees and a few credit charges sizzled several hundred bucks off the top–Money moves fast, disappears before you can count it. Been broke long enough, though, to know there's no use trying to hold onto it–When the machine registered the amount requested it flashed a message: `No Withdrawal Over [$200]` and knocked him back to the beginning of the process. Had to do it in chunks and even then the machine called it quits after a certain amount, displaying the vaguery: `Sec. Code–18XX9087X58.CWA.NC.0D//A34097.` From then on disregarding any attempt to re-type his PIN. Cash in hand and defeat dropping his face, Rohaan walked over to where the landlord and bartender were engaged in a politely terse conversation.

"Hey man, the machine stopped giving. I've got just short of a month and a half here now."

The landlord said, "Fine. Fine. We'll work out the rest later. Call this first and most of security and you can move in whenever. I'll drop the lease in your mailbox tomorrow. Sign and all that and I'll collect the rest when next month is due, how's that?"

"So, second and last on the first of May?"

"Yessir. First month'll be April, but the place is empty so go ahead and move in whenever."

"Alright, sounds–"

The landlord took a napkin from the pile on the bar, produced a pen from his pocket, and swirled a squiggled signature onto the soft square. "Call that a receipt for the cash, just write how much you're about to give me. Should be fine. Don't anticipate having to take you to court. Not a worry in my mind." Placed in the napkin's scratched center a key on a wire ring, slid it across the bar top to where Rohaan stood.

"Welcome to the neighborhood!" The bartender smiled, and from there everything progressively darkens...

This morning the air is kind on his face, rechilling the sweat that's warmed to slime on his cheeks. The same cannot be said for the sun, which drills its fire into his eyes with all the wrath of having been hidden away for so many overcast days. His guts feel better only for their being empty. Soon, however, they will roll voraciously into a bottomless hunger. In this strangely blissful confluence, shutting the door behind him and pocketing his new key, Rohaan breathes deep a phlegmy lungful and reminds himself that from the top of his spinning head to the tips of his numb toes he is miles away from the Jefferson Street Housing Project, the Jaspers, from Harris Park with its zombies, even, though not quite as much, from the Museum itself. An exhale and he allows his lips to silently form the closing cavern of the word *Home*. A smile.

This part of town, New City to some, the Fire District to others, and nothing at all to many, opens out of the commercial ruins that flow flotsamly down from 8th, along the length of South Murphy Street.

Continue from that intersection a mile-and-a-half south and, from the barren wastes of dust and rust and rebar, erupts hulking housing complexes, glassy and flat, screaming the sky back at itself and all around. Most of the buildings are empty, left over from a failed pass at gentrification that Cortland County to the north caught the crest of, but if there's a hip part of town, this is it. As Good As It Gets. Mostly bars and restaurants catering to tourists and college students. As Good As It Gets...

Stepping onto the sidewalk, uniform jacket wrapped around his waist, a slight limp from using his knees as skids along the bathroom tile and: "Oh boy, do you look like shit!"

The voice is coming from behind him. Registers the smell. Dry-throated, edgy-toothed odor of cheap weed rolled up with dusty tobacco. Rohaan turns around and there in full daylight is the shoulder-shaped man whose shadow he remembers the shadow of: The bartender himself, standing in front of the establishment's entrance, gate drawn closed, puffing on a joint, "Good, uhm, good morning." Rohaan replies.

"Is it?" Looks squintingly up at the blue sky and nods, "Yup, reckon it's close enough. You feeling alright there after last night, Mister, oh, what was it?"

"Rohaan... And yours was? I'm sorry. I can't remember much of a fucking thing at all–"

"Not a worry, my friend. Nothing wrong with pushing the edge if you're celebrating. You can call me Jimbo." Smiles and blows on the roiling cherry. A flurry of ash. "You want a puff? Make you feel better."

"Oh, no, no, no. Not today. Too rich for my blood, gotta get a move on getting everything moved in, you know."

"Sure, sure. Well, you go on and let us know if you need anything and all. Welcome to the neighborhood. Don't let the glitz get to your head, it's still as much Madiston as anywhere else."

"Alright then–" Forgot his name already.

"Jimbo."

"Right! Jimbo." Turning before the smoke brings up whatever his stomach's got left, "Alright then Jimbo, thanks a million. Reckon we'll be seeing you soon then. Thanks for your help last night." And it's down toward the bus stop. Heat rising to his cheeks as the embarrassment tears out from the pit of his being–Can't do all that again, can't let yourself fall into that hole. Jimbo seems nice, but they always do and then, Christ.

How the fuck are you going to move everything? Happening so quick. Hardly planned. Still have all your shit up at the Jaspers and, goddammit Roh, get your shit together! You're almost there. Almost out of the weeds. You got the place. That's all that matters. You've got the place, you've got a new home. A HOME for the love of it all! You did it! Just gotta get all your shit in there and it's a done fucking deal.

Bus should be awhile–Rohaan pulls out his phone, dials up Jawad, and leans his head against the shelter's glass–See if he's free today. It's a weekend, right? Yeah, Saturday. So, he should be free. He's got that truck. Get it done quick. Wham and a bam and a thank you ma'am–

Quick, sharp, impatient, and void of any brotherly warmth or welcome: "This'd better be good, Roh."

"What? Good morning to you as well, Jawad..."

Sounds of feet pattering over hardwood floors. The howl of a child. Coo of a mother's waning patience. "Roh, we're trying to get ready over here. Naseer won't leave his tie alone. I haven't had a chance to shower or eat or coffee or anything, so make it quick. It'd better not be an emergency. We've gotta be at the funeral home by–"

April

I.

"Quiet out here in the night?" Lungs filling with cool silence, Bennie looks to the deep navy sky. Orange streetlights and the threat of morning blistering against black. "Yessir, quiet, quiet, quiet..."

"Ruin it, you keep reminding it like that." The Custodian'd changed out of his coveralls when they were still in the basement. Now he wears a sweater marked with the College's insignia. Basketball shorts. Still in his boots–No longer looks the approachable and paternal underling. A humor about his bearded cheeks, cartoony and bearish–Frazzle-haired legs shining white and mooning from below the frump of his upper body–You'll have to get his name at some point. Can't just be in your mind as *the Custodian*. No uniform, no coveralls, and suddenly all the more a man just as you are, a complete other. Too late to ask though–"Didn't ever notice it myself, now that you mention it. Quiet in the night. But, then again, suppose, used to be here until near six in the morning–"

"Really? How's that?" A breeze through the parking lot. Reminds Bennie's wrists and ankles and–Christ, shoes as well–Of just how wet they are–Don't know why you would have grabbed a rag like that. Doesn't makes sense. Didn't think about it though, did you? Just brought the coffees in and, maybe just felt like you just had to maybe do something, you know? Had to jump in and get your hands dirty–

"Lots more to clean when the Ballroom is open–"

–A knife. A knife every time someone reminds you of how much that little change has changed. Hold your tongue against painting the big picture, no use. Museum filled now for a month almost with the heinous sounds of destruction and construction, decimation and fabrication, all behind the locked up doors of the Belchard's Ballroom. Contemporary Spotlights Gallery now, gotta remember to remember to call it that, get that in everyone's heads, make the Ballroom a memory so it can eventually be forgotten. Damned Suggestion Box full every other day for the first time in years with people complaining about the noise and smell and how it's all such a nuisance, how they all come here for peace and quiet and cultural edification and all they find now is chaos and darkness and you'll have to tell the Docents to stop reminding their tour groups about the Ballroom because everyone is just going to have to wait, aren't they? You put up the sign, so it's clear as day that something is coming soon, Dermot Putsch even, so, so, how's that for hats and rabbits? Just a few growing pains along the way is all. Nothing you can do about it at the moment because everything that could be done is currently being done, nothing left to do but–

"–Can't say I'm all too upset about it, though. Settled in, got into a new flow and all that. Worked out with the other guys some new scheduling so that we can all still get enough hours to claim benefits." Custodian's eyes fall to Bennie. Kicking pebbles of asphalt from the parking lot, gathering into piles with his sopping loafers. See if the managerial antennae set to twirling. "Had to let one of the younger guys go, to open up the hours, but–"

Bennie's phone vibrates in his pocket. Buzzing up against a clutch of key and coin. Thumbs the phone dead through his pants and asks: "Do you, uhm, you remember much of your childhood?"

Custodian smiles and puts a cigarette between his lips. "Yeah, sort of. Some of it anyway. Don't know that I had much of one, though."

"Ahh, yeah. I feel the same way, I suppose."

Smell of tobacco rises to fill the gap in the conversation. Then, Custodian: "So, how's the kid?" A boulder in the river. Divert the flow. Keep it all on the surface.

"Oh, fine, fine. Brought him home from the hospital finally maybe couple two-three days ago. Seems to be doing well enough."–Just screams and liquid and stink and tears and no more sleep and she won't let you touch it because you don't want to touch it anyway–

&&&

Mountainous peaks and valleys eroding to hillscape, wakeful waters bring it all finally to floodplain: Splashes up from the sink all down Carl's face. Washes the sleep away for an attempt to greet the day. Woke several heavy minutes ago to a dull ache pressing in his chest. Rose from the convoluted sheets clutching at it until he found himself in the mirror. Wide-eyed, skin drooping, cheeks sunken, sweat shining in the fluorescence–Not getting any easier, is it?

No, it's not. You were foolish to think it would. Couldn't honestly expect that not having a job, not having a place to be, would give you any more motivation than you already had toward being. No new leaves ever really get turned over and this life you live, like all lives ever lived this long, has been built on still ground, stomped hardpack. Only footprints in the clay are the paths you forgot to walk. Spade's too rusty now, too dull to turn duff.

Just have to keep reading, you know? That's what made it all bearable before so who's to say that it won't, yeah, sure, but who's to say that it will, right? Gotta get it all straight in your head and that's all probably part of the problem anyway, right Carl? Just, damn, be nicer to yourself in the morning. Life's hard enough when it's lived right, no need to make it any more than that, so what's that supposed to mean then? Life's hard enough when it's lived what? Lived right? That, yeah, that. You said, what's that *lived right* supposed to mean then? Was what you were doing before '*living right*?' Well, no it was, what was it then? Think that's why it's so hard to get up in the morning now? Because you don't have anywhere to be so why be? That as far as your formulation gets? That as deep as you're going to read into yourself then? Shit, what would Reggie say to that, huh? Think he'd ever in a million years just let that be enough of an answer? C'mon, wash your face, make some coffee, get set down to it.

No coffee. Remember? There wasn't any yesterday, or the day before, or hell, who knows when the last day there was coffee in that cannister that you still haven't thrown away, just sitting there in the cabinet like some kind of joke you keep playing on yourself, but yeah, when was the last time? Was it when, honestly when has anything been right? Do you remember what day you started in on reading? When your last day at the museum was or anything other than, bet you remember what page you're on though, don't you? One-hundred-thirty-two, just after the preface sort of section to the essay titled 'By Way of Delayed Introduction: Putsch in Letters' wherein it says:

...that this essay's inclusion is sheerly at the behest of this volume's editors. I would ask any reader who has committed to the slog of following my career in the arts to skip the next forty-or-fifty-some-odd pages for the fact that they should already know my stance in general on questions regarding individual identity as a category imposed by the social marketplace. Further I would ask anybody intent on reading not only to the end of this paragraph but to the end of this essay, if not the volume *in toto,* to consider during their reading and subsequent exegetics that I, Dermot Putsch, inasmuch as I am a mind or man do not exist in any real way outside of the works I've committed to the page and objects I've committed to reality, and that any critique or hermeneutical discovery that deviates from this line should be disregarded as rank contradiction to the point of dissolution. Rest assured, all, that any questions you may have about me as a man or mind will remain duly unanswered in the following pages. Generally, I find it distasteful when artists impose their meant meanings onto the audience's readings, but in this instance I'm afraid I must sin all the same. I am not here. I never was here. I will forever be there. That being said, to please the editors, let's get the biographical grist out of the way: I was born a human child on March 15th 19sometingandsomething...

Can't remember exactly what it was. Roughly the same age as Reggie, more or less. Roughly. Anyway, that's when you shouldered one of the stacks over, right? No. No, that's when Shah started in with all that goddamned knocking.

She's just looking out for you, can't fault her for that. Always been like that, never gonna change. If you'd be honest with yourself you know you wouldn't want her to change so, sure, but she's always just always–

Knock, knock, knock and the stack fell over and then jumping from his throat, "Just a minute!" sung all singsong. Brought then the halves of Putsch's tome together and laid the volume on the card table, centered it just so–She'll wait as long as you need her to, no doubt. Never in any rush, but always just stopping by. Always just in the neighborhood, Carl, just come by and thought you maybe could use something to eat, maybe figured just come by and check in like you can't take care of yourself or something but she's not ever yet just given you the time to take care of yourself so–

"Heavens to Betsy, what happened here?" She said stepping into the apartment. Walked around the stack rendered pile and over to the card table. Set then to unpacking the bags she'd brought with her–More of the soupy same as the same is the same as it always is. Those matronly sorts of dishes that put meat on bones and make your guts so heavy they drag you right back to bed all leaden and sleepy–Said then over her shoulder: "Carl, sugar, what you want me to do with this book here."

"Just leave it, Shah."–Can come and go as you please, hon, but you can't take over or nothing like that. Appreciate all the care you give, but sometimes a man's just got to, oh would you relax, just appreciate the fact that somebody out there still cares that you're so intent on being in here. Gotta look at the bigger picture, Carl. Appreciate what you've got and–

"Well, here then, I'll just put it on the chair. Need some space, I brought you quite the spread so–"

"No, Shah, wait just–"

Turned then. Greased lightning. Hands on her hips and, "I'm sorry, Mister Carl. Am I interrupting you or being a bother of some kind?" Shot a look. Deadly.

"No, no, Shah. I'm sorry. Here." Walked over to the table tail-tucked. Grabbed the book himself to make room. "Was just, just reading and you know it's very involved so–"

"Well, I'm glad you're enjoying it. Sorry to interrupt you, Mister Carl."

"No, no. No such thing. Just have to give me a minute to come back to reality and all."

"Mm-hmm..."–Never one to buy anything you're selling, you know that. She smells your shit a mile before she sees it. Don't even know why you try to get anything past her–Unpacked everything and fixed the plates before she brought up the pile again. "So, what happened there?"

–But you try nevertheless, don't you?– "Nothing. Was looking for something and I guess it fell over. Then you came knocking so I guess I ain' had a minute to stack it all back up."

"What were you looking for?"

"Something that was referenced in that other book, the one that was on the table."

"Did you find it?"

"No, no. I must have misplaced it at some point."

"Where you reckon?"

"Maybe at the Museum. They confiscated a book of mine way back when." –Praise be, that's all it took to get her off the subject, off prying your mind for signs of psychological abnormality. One mention of something done dastardly, by the Docent staff no less, and Shah could take care of herself for all the injustices she could extemporaneously unearth. Let her go, let her go, gonna use fixing you as substitute for taking care of herself may as well see if you can flip the script on her. Humor her and all that and she'll leave you be longer than if you put up some sort of fight. Let her get it off her chest and then you can get back hopefully to the text. Let her in and then you can be alone.

Don't know how he did it though, lived like this with all this reading and only reading. Can't have been the only thing he ever did but hell if you ever saw him do anything else. Maybe you just gotta *learn* how to do it, how to not let the words make your eyes tired, how to empty your mind away from wandering and wondering, maybe, maybe, maybe you've just got to forget yourself completely and that's how you let the books fill you is by becoming empty enough a vessel for them but goddammit can't even get the gumption up to get coffee to get the blood moving toward gumption enough to read!–

Back to the darkness of his bedroom. A tearful heat around his eyes. Bloom of a bodiless exhaustion he can't explain to himself. Carl's thighs hit the edge of the bed and he falls face first into the sheets. Cheeks that were so ready to crumble into sobs tighten suddenly around phlegmy coughs as the wind is knocked out of him.

Like punched in the stomach, Carl curls fetal and rolls away. Tears free now he feels around in the mess of fabric for the edge and heft that struck him. Rustle and resistance. Can't get his hand around it in any wieldy way. A deep breath against the sickening pain and he rolls to tear the linens away, revealing the book: Putsch's *Thermopoetics*. Had fallen asleep reading it last night. Must've laid on it. Fell asleep reading it, middle of the second essay, Uncle Reggie, as ever, impossibly far away...

&&&

The clutch of trees has bloomed back green, filling in their branches' network with leaves. A commendable effort toward blotting out this balcony's view of the highway and all of Cortland County's low concrete. Though the fast food signs are obscured, and the sun-sharpened glint of traffic's cruel chrome is brought a grain duller, the vernal blooming does little to assuage the sound and smell of it all. The tannic effulgence of motor oil and fryer grease still fills the air, trapping whatever heat may fall. Rubber and afternoon's bubbling asphalt. The hum of engines broken only at rush hour by the cry of dwindling car horn. Plastic and gravel. Smoke and roar. Gasoline and exhaust. Chime of broken glass. Solid, still entropy. All of it thick. All of it heavy. All of it always—A shame the balcony doesn't face the other way. Shame that the whole apartment complex isn't rotated so that when you lay out like this the sun is at least bouncing bronze off the rolling brack of Salt Creek instead of some semitruck's fender. Even then though, even there you can still see, moreover, still would *have to see* Madiston's crippled skyline rising out of its own smog. Shipyard cranes cracking the glass of the seaside horizon's pristine pane. Look up now and it's at least all crystal sky blue and spring's tearing greenery. So just lay back here in this faux-wicker or rattan or whatever-it-is little lounge chair and relax. Light a smoke and rest the book on your belly.

Got the apartment to yourself today. Don't let it go all to waste just because it isn't perfect. Nothing ever is, has been, or will be so don't get caught now hoping for impossibilities. Count your blessings, Aura, count them up as high as they'll go. Not as hungover as you ought to be. Leftovers in the fridge are still good, unless your belly just hasn't turned yet. Got a fresh pack of smokes. Sun isn't too bright. There's just enough chill on the breeze to brace your skin against this t-shirt, but not enough to make your toes cold. Haven't had a headache one since you left Mama's and now you've got the apartment to yourself today. One day a week when you've got off and he's just starting up. One day a week guaranteed, so quiet that nag there at the back of your mind, hon, quiet it down and tell it the dishes will get done when the dishes get done and if he's got a problem with a modest pile then he can be the one what cleans them. Shouldn't maybe have set the precedent so early on that he could expect to come home on your day off to having the whole damned place clean and spick and span and shining, but it seemed then that first week like thanks due enough. Mama kept on with all her calling and so he put you on his mobile plan and bought you a new phone and everything and so, well, couldn't just sit around and watch television and the situation, you're like a damned cat sometimes you know that? Like some street cat brought in from outside and now your fur stands on end and makes you nervous because you've been here so many times but still couldn't settle in enough initially to start reading or anything like that just had to clean and write it all off as thanks for, well thanks for what? Loves you, doesn't he? Yes, and you love him too as well so it's not thanks that y'all owe each other and making it all transactional like that'll give you enough reason to feel dirty enough to clean anyway so...

It just felt right, is all, isn't that right? Isn't that alright? Had a whole quiet house, apartment, yes, fine, sure, but still had a whole quiet apartment to yourself and can you really blame yourself for playing house a little bit? Scrubbed the days-old food from the dishes and reorganized what there was in the pantry, not much but enough to start a system or something. Wiped the lime and scuzz from the sink and shower and, hell, made the bed. Vacuumed and, the look on his face when he came home! You remember? It was only almost a month ago at the most. At the most. But the look on his face! Like he'd seen some kind of ghost or, or, or for a minute thought that maybe he'd walked into the wrong apartment! Jaw dropped. Eyes bugging and, "Holy shit, babe. You didn't, Jesus Christ, you didn't have to do all this!" And what did you say? No problem, hon. That you were just looking for something to do or getting antsy or something else that wasn't a lie at all at the time because it did feel like every smudge wiped from the mirror was a smudge off your soul, that the clots on the plates were threatening to clog and stop your heart, that the crud ringing the foot of toilet was the same stuff you cough up in the morning after a night of too many cigarettes. Mama's house was such a wreck and you never could do anything about it but now then here you could and you did and you wiped it all away and it was clean and shiny and smelling like chemicals and then it all got messed up again! Living throws everything into chaos and the next day off you have alone in the apartment you spent it cleaning again! And again... again... But now it's the perfect sort of afternoon to maybe read and relax, the mess that's been made is yours and his and since it's y'all's it's y'all that can clean it up so just lay out here now in this faux-wicker or rattan or whatever-it-is little lounge chair!

Perfect afternoon. Inhale the last and snub the butt and crack old William on open. See what the fuss is all about. Been staring you down long enough, damn near forgot you nicked it. Sitting on the nightstand performing its duties as coaster. Soak a hole right through it if you aren't careful so take this quiet before to crack it back open. Won't be like last week, won't be starting so late, so there won't be Derek coming home in the middle of it. He won't interrupt you in the thick of the introduction's prose. Biography and ruminations on the Bard's miraculously middle- to working-class upbringings. Critiques of his private business practices and sweet speculations of homosexuality. Theories on the identities of his Fair Youth and Dark Lady. Professor Reginald Lloyd diving into the lightless depths of a sapphire ocean of literary critique, all charybdic with dialectics:

> ...of course, as the critical line generally goes, the only thing Shakespeare *forgot* to write about was himself. Can his understanding of humanity be so praised as it is if he himself is absent from rabble he renders? Even here in the Sonnets, whether in the begrudging encouragement of the Fair Youth or the repulsive eroticism of the Dark Lady, in these seemingly most personal of works where, by the very nature of the form, the poet's pen *must* be present the poet himself is largely absent; a step further might even propose that it is the polar contradiction between the Fair Youth and Dark Lady that actually does the work of dissolving Shakespeare into so much dust and smoke. It is as a blow in opposition to this reading that the poems are here being presented in Shakespeare's own English, and not in what I will term 'translation.' This common critical line, that the Bard is less a man than ink, in some circles to the point of proposing a historical

and physical nonexistence, sheerly because of the antitheses presented by his plays and this specific cycle of poetry, should be for our contemporary sensibilities not only ludicrous but inarguable. We surely have come to a point in our feeble understanding of the human condition, which Shakespeare himself is often considered partly responsible for shaping, where we can comfortably tease out the full length of the twine from which these contradictions are knotted so nastily. That all seems simple enough perhaps, but here let's take one critical step forward and make a more daring case: Let's give the fuddy-duddies and sticks-in-the-mud, those ivory-shelled literati that cannot convince themselves of even the possibility of genius springing from the middle-classes (whether their underestimation of bourgeois intellect comes from proletarian pride or aristocratic arrogance is for our purposes of no consequence), their fair due and concede the fact that indeed William Shakespeare was less a man than the inclinations of his ink! But, let's be all the more mindful of the mechanism behind this argument. It is *not*, as has been badgered to death, that Shakespeare did not exist nor, as this argument ultimately serves to claim, that no *single man* could hold genius enough to produce such works as those to which his name has been attached, but it *is* instead that Shakespeare was *killed* by the works he committed to the page and stage! Not killed bodily by the labor of producing masterpiece upon masterpiece, nor in the fashion of romantic cliché, the starving writer dying midsentence and pen in hand. No, nothing so absurd. Shakespeare was killed in much the same way as Nietzsche (or perhaps even more to point: Mainlander) proposed that Man had killed God, in that the good Bard's frail humanity was superseded by the vision of humankind he had authored. Shakespeare could never be present in his works *because* he wasn't as human as the men and women he wrote. Though Shakespeare can be said, from a critical point-of-view, to have died at the point of his own transcendent quill, we cannot forget that we have spent the past five-hundred-odd years devouring the corpse he left behind. A eucharist of pure English euphony! We have subsumed the body of his work into our lived experiences not only at an individual level but on a *cultural* level as well; such as this is, we can say that we live in a world populated by men and women of a Shakespearean form. Now, with this true-to-pen edition of his Sonnets, perhaps we can impose a new and radical re-reading of these texts and bring forth in ourselves a Neo-Shakespearean, resurrected vision, a further transcendence from the groundwork the Bard initially laid-out.

To demonstrate the inner-workings of this new hermeneutical framework we will have to turn our attention to examples from the verse itself...

But then there was the sound of the door: Opening. Slamming. Heavy backpack dropping to the floor. Boots on linoleum. Boots on carpet. Squeal of the sliding glass.

Derek then. Arms crossed over his dirty t-shirt, something scrambling his face into a pensive pucker. Silent in that stunted, mannish way, begging to be asked to speak. So, you closed the book short of finishing the introduction, placed it on the glass table, and: "Hey babe, how was work?"

He reached down then and plucked a cigarette from the pack. Lit it. Squinted as the cherry glowed up and sizzled back. Could tell by the twitch set in his jaw that he was looking for the words. Few as possible. Simple. "Scooch," was what he landed on and snuffed the cigarette out on the textured glass.

"What?"

"Scooch, scooch." Lowered himself onto the lounge.

"Babe, I don't–"

"Scooch!" That time with a smile. Your resistance turned it into a game. No more naked emotion. Just pushing your buttons.

"There's not enough room on the–" Didn't even finish before he weaseled his way under you. Caught you up in his arms and laid your head on his chest. Rise and fall of sweat-stenched heaves. Asked him then after a few breath's quiet: "Everything okay, hon?"

"Just lay with me for a second, Aura."

"Rough day?"

"Yeah. David quit apparently, so there was just so much to, never mind. It doesn't matter. Just lay with me a minute."

"Alright. Okay, love." Closed your eyes then. Listened to the sounds inside of him: Fragile work and whir of fine and moist machinery. Life carried through channels and canals. Low rasp of lungs filling and the gurgle of a belly that needs it. Warmth giving greasy way to heat, the simple living heat of muscles stretched over bones, the heat of meat on ribs. Weathered rubber of tendon, churl of blood and *Ump-a-Bump* of heart pumping. Slow, languorous, thick, sinking, bloody. Every fall a chance to rise, and rise a guarantee of collapse...

A dark cloud has been setting to hover around his head. Explained it all that night, just the once: Jawad took David's exit as an opportunity to change things. Promoted Derek to a position like Assistant Foreman or something, the sort of promotion that provides no bump in pay but comes with a plethora of promises toward a future just far enough away. As he put it, at the end of the day it's a power play. David gets up and just fucking leaves and then there's a hole to be filled, that means fresh blood, that means new people kissing ass. Promotion is just a way for Jawad to find out if Derek's still going to kneel and pucker or if he can pivot and, can get away with all kinds of fuckery if your staff hasn't worked for you for very long, lots of aberrations can be made normal, all kinds of fuckery, Derek'd said. So, given his current state and all the stress and all you may as well really, really lay out today. Take as much of it as you can for yourself because he's gonna need looking after once he gets home. Doubt it's gotten any better. So, skip the introduction this time. Just get to the soul of it–

Props the book open on her stomach and reads down her nose:

From faireſt creatures we deſire increaſe,
That thereby beauties *Roſe* might neuer die,

&&&

–What could you have reasonably expected? Day off and of course everything goes to absolute Hell. Could smell him coming up the stairs *to* the entrance. Heavens to Betsy and back, it's thick enough here in the foyer to make a blind man's eyes water!– "Mister Buchanan!" Just enough boss-lady *umph* to scare him out of the haze. Nearly jumps out his shoes. "Mind telling me what's got you *all* the way out here?"

"Huh?" Heel turns away from the new sign out front of the former Ballroom's, soon-to-be Contemporary Spotlights Gallery's, shuttered and locked doors. "Oh! Shit, woah. Miss Shareese!" Telltale redness crackling the whites of his eyes, weighty sag to his face, and that fender-fucked skunk smell. "What's, uhm, what's up? I thought it was just Mister Rohaan working today."

"It is, sugar. It is." A smile held back but crawling beneath her cheeks.

"Well then what're you doing here then?" Watery smoke-fried eyes getting antsier in their sockets.

"I mean to ask you the same thing, Mister Buchanan. I was not aware that the foyer was a post that one could be assigned. Suppose the rules are different when I'm not around?"

"No, no ma'am. I'm actually on the, uhm, on the second floor today so–"

"It seems to me that you are very much *not* on the second floor at all–"

"Ha! Yeah, alright, got me, Miss Shareese…"

–At least he's sober enough to know that being stubborn won't get him anywhere. Always liked this Mister Buchanan. Perhaps he may be a little too relaxed to be reliable, but characters are always welcome, and he's at least got some personality to spare– "Who *is* on the second floor at the moment?"

"I've got, I've got someone watching it for me. Don't worry about that. I just had to uhm–"

–Ought to have planned a lie ahead of time, young man. Can't be sneaking around just to fold once you're caught. But, hell, you ought to let him go, let him off easy. You're not even supposed to be here, so let it come down on Rohaan if anybody. Attendants sure as Heaven is paved in gold don't run amuck like this on your shifts so– "Needed perhaps to make a phone call, Buck?"

A brief sparkle of knowing sobriety and, "Yeah, shit, phone call. Had to make a phone call and tell my, uhm–"

"Good, good. I hope everything is alright then." A hand on his shoulder and a slight nudge in the proper direction, "But let's get back to our assigned post."

"Yes, ma'am. No problem. I'll just–" And down the hall he goes.

–Middle of the damn day and these halls, the first place any visitor sees, are dark as blue-clouded dusk. Shame. No light from outside, no crystal-scattered, heart-burnishing glow from the bulbs of Eugenia's Chandelier. Nothing but dark until you get to the other galleries. Completely uninviting. And then there's this godforsaken racket. Sounds of saw and hammers, metal sheets maybe wobbling, shit being dragged from one end of the gallery to the other. Some secret being erected behind these doors, something new being built out of thin air and whimsy and without a whiff of concern for what it'll do to everyone else down here that's got to work here. Just have to accept that these halls will be loud and empty until the doors open again, reckon...

Used to be that all this marble and dark timber held on its face and grain the golden glow of faux-firelight. Shadows, visitor and employee alike, used to move as storm clouds over the settled warmth of heavy ochre spilling from the Ballroom's archways, gild cut by the pitch of human presence. Fairy-splotches of glittering rainbow floated about shoulders, freed refractions from the Chandelier and so much silver. You couldn't move an inch without the glint of something you'd never own galling you to gawk. None of that now though. Only the lazy grey of early afternoon on the walls. So, swipe your keycard and get to the basement. Plenty of day left to burn, shouldn't waste it being upset over things outside of your control. Just get down to what you came here to get down to–

Peers briefly into the breakroom, smiles and "How're we doing today, everybody?"

A volley of smiles in return from the few on break. None of the Attendant staff but a few from Secretarial and that one chinny man from the Preparator's Workshop that's always had a pleasant rapport with her. A fugal chorus: "Hey, girl, hey!" and "Ooo, that sweater is doing you well!" and "What on God's greenest has you snooping around here on your day off? Go back home to your man!" Responses fired off: "Hey, hey, y'all!"

and "Got it on sale, sugar." and "No man waiting on me, honey. Ain' a man in this world man enough!"

Chuckling follows her down the hall as she approaches Mister Bennie's door. Pleasant prelude to what always proves to be a miserable encounter:

Three knocks and no response–Told him three times that you'd be coming in today to pick it up, so no reason he shouldn't be ready for you. Always got the damn window blindered. Types like a mouse. Never takes an unscheduled call. No way to know if he's inside–Three more knocks, knuckled up in volume and followed by a singsong, "Mis-ter Beh-nee..."

Again, nothing.

A glance over both shoulders and Shah raises a flattened hand. Brings it against the door with a welt-summoning *Whap!* Hinges rattle.

Within the office: A muffled glassy crash, whoosh of papers liberated from their stack. Clatter of utensils rolling unruly, and a castrated whine. "Ahh, gah-dammit..." Shuffling as order tries to manifest out of chaos.

Three knocks and another croon.

"Just a," burbling brook of curses, "just a minute. One moment." Snap of lock and the door opens to Mister Bennie retreating.

"Everything alright, Mister Bennie?" Shareese bites the inside of her bottom lip against a rising chuckle, "Did you manage to–?"

"Yes, yes, Shah. Everything is fine. I found the, just give me one moment, please. Have a seat or something," bends down at the side of his desk to lift the computer monitor off the floor–Blow out your back lifting like that, Lord in Heaven–

Shareese takes a familiar seat on the other side of the desk. Chair too low to the ground. Knees kissing chin. "I don't want to take too much of your time, Benjamin. Just grab the book and be on my way, I reckon."

"Nonsense. It's no trouble." Sits down again. Straightens the busted-up monitor. "Nice to have a visitor every now and then, though, days off can certainly be busy in their own way..."

"True indeed. God's honest..."

"Don't I know it. Seems like more and more I'm begging to be in the office." Helpless little grin.

"I can only imagine, Bennie. I bet he's already getting big, isn't he? The little Anders..." Her eyes briefly drop to the sallow sink of his chest where, across the vertical stripes of Eastery blue and yellow, there is a thoughtless hand's smear of bleachy pink. "Quite a lot of trouble?"

"Indeed, indeed. But that's how we all were, is it not?" Up again. Rolling open drawers and slamming them shut again, "It's only just and right that we should have to put up with it ourselves on the other end, don't you think? Penalized for crimes we can't remember committing," lips tightening, whitening, and a roil of red above his brows, "now where the hell did I–?"

"I thought you had said you had it, Mister Bennie? That you'd found it."

"I did, or do. Just a minute." Jams his hip into the edge of the desk and, quick as a cat, catches the monitor before it can tumble again, "Ha! Bastard! Just one more moment, Shah. I do have it."

"I can come back another time, Ben. Working tomorrow, so it's no trouble. I'm sure Mister Carl will understand–"

"No, no, no. Just give me one sec." Filing cabinet drawers, "It's somewhere. Don't know why he would want it back though, trash that it is. Should probably be burned."

"It has, I think, more sentimental value than anything. I don't think he intends to ever–"

"Sure could quote it. Like a regular scholar, way I remember." Opened just about every drawer imaginable, gone around the whole office twice now.

"He was only–"

Bennie sits back down at his desk and raises a hand, pulling rank. "I've no interest, Miss Shareese, in digging up anything other than the book itself. Bygones be bygones and all that, alright?" Reopens all the drawers he'd already opened, guts them of binder and ream and, "Ah, there! Must have buried it, which is what I'd recommend done with it anyway. Pass that along to the good Herr Carl if you will." Drops onto the desk the volume's full heft. "You'll find it in the same condition it came to us in, not a mark made or a page frayed, not a vile word of it read. There's a lighter in this drawer as well, it seems, if Carl would like the whole book-burning kit..."

"That's all just as well, Mister Bennie. Thank you for digging it up." And she rises to grab the volume from the ruins about the desk. Big, clothbound in bloody burgundy, gold lettering on the spine: **MEIN KAMPF**. Shifts it in her hands, unable to get a comfortable grip–Honestly don't know why he'd want it back either, but that's none of your business. Just know that it might help to wipe that frown from his face, that godawful catfish grimace he'd had on last you'd mustered the goodwill to visit. Lips and eyes all droopy, snarling his words.

More and more distant the longer he's been out of work. Says he's keeping busy, says he's been reading and trying to fill his life up with the sentences he'd skipped, says he can feel his mind growing. So, all that's good, more or less, suppose. Only so much you can really do for people at the end of the day, especially when they aren't the ones reaching out; when there's no phlegmy tears on the other end of the phone, when the answer is nothing more than a terse 'hello' and everything thereafter is confined to the pinprick syllables of 'yes' and 'no,' resigning finally into a 'sure, I'll see you then,' it's difficult to know whether you're stepping into a warm and welcome hearth or a lion's den. He hadn't made the distinction any easier to parse with the way he'd opened the door, turning away the moment the latch let the hinges squeak:

The place was dark, lit only by the sunset's low glow and a little flickering desk lamp. The smell, that sour-tummied odor, had returned to hang its laurels in the air. Shuddered to think that the kitchen had perhaps returned to its prehistoric swamp state. One of the book towers that stonehenged the living room was collapsed and as your eye was drawn over to it Carl growled out some bullshit about how he hadn't been expecting you, and your unannounced arrival had caught him off guard, that he was perusing the stack for a reference text because: "There were some historical things in this book here," motioned toward the big white brick of a book on the card table, "that I just can't quite square. But I think I left the book I'm looking for at work... I mean, the Museum, you know."

Offered then to retrieve it. Least you could do, and the only way at this point to guarantee you'll have due cause to see him–

"You don't happen to have a bag or anything, do you? A bit big... Won't fit in my purse."

"Just carry it, Shah. It's a lot leaner than it looks." Bennie sits back in his chair. Feet up on the desk. Grins. Monitor wobbles.

"Alright, alright." And Shah turns, waving him off–Not gonna get riled-up over ancient history on your day off, no way in Hell–"Thanks again, Ben. I'll see you tomorrow..."

"Tell Mister Carl I–"

"Alright. Alright. Thanks again, good-bye." Shuts the door behind her, cutting Bennie's retort in two–Let him have his misery to himself, don't fight with people who've given up everything they'd had to lose–Makes her way down the hall, book up under her left arm. Up under the right as she again passes the open breakroom door. Into the Floor Manager's office without a knock.

"Christ! Who the fu–!"

"Just me, Roh. Just me."

Rohaan kicks his legs off the desk and puts his phone down on a stack of papers. "Scared the shit out of me, Shah."

"Should have seen me coming," nods over to the conglomeration of grainy, black-and-white cathode-ray television screens across from the desk. The all-seeing fly's eye on the wall of every gallery.

"Oh, you know I can't see worth a shit what's going on on these shitty little–"

"Don't have to tell me twice..."

"What's that supposed to mean?"

Drops the book on the desk. "Do we have any of those take-out bags anywhere, the white plastic ones?"

"I don't know...What do you mean, *don't have to tell you twice*?"

"Here, scooch," and she opens a desk drawer revealing a morass of plastic bags she's been meaning to recycle, "you assigning the foyer now?"

"What do you mean?"

Cinches a bag around the book–Dreadful thing...

&&&

Of course. Go to the bus stop, check the schedule notices and what? Yep, completely incomprehensible as usual. So, you bet on it being delayed. So, you light up a cigarette. And *boom* before you can even get a second puff in you see the motherfucker come rounding the corner a block away. It's all that kind of joke that if you told it everyone would catch the punchline before you even got the chance to make a fist. Been that kind of day though, so what else were you expecting? Should have held off on your little toke break earlier as well. Getting caught by Miss Shareese and all and reading that name, *Dermot Putsch*, having that spark a bunch of stuff off in your brain and, don't know, man, just couldn't settle into the high after that could you? Felt like someone was watching you. Perfectly good waste of perfectly good weed. Damn near scripted the way it all played out. Like a caricature of yourself. Kept looking up at the security camera there in the gallery. Hell. Doubt they even work. But still, weird day felt like, felt like the whole of everything was not necessarily conspiring against you or anything but more that the whole of everything had you in mind today, like that maybe the sun rose not like *for* you necessarily but with the anticipation at least a little bit of shining down on you or something, shit, just like as a joke though.

Light. Smoke. And *Boom*, there she comes: Northbound D. Know it from a mile away with your eyes closed just listening to it purr and smelling its exhaust. Know it all the more for its naked right side. Paint swiped off and never any advertisements over the dull silver scar. Don't know what it is about that turn off 8th and onto Murphy that makes it just can't seem to make it without scraping and screaming against the telephone pole there. Seen sedan, truck, and the clumsiest of vans handle that turn just fine, but never once have you ridden the Northbound D and not had it rub up against that pole. A snake sick of its skin. Whole inside of the damned thing fills with a heinous run away braking-train scream and the floor shakes and your head comes up off the window, jerked awake by the sound like the world being torn in half. Awake just in time to witness the city's disintegration:

Block by block buildings shrivel and brick gives way to plywood. Windows grow broken from their sills. Grass loses its war with weeds. The victorious dynasty never reigns wildflower. The brick that survives speciates to cinder block. Wicker devolves peelingly to plastic. A geological timeline of prehistory read backwards. Everything simplifies, reverts, and becomes somehow hardier and more precarious. And it stops at Harris Park. Off the bus then and it's just the sandy and fried expanse spreading pitifully out into the night, illuminated by a few orangely glowing light posts clouded and cluttered with gnats and mayflies and June bugs and mosquitoes and never the first thing you notice but they always materialize out of the void, more and more of them the longer you bear looking. The junkies or whatever everyone calls them. Some gathered in little clutches, counting change or passing a bottle of malt liquor and a kitty litter joint around back and forth. Others are strung out and slumped on the benches or at the trees' feet. More yet just pace, always pacing. One end of the Park to the other until, suppose you've never watched long enough to see whether or not it's true, but you pace like that and at some point you're going to drop, so suppose the ones that pace just do that until they don't anymore and then they don't until they do again. Wouldn't know. Don't want to, really. Do everything you can to just ignore that bit there at the end of this regressive history, last stop before the bus takes you to the Belchard Estate Grounds to turn around and do the whole thing all over, the same as the same is the same as...

But off at Harris. Get off at Harris Park and look past it all to find just a moment of quiet and let the day settle out of your mind. Because it was almost, almost like the beginning of a story, you know? A story you know, as well, one that you told yourself your life was going to tell so, so don't get all just let the day settle out of your mind because if you don't you might miss that it might be the beginning of a story. Maybe even a good one, right? Stoned out of your fucking mind staring at that sign, right? Thinking the whole time something about like where do you know that name from, like where had you heard it first because you definitely knew it and know it now like, *Dermot Putsch* is one of those names that every art school dropout knows or heard and knows that they should know but like, shit, funny because you couldn't think of it then, couldn't get it in your head that you knew that name because you held out for so long for this shit job at the art museum on the off chance that you maybe get the chance to run into one of the names that you know you know and you knew that name but forgot where it was from that you knew it even though the answer is obvious and what it was always going to be that the answer is you knew it because you went to art school and you forgot that you knew it because you dropped out of art school to go and try to be an artist by meeting maybe one day maybe meeting one of the names that they say you should know in art school if you want to be an artist and there it was, that was one of them, and you couldn't fucking remember that you already knew that already and then Miss Shareese said something and you near pissed yourself and didn't remember until just like maybe now or a few moments ago about where you knew that name from. Dermot Putsch. Feels maybe like something big is out there weaving coincidences together and maybe what really makes all those stories they tell you before you drop out of art school, as in maybe that's what really they should be telling you about all those stories, that it doesn't matter what sort of art you make or anything like that and that maybe it's really that an artist, like as in someone who makes art and gets called an artist for doing it, maybe what really makes an artist an artist is that they're the type of person who gives up everything to go fishing for coincidences, seeking out for themselves to glow as the nexus point between confluences of improbabilities and that the story has nothing to do with maybe like how they say in articles and movies, nothing to do with the setting out on your own and eating shit and dirt for three meals a day and getting really good at painting or drawing or writing or any of that stuff, got nothing to with finding the end of your rope, getting just enough noose together to hang yourself before the big break comes because maybe you skip out on all the rest of the pain and poverty that rests ahead of you in your future if you just keep your eyes open for impossibilities and coincidences and always, always, always bet when and only when the odds aren't in your favor because like, Dermot Putsch, man, you know that name because you've heard that name and now that name might be pretty close so maybe you get to where you just happen to get to know that name because you know that man or more that the man might get to know your name because you knew his or something like that because at this point it's got to be something at some point because Harris Park is big and there over on the east side there's already emergency lights flashing and soon some EMTs will drag another of these poor bastards into the back of an ambulance, seizing or bleeding or both maybe even not moving at all and the ambulance is just a courtesy because everyone knows the son of a bitch is already nameless and gone. Soon it'll be hot again and you and Jess'll have to swallow the full girth of your mistake as everything gets sweaty and you won't be able to think straight and the reality of escape will become some solid fantasy that you'll forever be bogged down in the dream of. Quicksand, quicksand, quicksand. Set up shop in a swamp and where you land is quicksand, quicksand, quicksand. Swallow you in the struggle.

But, but, but now it has to be home enough because it's what you've got so just light. Smoke and take the first steps–Off the curb, away from Harris Park. Keys in a fist.

Once inside his house: Nostrils flare. A needling sting plays in his sinuses. Quickly turns to burning. Vision blurring. Eyes water. Tries to breathe but the air has been replaced with something solid and hot that won't fit down his throat. From the side there is a chaos, a muted cacophony, as a vise starts to press at his temples. A slamming door, footsteps on linoleum. Then Buck is hooked around the neck by a strong arm and dragged kicking, vision slowly running hazy to purple to black at the edges, down the little hallway, past the bathroom, and into his and Jess's bedroom. He's dropped on the carpet and his lungs kick back. Wheezing, ragged, resinous, butane bong rip hacking. Vision reforming and a glistening rope of saliva unspools from his mouth onto the stiff berber carpet piles as he, choked into sobs, tries to catch his breath.

"Oh, oh, shit, shit, shit," a lighter touch about his shoulders now. Jess's voice at his ear. Rapid-fire pecks of placating kisses on his neck and she speaks again, "Shit, shit, I really thought it'd have dissipated by now, shit, shit, fucking shit. I'm so sorry hon. I left the windows and–" kiss "everything open and–" kiss, kiss, "I'm so, so, so sorry..."

A coppery taste in his mouth. Surprised the discharge isn't pink or red because it feels bad enough that he might as well be bleeding inside.

"What, what the fuck is going on, Jess?" His voice, a lazily deflating balloon.

"I know, I know. I'm sorry. It was stupid of me, I didn't think it through," she brings a wet washcloth to his eyes. The cool soothes the persistent but steadily dulling sting, "Bleach and ammonia. Should have known, it's like home chemistry one-oh-one…"

"Sure is." Another voice, but not unknown. David: "But it really should be fading by now. Windows are open and everything…"

Buck pulls Jess's hand away and uses the rag to wipe his mouth. His vision is clear enough for comprehension. David, boxers and t-shirt, is shoving a crusted towel under the gap at the bottom of the bedroom door.

"Bleach and ammonia?" Asks the room. Still hard to speak, "What the fuck was that for?" He leans back against the wall.

Jess is at the desk taking a big swig from her water bottle, hair pulled back and wet. She's glistening all over. Lingerie clinging and mascara running. David has completed his task of sealing the room and makes his way to the window. Wide open, pokes his head out to breathe and cool off. Camera on the desk and three empty water bottles.

"Well, followers have been asking for a long time," another swig, "So I figured we might as well do one. I mean, one ought to be enough I think; these fetish freaks don't much go for variety so long as you nail down the verité, you know what I mean?" As if she's being completely crystal clear.

Breath sufficiently returned now, the smell of it all hits him: piss and fuck and bleach and sweat, thick and rank and, sees then that his paintings, the three canvases, still line the wall they like to shoot against, "You guys didn't film in here did you? I, I really don't want my paintings in the shots, it's like cross-contamination or–"

"No, no, hon, we shot in the bathroom. Couldn't do it in here for the carpeting…"

"Oh, okay, cool, cool." Still a vise about his temples, "Can I get some water?"

"Oh fuck! Of course. So sorry, babe." Down on her knees, brings the bottle to his lips. "There you go, hon." Kisses his cheek. Smell is strong there. Ropey and hungover or only coffee all day. Bottle away and she plants one on his lips, salty and bitter. He locks his abdomen so that he doesn't pull away, but at the taste he can't help but allow a whimper of disgust to rise.

"Hey, guys," David's back in the room, nostrils wide and sniffing. "Guys, I think that shit is leaking into in here as well. Maybe, we'd better wait outside..." Picks his jeans up off the floor, slips them on. Out the window. A rustling thud.

Jess walks over to the window and is lifted out.

Another hack and Buck covers his face with the crook of his arm. Stands and walks to the door. Picks the crusty towel from the floor and opens everything up–Shit'll never dissipate if there's no cross breeze–He then climbs out the widow himself to join David and Jess on the porch. She's already shivering. Gives her the towel. Kisses her cheek.

"It's going to be a minute, reckon." David says.

"We should get some beer!" Jess chirps.

"Y'all got any money? I'll make a run real quick."

Jess: "Fuck, all mine's inside."

Buck produces his wallet and the emergency twenty he's had stashed in it. "Here, get a few forties."

"Cigs, too?" David looks at the bill. Wastepaper. "Inn't enough there for smokes as well..."

"You going to Mel's?"

"I don't know. I was going to just walk over to the gas station..."

"Nah, nah. Go to Mel's. It's nearer Jefferson Project. That way." Buck points out into the dark, "Get three forties and with the change, if it's the little Paki dude, Mo, if it's Mo tell him Buck wants however many loosies he's got for however much money is left over."

"What if it ain' him?"

"Then tell whoever it is that Mel lets Mo give Buck a few loosies for however much money he's got when he's got it. Whatever fell off the truck and all that. They'll know, they'll know."

And David makes his way away–Was that a grumble?–Back of his white t-shirt fading to grey, then joining the dark totally.

Jess's taken a seat on one of the lawn chairs that sits catty-wampus on the porch. Dry but still sticky. Wiping her eyes with the towel.

"You alright?" Buck asks. Picks through the dusty shadows in the ash tray on the porch's moldy card table.

"Yeah, a bit light-headed. Kinda sore. Eyes burn a bit from the—"

"Sorry babe," found one of the ones he'd only half-smoked last time the runs hit him hungover. "Shoot went alright, though?"

"It was fine. Just fine. It'll do."

II.

Naked and sweating. On the bursting verge. Headache and garbled guts—
Coming back to yourself is the hardest part. A shallow, dreamless, restless
slumber. Time travel to now where it's all ache and only ache. Slimy
withering. Fruit left out in the heat, bursting through the easy slough of
sun-leathered skin—

Dawn's creeping across the ceiling's popcorn stomp. Puffy spatters
casting long shadows, scars of a night's bruise. Orange out from the blue.
Yellow to drive it pink. Mountains over river valleys and flood plains of
dusky mauve, dustier every moment the shadows shorten. Room
spinning. Never completing a rotation. Sublating always back to its
original. Reconstructing itself. Every turn stronger a wall and firmer a
floor—Coming back to the world or is the world coming back to you?
Christ, reality somewhere in the rub. There's Jawad and Angela and little
laughing Naseer—

Hand over his eyes and Rohaan rolls onto his side. In the turn his
elbow strikes something firm and warm and slick. "What the hell?" And
the body next to him begins to slither.

Tan tortured back writhing a despondent sea of freckles. A few
groans and they're eye to eye. Black-and-blue eyeliner, smeared as if by
putty knife. Pits dug deeper by the brown of her eyes. Squinting, she
smiles and Rohaan finds himself pulled across the small valley of sheets
toward her. The bedding smells of sweat. The air of morning breath. Her
skin is salty on his lips as she presses him into her chest. "Morning,
sugar." Salutation's return muffled. Episodes of the previous night set to
sprouting in the soaked sod of his mind:

—Mold-splotched shower curtain. Off-white of a scummy tub. Piddle.
Puddle. Greasy drizzle as the faucet's hot water washed the night from
your shoulders. And hers. Hers. What was it you were trying for then?
Completion or closeness? Finger digging into warm places and her hand
hard around your uselessness. All one mass. Flopping against yourself.
Fighting for a way to fuck away the faint. Semi-conscious feeling of being
never quite almost, almost there. Filled to the clavicle with insides the

consistency of oatmeal. Her sounds were polite. Moaning as your stiff knuckles confused crevice and give, fold for hole, pleasance for pleasure...

She hummed your name. The diminutive anyway. "Roh. Roh. Oh. Roh." But, that's an easy enough mistake to make. If memory serves–A breast now pressed into his dry mouth. Choking toward purple–No way to know now if it does but you'd said very little in the shower as well. Perhaps a few unambitious, amateurly performative groans. Really couldn't get it any higher than she'd already shook it. Completely comatose below the belt. Just going through the motions you'd not gone through in longer than it's useful to remember. But, there's usually a response if memory serves. A *gently down the stream* for every "Roh. Roh. Oh. Roh," your boat and fuck if you can remember a goddamn thing– Tasting her now, dizzy and sour to the core. Cups the other breast. Cups it and squeezes it in his mouth, thick with morning after–Came tumbling into the bathroom. Could have been bad you know? Could have tripped on the rug and fallen full backward, hit your head on the toilet seat, cracked the back of your skull and gone out in a thick pool of blood like one of those College students who never even know they're dead. Could have bit the dust right then and there. Can you imagine? Buried not even a month almost after your father? Following the former Man of The House right down to the Home of The Damned, never having the chance to, but she'd gotten down to business and popped the full liquor limpness of your cock in her mouth before you'd even realized your belt had been undone. And you did! You did fall! You son of a bitch! Lost your balance grabbing the mess of her bleach- and dye-fried hair and nearly toppled over into the bathtub! Could have broken your fucking neck there as well! So many chances to have your last chance, to miss the landing and never again walk away from it, scathed or otherwise. Everything could have come to a fucking halt right then and there and you wouldn't even have known it! Could hardly feel her as she gargled you, as she squeezed your balls and coughed syrupy drool all over and, hell, when's the last time you even jerked off? When's the last time you did anything other than piss yellow and angry dribble? When's the last time you tried to–?

Now all the fleshy flavor is gone. Just the cured meat texture of aroused nipple on cigarette-sanded tongue. Raised edges around the areola and a certain givelessness of the skin suggests silicon. Pressing harder. Yeasty wheezings. A new welling of oniony sweat. There it is. By instinct alone. There it is again. A hand grabbing itself full of flow and sop and–She's got a bit more of you now. You've got a bit more to give. Whatever was hot in the pit, boiling tar and pitch, has moved aside. A new hollow. Something that suddenly needs filling, needs to pour out thick nothing, to spill eroding flumes down the sharp crags of a lonely mountain!

Before the bathroom though, Christ, how it all comes back in little packages of tinsel-wrapped shame. You'd turned the lights on in the apartment and proudly stretched out your arms. Grin glowing, cleaving your face in two. Behold! And all the rest. Here's the kitchenette and the living area and yeah it's a studio but I don't need very much, don't mind these boxes here, just moved in more or less, two maybe three weeks maybe, who the hell knows and yeah, work quite a lot, yeah, yeah. Just ladled the lie. Kept it thick. Haven't had the chance yet to unpack, and she leaned then, head lolling on her shoulders, tank-top strap sliding to shine the untouched sunless pale beneath. What did she say? Something cordial, like 'looks great, I can help if you want.' Or maybe it was nothing at all because it wasn't long after your display of prideful arms that she'd lost her own balance and knocked a stack of boxes to the floor. Spilled a collection of clothes and picture frames. Few books. That one they give everyone during recovery and, well, hell, you were both in a helluva state, if memory serves, and there's no way to guarantee that it does. No way of knowing...

But now! The only thing to know is that she's got you on top of her. Biting her bottom lip as she runs your rub-rashed tip through the gash of a sandy-shored gully. And how, oh how are these hollow waters now flowing! A numb buzz at your toes and, little light-headed, all blood rushing away, swamp draining to fill another turgid sump. It's like when you haven't eaten since breakfast, early morning, granola before the sunrise sort of breakfast, and you sit down with the bowl of something in front of you as night comes on, stomach gurgling, twisting itself into hot knots, but all the while your lips're tight against the steam and tongue curdled by the smell and, well, you almost have to shove the food down your own throat, spoonful by piking forkful, wishing the whole time you could just cut your belly out with a knife and fill it by hand, a bag of sand, and get the whole thing over with. But all it takes is a few bites before your body remembers what it's for and the fear flies away. All it takes now is a few strokes and a cooed invitation before you told her you'd never been *man* enough. Floodgates open on that one, Christ Almighty. First time maybe you'd ever said it out loud. Standing outside the bar, a little late-night drizzle as the air cooled enough for the humidity to glom and fall, one of her slim cigarettes between your fingers. Face crinkled up in that stupid drunk way, where the tears flow before you even know you're crying, convinced inside that you're talking complete sense, just about how your father died recently and well, the world's a bit empty without him, seems anyway, and that if you had one thing to say it would be why on Earth has everything gone blurry and no, no, no, I'm fine and all that, just you know, never felt like I was man enough, you know? And now what's the point of grabbing for it? What's the point of keeping it together and cooling your head and holding everything under calloused hands of control if in the end it leads to the same monstrous conclusion? You know? You know? You've done so much work to get away, to outright quit. Held up the cigarette then, as prop and proof. To outright quit the things that were supposed to kill you, right, all the things that disappointed him, all the things, the lovely blissful things, that were symptomatic of your overall weakness just to... You made yourself strong, you put on the shoulders of manhood and breathed deep sober breaths, exhaled gusts of storming wind, all to watch him die, doped-up and blissed-out on the very same joy that flooded your veins to ruin your life. And now... and now... and now the man is gone... and you're still not man enough to fill in the hole he's left behind... and now... and now—

Her legs wrap up around him and her hips take over, grinding in a way that's nearly painful. Her eyes are closed, jaw clenched, cords stand in her neck. Beneath a caesarian keloid her abdomen twists. Hands strong on his back, nails cutting against his shoulder blades. All beneath him, quaking and aching and finding every grind a finer finish. Chest rising, chest rising. All beneath him. Chest rising and breath shortening. All beneath him and it's all then just–Another day. Off at the bus stop ten blocks down South Murphy Street. It's started to take the shape of a routine, the left turn relinquishing its relish. Past few shifts the D line has arrived before your blessed B, so none of the underlings get to see you hop on the better bus. Walked then the block and a half or so further down and popped into the bar, not yet packed with early tourists, to say hello and have a quick one. Jimbo was there, greeted you like a friend and cracked a bottle before you could ask: "Howdy, howdy, Roh. How goes it?"

"Not too bad, all in all. Just another day in paradise." And you sat down.

The few others that were in the bar were seated at the tables along the wall, nestled away. Only one other person sitting on the stools, sipping something complicated and blue in a scowling tiki. You sipped away at your beer, but it wasn't long before Jimbo interrupted the silence with: "Hey there, Roh. You grew up here and all, right? Got someone visiting," motioned toward the woman. Tank-top, short-shorts, an out-of-season tan. "Wants to know what's worth knowing. Let me introduce you–"

&&&

Odds are nothing will come of it, but that's how the story always goes. If the story is going to go in any which way at all, that is. This is the way that it usually goes when it gets told. Struggle, struggle, struggle, hit the bottom. Landlord breathing down your neck because you damn near poisoned the whole neighborhood, cops and ambulances and even firetrucks for some goddamn reason. Luckily, no one had to get hauled off in any of them. But Jesus Christ close enough. Cops didn't even ask to come inside or anything. She showed them the raw footage on her phone and, though the landlord thinks y'all are cooking now, so that's a pain in the ass. Hangs around a lot more. Suddenly the neighbors' houses need fixing up and the way the bastard looks at you could make your fucking blood boil out of your ears, bothering Jess all the time too when you aren't at home. Probably peaking in windows and, wonder if he's seen, wonder if he knows where rent has been coming from. Haven't seen David since fuck, fuck, fuck, there's no use in getting all torqued-up about it this early in the morning. If this is your story, if what you're living now will one day be fit for a story then this is the bottom, the low point, this is where you really start getting it *to-fucking-gether!* You know? This is the montage. This is sudden sobriety and early mornings, hearty breakfasts and kinder words, reassurances in the mirror and deeper slumbers!

Though, it's hard to do anything perfectly, or like you remember seeing it done, especially with the set up you and Jess have currently got: single non-stick fry-pan, the proper dimension for a grilled cheese, with a fussily loose handle and an inexplicable dent in the basin is all you've got other than one high-walled pot fit for stew and little else. So, it all always gets done in one, either altogether or one portion at a time, always sharing a pan so no matter what really, unless you want to wash it in between, which is a rigmarole of its own, it all ends up tasting the same in the end.

That's what's so reassuring about it though is that if it's going to go any way and be a story worth telling, there's only one way in which the whole thing can go! You look up from the bottom, a pit you've fallen into, right? Look up, black-eyed and broken-boned Bucky, and what do you see? A shining marquee! The name of a master: the one, the only, the legendary Dermot Putsch. Installation artist responsible for a movement of his own, a true original, that's what every book or article or anything about anything he's ever done has said about him!

The trick is to let the bacon grease cool a bit. You know that. Once the heat's settled out it won't jump and bite and burn up everything like it's doing now; instead, you can get a gentle fry going, a steady crisp. Not have it wind up like this, where the edges run back toward the center, bubble and collapse into cinders. Christ. Fuck! Comets of grease jumping up onto your hands. Bacon's already fucked as well. Shriveled like adhesive bandages in the sun, centers still soft with a wound's weepings. Thick cut shit charred to brick, complete waste of a couple extra bucks. Can't do anything fancy at all, can't get any better if the tools you're working with aren't cut out for the job. No matter how hard you guys try it seems like, just fuck, fuck, fuck!

But that's the way out if there is one. No doubt the museum will do a gala sort of thing, an opening like they do every rotation of the second floor gallery and, it's an outside shot sure, but you never know, and everyone likes to be flattered. Make sure the work is up to snuff and find him and they always have Attendants work those events, show off the staff, gives everyone a few extra hours every couple of months and sure, it's an outside shot, but if anything is going to happen then this is the way it's going to happen. Just gotta make sure the work is as solid as can be, make sure you're ready and montage shit, this is montage shit, champion, king, genius, all that montage shit, get it all done so you can get Jess out of all this fucking, no! Don't run it under the, bullets now, leaving smoky arcs in the air, stuck in your chest and hair and, ow! God-*Fuck!* Clatter and bang like a break and enter. Knife falls from the counter. Just barely missed you, fucker. Could've lost a toe, you know that? What the hell is wrong with you? Get it together! Just, you did this to yourself you know? Stay up all night nipping at a bottle, run through a whole pack of smokes, gonna burn a hole right through your throat you don't get this shit together and move with some semblance of grace and intention and, yup, skin there already starting to puff and blister. Awful greasy smoke. Thick. Settles like soot on your face and watch it get all infected now, just you wait and see. You absolute fucking moron, you complete fucking waste of fuckin goddamned trying! Head hurts and you're tired and you're trying and you were–

"Buck! The fuck is all this?"

"Sorry, sorry, I was trying to–"

"Here. Jesus, B." And she weasels between him and the sink. Cuts off the flow, picks the thick dripping pan off the floor. "Fuck it's hotter than," clatters again.

Buck leans against the wall, gathering full sight now of the catastrophe he's rendered where the kitchen used to be. "Sorry, babe. I was trying to–"

"You can't like, you can't like just fucking pour grease down the drain like that, B. It'll get–"

"Clogged, I know. Sorry. I'm just tired and–"

"Can't even believe you're up, babe." On her knees now. Unwashed panties loose in the hollow between her legs, white t-shirt worn yellow as a habit over the rest of her. Wet washcloth spreading the snotty grease and its flotsam in thick smears over the linoleum. "Christ almighty. What time did you–?"

"Won't work if it's wet, Jess." Buck down now, jeaned knees soaking up a portion of the piss-warm coagulation. Takes his own shirt off. A long johns top. Still cold in the mornings. Balls it to sop up the clotting slop. Kisses her forehead. "Sorry, hon. Smells good at least, right?"

–Hand on your cheek. Her lip twitches as to smile, then stills as to worry. Her eyes are green, butter-mint green.

&&&

Just need to take some time. Just get outside and clear your mind. Take in some of this spring air and let all these new ideas settle sedimental and, yeah, deep breath now, deep breath. Should've brought your fishing pole. Don't know though whether it's really public like where you can go fishing in it or public where you definitely aren't allowed to go fishing in it–

Slugging brack sludging back out to sea. Curdling foam at every rough and oily shimmer along the shores. The bank drops steep into the water. Not much shore for the shimmer. Trees hold the cliffing soil steady and keep the Creek from running off with the path all of everyone is meant to walk on–Wouldn't swim in it, that's for sure. Wonder back then when all this wasn't so friendly to everybody if you would have thought to swim in it. Fished it. Definitely fished it once or twice. Come out here with Uncle Reggie when he for a while had the time to take you out here to fish and, judging by the memory of how fast and far down the current took the bobbers on the line seems like it run a lot quicker back then. But, water hides its truths. There's something Putsch would say. Some long essay about the essences of materials, though not in a sense or way at all mystical and magical, but that, and he wouldn't be wrong if you could say it without any poetry, everything's got an undeniable thing-ness to it. Seems simple enough until you start trying to list those qualities though, right? Water hides its truths. That's one of the qualities that it has inherent in its substance. Water is a liar, then? No. Not like that. That would be poetry perhaps. That water is a liar because it hides its truths. So, you have to change the formulation then, right? Right. So, it's not that water hides its truths it's just that you can't see them without investigation. So, water doesn't tell its truths without, no not exactly that either. The truths of water are completely and utterly visible only if you know about what water is and what it does and how it does what it does and becomes what it is, which is necessarily an investigation not of water itself but of the world it wets.

But there were never very many fish, if you can remember that about the water. Remember that's what Uncle Reggie would say to start it all off, that there aren't many fish because of the highway, because of all the rumbling grumbles from the bridge and that fish don't like water that's not one or the other, that they're particular. Fish are particular and water hides its secrets. A match made in nature. All the fewer now you'd think what with the–

Low concrete and corrugated metal. Cyclone fences and cinder blocks. All the failing industrial ugliness necessary to keep the suburban roosts up and running. Rest. Stop. And pouring all this oily shimmer into Salt Creek. Grass can't hold the north bank's soil at bay anymore so–It's gotten wider, that much you can say for sure. But, secrets of the water, wider would mean faster? That the whole thing would move faster because it's more spread out or maybe it's deeper as well because this shoreline here the Madiston side just *Foof!* straight cliffs down into the water but that's whether that's because the shore has sloughed away or because the Creek's now deep as the Bay is hard to say and harder to tell from where you're standing now because your foot's fallen asleep sitting hard on this bench here along, what was it the sign said, twenty-seven miles of hiking trails? Don't know whether that's a whole lot or not very much at all. Fitting though, isn't it? Everything a secret because you keep asking the wrong questions and no one has taken the time other than maybe Reggie who relished in the don't know, don't know, impossible to tell if it all has ever thought to tell you how to ask the right questions about anything. Can't blame anybody but yourself though. Gotta learn to finish the book first, you know? Got to sojourn the whole thing before you interlocute yourself into the particulars.

The land seems cleaner though. Less trash. Remember a lot of trash back when you and Reggie used to for a while when he had the time to come out fishing would go fishing. But back then the water was green like stuff was living in it and even though there were never very many fish at all because of the rumble and grumble of the bridge up the way over the Creek there would still be little shrimp or crawdads or minnows all in the shallows along the shore. More trash sure. Cans and bottles and cigarette butts and boxes, but the water was still mostly water. Now it's— Slugging brack sludging back out to sea. Curdling foam at every rough and oily shimmer along the shores. The North's glades have given way to development and South's forest has been allowed to stay—But now the air stinks. Not with the fishy or briny tinge that might be a welcome sea breeze passenger, but with something sewage, stagnant, a deep and still rot, an unremitting:

...triumph of the World over itself!

We've managed to manufacture materials that, through the laws they seek to break, supersede Mother Nature's guarantee of nurture. Structures seemingly separate from the demands of decay now pock the surface of our planet and have even, according to some studies fixated on microplastics (which, not to laugh in the face of doom, but can you imagine entropy's embarrassment at the revelation of microplastics?), begun to actively replace the plane they rose from. At the end of it all is inertia, at least as far as our conception of the end it all will carry us. One must here, however, take enough of a breath to ponder the preponderance of YHWH on that seventh day, fully freed from the strictures of his Elohistic plurality, found singular and omnipotent on that day of rest, when it was all to be good and good forever at the very least. Ponder now the sound of that first question from the lonely man down there in a garden made for him to hush-up in. How it must have stuck out against the whisper of wind and the by then already clichéd babble of brook and stream. How strange it must have seemed against the certainty of bird calls, where every waver and warble serves the purposes it's ignorant of singing for. Maybe it was the man's recognition of his unlikeness to the world around him that spurned the first question; perhaps he stumbled upon a chimp or gorilla or spat out the water where Narcissus would have drowned and saw himself ultimately as something different and apart and he directed a thought, a query, up to the sky, to where things seemed as unlike everything they were held over as he felt in that suddenness to the things he was surrounded by. How God's eyebrows must have twitched at a sound so like his own, how his heart must have kicked to realize he'd made something just as alone, how furious he must have been to hear his own impulses echoed back to him. So too do we confront the plastic forevers we've guaranteed ourselves...

I once heard a man cry, 'None of this ain't going nowhere!' on an oil-stained driveway. I can't remember a lick about where I was. I know that I was searching, though. Searching and looking and seeking and trying to find the sorts of things I remembered being sold at garage sales. To my recollection I don't think I found what I was looking for that day, but I did receive a memory I'll never forget. To call it formative would be perhaps to give it too much credit, however I can't help but dredge it up here. Perhaps, Dear Reader, we've gotten too close now with our earmarks and pet names. But, if feelings of intimacy aren't simply an assumption on my part, if we can really trust each other, allow me here, for just a moment only, to break from this academic mode and slip into something more comfortable, something a touch more prosaic... There. As I was saying:

He said, 'None of this ain't going nowhere!" and rose from his lawn chair. He then walked over to me with his hands on his hips and leaned across the table to speak a little closer. He asked me then something like, 'Going to buy something, son?'

On his breath I could smell cigarettes and vodka and, since the day was falling away from its peak, beer as well. Thinking back now to how much I myself was smoking at that time, may even have had a cigarette pinched or dangling during this confrontation (I can't remember exactly most likely on account of the regularity), it's a miracle I was able to smell any of it all.

I was a young man, then.

I ignored him best I could, and my hand found a figurine made of the sort of porcelain a girlfriend some years later would inform me was called bisque.

'Gonna buy that?'

I must remind you again here, Dear Reader, that I was a young man when all of this happened and I now hold it a sacred tenet to never take advice from or mimic the actions of young men; all to say, I recommend now as an older man that you salt this exchange as heavily as you can.

'I might,' I said.

'It's going to be–' and then he said a number that was far outside the prices usually demanded at sales such as these. At that time yard sales and garage sales or whatever it is that your region terms them were the sorts of events people held to empty their lives of excesses, and that you as a shopper attended to empty your pocket *only* of the change that jingled against your keys. Haggling was a formality, a game the seller was set up to lose with grace and good faith. So, I counteroffered something much lower, something that would require no paper, something that might get lost in the couch cushions.

'No, no. Gotta have–' and he said his absurd number again.

I was a young man then, so I looked this drunk in the eye and saw there what I could see. For me, in his haze, there was a moment of clarity. Some early forms of the ideas I'm currently obsessing over began to take their most rudimentary shapes. It seemed to me then in that moment that this man was trying to get rid of a world he'd made, attempting further to exchange it for the value that he'd spent in its making. One cannot now and could not then fault him for that; it's a perfectly reasonable and desperate thing to desire. However, it struck me then that regardless of how much value he perceived himself as pouring into this world that now, and this is important, he desired to be rid of, the world in question no longer held that value in its form and substance. There is no Marxian or economically materialist point being made here, this is pure eschatology.

The simple fact is held in the statement he slurred at me while he was still laid out on his lawn chair: 'None of this ain't going nowhere.' Ultimately and in short, the point is that the world he'd built up around himself, that he was now in that moment trying to exchange for the value of a potential new world, had already not only ended for him, but was fully inert for everyone else as well. All the more, for everyone else, it may as well have never been at all! The world he wanted to be rid of was already over, but because of his hands alone it still held the hollowed shapes of its previous existence.

I must remind you once again, Dear Reader, that I was a young man.

'No, no. Gotta have–' and he said his absurd number again.

I held up the little porcelain figure, rosy-cheeked and bo-peeping, and said, 'You want [insert dollar value] for this?'

'I said it in plain [insert county name] English, didn't I?'

So, as a young man, I throttled the figurine down to the driveway. It shattered to several and thousands. I pointed at the little dusty impact pile by my foot and asked then, 'How much for that, then?...'

Never really got to get any of what it was before, did you? Only those few times fishing before the city come out and blocked the whole thing off, adjusted the bus route and, well, heard it in the halls at school there for a while. Upperclassmen complaining all the sudden about how now there're cops up around the grounds and the house up there on the hill is all locked up and how, remember how it all started when that poor kid got arrested smoking a joint in one of the Belchard bedrooms? Suppose it was a rite of passage sort of thing. Get to a certain point and then you get to go party at the abandoned Belchard Estate, have a kegger and lose what you've got left to get rid of before you grow up.

Robbed of it now that you're thinking about it. Estate falls full into public hands and yeah, probably best to assume that they wouldn't take too kindly to you trying to fish in all the muck because the moment the Estate fell full into the hands of the public is when there were suddenly cops everywhere around it and you couldn't have ever even have gotten the chance to come up and smoke a joint or drink a beer or huck rocks at panes of glass or have a kiss or two or three or four or more. Go down to the grounds and drink and smoke and fiddle with each other's newnesses, all under the roof of a mansion getting ready to collapse. Chandelier all on the ground then probably and still maybe valuable silver in the drawers.

Never got a chance to haunt the house up on the hill–Now: Pristine. Empty. Ensconsed immaculately by its garden. Gleaming plantation-white for all to see.

&&&

Bedlam. Bennie's eyes open to the unholy sound of chiptune chimes. The dark fluorescence of the office unfolds–Your fucking prison cell–Before him: candy wrappers and take-out bags, the fetid filth of half-drunk paper cups of coffee run soft and cold. The shattered monitor staring at him. Hood-darkened, voidful face of Death. His phone skitters and chirps.

"Morning, hon."

"You are coming home this afternoon, correct?"

Smell of nicotine tar and bleach on his fingers. Hangnails have started variously peeling from the tips.

"I should be."

"Should be? I have to make some errands today. It will be easier if you can watch Anders while I do."

Eyes burn bleary, singed with restlessness and cleaning fluid fumes. Discovered that a specific brand of floor-cleaner gives him nosebleeds. Stomach empty of everything save coffee and powdered donuts from the vending machine. Her voice. Whiff of soured milk–But you can't watch Anders because you're already watching Anders and there can't be both of you all because, no wait. You can't watch Anders because you don't want you to watch him. Both of you all can't just–

"I know. I'm sorry. Work has been very busy lately, Heidi. I've got–"

"You've got a child, that is what I know! It will be a great help if you can come home this afternoon. You said that–"

–You've already got the child, so why do you have to go and hold it as well. Can't you just, you said that you wanted to be the one to–Places the phone on the desk in front of him. Her voice rummages. Elbow props up a hand to hold his head. He watches a wash-softened finger trace the edge of a shard still hanging onto the desktop monitor's frame.

Her voice empties.

"Uh-huh, I know, babe. I know." He says.

Rummaging again. Riling into a squeal.

A muttered 'Christ' and Bennie picks the phone back up–Try to talk her down. No use in explaining any of it, all this feeling in your guts, don't even know if you can, but try to talk her down at the very least. Mention hiring a wet-nurse or midwife or nanny or whatever it is that she needs to keep you and the kid quiet and away from each other enough while you figure out just what the fuck is happening inside–"Hey, hey, hey! What the fuck is this?"

Godawful digitally chipped-out and ring-modulatingly fried cry. Squelching siren. Caterwauling so hard can't even catch his breath. Little ribs. Rubber accordion. Screaming squeezebox. Mucous hitch and a bubbly gasp followed by another keen fit to rinse fat from flesh.

"Hey! Hey, Heidi! Fucking, Heidi!" Apparently put the phone up to the child Anders' ear. "Heidi! Get back on the, motherfucker! Heidi! Heidi! Goddammit, Heidi, get back on the fucking–"

Her voice suddenly back on the line, not a hair of quiet or fumble between the fit and fury: "Ben! Ben! Why do you yell at him like that? He is your son and you are yelling at him like this and, why are you yelling at my baby like you are angry with him when you are not even here at all, Benjamin? Why are you–"

"Hey! Hey! Watch it!"

Teeth grind on the line: "Benjamin."

Closes his eyes against his name. The warmth of the lids meeting is an ineffable pleasure. His shoulders drop. "Yes, Heidi."

"Are you coming home?"

"Fine."

"Tonight?"

Warmth blooming, cut with soft salt. Holds his answer in his throat for fear of her hearing the watery shake of his voice. A thumb ends the call. Phone screen-down on the desk and a prayer it doesn't start buzzing again. Wipes the water from his eyes. Smiles at the shine it leaves on his fingers.

Index again at the edge of the shard–Always thought the glass was clear and that it was the box inside that was dark. Wouldn't make much sense, guess now that you think about it–Tinted a greenish-brown, dusty on the concave side–From the tube breaking? These things use a tube? Would need to know what a tube is in a way other than as an item on an invoice to know though to know that, wouldn't you? Yeah but, fewer sparks than you'd've thought when it fell, much less of an event. Dust inside. Known that and you'd've knocked the thing over sooner, especially considering that there hasn't been a ring from one from the Secretaries. No note or knock of anybody coming in to check up and say hey hey how you doing, everything alright? Was wondering why you've gone silent. Up top they're saying they need your approval on something, some new, oh I don't know, how am I supposed to know what all it is that y'all monkey around with, just passing it along, sugar. What you want me to tell them?

You'd tell them then to tell them that during your first year at the Museum, fresh in this line of work, new to the nuanced concerns of the 'art world,' that during your first year the Second Floor, the Rotating 'Special' Exhibition Gallery, hidden gem of Madiston's Municipal Art Museum, overshadowed only by the ostentatious and gaudy display of antebellum decadence that is, *was* now, but *is* then the Belchard Ballroom, had for its autumn showing an exhibit by the late and great oh, Christ what was her name? Do you remember? It was only eight or nine some odd years ago, can't believe where the time goes can you? Just rushes away no matter what you do. Try and keep track and just, well, it's all history now and if it's worth remembering you can only hope that someone managed to get it written down. Shame though, now that you're thinking about it, really should do more to remember as much as possible about everyone that comes through here, the voices you all give the floor to, the *great works* by *once-in-a-generation geniuses*... Ever stricken by how many once-in-a-generations every decade seems to produce? All these names just vying for a place in history... Guess what you mean is that Homer didn't write any of that stuff, that a lot of other people did, wrote it all after him if he was ever even there at all. Same goes for people like Plato maybe and even Jesus, though don't you let anyone catch you saying that around here, Lord A'Mighty and all that, but what you're trying to get at is that you'll have lost them by then, no doubt. Probably need to double back and slow down. Lay it out piece by piece and watch their brows for when it finally catches, stop then once they've got the hook in their mouth. Lay it out, floating in the clear still sea. Tell them to tell them:

The Second Floor exhibit during your first season here at the Museum was a series of 'sculptures' that were to serve as 'meditations' on the 'progress of technology' or whatever. Most of them were tube televisions, either set to a static station or with a short film looping or simply a still image of some kind. Family at a dinner table. Kids opening gifts at Christmas. Canned Americana. A heavy-duty, not-fucking-around, industrial magnet duct-taped somewhere on the body of the thing then to distort the images, jam the cathode or something, twisting and maligning the whole thing into a shape similar to the truth the lie was meant to hide. Ancient technology and Jesus, what you're trying to tell them to tell them is to tell them that pleasure is prelude to pain. Convalescence is the epilogue. Life itself, the story part, where you think everything is happening is just—Blood running down the shard and pooling on the plastic frame that for so long masked the hollow inside.

"Shit." To himself. Wipes the gathering ruby gob on the hem of his t-shirt. Wraps the fabric around the digit. Pain dulls to a nuisance.

—Gonna bite like a motherfucker later. Sting like holy hell next time you get that sponge in your hand. Wipe up the yolky yellow of dried piss. Stubborn crud of heeled scuffs. The day's caking failures shunned with corrosively omnipotent swipes. Brought shorts for last night and the bathroom tile pressed its grouted grid into your knees, raised red crosses that still achingly pock those hair-capped hilltops. Wanted to be prepared, but not presumptuous. Yet to endeavor the purchase of your own set of coveralls.

First time into the breakroom was empty. Same goes for the second attempt. Third time though, the charm, always the charm. Some rules can't be broken. Caught the fella walking down the hall in the opposite direction, just coming off the employee stairs. Met at the door and, like old friends, shook hands.

"Ben. How goes it?" The Custodian raised his paw and motioned into the breakroom. "After you, boss."

"Thanks, uhm, thanks." All you could think to say. Slunk then into the room, ducking down despite the clearance. "How's, how's everything in your world?" Over your shoulder.

"Fine, fine, fine. Would be ungracious to complain, so I won't." Brought the coffee machine away from the wall, centered it in front of him.

"That's good, that's good. Yeah I've just been just—"

"See you're dressed for comfort today, boss. Must've been a hefty one." From his back pocket then, a paper bag of coffee, sealed by a rubber band. Grounds rattled. Smell filled the room as the band snapped away. Lips of the sack opened to sigh a morning breath.

"Smells fantastic, Chief." *Chief,* an overworked fart.

"Welcome to a cup, as always, boss." Machine gurgling. Steam curling. Thick dribbles sputtered into the urn.

A cellophane tube of donuts fell behind glass. You turned back to the Custodian. Pressed one of the arid pastries into your cheek, and said with a muffled, casual air: "Wer lash nigh?"

"No, no sir. Thank heavens." Lined up two paper cups on the counter, "Lucky to have more or less a normal schedule when it comes to weekends. Seniority'll get that for you, reckon—"

You knew he hadn't come in the night before. Sat in the breakroom licking powder from pastry, picking coconut and marshmallow from bunny tails, investigating the fractal fragility of cinnamon bun icing until almost midnight. Guess the other Custodians don't make such liberal use of the basement amenities.

"—Makes time with the kids a bit easier as well. Wife works midweek to Monday at the hospital so it's good I can be home when they've not got school."

"You've got kids?" You sat down. Looked up like along the tear of a tower.

The Custodian didn't answer immediately, just poured up the sludgy coffee. Thick residue on the urn's glass.

It hit you once you managed another mouthful of ornery cake down your throat. "Shit, that's right! Twins, is it? Twin b—"

"Girls, twin girls. Daughters, little monsters, telepathic freaks, my two little Martians." Walked over with the paper cups tiny in his hands. Smile growing under his beard with every epithet. "What about you, boss? How's yours?"

"Oh," laced your hands around the cup, "bigger every day."

&&&

A quiet lunch. No use wishing for what you can get for yourself. Then, a quiet lunch without having to hide away like this. Better suited for a prayer–

Shareese sets to unpacking the sack item by item. Yogurt. Bag of salted nuts. Banana beyond due. A PB&J already given way. Flattens out the brown paper and lays it all out on top–Cooped-up like this, hidden in the walls of your and Roh's office, clenched against the clutter, just isn't fair. Feels wrong. Wrong to have to hide away like this. But, there's no shutting him up anymore, is there? Like he's got his own cameras or something, like he's watching or, worse, maybe, constantly peeping out and popping back in like some predatory vole. Something's gotten into these men, that's for sure. Roh's daddy died and he then comes into some money he's never had and very obviously doesn't know how to take care of himself with. Worse every time you see him. Bennie just as bad, though. Like he doesn't ever leave it seems like, just always here and ready to pester you with platitudes. You got all the savior you need, thank you very much, and don't need any preaching from nobody else.

Grim though, staying cooped-up like this all day, just watching these screens. Suppose you'll get to walk a bit when you let them all off one by one for lunch. Twinge in your knee though, all that hoofing over to Carl. Can't ever once be bothered to leave his house to come over your way, can he? Come have a sit down in my miserable, dark, unfurnished but don't touch them books! No sugar, I've got them in order like I like to have them and got it all worked out and situated just the way they need to be, see, and can't have them getting all jumbled unless you just, "Look at the state of this thing, Christ A'Mighty!"

No smile. No thank you. A whole lot of nothing when you'd put that awful book in his hands. Nothing. Just took it and flopped it around. Brushed the spine and walked it over to the window. Examined it in the dusking orange failing light and said, "Look at the absolute state of this thing," And blasphemed.

Rolls the stomach just thinking about it. People can be so ungrateful when they feel like they know you well enough. Displays of affection fade in marriages, and the same goes for friendships. That's why people go and drift apart you know, because they stop holding onto each other. Why Jesus got down on his knees to go and wash the feet of his followers and all that, to hold onto them. Good Shepherd's always got his crook so you just go on and Come Lord Jesus. Go ahead now, don't you get riled up about what's not got to do with you. Fold your hands and don't you scoff none at what you've been given. Be our guest. Lord knows it'll always be enough. And let this food. You might feel hungry, might get a growling pang or two, but you'll never *be* hungry. To us be blessed. Every stone that stubs your toe, trips you on the narrow, will one day be the bread of your salvation. Thank the Lord, for meat and drink, through Jesus Christ, Our Lord Amen... Amen—

Eyes open to nothing changed. Shareese looks over at the grainy television screens on the wall—Dinner and a show—If only for the sake of something moving. Something splotchily alive. But, her eyes dart back to the door. Looks away to take a bite of sandwich or drink from the cold milk-cheesed dregs of her coffee—Can't think to muster the gumption to go make another pot in the breakroom, getting caught up in conversation with him for even the length of a drip seems a bitter eternity—Back to the achy screens. Door in her periphery—Any minute can imagine him wanting to come knocking. Need to get something off his chest or worse have some thought re-burble about a screed from days or weeks before, an addendum to add to the already inflamed area of your brain allotted specifically for his drivel. Just come and bang on the door all bossman and you'll bite your tongue and suck down running slugs of blood while he blathers on and on and on.

Could have chewed him out years ago, you know? Laid the law down and drawn the line. Set a standard. Instead, the inside of your cheeks are calloused from holding back your words. Tongue scarred from the staid insistence of your teeth. Voice garbled for swallowing so much venom.

"Not. Your. Job. Mister. Carl." He'd said years back, right after you had been promoted. Said it just like that too, every word a sentence of its own, punctuation marked out on the back cover of the book by his knuckles. "No one has ever asked you, Carl, to ever do any research on anything ever. Not. Your. Job. Mister. Carl."

And you just stood there the whole time. Silent. Coppery pain in your mouth. Hands stitched together behind your back to keep from getting thrown. Never a violent woman now, you know it and better believe it. Full up with love for the sinner. Punishment and justice are the dominion of the Almighty alone. Retribution is no responsibility of yours, but dammit if you didn't want to skin that pasty sonofabitch, bring the hammer down on his peeled-potato looking ass face for talking to your nearest and dearest like that. Hard not to just jump over the desk and see how red Bennie was beneath all that righteousness.

"I'd just thought–"

"Again, Carl, that's not your job. It's nowhere in the description or employee manual or anywhere else at all."

Just watched Carl's shoulders rise. Oversized uniform jacket, a snail's shell sucking all the soft stuff inside.

"You aren't paid to think, Mister Carl. Is that clear? You can do all the thinking you want outside of these walls, but when you're here, the word isn't simply mum, it's absolutely *none*." Had to have rehearsed that one. Came off the tongue too easily. Vindictive little shit had the nails already in his pocket. Always something smart to say to anybody quiet enough to give his hammer the time to swing. Put you on a cross faster than you could say:

"Bennie, if you'll just let me explain what I was trying to–" Carl had reached across the desk to pick up the book, but Bennie jerked it back into his lap. Leaned back in his chair and began to flip through the pages. A whole passion play. "I've, I've got some pages dog-eared and–"

"Oh, I can see that, Carl, and believe you me I've read through them and it's just awful stuff. Truly heinous."

No way he'd had the time to read a damn word of it. The Docent, whatever her name was, something WASPy like Jeanine or Margaret, had snatched it pretty immediately from Carl when he'd interrupted her spiel about the, what was it Carl'd said she'd gotten wrong? The fascism inherent in the expressionist whosiewhatsit or something like that. She'd snatched it and said "That's enough of this!" All shrill and wide-eyed, with flat clapping, stiletto-snapping indignation, "That's enough of this! I simply won't have it anymore!"

Brings a smile almost to your face now imagining one of the Docents all *verklempt* over someone as harmless as Mister Carl, sweet old geezer. Indeed a different place when he was around. Even in this short wake of his absence there's been a miserable pall fallen over everything. No more of him raving at the Ballroom's entrance... Can at least count his reassignment to that position as one of your greatest managerial achievements. Saving his ass from Bennie's warpath that day, flipping Carl from nuisance to pedantic mascot, charming in all his performative intelligence, wearing a hole in the marble of the Ballroom floor, bellowing husky welcomes and welcome backs and who's the little one heres and oh we haven't seen you in a whiles and tongue-in-cheek don't be afraid to ask me anything at alls... All replaced now with the dull clatter of whatever it is that's happening behind the Ballroom's boarded and locked doors–

One of the screens in the cluster has been privy to the former Ballroom's baroque deconstruction. Through grain and warble, fuzz and flicker, fog and stars, she's watched it all come away. So much to be taken away. So much not there at all. She didn't see the Chandelier come down, but watched one day as they cracked into the display cases. Watched every little trinket find itself nestled into foam and padding specifically molded for its keeping. The marble floor came up, slab by perfect slab. The big ceiling rose was lowered and sent off, leaving nothing, a hollow, an echoey void closed off from the world by massive oak doors. Then, starting last week, there was metal. Sudden screaming metal.

III.

Make a wish:

"What's that?"

"Eleven-eleven. Make a wish." Craig sets a hefty shot at the edge of the book. Gold rolling over the glass's lip.

"Careful, careful." Aura lifts the volume off the bar top. Palms her sleeve cuff. Wipes away the glittering spillage.

"A *thank-you-kindly-Mister-Bartender* would have sufficed just as nicely, you know."

"I know, I know. Sorry. Here..." Sets the book back down, sensitive pages pressed to the wood. Aura raises her glass, "Cheers, Craig. Sorry. Make a wish."

Over his shoulder, at the bar clock above the racked bottles and mirror: "Little late now, reckon." His drink aloft. A bottle of Belchard's steadily nursed for the last hour. "Late never bothered me none, though." Clinking rims. "You need another?" Points to her finger-smudged pint glass. Only a piddle left.

Aura checks her phone. Screen bright and fuzzed. Squints and winks. No word yet—Could always catch the bus down, catch the B, but—"Yeah, sure. Not the shot though. Just another beer. Derek should be here soon enough, I think."

"Alright, sounds good." Off down the bar. Shimmery flip of an empty pint and a heady pour. Back again and the dribble finds its coaster. Taps a page with a jet wet finger: "Never could get very far into that stuff."

Aura rises from the book. "Yeah, it can be a little hard sometimes. Sometimes it's like reading something written by an alien—"

"All those *thees* and *thous* and *thines*—"

"Yeah it can be a trip, but that stuff is at least consistent. Just gotta get used to it. Like read it slow and with the rhythm, because there's always a rhythm. The Sonnets are nice because—"

"That what you've got there?" Plunges an empty pint into the dish pit. Piled high tonight even though it's been slow. Shortness of his speech and busy-ness of his hands indicate that he's pulling back, regretting having let the dishes stack.

"Yeah. They're different. Like shorter. Like little blocks of–"

"Sounds good, I'll have to check them out one day." Craig wipes suds on his pant leg and looks long toward the taps. "Shit. Somebody needs something. I'll be right back."

Aura's eyes follow him down the way and–Only patient regulars. There since you came in after work with Buck nearly four hours ago. Caught the tail end of Tanisha's shift. She'd come around from behind the bar as soon as you and Buck walked in. Big smile on her face, arms wide, took him up like to tackle him to the ground. Got him up in a big hug and started in on all that, "Where in God's greenest have you been, honey?" and "Haven't seen you in so long! Thought you were dead or something!"

To which Buck responded with a squeak, "Just taking a, a breather is all."

Tanisha dropped him and turned to you, "Don't you look so gloomy like you're about to piss on a parade. I got one for you too!" And her arms wrapped around to squeeze you. Cooing into your shoulder, "Enough love for everybody, sweetheart."

Once at the bar she started pouring and prying: "Where you been? What's going on?"

"Only been M.I.A. for like a week or two. Relax." Blushing as the whiskey flowed.

"Week's a long time in this world, B. Lot can happen in a week."

"I know, I know. Aura could have told you I was fine, though. Isn't that right?" Turned to you and yeah, you could have and you did when she asked but it's not your job to lie about things you don't understand or cover the tips missed from his hands. Besides, it's difficult to cover someone else's ass when your world is crumbling just as fast.

"Well, I'm glad you're okay. But you owe me an explanation!" A joke, sure, but truth in every gibe. She depends, like all bartenders, on her regulars. You and Buck pay fuck-all for drinks most of the time, but it's the hundred odd dollars you leave in tips every week that adds up.

"Alright, alright, but only because I love ya–" And then he goes into some rehearsed diatribe about trouble with his landlord and hidden fees or something, all shit that he's kept just obscure enough to make commenting on it impossible. Only wears the emotion of it on the outside, all prickly so that even if you ask like you care, which you do and he knows that so why's he got to act like, all prickly so that when you ask he can just poke you with the pikes and then soften suddenly at your bleeding, apologize, and then you aren't even talking about what's got his face all droopy but about something much bigger and all the more inconsequential for its ineffability. And Tanisha shook her head through the whole thing, arms crossed in disapproval and solidarity. Nodded when the tale obligingly transmogrified in a rant about slumlords and labor politics. Reticence bloomed raconteur, and Buck's gesticulations began to run wild. Trouble left behind, he entered the realm of the conceptual, no longer facing the facts about what had actually happened or how slick the shit he was in ran. Could rant and rave himself into a register not of fear but of wizened authority. Where he likes to keep his speech anyway, lofty. Always the one to dole out advice, to listen until he knows exactly what *you* need to do. But, godforfuckingbidit if on the occasion that he slips on his own mess you pose to offer *him* a recommendation!

You'd suggested when he told you some mangled version of the unutterable thing that had happened a few weekends ago that he and Jess start figuring out how to move or something, maybe find a place closer to the city or nearer the College or get out of that swamp and away from the Jaspers and Harris Park. And he'd barked you down. Lost his cool:

"Fuck you, that's not the point! It's the whole principle of the thing in the first place! It's got nothing to do with any of that–" You two stopped there on the corner of 8th and Smith so that Buck could light up a cigarette. Sweating through your uniforms in the early spring curtain of musky mug. "I mean, Aura, miss me with that 'maybe find a new place' bullshit. It's not as easy as that! I mean, we–"

Can't say how many times, piss drunk, hung out to drown in the night because Jess was 'shooting,' Buck had put his hand on your shoulder, assumed the wobbling posture of paternal wisdom, and said the exact same shit to you: "Sounds to me like you've just got to fuck-off, you know?

Tell your mom or whatever to suck a fat one and just get the hell out of there…" Sweetness of his sympathies growing edgier the longer your problems lasted. Love him, but there's an air about him that you just can't gulp through sometimes. Strange victim complex. Allergy to triumph or, oh, who knows. Just needs someone to listen, is all. Most all anyone needs is someone to listen to them when their words don't make sense in their own heads. No one ever wants to hear what you've got to say once they've gone and said what it is that they wanted to go on and say. It's all purge. Best to clothe your soul in fabrics that don't stain for that very reason. The world mostly pours itself into people, fills them up until their levees break; at which point they flood over into whatever reservoir you've let them know you've got. Everyone's secretly a floodplain just hoping against the dam. Thing is, though, your drowning in their misery's rarely a concern of theirs, especially if they're full-up to burst. No, they want it all out, that's it, just let it all out. Doesn't matter much to them whether you hold onto it or not.

Desire is often less to be heard than it is simply to speak. Like what Craig would have heard what's interesting about the Sonnets, particularly the first seventeen leading up to the one everyone thinks they should say at weddings or on concupiscent picnics, with the comparison to a summer's day or whatever, that what's interesting about it is the reason anybody ever thinks to read them is that they think they're love poems or whatever, that they're like the greatest love poems in all of history or like that it's one of those things where Shakespeare did it the best and you should read it because of course he did it the best and y'all're all very lucky that history has seen to it that you still get to read them, but even though they're a little blurry on the page from the several unplanned-for pints and, where the honest fuck is Derek? Working later and later and later. Understand that things are tough with new hires and the senior staff taking a hike, but Christ Almighty. Tell Jawad to go fuck himself and this edition plucked from several others, thumb-greased and crinkled and barbarically marked-up with soft lead pencils or in a few cases even, goddamn couldn't hardly believe it, pen of all things, maintains the quirks specific to the Bard's own English, with all what the introduction says are called long S's and misspellings, possessives made plural and the introductory essay written by, oh who was it now? Dr. Reginald Lloyd, Art Historian saying he specialized in think it was something about the history of the printed word or but not from like a technological perspective or even a strictly historical one but what he called a maybe aesthetic one, something about the shapes we choose to convey meaning and how they've changed and why they change and well, but in the essay he basically spends most of his time pointing out the quirks in old William's old English and how maybe it's best we leave it like it is even though conventions have changed because maybe there are what he said was wordplay allowed only because of the centuries that lay between the pen and eye and ear and page, that the associations pressed onto the words or meanings erased by our current English that basically all said the poems maybe get richer over time but only if they remain in stasis as they were originally penned or something like that, like how everything is always better in its original or like the way grapes turn to wine and that wine if it's good wine and kept well won't turn to vinegar but continue on and transform into something truly special maybe it's all jargon and hard to parse but read them and there's something like that in there maybe like the heat of a whisper–

But, now she's drunk and even the inner voice is slurring its speech. Gripping the sides of her barstool, Aura turns to hang her feet over open floor. Plops down and for a moment the world wobbles on its axis. Her head is heavy, full of sand. A quietly leaden unpleasantness. She can't speak it, but that's fine for now. Her tongue is too thick to find most of the words she already knows.

A voice from down the bar: "Hey! You okay? Want some water?"

Raises a hand and pats her uniform's breast pocket, "Yup. Goin' smoke..."

–It all hits you at once when you stand up. Could sit and be drunk for years, remember everything and never get sick, but stand up and it's a mind-wipe, a liquid world, a sudden–

Outside, fumbling in booze-blunted slow motion. Body and mind connected only by a long, thin leash of awareness, each one liable to go off its own way and break the tether. The world presses down on her. Weight of the sky brings stumble to sway–Must be a sight to see from the outside. Stringy-haired girl in an oversized jacket, dragging her feet on the cracked sidewalk in a drizzle, attempting to set a cigarette aflame, unaware that it's already too soaked to catch... You're a subject fit for oils in a smoky studio. Inside though everything is inky and black and angelic tracers, meteoric flashes, loamy turnings in your belly–A jubilant tumble onto something hard and wet and cold and stony and then she rises. A poem from the page. A voice she knows is safe: "Hey, hey, babe. You okay?"

"Get, get off of, of me!" And her palms come to a hard shoulder, sending her free again to the streaming wall. Turns against it and brings the lighter back up to the broke and soaked cig. Orange flash without a catch.

"Hon, here. Are you okay? Let me see," turns her back to face him, "let me see your face. You just ate shit."

"Nuh-uh. No, I–"

"Oh yeah you did, babe. Went down hard." Derek brushes a strand of hair from her strawberry-rashed cheeks. "Lord, hon, what did you–"

"You smell like beer."

"No, babe, *you* smell like beer. Hold still. Let me–"

"No!" Rolls away again. "I want to go home..."

"I'd like to go home too, Aura. That's why I'm, can you stop this? Jesus, you know how bad this looks?"

"Let me go!"

"Babe, Aura! Ow! Fuck! Fine!"

Stumbles again but catches herself on the parking lot's cyclone fence. Silenced sepia. Slapstick.

"Aura, come on, let's–"

"I want to go home."

"I know babe, me too! Let's go on and go then!"

"I want to–"

"Christ Almighty..."

Hands on her shoulders. A scoop to flight. The soft, heavy stuff inside left behind. Husk dumped in a stiff fibered seat. Smell of stale ash and body and a violent pouring, a stinging speech, onto the glistening black. Holy chunks...

    –Look in the mirror. Look in the mirror and tell what you see that it's time to make itself something wholly different. April of your prime. Famine where abundance lies, setting even yourself on fire. Refuse to bloom, bury it all, a glutton eating the world's due, swallowed in death by the ground. Thyself thy foe, to thy sweet self too cruel. Who are you so fond of the tomb? Thy mother's glass? Herself in thee? Die single, live remembered not to be. Unthrifty loveliness. Nature only lends, and only to those who are free. Hideous winter. A liquid prisoner. Walls of glass. Ten times happier, ten times ten times thyself happier than thou art. What could death do should thou depart? Too fair for free will? Golden pilgrimage. Highest pitch. Feeble age. Gracious light and a burning head, why do you hear music sadly? Sweet wars not with sweet and joy always delights in joy. A speechless song: thou single will prove none. The world is thy widow. Beauty's waste. The user destroys. Seek the beauteous to ruinate. Hate shall be fairer lodged and make thee another self. Make thee another self: Harsh. Featureless. And rude. Lofty trees of barren leaves. Nothing against time's scythe. Find now determination. Yourself again. Who lets so fair a house fall to decay? Barren rage of death? Winter's day? You had a father, you had a father, you had a father. Thy end is truth and beauty. Doom and date. All in war with time. Make war upon this bloody tyrant, time. Give yourself away. Keep yourself still. A poet's rage is an antique song. Live twice! This poet lies–

    Her eyes open at a fresh burning, and a groan brings her up. Blinking through the intervals of orange, the world returns lazy and empty: "Oh, fuck..."

"You okay?" A voice she knows is safe.

"Huh?"

"I, are you alright? Do you need me to pull over?"

"Whu–"

"No, no! Fuck! Babe! Not in the–"

"I don't feel..."

"Shit, let me just, here..."

It goes all the way out here. From this bend to cross Salt Creek, the bridge, where the highway merges with the Loop, it opens up into the great grey of the ocean. A still, moonlit mass. All tumult a secret until its telling. Deep topography hidden by immovable motion, every tide a what-will-be being what-it-will. A blast of lightning reminds the horizon, and Derek holds Aura's hair back as she pours out onto the highway's gravelly shoulder. They are suspended by concrete over the laze of the tide-risen strait. Petrichor among the salt the breeze carries. Fumes of reified death from the cars passing behind them. There's a storm out there, this rain now only its herald. A massive thunderhead hidden by the streetlight-blotted starless night. In silver flashes its haunches briefly rise: the back of a beast turning away or the barreled chest of one bearing all down? Probably break before landfall. Or maybe it'll swerve away to amass again over the soft sea, feeding from the forever-full ocean, always more and more and more for the sky to gather and pour...

&&&

—Though the storm woke the poor thing, the drizzle's sent it back to sleep. A basic principle you took note of years ago, decades now even maybe: They need things to be steady. Pattered rain. Circling lullaby. A heart's constant beating buried beneath the draw of lung.

This here Winston, a lifetime of Winnie ahead of him, is proof positive of that, sleeping lumpen and limp after so much of a show just moments ago. Too big for his mother in every possible way. She'd come to you two-and-a-half-maybe-three years back, arms wrapped over her belly even though she'd not yet begun to show what she still secretly considers a shame. Rattled the screen door on its frame with wristy whacks, face all hard against tears, sun setting behind the cloud about her. Little thing. Twenty years old, freshly free from her parents' house, knocked-up and back down into what she thought she'd stood to escape. Found you only after turning every other way, running finally into someone with good and solid enough faith to say, "Call up my Auntie Shah. Have a talk with her. She'll set you straight." Works nights at the hospital now a few times a week, so you come over to watch Winnie grow and fuss.

Little thing, so fresh as it is, is going to cry. Understandable and expected and normal so, going to have a hard time at night. Needs Mama to be there, ready to hold him and press him to breast, feed him and fill him up and get his tummy all ready for all the things that will make him strong and big and big and strong one day, isn't that right? No need for you to bother with it because it's her that he needs. Lightning in the sky makes day so suddenly, and then falls back to night with a big clap, the dark crashing back. One day he might be your child and then he'll get to know exactly why, he'll understand what it is that's happening in the sky, and then he'll be able to answer his own questions as they come to him. But right now, he's too fresh and soft and little. Still grabby. Still grips hard and tight and blind even though you'd bet his eyes have been open for weeks. Mouth all puckered-up toothless and begging for either milk or something new, something to garner a giggle. Nothing of a father in any of it.

Going to cry and there's no use in getting all torqued-up about it. She can't reasonably expect restful nights for quite a while now, whether you're there or not. Best get used to being jerked out of bed. Going to have to rise every time there's a storm or the little fucker shits himself. Going to have to jump out of the bed and, if you were there it would be a race to the cradle and you might trip over your sleeping feet and it's only hope that could get your hands on the little bastard enough to prove your presence, lift him and pat his back and go all 'Anders, Anders, Anders, it's okay, little one... Is the little thing hungry? Is the little tyke in need? Hungry? Thirsty. Can I get you anything?'

"No, no, nothing for me, boss. Can't stand to eat when I've still got the smell of this shit in my nose..."

So—Bennie puts the cellophane-wrapped pastries on the bathroom's windowsill. Coffee's dropped to the side of them. One for each hand. One for each man. Had walked all the way down the inky nighttime halls with the hot sludge dripping over his knuckles. Scalding beneath his wristwatch. Snack cakes shoved up in his underarms, threatening to fall the whole way down. Rivulets running to ring. "Yeah, I've put in a request with Inventory that we change up the brand we're using. Something unsettling about the smell isn't there?"

"Don't know that it's unique to the brand." The Custodian leans in the doorway and pulls the yellow mop bucket closer to him. A splash of sudsy puce fluid sloshes onto the tiles. "All those chemicals are gonna smell like that. Doesn't matter who makes it. All the same."

Bennie perches himself on the marble windowsill alongside the snack cakes. Leans against the cloudy glass. Downpour pounding rat-a-tat against his back. He plucks from the cluster a white-iced cinnamon bun. Strips it of its wrapping and presses fingers into its sugary mass. Flakes fall to the watch-your-step wet floor. A shattered monochrome mosaic. "Got a bin or anything?" Holds up the crinkled ball of plastic.

The Custodian nods and disappears briefly into the hall's dark. Returns with his hand round the rim of his big trash bin, his vocation's familiar. Drags it in. Onto the tile with a spin on its rickety wheels. *Clack, clack, clack.* Comes to rest between the stalls and sink.

"Place your bets!" And up rises the ball, "Place your bets!"

The flight is high of arc and short of distance. Lands far from an admirable radian away from the plastic-lined maw.

"Shit." And Bennie's feet come to the tile. Bends to the fallen ball. Notices then the grimy grey marks all over the bathroom floor. The shape and shame of his own feet. "Oh, damn, look what's, look what I've done to your, to your floor." Eyes up to the Custodian. "Here, I'll, I can't believe I, uhm… Here just let me go grab some sponges and I'll, shit." Pushes past him in the doorway, leaving more blemishes of his presence behind. "Just let me get some sponges and I'll, supply closet is down this way, right?"

"Yessir, it is."

"Alright fine. Here. Go on and have a snack or something. Some coffee. I'll get this fixed in a jiffy, no uhm… no harm done, right?" So— With something burbling like a panic or brightening like excitement, either way calling sweat to your brow, you would rise and plod down the hallway, arms out front into the dark, sleep torn from your eyes. Autumn leaves in an unseasonal tempest.

And she'd come up quicker from behind and push past you, clipping you into the doorway.

And it would be all, "Hush, hush, hush, little one. Hush, hush, hush…"

And you'd be: "Fuck, fuck, fuck, goddammit. Shit, shit, shit!"

And she'd hiss over her shoulder the same as to the child but harsher, "Hush, hush!" And then some language you'd sworn to learn years ago.

"Alright, fuck, my hip. Okay, okay..." And you'd back out of the doorway, palms up in feeble surrender, ready to accept helping hand and damning nail all the same.

She'd continue then to natter on native, enmeshed in song, as Anders' globular, shining eyes would look up at her, his mother's, mouth. Jaws at one end cutting from the air a tune and the other suckling soft and jejune, all while you stand mute, deflated, and defeated. Empty-handed. Tone-deaf breath. Sleep tugging at your ears. Ache like a heart in your rear where you'd confronted the architecture. You'd look through the window that gives view to the porch where she'd stand under the buggy light, a breast fallen, swaying to her song as little hands at her clavicle claw–

"Enough now, child." Nuzzles his roll-chocked neck. Whispers it again into his ear. "Enough now, child, enough."

The rain and all the commotion that woke him has stopped. Only streetlight-gilt glistens dribbling from the powerline and budding trees. Rhythm growing erratic, though quieting. A choir of frogs grumble at the rain's cessation.

"Hear all that, Winnie?" And Shareese presses her lips to his chubby cheek. Blows a big wet raspberry. "You ol' frog, Winnie. You just an ol' froggy coming out after the rain, ain'tcha?" The child gets his giggle then. No evidence of the caterwauling of before, that cantor's howl of being ripped from sleep by storm. "Just coming up out after the rain, huh?"

&&&

–Perfectly timeless when the lights come up. When the music stops and the door locks, when the air fills with only the sound of motorized brushes sloshing in the sink and the ding of that clanging machine, the ancient manual cash register. When Jimbo takes the bundles of cash from their pans in the drawer, stacks them all into a lockbox forever overflowing with receipt paper pocked black and blue, grabs the lip of the fishbowl they use for a tip jar, **'Yacht Fund'** written in thumb-crumbed chalk marker over the bow, and says over his shoulder to Gene the Barback, "I'll be in the office doing money. For the love of God don't need anything..."

And Gene says, "Aye-aye, captain. Never have and never will." And turns back to the sinks. Two pints in his hands, filmed with the solidified froth of dregs. Dunks them into the steaming churn and rinses them in an ultramarine sanitizer solution. Holds up the shining clean glasses, looks over his own shoulder in the direction of the office and says, invariably, grinning under his greasy blonde mustache: "While the boss is away—"

Which you invariably fill in: "The children will play." Words heavy on your tongue and lips. Mouth can't move fast enough, can't get out of the way. Verbiage spills. Cottage cheese, clotty and flavorless.

"That's what I like to hear," Gene spins the glasses gunslinger and turns to the taps. "Buford?"

"Always," and just a few moments later an over-foamed pint of the local stuff is slid in front of you. Call it the fifth pint past the one-too-many mark. "Thank you kindly, Gene."

"Not a problem, sir." And y'all clink glasses.

No doubt about it, that feels good, that *'sir'* there. Gene's a good kid, no doubt about it. Respectful. Knows his place. Doesn't seem ambitious enough to fail, nor unambitious enough to end up at a dead end. Can only hope that he doesn't end up like you. Sometimes there's just nothing that can be done about it, fuck up too early in the game and spend the rest of your days climbing back to the beginning. Find it empty then, though. Shouldn't measure yourself against others. Yeah? Who then? Who do you measure yourself against then? Yourself? Horseshit. You ain't shit without others. They all decide what it is you are. Like Gene, a good kid. Employed, making his own way. Quick on his feet, that's for sure. Little skittish, maybe. Could use a visit to the dentist. And a dermatologist. Nothing can be done about that though maybe; scabs and spots are genetic sometimes. Not everyone is cut from the same cloth. Some kids can be skinny like that and simply fine. High metabolism and all that. Used to be that way yourself so don't get, you weren't eating when you looked like that though, just drinking and smoking and letting gold run through your veins. Not a worry about ol' Gene here though, is there? Shifty and skittering and thin, all ailments of a young man working too hard. Working too hard is good for you at his age, though, isn't it? Working nights like this'll make you appreciate the day. Put you right in your place! Love that, that *'sir'* there. Good kid, good kid...

Gene looks up and to the side, toward the door. Looks back at you. Swaying on your stool as your thoughts jumble and collide. Motions with his head in the direction that he looked.

You smile, "*She* there?"

Gene nods, "Yessir, it seems like it..."

"Old bag-of-bones bitch..." Point to the hours-empty shot glass in front of you. Mouth wet-lipped the words 'one more.' Whiskey splashes. Toss its searing down your throat. Open your wallet and smack two twenties on the bar top. "That's all you guys, Gene."

"Thank you, sir."

"Now let me out so that I may," big cinder-rimmed belch puffs your cheeks and burns your nose, "meet my maker, as it were."

Standing out in the streetlights' hazy orange: sweatpants, hoodie, flipflops, shivering a touch it seems in the wake of the modest spring storm that blew through an hour ago. Saw that stumble that very nearly caught you on the way to the door. Raises her palm to rest her embarrassed face in. Can't believe this is what she's rendered for herself. Just looking for a bit of vacation, she said, celebrate the finalization of the divorce, cut loose like she never could. Got a tan, got hammered, partied a month away and has now spent the past two weeks cleaning up after you, another broken man, another buffoon. Goddamn born-again boozehound. Listened to you tell your sob story over and over again, and now, key in lock, drunken fidget figuring which way it needs to be turned to disengage the bolt, and finally the glass door opens.

"Roh, will you come on? Jesus Christ."

Out the bar and into the street's humid fog. "Would you fucking relax, babe? I don't work tomorrow, lay off me..."

"I don't care if you work tomorrow or not..." Walks over to turn you toward the door that leads to the stairway, "I don't want to have to be your fucking mother all day again..." Pushes.

&&&

Tiny, precise chips. Tedious work. Coming at the paint with housekeys first brought it from the canvas in cloddy chunks and fibrous tears. Threads and tufts ripped up and stuck to the underside, canvas itself running more toward translucence as the pigment's face fissured and gave. Thought then perhaps to let some linseed or thinner set into it, see if it'd soak all back to a liquid and then maybe you could just scrape it away. Worked a little a bit, but the reconstituted paint rivered together and turned baby-shit. All the greens and purples and fiery swipes purged of their differences left an unworkable stain on the canvas beneath. Wanted it white as possible so as not to get caught making the same thing over and over. Thought then to use a razor. A dull one, plucked from the bathroom trash bin, pried from its plastic head, and revived into some sort of useful life—

With the weathered edge he's now slicing crosshatches into the thick globs. Pinkies a conservative sheen of linseed over the brusque-brushed surface to soften it. A few short, shallow, quick *snic-snic-snics* and he flips the canvas over to make sure the blade hasn't insisted itself full through. *Scrape-scrape-scrape* and the paint comes away variously in boogers and flakes. A powdery residue is left in the wake.

The hand-cramping tedium brings a welcome shroud over his mind— Know that if you stop to crack your knuckles or flex your fingers or anything at all other than what it is right here right now that you're already doing you'll be clobbered by the realization that this is a fool's errand. Whatever is left of the canvas, whatever integrity it's still got, very probably won't be anything useful but, but, but you've already set about it for an hour or two now and the weight of failure before finish would be, this early in the morning, too much to shoulder. Press on and hope for the best.

Haven't slept a wink. Jess'd already been hours deep when you stumbled into the house just before midnight, all heavy with smoke and whiskey. Her shoots are getting more demanding, sucking more and more out of her the more she has to shove up inside. Few days back, after she returned from the bank with a wad of cash for the mason jar perched on the desk, you'd looked at her profile for the first time in who knows how long. Getting into some intricate territory. Seems to be the trend with this stuff. Can't just rub yourself with produce and toys and keep a following. Just the way it goes. Deeper and deeper down the hole until there's no more hole left. It's just work. What she does to make ends meet, *our* ends meet—

The rain's done nothing to knock the mug from the air. Buck raises a cigarette to his lip as he greets the sunrise—Smoke does amazing things to the pinky blues the sun's brought-up with it this morning. Haze holding the light's every moment a touch longer than it would have lasted without it, piling them up as they fade, glow amalgamated out of a single source, honey from nectar, jam from fruit, booze out of barley. Eyes heavy with that blissfully dehydrated, over-smoked leathery feeling. Tongue a strip of sandpaper. Salty silted fish film on your skin. Come away green-grey in a shower. But can't sleep. Couldn't hours ago and definitely can't now, not until those canvases are as blank as can be.

Gotta get some new stuff ready you're going to get Putsch on the hook. No fucking money to buy materials so just have to repurpose the old stuff. But, that's the story, right? That's how the story goes whenever a story is going to go at all. Gotta get all the way to the bottom and start weaving coincidences together. Had the idea while you tossed and turned with the comforter clinging to your skin, sobering sweat pooling up under your arms, knees, crotch, and eyes. Kicked the sheets off and jumped from the bed, heart kicking up a new revelatory storm. Start over. Start all over. Make it better. Going to get Putsch on the hook, gotta start all over.

"Yo, Mo!" Bell clanging behind.

"Ah, fuck you and slamming the door again! Don't slam the door, fucker!"

"C'mon, Mo. I don't get a hello?"

"You get a hello if you don't slam my fucking door!"

"Jesus man, what's up your ass?" Leaned then on the counter, loose knee displacing several rows of candy below.

"Had to go and get a new door. Jasper kids came and threw rocks at the old one, broke the glass and, no reason! Not a brain in their heads!"

"Shame, Mo. Can't believe it." Was bright as Christ inside the shop. "Hey, let me get a–"

"Ah! No, no, no! You don't get shit, Bucky! You don't get shit until you pay me."

Felt like your guts had been blown out your butt by the walk over. Fabric filled lungs. A few flashes out to the, what was it? East? Yeah, always east. Portending of that storm that's always being prophesied but never flows to flourish. Bang always less than the buck. "The fuck are you talking about, Mo?"

"Weeks go by and you want to come in here and start asking me for shit when you don't even have the money for what in the fuck I already gave you?"

"Mo, honestly man," lights flickered in the shop as blue day suddened outside. A crash, the night falling back. "Shit. Look man, I don't know what you're talking about. I gotta get back home before all this shit, I mean, it's about to come down and I don't want to get caught in it, you know? So, can I just like–"

"You owe me ten dollars, Buck. You give me ten dollars and I'll give whatever else you want if you've got whatever else it's going to cost. I have a business to run and I can't keep–"

"Mo," passion of whatever it was that had ripped you from bed was beginning to fade. Another crack of day and thunderous applause for the implacable darkness. "How the hell do I owe you ten dollars? I haven't been over here in, like you said, like over a week, two weeks probably–"

"But your friend, your big guy friend that came in here smelling like my supply closest, like bleach and whatever else, come in here smelling so bad it made my eyes water. You send him to come in here and he goes all, 'I have got to talk to Mo' like he fucking knows me or something. So, I say to your big fuck friend–"

"Oh, shit..." Had gotten so caught up in the debacle that you'd completely forgotten that David was even a part of it. Forgot about the run for smokes and booze entirely. As your breath came back, burn in your lungs subsiding to a rolling prickle, and Jess shivered in her pissy shellac, can't believe it had been that cold that short a time ago, lights on in all the houses of your sunken clutch, frustrated male voices and warbling wives and cry of kids and then, like caught in a conflagrating cornfield, heinous coughs abound. The noxiousness of your home had blown out and pooled in the humid air, spreading like plague in a petri. "Fuck, what did he–?"

"Came in and bought three magnum Bufords and then a pack of–"

"Ten dollars?"

"Three magnums and a pack of–

"Alright, fuck me then, here." Slammed the crisp twenty on the counter, "Fuck dude. I guess then let me also get a pack of golds and, shit, what's the cheapest forty you've got?"

"Belchard's Lite is two and seventy–"

"Alright, fine. Piss..." Turned then to pluck from the shelves a plastic, shatterproof forty of Belchard's Lite. Came back to the register and Mo was reaching up on the cigarette rack. "No, no, no, Mo. C'mon, gimme the out of state shit. I can't throw down like that."

"No golds fell off the truck this week," and grinned.

"Well, Mo, what did *fall off the truck* then?"

Mo looked briefly, performatively, under the counter. Then said: "Only Rezzies–"

"Fuck you, that's not true," government issue, covert ops shit, chemical weaponry, "pretty sure those things'll give you cancer just looking at them."

"Well, that's all I've got, Bucky–"

"Fine, fuck, fine. Ring me up then."

"Golds?"

"Yeah, golds..."

"Okay, ten dollars for your big fuck friend, seven and fifty for the golds and two and seventy-five for the beer and, call it twenty and ninety-seven."

"Fine, here's twenty and I owe you a dollar–"

"Plus interest this time!"

"Fine, a dollar and a dime, fuck you very much." Gathered your things just as the night again exploded briefly into noon. "Jesus Christ," nearly dropped the forty.

"Next time you come in with a better attitude, Buck, or I don't sell you anything anymore."

"Alright, Mo, alright." Bottle up under your arm as you got the door handle in your grasp.

"And get better smelling friends!"

"Fuck off, Mo."

"And don't slam the door!"

Let the door slam on its own then.

The rain had come down like a cliché the moment you made it to the middle of Harris Park, just as you come up on the central fountain, dry in every season so as to disincentivize its use as a public bath for the unhoused. Too far from the Jaspers or Mel's to go anywhere but home. The park's inhabitants didn't seem to mind it one bit. Those that slept under the trees or gazebos stayed just as splayed or crumpled as they had been, sinking into the swallowing mud or acting as unweatherable obstacles as the sky's water flowed over the concrete paths. The others, those walking in their plumbed daze, sought out no shelter from the rain, only let it wash away whatever it was they paced to escape. Crud and gunk of all sorts sloughed from the skin and hair, revealing for the night what it had all gathered to hide. Gaunt and sad faces, sullen skulls, clearly colored eyes. The clothing, soaked and sagged, gave view of the frail frames they, in drier times, gave shape to. At the peak of the pouring, you cast your head down, watching only each footfall deepen in the increasing inches of earth-browned water, eyes away from the human truth that abounded all around.

—Once home, he stripped down to his underwear on the porch, cracked open the warm forty of Belch, lit up a smoke and fantasized about his new plan to make something of himself—

The clothes are still piled up on the porch's boards and the morning's sun is making your nudity apparent. The partition offered by the storm now only a strange, half drunk memory. Your hands are covered in paint and little plasma-crusted cuts from the razor. Something is clarifying as you rub your palms together. A stinging friction that showers flecks onto your bare feet and it all just now seems that. Shit, all up under fingernails and marking out the lines in our palms... Shit... Can feel it over our skin, in our pores, climbing all the way up our arms... Shit... Gonna be fucking impossible to wash out... God, can't hardly fucking breath in this fucking humidity!

–Inside, Jess is standing in the center of the bedroom, feet planted in the cruddy collateral circle of paint chips muddled into the carpet by wayward knees and elbows and thumbs. She's holding the only canvas not yet destroyed. The other two lay dead. Fetal. Miscarried. Tossed away. Her mouth is slightly agape, neither readying for nor returning from a morning yawn–But more as if she's realizing now for the thousandth time just how far away we are from home...

Her eyes rise from the painting to look at us. She says: "Are they done now, Buck?"

&&&

The Thermopoetics of Plasticity:
The World as Human Byproduct

The *plasticity* of an object is the measurement of its here we go again. Why make something new when we can just insist that something old doesn't mean what it meant? Not a fair complaint in the long run though, because then we'd be complaining that we have to learn all these new words instead of complaining that the words we already know are now so different. Problem is when we read it our immediate thought is does this new meaning of this old word change the way we use it now or does it still fit into the context from which it's being corrected? Like in the case of this, of this opening here this the *plasticity* of an object is the measurement of its aptitude for formal change despite its tendency toward eternality, does that mean that we now have to use the term plasticity more seldom than we'd already been finding cause to use it for fear of this being its new definition to the point of cutting us out the fool in every thought it was previously thunk within? Probably not because, again sometimes to read is simply to watch and listen, so probably not because it seems that Putsch may have anticipated our question as the next sentence in line here is: By *tendency toward eternality* we are referring to something that to this author's knowledge has not yet found for itself a common name. Whether through the Tao or Hegelian Synthesis or any other codified nonsense, it is generally accepted as unverifiable fact that the existence of anything at all necessarily dictates the existence of its opposite. So, since there is most certainly a tendency within creation toward dissolution and decay and inertia, namely entropy, so too there *must* be, at least conceptually, a tendency toward eternality. Sisters in time and space. But that's just poetry, right? Sisters in time and space? Bet any dollar amount that he'll wave such an accusation off in the next few sentences though. Has definitely expended a not inconsiderable amount of syllabage toward covering his ass where anyone with any degree of expertise would have his tail tucked. The sort of thinker that gets lost in the art of it all and then insists that his map is just as, if not more, accurate than those of the scholars he seemingly so wishes he was in the ranks of. Maybe though, maybe because it takes two to tango and reading is a dance of its own, maybe we're just not in the mood for it right now and maybe it's not his fault exactly in the way that we'd like it to be. Maybe, as usual, when we take a moment to step back and slow down we'll stand a chance of seeing something that might actually be there instead of all the stuff we think ought to be. Because by tendency toward eternality we are referring to something that to this author's knowledge has not yet found for itself a common name so maybe it stands to reason enough that it won't immediately conjure something concrete in our mind, and furthermore that that's alright and just fine because it's not like anybody else would know what he doesn't know if he's talking about it clearly or not any more than we do now. He's asked, right? He's asked right here in the text as it stands for us to breathe deep enough to broaden the scope of our imagination enough to at the very least make room for the thoughts he's trying to think, and inviting us to think right alongside with him, no honest wool over the reader's eyes so go ahead now and let's trust that these new things are indeed in fact sisters in space and time. Insofar as it is possible to imagine a conceptual object which embodies a tendency toward eternality, it seems to this author that there are two positions readily available which to take.[1] The first is an object of abject instability, one which moves through time with all the grace of a stuttered insult, that wears on its face a chaotic glower and moue. The second object, and the one which we will favor moving forward, is one of complete and utter formal serenity. A moment before diving into our favored object to offer explanation for why the former should be resoundingly disregarded: The coexistence of these objects, the object toward decay and object toward eternality, depends on a conceptual universe in which both of these objects are safe from the strictures of having to break rules in an effort to exist alone. The general law that guides this universe, *Entropy*, which makes most objects, or all in the case of the shadowed corner of the cosmos we occupy, tend toward decay, cannot be broken by the theoretical object tending toward eternality. It is part and parcel with this law of entropy that any and all expenditures of energy are subtractive from the expending substance's whole, and therefore falls in line with the tendency toward decay. All to say, hopefully with some semblance of clarity, that an object that tends toward eternality must be wholly still and at peace with its corporeal self, that whatever changes it incurs must be sourced from without. This is the essence of our usage of the term *plasticity*. The object toward eternality's plasticity is its ability to maintain in the face of the changes brought about by the entropic environment by

---

[1] There is, of course, an unlimited number of positions to take on almost any issue, all the more when the issue in question is the theoretical geometry of a completely imagined object. However, this author personally believes that it behooves the thinker to set about the particulars of their paramatizing before blithely allowing the mind to run wild. A bit sober of an approach to something so scintillatingly nonexistent, sure, but we stand to lose sight of the proposition of the object if we blur our vision so early in the process of imagining. So, here for this object that tends toward eternality, we must decide whether or not we're imagining an *opposite* or an *inverse*, perhaps even a *reflection*. We also must put our foot down steady and hard against the rising of a recreated concept of *creativity*, as though it may seem sororally linked to decay its relationship is much more avuncular.

chaotic objects toward decay. Plasticity, as we would assume by our given associations of the word, though let's reinforce it here nonetheless, is the quality by which an object's shape may change without its form incurring any of the qualities of that change. See, it's this shit though, getting lost in the poetry of it again, feels like distinctions are being drawn where in reality there are none. But, of course we've got to constantly remind ourselves that nothing printed on the page is any way a reality in the way that it claims to represent. Shape and form, though synonymous in conversation perhaps, are in fact two different words, so much to the point that don't even dare share any letters... Wait, this what all this has done to our brain? Gummed up the works so much that we're willing to argue with ourselves about the difference between two words like shape and form for him? Putsch doesn't even have to try at this point, does he? We could write the rest of this ourselves! Adopt the scholarly tone and just conjunct contradictions: It's perhaps in the essence of these terms, shape and form, and the ticklings they take on our tongues that trick us into thinking them similar when in fact they could not be more different. Water may be the easiest example to grab onto, but matter all the same would do just fine. It's the familiarity of water in our world that makes it a perfect example, the fact that it takes in terms of its matter so many forms and in terms of its general fluidity it readily takes, in conditions we are doubtlessly familiar with, it takes the shape of its vessel. So, with regards to water we are all the more able to imagine the coexistence of the two different aspects that are shape and form. Shape, for our purposes here and maybe also in life and reality outside of this page but that's not for *this author* to dare to say, will stand to mean the dimensions of a given object, all that numerical geometry and mass and weight and so on and so forth, though he'd never write so on and so forth like that, have to think that maybe his notes would include little scratchings of that sort, placeholders for poetical configurations that need to be tinkered with before they get really written. And form stands to mean where he wouldn't falter, but we certainly will here and now, where it all depends on the wittiness of the words and memorability of the phrases, where what needs weaving is an aphorism more than forcefully injected insight, and odds are even he'd put here another footnote.[2] And boy, does he love his footnotes! Something about the forms of shapes or shapes of forms or, back to the beginning of this turn: Plasticity, as we would assume by our given associations of the word, though let's reinforce it here nonetheless, is the quality by which an object's shape may change without its form incurring any of the qualities of that change. That is to ultimately say...

---

2 Some murky soliloquy to clarify what had been lost in the mess above. Down here in the prose's basement, the air humid with run-on run-off and walls mildewed in a thin paste of afterthought, the author can set about a flaccid apologetics for the nonsense that weighs so heavily over us. The hope is ultimately that the reader disregards the wobble this well adds to the foundation and moves on through the rivering words all the same, never stopping to read this canned paroxysm. Worst though is when they're chocked-full of cryptically comma'd and dashed references. Treacherous place, the footnote. Tempting for the author like our Putsch here, who never seems to know when he's got no more to say, knows even less when he's got nothing at all to begin with. This is the empty pan from which the fumes rise, the source of the kitchen's stink, the place where secrets are hung from hooks of admission and skeletons dance out of their closets.

May

I.

Midday and nothing. From the passenger's seat: a crackly blacktop bend off the state roadway opens to the little development's barren stretch. A single dead-end street, not quite a football field's length. Seven grey driveways branching off, leading to the closed garage doors of identically vinyl-sided ranch houses. The dead end sprouts a few tufty attempts at greenery. All around is sandy farmland, erred arid. At the furthest the eye can see, along the horizon's wobble, there rises from the loamless earth a rendering plant.

We bring the car to the curb, where the asphalt gives over to parched lawn. Shift the vehicle into park and place our hand on the keys dangling from the ignition. Stop short of cutting the engine. Hotter than a whore in church. First heatwave of the season's come early. Don't want to cut the A/C if we don't need to, took it near halfway here to get cool in the first place. "You, uhm, want us to go in with you, babe?" As she digs in her purse for keys.

"Don't see why I would." Finds them. "Can't imagine you showing up would help much." Smiles.

"Fair enough," Nod and offer a nostril's terse jet. Roll with the punches here, should be the last time we need worry about any of this. Godawful way to spend a day off, but so it goes. Just let her get the things she needs, try and make her peace or whatever, and then it's over with and we don't ever have to drive her back here again. That was the deal. Just needs some things, is all. Sentimental or whatever. "Well, I'll be right here if you do need me. Otherwise–"

"I won't be long, D." No need for eye contact, just get out and get it done. Convincing him to get us out here in the first place was enough trouble, no use digging any further now. Like to just turn around and leave us here. Promised him that after this it'll all be settled, that we just have to get some things that were left behind so that *his* apartment could start to feel like *our* home. Bout blew a gasket at that though, didn't he? Like we were insulting his way of living or something, spitting on the face of his essence, but that's just not what we meant, babe! That not what we mean, but we live *together* now and that isn't ever going to work if one of us doesn't feel like we're able to really *live*, because then it's *not* together, you know? It's not living together as two people sharing a life but it's only one person *keeping* the other person, you know? No, that's not what we meant. No, we don't feel like we're being kept or anything and we know, we can leave whenever we want, so maybe you don't make that fucking suggestion because maybe we will just go then! And don't fucking call us that! Don't you ever fucking, I swear to God if you ever call us fucking crazy or just like our mother ever again, we'll fucking, in retrospect we didn't have to slam the bathroom door that hard. God's honest, didn't mean for the mirror to break like that. Just goes to show though how cheap everything in that place is though, in those apartments. We should try to move into the city, down to Madiston, both be closer to work and maybe we could try and enroll in school or something and we could, know it's expensive but maybe, just maybe, fucking Buck and Jess live in town so why can't we? "Don't worry, hon. I don't want to be here anymore than you do…" Shut the door behind.

No matter what they do to us, it's impossible to forget family.

The latch clicking gives birth to that air-thickening woof, the bass-burble of the television in Mama's living room. Loud as ever. The only sound other than the idle of the car's engine. No birdsong for there being no trees. Nothing for the wind to whistle off…

Could blame it all on the heat, on the soup that hangs in the air, but that would be dishonest. Step away from the car. Sweat springs across our forehead, beads to pour. A knuckly hollow kicks in our belly. The nauseous desire to purge, that animal anxiety and urge to lighten the load so as to make the inevitability of flight feasible. Swallow against it. Push the rising sour back down.

The fear is obviously of violence. Yelling can be tolerated, and has been for years, as explicably symptomatic of whatever ailment has weaseled its Latinly ornate syllables in our mother's brain. Heard the hail almost every Friday night for the past just-over-half-a-year, always greeted upon our return by hard, obsidian-tongued words. Hell, used to yell and shout and holler, fall into paroxysmal collapse, fits of floor-biting madness, long before Papa left. Probably why he eventually did. Never got a full explanation as to why he fucked off but we can't blame him for having had enough. We've done the very same to her now. Never a memory of real violence, though. Sure, after Papa absconded in the night without so much as a note there were, for a short period of time and infrequently recurrent, episodes of wine bottles flying through the house, breaking to millions against the drywall, but, so, wore a pair of flipflops whenever we went into the kitchen. What's a few shards in the sole once or twice? Only blood ever spilled in any meaningful way had been Mama's own, by her own hands, and all within the realm of reasonable accident. Though, the words uttered in these episodes were reason enough to take pause. Threats of violence toward 'Him' should he ever show his face again. Swore that she'd kill him, wring his neck, or stomp his face. Cave his head with a frying pan. Gut him with one of the duller kitchen knives. Beat him to death with the golf clubs he left behind. Do something, hurt him for abandoning her and, well, we followed suit so it may be fair to assume that all precedents for prediction of Mama's behavior when we set foot on the welcome mat are now moot and useless. But the conditions here are different in several important ways. Right?

Slip the key into the deadbolt. Should we have had Derek follow up behind?

Wrist flicks and the latch doesn't give. Wasn't here that we expected to meet resistance. Knee comes up and collides bare with the door. Really thought it would just open. Hop on one leg and spin the throb away. Key ring comes with us and shimmer and jangle falls to the sole-worn welcome mat. Take a look. Used the right one or, yeah, no, that's the one for the front door. Must be something wrong with the lock itself. Wouldn't be surprised, maybe. Lots of rain and maybe, we don't know, rusted over inside or something? Maybe she hasn't left the house through the front door and it's jammed up from like lack of use? Makes enough sense. If she were to leave it would probably be through the garage, in the car, so... check the back. Plus, don't want to mess around too much and startle her. Maybe she won't even notice us come in and we can sneak by and get our things and then just quickly like say hi-and-bye because we can't just not say anything right? Just make sure she's okay and all because, well, we can't just come home after what, a month? Month and some change?

Who's counting? We can do whatever we want, first-off, and she, or he, can't do a damned thing about it!

From the driver's side window, rolled down a crack to let the smoke slither out: Keep eyes on her. Don't trust this whole endeavor. Never met the woman, her mother, but've certainly heard enough about her, wiped away enough of the tears she's caused, enough arduous come-down conversations after the panic attacks she's been responsible for. Panic attacks are a motherfucker, poor girl. Migraines and panic attacks. The panic is lessening though, only comes about when enough of a cause has built up. Hasn't seemed to have a significant episode since she moved in, so maybe all that's behind us. Migraines though... Lord knows how someone is supposed to navigate life, supposed to plan for anything, when at any moment their brain could just, don't know, it's like it falls in on itself or something. Sometimes she'll go totally nonverbal. God forbid she ever have like an actual stroke, because we sure as fuck wouldn't know the difference... Flick the butt through the window crack, onto the asphalt. She's leaving the porch. Abort mission. Hell yeah, thank God. Sit up straighter and get ready to slack our face into brow-bent inquiry, 'Everything alright, babe?' But, wait, wait, she's rounding the corner of the house, disappearing behind it. Out of sight. Stomping.

The television is quieter on this side of the house. On account of the laundry room. At the back door now, stand on tiptoes to look through the textured glass window. Cup hands to block out the beating sun and, looks dark inside. Can't see exactly anything, all is fuzzy and warped and out of focus. Pulsing blue glow from where the kitchen opens into the hallway offering the option between dining room and living room, but all else is dark...

Key ring in open palm. Should be the same as. Yep, slips in fine. No snags or catches or anything. Really must have just been the front door. This just, hold on. Press thumb red and white and burning. Edges dig into the soft of our hand and, Jesus fuck, what the hell is going on? Another try at twisting and, there it goes! Easy now. Twists all the way to, no click, door won't give... Look down and see the shaft has broken. A torqued little nub sticks out of the lock face. All now between finger and thumb is dropped all again.

Both hands lunge for the knob below the bolt. Try to turn it. Gives nothing away. Hands off, wipe 'em on our, just sweaty is all. Nervous. No need to make any more of it than there is here, just hands dry enough and again take up the knob. Palms don't slip. Met still with just as much refusal. No, no, no, fucking no! What? Both hands, digits laced and braced, and the motherfucker still won't give. What the Hell is all this? Why won't it shake in its frame as we give up on twisting and commence to jerking it back and forth. Tonguing a stubbornly loose tooth. Couldn't have meant it! Couldn't have meant it! No way she'd be that fucking cruel! But, of course, she'd said it. She'd said it again and again in endless variation. Spat it through cabernet-stained teeth, spittle sizzling on her lips the color of clotted heart-blood: "Can't just come in and out all you like, you know that? Ain' a damn barn, so don't you go thinking these doors'll always be open." One day, one day, she'd said on the phone last we spoke, one day you'll see you little shit that you can't just go having everything every which way that you want it! One day, one day, she'd said the first time we'd come home late, the first time we'd slept a night in Derek's arms, one day you'll see you spoiled little bitch that all a man can ever do in the end is hurt you. One day you'll see how they always break you or leave you, how they always take something from you. That's all they come around for anyhow, just to come and take something from you until you've got less than nothing left to give and then they one day, one day, she'd said when we hung up the phone, some velvet-voiced woman named Shareese just having told us that our application looks great, asked us could we come in for an interview, that it'd be wonderful to see how we'd fit, one day you'll see you brat you stupid little child that there ain' an ounce of work in this world worth doing, that they always take more than they give back, that whatever it is you think that you're going to be right now, that it just ain' gonna happen because that thing you think you might be one day ain' even a real thing in the end, it doesn't exist, nothing exists like whoever's telling you it does tells you it does, it's all fairytales, worse than fairytales you shit-for-brains because it's all the lie that they all made the world out of, don't you see? Don't you see that there ain' a thing worth doing because at the end of the day, my sweet Aura, because there ain' a thing in the whole world at all after all.

"I can certainly understand all that," with a flat generosity, an air of acknowledgement, smoothing the rough surface of the conversation. Palette knife over buttercream, "But, Miss Sherry, we must never forget that at the end of it all a mother is still a woman, still a human being."

"Surely, Heidi, but again," Shareese's attempt and failure to match the disinterest in the expectant's tone only drew them into starker contrast in our wracked mind, "a woman with a job to do. At the end of the day, the job getting done is where a mother's measure must be taken–"

Out on the ocean the sun was caught, volleyed between the crests of waves still a ways from breaking. Every glint like a razor's blade through the kaleidoscopic murk murmuring in our brain. Cool steel, the sort whose slashing brings about an initial pleasure, first flow of blood some salient warmth before the flood of it shortens our breath. A rhythm to the pain though, a deep lifeless vitality in the tide, whole planet heaving its truth as dead rock and water. The hollow poetry of a mothered Earth.

"I do not see how all that is still worth losing yourself because of." Heidi's hand fell atop her bump. "What is a child to think when he is all grown up and his mother was never anything but that? Do you know what I am trying to say, Miss Sherry?"

"I suppose I do." A look over at Aura then. Some time to generate a response. Strange girl this one, just staring straight-backed out at the sea, growing pale in the sun. "But still, I just can't bring myself around to the idea that woman loses anything by being the best mother she can be."

The pain started up once the first wave had sloshed over our shoulders, once the ocean had stuck its salty fingers up into our nose. Fiery, fishy snot down our throat. First bolt. A rusty rebar run right through our skull. Tried to fill our lungs with air and got foam instead. Shouldn't have been surprised. Was well underway when we rose that morning. All telltale: shimmery peripherals, lazy tongue, a tummy simultaneously bottomless and full-up with rancid butter. Pounded enough coffee to set a horse on fire and took a clattering handful of over the counter pain pills. Couldn't miss it. Couldn't miss the opportunity to get as far away as we'd ever been. Rode the southbound cross county bus green-faced and dizzy. Hadn't eaten breakfast for fear of it coming right back up and, just couldn't miss it. Whole life in Cortland County, our whole life in the heat of it, sweating and flicking away globby bottomed mosquitos, waving gnats away as they swarmed our eyes, ears, and scabs, never once made it far enough out to see the ocean that all this was for in the first place. Couldn't miss it when the new job told us that they'd pay for the ferry ride, bring food and snacks and all that, that they just wanted everyone to get to know everyone before the school year started and fall season kicked off. Caught us by surprise, though, that the waves carried with them the whole possibility of the ocean as far as we could see it. That the floor, the sand, the earth, moved with it, out from under our feet, the whole planet in retreat, shrinking and pulling back just to get a bit more momentum to knock us back down. When our foot didn't find the bottom we slipped full under, taken by the slimy roar, pain rising in our head as to burst it, to split us in two and spill our own salt for the sea. Come up then for what air we could find and the next tumult tossed us grittily to shore, sand settling for home in places we wouldn't be able to publicly pick. So we rose, followed the beach's slope to as far as we could get before the migraine forced us still. Miss Shareese soon followed and set up a worrying camp around us.

"But, don't you see that? It's that there, Miss Sherry."

"What is it?"

Could feel those sidelong glances grazing our cheek. Shoulders even fell slightly at the reassurance of being seen. Not judged or measured, but watched over, looked after. Worried about. The great indifference before us flashing its daggering glints, wild white flashes of hot absence. Briefly privy to blind eternity, we forgot then to breathe and found ourselves gasping through our nostrils as the groaning pit in our belly finally imploded...

"The best mother that *she* can be. You yourself said it." A sip then from her bottle of mineral water, "At the end of the day, you know, it is still *she* that has to be it. And no one, you know, can be expected to—"

"Pardon, Missus Heidi, but I don't see how—" Not like us to interrupt, but you don't just come into someone else's house and start rearranging the furniture because you've different opinions on decor, "I don't see exactly what it is that a woman's got to lose by doing right by her children, by doing the damnedest," not like us to curse neither, "by doing her damnedest to bring up the best that she can render."

"Again, Miss Sherry, I think we might have a misunderstanding where we don't quite see it..."

"That perhaps may be true but–" The sound was kids making mudpies, a thick slurry pouring out onto itself. We broke by instinct alone it felt like. Poor girl must've swallowed up some saltwater or something, stuff'll make you sick no doubt. Just a soup of fish poop and rot and whatever it is that comes out of those big boats always passing by and taking up space in the Bay. Poor thing. "That's alright now, sugar. You go on ahead and let it all out. Don't you swallow none of it back. Wants to come out for a reason, sugar." Grabbed up Aura's hair then, pulling the stringy sea-scummed locks into a ponytail as another round of thin, brown vomit rolled over her lips.

"Oh my!" And Heidi shot upright, knocking the bottle of mineral water over from its champagne perch in the sand. Foam cutting a soft canyon in the beach. "I will go for the lifeguard and go to get a doctor!"

"No, no, no, sugar. You sit back down. Nothing to worry over. Isn't that right?" Turned then our attention back to the one who needed it, Aura. Leaning forward on her knees, holding herself up over the beach towel, no longer spilling, but spitting and gasping. Ribs like bellows beneath her pale skin, expanding and falling again at a rate giving reason enough to worry. "Now, now, hon, don't you get all worked up. It's gonna be alright, sugar. You just breathe and make sure you ain't got nothing left in you that wants to come out. Don't you worry about anything else." Held tight the hair, look over our shoulder at Heidi, still standing in awful shock. Cooed then: "Honeybee, would you mind getting me one of those water bottles out of that cooler there?" Calm as all. Calm as all ever was.

Poor girl, color rising rosy back to her face, dawn through a green swamp fog, hardly knew anybody and was no doubt, had to have been, embarrassed to no end. Couldn't imagine her sticking around on the payroll after going through all that. Eyes all glassy with tears, beet red and, yep, embarrassment gave over to panic and that awful mouth stretching back over her teeth, baring it all because, but "I know, I know, sugar. But you've got to trust me." Whispered in her ear. "I know, I know there ain't nothing else to do when the world gets like this but to cry and that's okay, so you go on ahead and cry, you hear me, honeybun? You just let it all out, okay? Get rid of it all–" that poison, all that venom and fear and bile and we could see it in her face when we'd said it, when we'd said "Yes ma'am, I think you've got the job." The way her eyes lit up, smiling like she knew she should be hiding it, all giddy. Tears even then, though they didn't fall, they sure did try and come up and her cheeks got all red, ruddy and ruby then, strawberry pie or something, sweetened her smile and oh, her hand was clammy when you shook it, said thank you very much Miss Shareese and we said go on and call me Shah and decided right then and there that we were going to keep an eye on her, add her to the list, because nobody smiles that wide for a job this pointless unless they've really got a reason to give up eight hours a day, unless they've really got somewhere they really would rather not be, unless they've really got something to run from...

That's what they'll never really understand about it all. To get your arms covered in someone else's putrescence, to never hold your breath against the rising of another's fumes, to ignore the smell and gunk of it all, get your hands dirty on account of another's well-being, you've got to first off forget about yourself as completely as possible. That's what's so worrying about it all... Not to set about ordering a stranger's home, prescribing means and methods to problems we only truly know the appearance of, but nobody seems to want to forget themselves enough to realize the fullness of everyone else around them. Seems scary, can certainly understand all that well enough, but, and it inn't just got to do with motherhood, that's a whole other piece of the pie everyone skips the crust on. Taking care of people's got nothing at all to do with being a mother, or acting like one or what have you. Ought to take it from us easy enough on account of we ain' got a child to our name, so what in the end can we know about being a mother as such? Wouldn't ever talk about being a mother in any real way, wouldn't know what sorts of salves to prescribe for what sorts of pains. But take care of our own, family, friends, whatever else, that's something the world ought to silence itself to hear coming from our mouth.

Secret is, cut that damn television off, been flashing those awful not-the-father programs all day, can't stand them, don't know why we waste our day away watching them, though, secret is that the less of you you can keep for yourself, the more of you you've got to give and, secret is, the more of you you get back in the end. And it's only the good parts. Problem is everyone tries to keep their good parts for themselves. That's the real problem of it all. Rise from this recliner. Getting old, Shah, all that knee-popping and back-begging. A kind bend then. Be careful, we might get older. Real problem of it all is that when you go around keeping all your good parts for yourself and only yourself all you end up sharing with everyone else is the bad parts. Everyone knows it. Lumps of coal for Christmas. When you go giving everyone else only your bad parts, well, that's what they want to give back to you, give you their bad parts or give you yours back and then you all start to hate each other because everyone's trying to get rid of their bad parts and give back the bad stuff they've been given by everyone else! And you hold tighter to your good parts because now they're precious because you can only see that all anyone else has to give is bad stuff, so you hold onto your ushy-gushy soft stuff, shade your shine, and can maybe end up crushing it all to powder, blows away in the wind, and then you're only left with, in the kitchen now but not hungry.

Couldn't bear to have another cup of coffee. Jittery already having nothing to do on a day off. Ought to relax. Ought to take this time and rest up. Should've slept in. Maybe read a little bit. Crack open the Good Book and finally get through Leviticus. Pastor says it's alright to skip around, but just doesn't feel like we should. Wants it read in the order it's given, otherwise why give it in that order? Could maybe go for a walk or something. Should revel in this one peaceful day out of so many that have been so distraught lately. Museum is chaos at the moment and no, no, hon, don't call Roh and check up on them or anything, he can handle it and if he can't then we can talk to him about it when the walls finally fall. No use in bickering if nothing's yet burning.

Secret is, though, that everyone's good parts are the same. There ain' nothing precious about them other than them being the good parts. So, everyone spends all their time hiding their good parts away from everyone else and getting badder and badder until, well, they've finally got no good left to give without ever having really given any in the first place! Then they beg for good from others and, well, nobody else has any either. And what's supposed to happen then? Someone's got to have something good to give, and it ain't about losing ourselves on account of it neither. Give it and get it. Law of the world, so far as we know it. Give time, get time when you need it. Give kindness, get it back by the bucket. Give up your life and some say there's a better one on the other side. Or, hell, you'll be remembered at the very least...

Fridge is full up. Could make a stew, maybe. Boil up these ham hocks and, maybe, yes! Cook up something hearty and, let's see, ham-hocks and celery, onions and carrots here, garlic, got some dry peas and beans and, could make something real nice. Isn't that just the best? Brew up something nice and thick and give some folks a call, see if Tash and Winnie want some, see if, give Carl a call, see if that old grouch is hungry and in need of company...

&&&

Best here to jump to our conclusion. No use futzing around with an argument if we can't bring ourselves to stomach the world we're arguing for. If you, Dear Reader, are not ready to accept your responsibility toward the world to come, best close this book here and now. Otherwise, let's get to work:[1]

It has become increasingly apparent and undeniable to this author that the world we live in, this realm we call home, this material abounding around us all, the *literal truth,* is fundamentally less than us. We, of course, do not mean this as some sort of ontological presupposition in that increasingly unpopular anthropocentric and humanist fashion; let it be duly noted and said once more over upon the last that your author here has no *a priori* love for humanity whatsoever in any way imaginable.

---

[1] Christ Almighty, nearly knocked it off the table there. Heavens. Just let it go to the machine. Know who it is. Always know who it is...

[2] The assertion of the World's being less than us is not one of superiority on our part, it is not *lesser* than we are, nor are we its better; it should be just as obvious to any thinking person that this world-the-less will just as well be our undoing as we have been its continued assertion. There's the truth of the relationship, simple in terms of thermodynamics,[3] that we being the originating source of our world's assertion, meaning that we are the ones so bent on continually insisting that the world is here at all and that, the more vulgar among us anyway, we are in fact *in* the world, that it is around us, containing us, that it defines our limits, both internal and external, that for these facts alone, since the world without is wholly and totally sourced from within us that it must be, in *gestalt* and nominal totality, less than us. I'll even go so far as to say that something fundamental is lost, made moot and useless, in this process. Here, 'energy' is converted into cosmic motion, expended, and therefore lost, as dictated by those three immutables.

---

2 Is that? Come on, Shah. Come on! Just, we'll, we'll call you back or something later. Need to finish the chapter up. Getting real sick of this book and haven't even got to the part with Reggie yet so, just, fuck! We'll call you back. We're fine and, it's starting to feel like the same thing over and over again and, just let it go to the machine again. She'll leave a message always does...

3 Always some benign and kind sort of, 'Hey there honeybee, sugarbun, sweetie, child, little one, hon, etc. etc. Just checking in on you, see if you need anything. Just happened to cook up something and made too much for little ol' me, so just wondering if you were getting hungry at all. I can bring it on by or something like that, you just let me know if you need anything and I'll be right over and all.' Sometimes enough to make us feel like our world is falling apart and we don't know it, that there's something everyone else but us can see and that we should be scared, more scared than we already are...

It is, however and praises, in this fundamental loss that we can find the final hope of doom.[4] It seems relatively consistent through human consciousness, and our conception of the world we are only just recently beginning to realize is not only in our hands but of them as well, to hold true the fact that this place, realm, reality, planet, or universe is failing or falling or, in some traditions, already fallen (the philosophies and belief systems that differ on this point have been roundly silenced by the current hegemony, and though we may hope for their return to the fore, we must acknowledge that as simple hope and hope alone; the world we've made fosters little room for such naïveté). Through all human history it has been accepted that the greatest hope we have is the end, the final reckoning of ourselves with greater realities; in the current hegemony, this would be a literal 'come to Jesus' moment.

We will put no effort here toward challenging that prognosis, but we will raise this question: What is it that we portend the end of? The common assessment here is that what we fear is the end of existence itself, the final heat death of the physical universe, the collapse of matter, or whatever the opposite of the Big Bang would be. Though this is exactly where each of our minds went (no wool over my eyes, Dear Reader; I can't even see you, I'm not even here), we all perhaps know at the same time that this isn't remotely what we fear reaching its end. If we were honest with ourselves we'd have to admit that it is not this world that we are attached to, though we've certainly become addicted to it. What we

---

4 But we're fine. That's the crazy thing, maybe. Maybe that's the crazy thing that's got her so worried is that we think we're fine when we're very obviously not, but, but look we're doing whatever it is that we think we ought to be doing to be okay and, well, why can't she just let us be? She's just gonna come here and see everything and point out how maybe some things have gotten a little bit messy and how, yeah, okay, sure that pile of books is still a pile of books when it was for a little while actually a stack and we ought to go and pick that up but, we're almost done with this one here and maybe the next one we needed was in the stack, like in the middle, and it'll actually be a bit easier now that it's all spread out and collapsed to find the one that we'll be looking for if we ever finish this fucking thing...

fear fundamentally is the loss of ourselves. We fear our own creation rising up against us, taking our thrones from beneath our bottoms, and not just throwing our kingdoms into disarray but razing them totally to the ground. We fear that what we have rendered for ourselves is ash in progress.

In our stories and myths, the prophecy is always for a return to order, a reassertion of reason and birth of a world in a constant state of ever widening ought. In our stories and myths, we give over the 'is' entirely, give it up to the rearrived reign of something much higher than ourselves. This traditional eschatology no longer serves its necessary purpose of orienting us toward a future,[5] of giving us a place to carry our world toward. We must now endeavor to develop a contemporary eschatology,

---

[5] But she can't keep, she can't keep calling us like this just to check up on us because we don't owe her anything, not like money or anything like that and if we needed her she's got to trust us that we'd reach out and ask her over and make our desires and fears and hungers and thirsts and anxieties known but right now we're where we've always been, right here in the book trying to finally, actually for real this time, get to the end of something, so if you could just kindly leave us be so that we can get to where we're going, we're starting to think there might not actually be a last page at all...

one that puts us[6] in the throne we've resoundingly rejected, one that puts the future in our hands.

To do this we must first, however, insist upon the existence of a future with us in it.[7] We must make a new world for ourselves in memorium of our progeny...

&&&

Fine mist floats to alight on the glass case, bringing the jade teapot and velvet pedestal out of focus. Foams and runs its legs down. Found it's best to let the bubbles settle out before starting in to wipe it away, keeps it from going streaky. Degreasing, polishing, disinfecting. Three-in-one action, says the label on the nozzled bottle. Label inside the case lists its own slew of attributions: Teapot, Jade, Ming Dynasty, Craftsman Unknown, and all sorts of other etceteras.

Wonder how often the visitors actually make it up here. Third floor, East Asian Art Gallery. Can't imagine the Docents having much to say about all this glorified crockery. Gotta give Curatorial their due though,

---

6 That we're going to be stuck here because when we look outside, out our window down to the Park it's always the same thing. It's rerunning as bad as television, every sunrise is as canned as television laughter and we've almost got it figured out that why every day seems to be the exact same, always delivering the exact same punchline but with a different premise, that what we're really scared of is that we're almost afraid that the comedian in charge of all of this is going to run out of premises and just start in yelling the punchline over and over and over and over again, that it really is always going to be like this, going to be like it's going to be right now, and it's never going to stop being like this so please, Shah, just stop and let us be and be like the rest of the world and forget that we were ever here so that we can finally get to the point, so that we can finally get to where we want to answer the question asked...

7 Why does Mister Carl keep reading? Don't know, why? To get to the other side. Ha-ha. Ha-ha-ha...

certainly managed to put a spin on a dearth in the collection. Plaque on the wall, like every gallery's got, gives an overview of what the holdings on display represent in their gestalt form, answers any unasked questions about why it is that the room is populated with these specific objects. The objects are few, all enclosed in glass cases. Mostly household items of sufficiently alien design and ancient designation. There's a few silk prints on the walls, all from different regions within the greater geography the gallery ambitions to represent. The plaque at the entrance bears the title: **Feng Shui and Wabi-Sabi.** Wonder how many people actually read it. Gotta be less than who actually makes it up here. This is the third floor's only gallery. Can't imagine the disappointments of the bottom two floors do much to encourage the climb. Ballroom completely kaput now, slipping into a grave silence, the sound of raze and rise having come to subside; we've still not got a glimpse of who or what's been responsible for all the clatter and clang.

The walls here are meditation blue and, judging by the softness of the light against the night, the gallery is lit mostly by the day itself. A kind sheen off the porcelain and jade. Sunset probably looks pretty great from up here. Slip the grime-blighted rag into our back pocket. Walk the few steps over to the eastward window. Streetlights down below suggest a landscape. Blotted out by the night, Madiston like one of those undulating gelatinous creatures that float blind at the bottom of the ocean, the complexity of its form given shape only by nodes of bioluminescence. Does our heart some good to see that the city is still alive like this in the night, blasting the stars from the sky, canopying itself in a heavy and inky pall. Cars move to and fro and there's a few purple shadows of people walking. All awake, all alive, refusing to drop their eyes and fall into dreams, to give up for the lack of light, to rise against the World, the great All There Is. Does our heart good to know they're all still awake, rubbing sleep from their cheeks, but awake all the same. Ignoring what the little monkey in their brain begs of them, that bouncing bastard that says come back to the trees, give it all up, honestly it was better this way, your nakedness wasn't the mistake, it was clothing it in the first place. Wonderfully workaday ignorance of body and mind, the embrace of wordless time, silence until the very moment that something starts to scream. Does our soul good to know that we can't be the only one that's this tired, morning, noon, and night...

Dragged our feet down the hallway, new boots already a heavy strain on our calves. Biting at our heels, rising raisins of tenderness where blisters were bound to erupt. The new coveralls were, still are, Jesus Christ, heavy about our shoulders. Sweating through the suffocatingly stiff fabric, seams bunching up under our legs to rub raw spots we'd forgotten we had, we slugged ourselves into the breakroom and leaned against the counter, arms a tad shaky. Hadn't eaten all day. Couldn't pry ourselves off the floor until we heard the halls outside fill with the falling feet of everyone leaving. Hard hand against our face to wake us further. Produced from our back pocket a bag of coffee grounds, cinched and sealed with zealous rubber-banding. Pulled the squat drip pot away from its resting place against the wall. Smell of stale coffee and mildew in the machinery. Went about the ritual of preparing a brew: filter, grounds, water, rinse the urn back to a shade of tobacco brown, two paper cups. Gurgles began and we sat down at one of the round tables, boots big and clumsy under the fold-out legs' arcane network. Again, for the umpteenth time today, our eyes fell leadenly together and our forehead found the crook of our elbow...

Rose then from a dream-quake in the dark back to drop-ceilinged fluorescence, a vice on our shoulder and skip in our heart:

"Hey, hey. Rise and shine."

A blast to our back.

"G'morning, Boss. See you're ahead of me this evening."

Looked around the room, found the earth beneath us, the same place we'd forgotten leaving. Dreams black as a quick-felled night after a stormy day, black and cold and wet and, bunched a wad of coverall sleeve's stiff blue into our palm and wiped away a clot of gargle that had set to drip from our lips.

"Alright, alright, here it is..." The Custodian placed one of the paper cups we'd previously, before drifting away to wantful nothing, set up. Filled to the breaking brim with obsidian. "Should get you right."

"Thank you, thank you," and brought the steaming brew to our lips. Sipped past the singe.

"Looking sharp, by the way," the Custodian said and, breaking with standard procedure, plopped his gargantuan mass into one of the table's chairs where he normally would have kept a friendly distance by leaning against the counter.

"What's that?" Hadn't yet fully come to our senses. Hollow bellied, everything seemed to be moving slower than the usual rate.

"The new duds, brother." Custodian leaned across the table and pinched the thick shoulder seam, jerking us into the edge of the table, "That's high-quality stuff you've got on, no corner cutting bullshit. Boots too, finest shit-kickers the dollar can buy."

Shit-kickers. Called them shit-kickers. The big lugs tearing up our feet like they're walking on dogs' teeth were shit-kickers. Forehead against the southern window's glass, leaning. Fog from our breath climbs up to cover the pane in front of our eyes, clouding away every shape below, leaving only the light.

Sun on our cheek. Bottom of a skillet. Light pries the lids open. Crusty. Rusty. And a gasp of sudden terror. Lung dust. Groan into and at the morning. Roll over now. Roll over now and just scoop her up in our arms. All slimy and salt-skinned just like the rest of us. Grab where she's softest. Pull her across the sheets, across that fetid linen swamp. Hold her now. Her now against where last night dropped its bombs. And there, here her hand comes up, breaking from its prayerful pair to lace its fingers through our hair and, pull her closer then. Arms tight. Full round. Against all odds and the sludge-blooded tingle in our extremities:

"No, no. I can't, B..."

A kiss on her neck then, through the rancidity hanging behind her ear. Smell of the night before: Cigarettes, turned-over perfume, oniony sweat, morning breath. That godawful grime laid over us all like fish skin. Say: "It'll help with the hangover" and grab the sharp handle of her hip, "get the blood flowing again and all that..." Would be an embarrassment of a session, no doubt. We know that. Got to sometimes just pretend the pain isn't there.

"No, babe. My head is killing me." Reaches to grab us where we're growing. See? It's worth a shot at the very least. "Plus, I think Obbie crashed out on the floor and–"

"Obbie? What?" Rocket up, flinging sheets, and our head rings like a gunshot struck bell. "Holy shit." Laid out in his boxers and nothing but. Head on a stiff couch pillow. Snoring, hog-in-hand. "Did we, fuck, did we drink that much last night?"

Eyes still closed, she curls back into the pillow, drawing her knees up to her chest, "You two morons definitely did..."

It's coming back in brushstrokes and spills. All leveled without a subject, but nonetheless in search of one, ourselves in the mess, something clean there that we sought to erase. Certainly feels like we drank our fair share. Find ourselves in the holes between everyone else. Remember the hue of the night, the mood of it, that overlayered and super-smeared purple on the porch. Everyone else, all of them, the real nodes of this life we didn't know we chose, brought-out chiaroscuro behind cherrying cigarettes and streetlight. It's the orange then in the blacked blue that makes it purple. Laughing because we all just realized with our widening eyes that the words we're saying are making less and less sense and that if we can careen completely, keel-the-whole-hell-over into incomprehension, then we might stand a chance of saying something we'll all understand, we might babble the truth right out of ourselves. Adrenaline from waking so suddenly subsides and, oh God, take her again in our arms as the revulsion rises at realizing a body in pain. Erection falls toward the mounting pressure of bladder. Gotta piss. Sit up, sit up. Curdle the shame. Get all sweet last night? Start telling everyone how much we love them and how we've forgiven them for everything they didn't know they'd done? Tell the same story again and again or settle for interruption over true conversation? Did we cry? Did we tell everyone at some point that we really wish we would just wish we would die? Admit that we don't know, that we really don't know anything at all really and haven't honestly painted anything in forever, that we've never really even felt like we'd ever really even painted anything at all, or what is it just cans of Belchard's Lite strewn about the carpet like semitrucks in some improbable interstate pile up? Crushed and trounced flat, dark spots of moisture radiate out and into the carpet. Yeasty musk in the air now. Jesus, snubbing cigarettes out on the carpet as well? Fucking Christ, what the hell got into all y'all? Plastic shooters, oh God, can still taste it on our tongue, on our breath, still burning our nose, silver tequila. Plastic shooters scattered as the pearls of the proverb, glistening and empty. Obbie Walters there among it all, another fallen titan.

Last clear thing before this nightmare morning: All on the porch with the sun setting behind, settling the debate about whether we'd gathered enough booze yet. Aura and Derek had only brought, Aura and Derek? Who else was, oh Christ... let the shame rise, hot on our cheeks. There's the sweat. There's that panicky slick, that tummy tumbling roll, "Oh fuck, Jess..." Fall back to the wet sheets, "Oh, fuh-uh-uh-uck me..."

"Shh, shh..." She says, "Shh, shh... Quiet down. Don't be a baby." And reaches again behind, nails and fingertips feeling blind to flail and find fast to zip our lips, "Just go back to–"

Heart, heavy and slow, audible in our ears and unswallowable in our throat. Right on cue, there they are: the shakes. A world gone boilingly frigid.

"Just go back to sleep, B." Blue of screen mingles with the sear of sun, "It's like not even noon yet, hon. You should be dead asleep right now."

"Jesus fuck." The cataclysmic simultaneity of everything inside is putting the pedal to the floor while the fuel gauge screams empty. We would cry if there was water enough for tears.

"Only been asleep for like three hours..."

"You gotta be fucking kidding me–" Can't just black out like that and not pay for it when our work schedule's got us trained to kick on at the ass crack of dawn. Never be able to sleep it off, just have to live a whole day like this. Crippling agony. All the while she's gonna laugh at us. Tell us about how it's our own damn fault, and we should have stopped drinking before Obbie brought out the shooters, before he disappeared during the sundown deliberation only to crash back onto the porch with a gallon-sized Zip-loc full to bursting with those heinous, ugh, God, don't burp, don't burp, mini-bottles of tequila.

"Always," he'd said holding it up for everyone to see, smiling all shit eating, "always, and I mean fucking always, flirt with your stewardesses!" Threw the bag down onto the card table, knocking an ashtray and bag of rolling tobacco to the porch floor. "Problem fucking solved, bitches–"

Almost jumped into Derek's lap at the collision. Definitely grabbed his arm. Spilled a little bit of his beer. Whatever was in the first spliff had made us jumpy as all hell, pushed us into the resonant quiet of our buzz brined mind. Lots of men. Lots of very male energy. Glad we could show up and rescue Jess a little maybe. Derek and David mean-mugging each other across the table, a forty of Belchard's Brown, Buford Heavy, each. Jess rolling her eyes near to knock herself over at how far gone Buck and this Obbie character were. Heads lolling, time frozen and everything speeding up and then Obbie's fucking grin and slamming that bag of booze to roil the row.

We'd all heard of him. Knew him as the guy that got Buck all the crazy shit that we sometimes ended up smoking out front of St. Never's. Knew in some wise that they were tight, old friends that went way back to before any of our histories intertwined. Knew all that, sure, but didn't know anything really about Obbie himself. All had, reckon, our own vision of him in our heads, save for Jess because she definitely already knew him and, now that we're thinking about it, changed the topic of conversation every time Buck riled himself into telling the tale tall of one of their escapades. All had our own idea of who Obbie might be and pretty clear last night how wrong we all had to have been. Certainly didn't expect long blonde hair braided in French twins, hand tattoos, scruffy beard. That necklace. That's what killed us about him, that fucking necklace. Black and red and white and orange clay beads strung together in support of an eagle shaped pendant; the sort of thing for sale in like a national park's gift shop or something. Fucking leather vest with all that fringe shit, tassels dangling. Music festival t-shirt. Rope sandals. And what a fucking performance! Bottles all clatter and everyone shocked silent:

"Always, and I mean fucking always, flirt with your stewardesses, man. Problem fucking solved, bitches." Produced from his vest's inner pocket a blunt like a billy club. Perched it between his lips and lit it. Puffed and said, taking his seat: "They get crazy lonely up there in the sky all day, you know? It's a wild way to live, but it inn't much of a real life. Know what I mean? Like, look, I was flying back and forth for a while last year, back and forth between Cackalacky and Cali, took a few dives down into the Rockies between for that stratospherical mountain shit. Research and all that, you know? Like checking out what some boys I knew out there were growing and like you know, nabbing some trimmings or whatever for myself. Shit's like making a stew, you know? Sometimes the best way to go about it is to just like throw a bunch of shit together, crossbreed strains like a motherfucker, just sit back and let it simmer to see what'll happen." Smoke pouring out from the blunt's flame-flowering tip, edgy with resin. Obbie coughed and held it out in the center of the group to initiate the puff and pass, "Takers? Here bud," up under awkward David's nose. "Only ones here unspoken for looks like, so let's live a little." David nodded, said nothing, and ripped away staring down at the floor. Avoiding Derek's eyes, set scowl-sharp beneath a not-yet-liquor-loose brow. "But, yeah, nah, what I mean is like that those flight attendants like only ever land and take off, you know? They all live somewhere or whatever, but they never really get to go home so, and it's not like, usually anyway, some of the older ladies it might be, but it's not usually like what it's like when you like think of old sailors or pirates or whatever, you know like a woman in every port, whore on every shore sort of thing. No, no, it's not like that at all–" Blunt then hovering in front of Jess. She took it and had a casual, taster's puff. Could tell she knew the night ahead of us portended no end. "They're like completely alone up there, always a different crew most of the time so they don't even have those like terrible work friendships that are the only things keeping so many people from drinking drain cleaner. Painting their bathrooms with their brains shit. It's absolutely fucked, man. And they all, like, they all get into it for the same reason, you know? It's always the same reason whenever you talk to them, and they'll always talk to you. There's dudes that make it like their whole thing to like talk to the flight attendants, go back to where they sit in their jump seats and just chat them up and well," motioned to the saggy bag of bottles, "you know it pays off in its own way, you know? Always flirt and they'll always get you like an extra coffee or some extra nuts or cookies or whatever. Get good at it and you can score big like this. They've got no real stake in it, especially the older ones. Because they like full on, straight up hate it. They're hip to the lie, you know?" Jess passed the blunt to Buck, whose head sank further into his chest. Had to tap him on the thigh a few times before he finally took it. Examined it long and lazy enough for the coal to run cold. "Because they all like get into it for the same reason, you know? They all wanna fly so they can see the world or whatever, all some romantic idea about travel. They're almost all from the Midwest these days as well, from cultural wastelands in general, hungry for something different and, I mean, they do get to see the world, but it's classic devil-and-crossroads shit, Faust or whatever, you know? Genie in a lamp all like, sure, you can see the world, sweetheart, you can see the whole world all at once from way up here, where you can't talk to anybody down there and everyone up here with you is just trying to get somewhere else. You can see the world, but you don't get to live in it anymore, you know? All the older ones are hip to the lie, though. They'll like give you whatever you want just for some conversation–"

Blunt came to us then, cold and smokeless. Thankful for that. Didn't even have to pretend to smoke it. Just passed it over to Derek and let him do whatever he wanted to do with it. Already by that point feeling the beer undoing the threads of our memory. Probably would have blacked out then if we'd have smoked anything so, disregarding the headache now at this cruel morning, can go ahead and pat ourselves on the back for keeping it relatively together last night. One of us had to.

No more be grieved at that which thou hast done. Roses have thorns and silver fountains mud.

Got so sideways last night he even let us be the one to drive home. Had his little big man scrap and then drank himself to darkness. Crashed out in the car on the way across the creek and wouldn't wake up when we pulled into the complex's parking lot. Has us now swampy against his chest since he got back in bed. Rose an hour ago maybe to groan and piss. Pulled us right into him when he laid back down, right in, oyster around a pearl sort of situation now. But pearls don't need to breathe, Derek. *We* do. So, how about we loosen this hold a little bit and we can all maybe sleep this thing off?

Clouds and eclipses stain both moon and sun, and loathsome canker lives in sweetest bud.

Obbie took the silence as tacit approval toward a sequel monologue. Jess looked long across the card table and made eye contact with us. Motioned with her head, a 'wanna split?' twitch, and smiled.

We nodded and rose.

Jess followed, and said, cutting Obbie off before he could get rolling again, "So, what was it then? A thirty-rack of Lite?" The boys grumbled. "Cool, cool, cool. Aura and I'll make a run then."

Approving grumbles. Something slurred across Buck's spit-thickened lips.

"Alright, uhm..." Jess looked over the group, sighed, and, "Davey, baby, you're in charge. Don't burn the house down while we're gone. We'll be back shortly. Someone get Buck a glass of water or something..."

Could feel it in the air, the tension relieving itself of Jess the further we got from the house. Shriveling and sloughing off. Week old sunburn. Flakes falling for every step. Whether it was Obbie's grass taking hold or what, we were at the least gladdened to see her shoulders find their way level, down from around her ears. Hate to see her as she had been. All torqued-up and edgy.

As we came up on North Murphy, Harris and the Jaspers materializing in all their immutable flint-sharp apathy, we turned a touch to speak but Jess beat us to the punch:

"Sorry about him," onto the asphalt, flip-flops flicking gravel up under our heels.

"No. Don't. It's–" Never known her to be particularly apologetic. Strange. Never known her to give much of a shit either way. "What can you do? Boys are, Buck says he's his best friend though, so I guess you marry the whole family sometimes and–"

"No, I mean Buck. Totally just like, fuck man–" Bitter annoyance on the back end there.

"Oh. No, don't, uhm, don't worry about him, Jess. I've seen him much worse, you know. No biggie." Should have been an assenting laugh there. We've all held each other's hair back, called each other cabs, taken care of one another in the throes of carelessness.

"This is different though," lifted her t-shirt collar and produced a beaten pack of cigarettes from under her bra strap. Lit one and, "Something's different. He's not as like, I don't know." Made two fists and held them up pugilistic, "Scrappy or whatever, you know? Like he used to be so, like–" Jab. Jab.

"Oh yeah, I get you. I think he might be, I don't know, you know him better than I do, so who am I to weigh in, but he might be just–" Concrete path into the Park.

"You know," passed the pack over to us, "you know he went over my head on this Obbie shit?"

"What do you mean, hon?"

"Like, maybe *over my head* isn't the right way to say it. He can do whatever he wants. But he didn't like *tell* me, you know?"

Sucked on our cigarette. Silence to urge us into deeper waters.

"And, look, I get it, right? Like I'm not his fucking mother and so, like, he can do whatever he wants, you know? But we like live together and love each other and whatever and I guess just like, I don't know, let me know, you know?"

"Yeah, I get it–"

"Like don't just not tell me and then when I like come home from fucking grocery shopping or whatever I find you two numbskulls starting at your fucking paintings, stoned right the fuck to Jupiter, like not giving a fuck and, it's just like, I don't know–"

"Disrespectful?"

"Yeah, maybe. I don't know." Flicked her butt away. "I get it though. Like I can't be *everything*. I can't always be there in the way that he might need. So, like, yeah, call your best friend, have him stay a few days, it's fine, be gross arty stoner boys for a little bit, but like maybe a heads up or something at least, maybe? I mean like–"

"For sure, for sure. I mean, you've got your own things going on, so you at least need to know what's up so you can adjust–"

"Yeah, no, I guess it's not about adjusting or anything though, but that it's–"

"You know what I mean." And she was kind enough to touch us then, bring us back down to where we'd forgotten ourselves. "A heads up. I get it. Like you said." And then we allowed a silence between us as Harris Park opened its wastes. The sky above was, a beautiful night last night, honest, clear, steadily purpling, falling at the same pace as the junkies around us rose from beneath their shading oaks. Most of them, from what we can tell, sleep the afternoons away and start up with sunset. She spoke again though, like a halt in the breeze: "How's *your* work going though, Jess?"

Love her to bits, honestly, but she makes us regret the airs we put on when we all first met. Slipping into last winter, Buck trying to make his dream with us right alongside. He was still painting and we were gonna make some short films or something maybe. That's what we told Aura then at happy hour after Buck had finally been hired after finally looking for a job and we did it with all that self assured optimism that someone with the gall to call themselves an *artist* must have. Said we were working on some experimental stuff, that we were a *filmmaker*, that it was hard to put into words but we were so inarticulate in our imaginings that we never got there, did we? No, we got right here again and stayed here with him next to us in the sweaty bed shivering at the morning he made.

Turn to be merciful. Just a little bit because we know he'll never get back to sleep without our pity. Can't yet stoop to honesty with him, can't yet tell him that he makes us feel like all hope is already lost and that our life has been made by his refusal to make anything. Can't tell him that we feel trapped when we hold him in our arms. Can't tell him that this feels more and more like a chronic condition every day that passes. Can't yet tell him that we're so tired of it all, so tired of being tied to this life he's trying not to live, sick of aspiration, so nauseated at the very subject of him that we went so far last night as to just finally show her, show somebody other than him and David, what we've really been *working on*. Can't tell him now while he's in this absolutely pathetic state that we showed her because we needed to know whether this was a thing that needed to be done or a place it all had come to. Can't tell him that when she asked us last night, when she asked with that shimmering kindness in her eyes, "How's *your* work going though, Jess?" that we said: "It's coming along, I suppose," and lit another smoke.

"Do you, uhm, do you have anything to where maybe I could see some of it?" Passed the pack to her again. "Like, not to pry or anything, Jess. I get it if you–"

Can't tell him how we're so in need now of being seen for what everything around us has come to be that we said, "No, no, it's nothing like that, Aura. It's just–"

"I get it. It's personal. But, like, just saying, I'm your friend. I *am* interested. So like, whenever you wanna, don't know, don't want to pry and if you're uncomfortable with it, like I get it so–"

Can't tell him how we couldn't speak, how we couldn't fill that silence with something shifting, how all we could do, all we wanted to do, what we needed to do, *needed to* so we did and there's no going back now and it's her secret to keep along with us or whatever, but someone other than us needed to know so we could gauge how much further there is left for us to go so we set to digging around in our pocket. We found our phone and the tangled mess of our earbuds. Our hands were sweaty, and we couldn't fumble the knot out of the wires. Our heart was beating to the beginning and back, every valley the shadow of death, so we unplugged the cable and passed the morass over to Aura. "Untangle those."

We'd made it by then to roughly the center of the park, where the cracked concrete paths meet around the central fountain drained of its water. We sat on the fountain wall. Aura frustrated the cables and we scrolled through thumbnails. Scrolled and scrolled and scrolled and turned away to make sure Aura couldn't see any more than we already didn't want her to. "Gimme just one second here."

"No problem, babe," and the cable finally came away from itself. "Seems like you've made a lot, though. Always used to sound like you were chugging away on something big or like, I don't know–"

"Yeah, you kind of have to make a lot or else–"

"I'd imagine. Probably best to have a catalog going. Lots of options or something like representative of all the different things you can do, like a–"

"Yeah... Something like that." Scrolling. Scrolling. Scrolling as the orange streetlights kicked on to throw the park into negative relief with itself. Human figures rising all around from piles on the ground. "Alright here." And we finally put the phone in Aura's lap. When we stood, our hands were numb. "Just, uhm, yeah... Just be honest with me, okay?" Can't tell him our eyes burned. Can't tell him our chin quivered. "I'm gonna, uhm, gonna walk around for a bit while you, just please be honest with me..."

"Alright, hon. Sure, sure. I'm sure it'll be–" But we turned away before she could finish. Sunk into an oak's shadow. Off the concrete onto the crabgrass-woven sand. She put the earbuds in, and we saw her face light up blue from the screen and, "Hey! Hey! What's your passcode?"

And we ran back over, snatched the phone, entered the code, and dropped the phone like it bit back into Aura's lap.

"Sorry, Jess... I just..." And her eyes fell to the screen: Frozen image of a woman in a red dress. Plunging neckline. Standing in front of a bed. Thumbed the play button floating over the woman's midsection and:

Nothing. Then a hazy something. A beginning beginning. Fade *from* black. Out and from and then enough of it comes so we're into the room. Walls, bed. Floor out of frame and windows curtained over. Unnatural light. Manufactured. No, synthesized. A replacement for the sun. A replacement for the sky and everything higher than this right here on the screen. Can never forget that because it's in our hand. We're holding it and, just like reading in a way, but different ultimately because music then, soft and like air. Nothing to breathe on the screen. Unnatural light. Floor out of frame. Windows curtained over. And music to fix the air, to fill the space in our brain. Faint. Low volume, without a bottom. Synthesizer chords and slippery cascades and rat-a-tat snare and hats and there's a little subby woof sort of sound. *Drops* they might be called because they fall all the way to the bottom of the spectrum, but the floor is out of frame and the windows are curtained over and when she walks in, flicking her hip, hand perched atop, knees rising slightly above the frame with every step so there *is* a floor, there is *something* else down there and, head out at the top so there *is* a sky, there is *something* above. Above and below though not in frame and the music fades out, *out*, but is replaced by the stale frazzle of ambient space around her now facing full-on and forward but face and foot still out of frame and, neckline dives all the way from shoulders to belly, just above the button where soft abdominals twitch and roll as she sways side to side. Light, artificial from some fixture way off screen in a place where it's not supposed to be seen as existing, cuts shadows over her dress incredibly short, knees out of frame, and still miles of flesh on screen. Body. Everything cut out and, body drops presumably to its knees and suddenly a face is framed. And there she is. Smiling like she shouldn't be. Wry and glossy. A look up and to the left as another shape enters...

So, hold onto her. We've got to just keep a hold on her. Tight as she'll allow because we know what happens now, know what happens when life falls apart into its living looseness. It's not paternal or anything so stop worrying about that. It's just, who would want it like that? Who would make that choice unless they absolutely had to? And that's why we've got to hold her now, get the other arm another elbow's curl around here, and that's why because it's not about if she would ever go there, if she, Aura, our Aura, would ever sliver herself digital to sell through screens, no, none of that, it's about instead, instead it's about making sure that she'll never *need to* do anything like that, that she'll never have to work that way or preferably at all ever again if we can really do anything about it, if we can do what we want to about it she'll never need to *do anything* and then she'll be free to want and then she'll be free to do the things she wants and she'll look at us with eyes that know we were the one to feather her wings...

"Alright, alright. I think I get the picture," pushed the phone out of our face, screen glowing between the breaks in our fingers. Jerked our head to pop out the earbud. Tiny tinned decrescendo of moans. "Yeah, alright. Alright."

"So, yeah, anyway man, that's like, do you get it? That's why I bowed out you know?" David pocketed the phone and stepped back onto the asphalt. "Like the money isn't bad, you know? She cut me in pretty fair and, well, feel a hell of a lot better the next day..."

Thank God for the night, for the city letting this part of town go to absolute shit. Don't know if we would have been able to handle it if we could see his groveling face. Know he thought we had asked him away from the porch to fight, but we don't do that anymore. Waste of time. Just wanted an explanation and maybe an apology for why the fuck and how the fuck could you just leave your boys in the lurch like that? Just fucked up man and, got the explanation, but not a lick one of apology in there. Nah, something worse, a begging for approval or something like that, wanting the explanation to lead to our understanding to lead to our, what? Blessing? Nah, not gonna happen.

"Like *a lot* better..." Tried the same joke again. "And, get this, none of it is my idea, right? She just like, I mean can you believe that she's fucking asking me to–"

"Yeah, man. I don't know." Patted pockets for our cigarettes. Had to do something with our hands. "Makes it like worse somehow, right? Feel like that makes it worse."

"What're you talking about, man?" Pulled the phone back out and started scrolling. Screen lit up his face, eyes all buggy at the blue-hued luridity. "Here, look man, look."

"Nah, nah, nah, just–"

"No, fuck, dude look!" And shoved it in our face, "You see that? See that number there? Those are her subscribers, right? That's free, can subscribe to get updates on the content she uploads, little free videos and the longer one's for like real fucking money. A solid third of these dudes though, do *that* math, a solid third of these little pervs pay a *monthly* fee for exclusive content, pay to watch her get the absolute living shit fucked–"

"Alright, alright. Man, lower your voice. Jesus Christ. I get it, believe me. I definitely get it." Took a drag and, old habits, feet subconsciously found their square on the unlevel, rain-ragged street beneath us. "Don't give yourself too much credit there, stud. Not exactly the craziest shit on the–"

"Don't know man," phone back up and scrolling, "we did one video where we–"

"Nope. Nope. I don't, don't show me anything else or I'll knock your fucking teeth out."

"Alright, Jesus, bro. Fine. But you do get it, right?" That pleading sag. Nah, not gonna happen.

"I mean... no? But yeah, I–"

"It's the easiest money I've ever–"

"No, I get that. Trust me. That makes sense but like, dude, does Buck know?"

"Yeah! She told him about it before and I ran it by him a while back before I ever–"

"Jesus Christ..." Pot, Belchard's, and *this*, it's amazing we didn't barf at it all.

"It works out for everyone, I think. It's like, I mean, not to like dole out advice or anything but Aura's not bad looking either and you two could–"

Old habits. Dropped him in one. Unseen punches well placed in their coming, doesn't really matter how hard they're hauled off if those two things can be managed. Knees give out pretty easily. Not that we *didn't* hit him hard, hit him fast, that's for sure, not a stain one on our knuckles, doesn't take much to get a nose to give its blood over, though. Hit him hard enough. Hard enough. Didn't break anything but a few vessels and his train of thought. No teeth spat out with the apology, so we've got nothing to apologize for ourselves. Didn't really need the whole performance when they got back from the beer run:

"Jesus fucking Christ! What the hell happened?" Derek and David alone on the porch. Derek leaning back in his chair, blunt from before relit and dangling. David, Jesus Christ, David sitting next him, head thrown back and pinching his nose with a hand caked in velvet thick blood. We just, Lord in Heaven, can't leave these men alone for a minute without them trying to kill something or each other. Just, "Davy, hey, are you okay? Here, let me see?" Moved his hand away for the flow to start fresh. A bruise beneath his left eye bloomed dusky. Christ. Good thing his face is never in the videos. "Alright here, let's go in and wash you up. The fuck happened?"

"Nothing," stood up, "just boys being—"

"Shit, where are Buck and Obbie?"

"Uhm... I don't..."

"Derek?"

"No clue..."

"You guys... Christ..." And we took David in. The door opened to a torrential, noodling squall of jam-band music. Our heart settled out of its frustrated ribbings, no longer were the two numbskulls lost. Took David to the bathroom and splashed some water on his face. Left him there to tend to himself. We found the boys, Obbie and Buck, right where we'd first found them earlier in the day:

Sitting cross-legged on the carpet, a joint rolling wasteful over the bowl of a bent Belchard's can, and Obbie thumbily manhandling one of Buck's canvases while Buck stares glazed and amazed at the sequined thread of praise sewn by Obbie's ranting teeth.

"Yeah man, I mean like, I'm not one to like, you know, just lay it on thick or anything," rubbed the stubborn smears of the razor-scuffed painting with his fingers. Powdery effluvia flaking away. Sand from beachy soles. "But, goddamn son. This is like, you know? I don't want to say it, don't want to like gas you up or anything—"

"Shit man, thanks. I really—" Stopped midsentence to pinch his teary eyes closed. The other hand rose blind to Obbie's shoulder.

"Nah, brother, I'm not kidding, you know? Like, you know me, I don't fucking dish out compliments and like, this shit might just be a work of something like genius."

"Nah man, don't say shit like that. That's ridiculous, don't fucking–" Joint up from the can and a slow crepuscular puff.

"I'm serious man. I love this whole like, don't bogart that shit, pass it over motherfucker, but like this whole make-something-to-break-something sort of thing, really fucking cool. Apocalyptic. Just like, shit, you know what I mean?"

"Yeah man, I do. But, do you know what *she* said, man? You know what s*he* said? Said I should take them over to some fucking coffee shop. That I should hang them up there and sell them to like whoever buys art at coffee shops and like, I mean you said they're–"

"Genius. Or at the very least very near it, brother. I mean like, congratulations man, it's big, man, it's like–"

We've never said they weren't genius! That's never been our take on any of it! Tell him all the fucking time, literally every chance we get when he brings it up, that we love his work, that we think he's got something special! All we've ever said is that he should take it and show it to someone that isn't just us, isn't just people who already know him and like him and are gonna tell him it's good anyway! Can't act like a struggling artist or whatever, an unheeded prophet or something, when you never even take the shit to be seen by anybody other than people who already fucking love you! Who already put up with all the shit you think you have to do to make this shit and still congratulate you for it! Who never complain about all this drinking and smoking and sleeping in and putting off getting a job and adjusting our own lives to fit the one you want to one day be living! Who never interrupt or intrude or correct you or say from behind, from the doorway, from the *world*: "Hey boys! Is that, oh my God, Obbie Walters! Hey!" And held out our arms for a hug. Obbie rose to meet the embrace then. Locked eyes with Buck's ruby-red stare over Obbie's shoulder: "I wasn't expecting you!"

Broke away and did that thing where he touches our cheek, patronizing little shit he is, and said, "Oh yeah. Bucky here called me up last week. Said if I wanted to visit best do it now since the summer season's just kicking off and the beach isn't packed yet. Said that, what was it? Some island?"

"Riley, yeah," muttered into the carpet.

"Yeah, Riley Island or something. He said it's gorgeous and–"

"Oh, yeah, we've heard the same things." Heard because we've never yet managed to get out to Riley. Too broke. Too busy. Too wet. Too hot. Too far. He needs to paint, and we've got to stream and, "Well, I'll leave you boys to it, then. Gotta unpack some groceries and, it's nice to see you, Obbie and–" Our ears burned as we skinned the week's rations of ramen and eggs and oatmeal of their shopping bags. Not enough for three people for any significant amount of time and, called up David because fuck it. Hadn't spoke much since the little incident. Just dropped him his weekly earnings through that banking app, his cut of the videos. Suggested that he come over and hang out for a bit tonight. Been a while. Buck's friend is in town and it could be fun to all have a little party or something, drink the truth out.

"Speak of the fucking devil," we said as David's car rolled to a stop on the street's shoulder a few hours later.

"That the guy?" Obbie asked, cracking a fresh can.

We were on the porch stoop, soaking up the sun's first sinking. Slant gold through the trees. Ramping up our drinking while Jess conducted her afternoon stream inside. Pulled it up on our phone. Had to show someone, and who better than motherfucking Obbie-fucking-Walters? We don't have an account on the site, so our viewing just showed up in the chat as `[anon_user#357] has joined`. She even said, 'Hey there, Anon. Feel free to make an account and subscribe.' A knuckle further for each latter syllable. Needed someone to see how wild this shit had gotten, tell us whether we were crazy or not for thinking it.

"The *fucking* devil." And smiled like we weren't trying.

David exited the car and stepped around back to kick open the trunk. Pulled out a shopping bag stretched translucent with darkly sloshing forties of Buford. Glass. Good shit.

Hollered at him: "Hey fucko, you owe me money!" and elbowed Obbie to extract a chuckle. But he was eyes on and locked like a hunting dog with the writhing on the phone.

"C'mon, Buck." David stopped and held up the grocery bag, "I didn't forget! Here look," dug into the bag and threw something the distance between us. "Didn't even smoke 'em!"

We missed the catch but picked it up off the steps' concrete. "Oh, clutch. Very nice. Alright." Pocketed the smokes, "You're off the hook for now, motherfucker." Winked. "What the hell happened to you that night, anyway?"

"I don't fuck with the police, man. Started to come back and saw all the lights and shit, no fucking way, dude. Nah, nah, nah..."

"Hey!" Obbie's eyes up then, screen black as the broadcast came to its close. "You're new!" Stood up and held out his resin- and nicotine-stained hand. "What's your–?"

"Davy baby!" From up and behind. Sound then of the screen door slamming shut. Jess in a t-shirt and jean shorts rocketed off the porch and took David up in a hug.

"Hey, Jess... I thought you'd, uhm, yeah, long time no see–"

The party grew out from there. Aura texting us apropos of nothing once she'd got off work, asked if we wanted to meet at St. Never's while she waited for Derek to get off. We suggested they come by our place instead. Then, it's mostly dark. David showing up out of nowhere had us hitting it all a lot harder and faster than we'd anticipated. Obbie's little Mexican surprise didn't help a lick either and, Jesus fuck! Can't get back to sleep now. We're just here again...

Morning breath and detox sweat has rendered Jess's kindly ump-a-bumping chest unbearable. Every time the piss-wet blanket of our sour sleep settles about our shoulders we jolt awake again with a gasp and heart punting. A square wheel. Sit up now. Sit up now and wipe the sweat from our face with hands that smell cruel and feel like they're covered in a stranger's skin. Gotta piss. Piss and then get some water and then, discrete steps piling all a Babel of driftwood, rocking and teetering on the shifting sands of a rising tide and, okay, okay, okay, just piss. Just get up and piss and naked, we're completely fucking naked. Fuck it.

Smell of the bathroom is an intestinal Armageddon. And that's through a nose that, judging by the lead in our lungs, smoked enough cigarettes last night to fry every olfactory nerve a couple times over. Feet on the bathmat kick empty tequila shooters, sending them skittering under the sink and clattering off the tub and commode. Lift the lid and seat and there's the culprit of the criminal effulgence, the fecal haze. A concerningly colored bog, frothy and islanded with floatsome flotsam. Legs of shit run down the bowl's bow, the swirled glass of a demonic sommelier. In the middle of it all, shimmering silver bullet in the wound, yet another glimmery plastic bottle. A raft capsized in the mire.

Take aim and fire: Piss comes thick and burns its way out. Acid blood of a space creature. Cuts canyons in the bowl's muck, bobbing the bottle up and down, disappearing and then breaching back through the grime again. Piddles and paddles, splash and drizzle, as the stream weakens to a drip, drip, drip, and *flush*...

Sleep comes a bit easier now. Don't wrap up in the sheets. Let the air cool the sweat on our skin. Eyes closed and, let the headache rise warm behind our brows. Gonna be a rough one today. Gonna be real fucking hard to–

"Ah, Oh! Jesus Christ, what the fuck is–?"

No end to it. No relief. Nothing is ever as easy as it ought to be. Back awake. Sit up. Obbie's up. Jess's up.

"You smell that?"

"Smell what?"

And it pours in from under the door.

Relentless filth.

Low tide.

III.

Awake again with a snorting start. Never feel it come over us, just nothing and then nothing at all until a gasp and a parade of panic and no dreams, never any dreams. Gunky lips and a mouth-breather rot-fuzzed tongue. Something's cracked off the desk, but that's not what's woken us...

It's all the same. Water-stained drop ceiling and painted cinder-block walls. Bulging filing cabinet and stiff short-piled carpet over cement floors. They say that sleeping on the floor is actually better for the back, better than sleeping on most beds. Sure, there are some beds that are better than the floor, but the revelation is of course that most beds just won't do despite them being most beds actually. Nothing worse, though, can't imagine anything worse than this hunched-over, barely breathing, think-we-were-dead sort of sleep we've been getting lately. Shattered monitor screen. Jagged glass, mean as teeth. Succubus is the demon that sits on the chests of the sleeping, right? Sits on the chest and sucks the soul out and, no, no, succubus is a sexier sort of demon because women get called succubus a lot by men who hate them. Wonder if, shattered monitor screen, guard dog, gargoyle. That's it. Gargoyle. Been on the floor once or twice. Maybe more. It all runs together now, doesn't it? Bad days just getting badder. The same is the same as the same is. Can't recall ever exactly how we get down there when, after, when we wake up after having fallen asleep down there. Worst part about it all in all. The sourcelessness. Can't point to anything in particular being wrong *inside*. Never sick the same way twice. Same as the same is the same as. Never feel sick the same way twice, so it's not like the wires are crossed up there or anything, it's not like we've got something toothy and ambitious tying us up into our own belly, like trying to burst out and replace us. Never works like that. Nothing wrong on the inside, never sick the same way twice or whatever. So, it's gotta be something on the *outside* then, something wrong out there in that noxiously atmosphered world around this pristine mini-fridge hell. So, yeah, so, wipe our mouth now, and all that drool, fucking *child*, wipe our mouth and be thankful, be thankful for these walls and that water-stained ceiling holding the Museum up above our head, be thankful for this little bunker here, for our shattered screen and disconnected desk phone, dead cell, carpet over concrete, windowless view. Be thankful for the way the air-conditioning whines through the vents all *BAM! BAM! BAM!* to damn near knock the door off its hinges...

"Benjamin?" A voice we've not heard in forever but fear enough to recognize. The Director: "Benjamin? Are you in there? Open up this door!"

&&&

Really should have waited until the morning. Shouldn't have brought it up crossing over the Creek, but there's always that thought that maybe she'll be more open, more willing to reason, have a back-and-forth about the whole thing once she's had a few. Problem is we never know how many she's going to end up having, never know how long we're going to have to end up staying and shit, c'mon, we've gotta get a key made or something, replace the lock, make sure this isn't a possibility anymore. Make it so she can't just hide away in the, Lord, didn't even give us the chance to piss either. Just immediately: out the car, up the stairs, round the corner, at the door, in the apartment, and *Bam! Slam! Fuck-You-Man!* It's never going to get any easier if we can't talk these things over, if she can't be relied on to articulate her feelings in a way that doesn't make us want to just, could get a screwdriver and pry maybe the frame away, shed some light on the bolt there and slip a credit card or knife in or something...

No one around. No one right, no one left. Just all this same darkly carpeted hall that's always been here. Never not had a knock answered. Wonder maybe if, well, we don't know anybody else down this hall. Maybe they wouldn't take too kind to strangers knocking at their door. Think it's maybe debt collection or repo or taxman or something it just inn't worth much to give anybody a scare that doesn't deserve it but, Lord, Tupperware's leaking in the bag ain' it? Damn and hellfire, shit, no, no, no use getting upset here where there inn't a thing we can do a damn about it. Another knock maybe, maybe a just, set it on down and get the container level so it'll stop seeping out the rim like that. Least it smells nice, made a good one this time around. Last time overcooked the potatoes and the whole thing ran pasty after a few days, all thick like a chowder, but it all tastes the same, same ingredients, just cooked it a bit too long and, another knock makes it a burden but you know if you'd just answer the damned phone then we wouldn't have to come all the way out here to the edge of nowhere just to check up on you, could've told you the good news on the line. Can't get mad at no one for caring, that's the Gospel. So, so, so how about you just open on up and we'll give you this here stew, make sure you've at least got something to eat while you mull over the fact that, can you believe it, Mister Bennie got fired today! And they put us in charge of everything he was in charge of until they go and get someone else to be in charge of it, but whether you eat it or not is between you and the Almighty, but we're not gonna let you go without just because you're stubborn as a hog. So, just one more, just one more knock then.

"Aura? Come on, babe. Open the door. We'll talk in the morning, but just open the–" Probably all curled up in the bathtub, knees at her chest, cramped into a cold porcelain womb and, just really, honestly, no shit want to do what's best for her, want to take care of her and like the only way for that to happen is for her to allow it to of course, can't force her to let us or whatever or something or anything but, Jesus-Fucking-All-Of-It there's only one reasonable thing to do here and what we're asking isn't all that hard just like we can't keep coming to pick you up drunk and sure, yeah, fuck, maybe we could have, should have like phrased it better or something. Don't know. We don't know! What else are we supposed to, maybe she should have, don't fucking hit the door like that, dude, just going to end up fucking it all up even more, making it worse and could tear the motherfucker off the hinges. We could just like, work boots, shit-kickers, just fucking knock the motherfucker off the hinges just *BOOM!* but that'd be unreasonable and she'd like scream or something or start crying or even like maybe even like fucking maybe call the cops and if there's one thing we don't have time for it's having to deal with the fucking cops. What else are we supposed to do? It doesn't, it shouldn't matter, but it does, but it shouldn't and doesn't so let's be reasonable, it doesn't and shouldn't matter how we asked, how we brought it up, what our attitude was because what we brought up and what we'd asked for is completely reasonable! If we could, goddammit, if we could buy her a car, if we could buy her a house and car and, don't fucking know, a garden or something, if we made enough money to just give you everything you needed so you didn't have to also fucking have to work, if we could, we would. You've got to believe us there. Maybe that's where we should have started though, yeah, check the knob again, fucking moron. She's definitely unlocked it after we nearly knocked the thing off its hinges, definitely given into our superior reasoning there, fucking big-brain doofus, but maybe that's where we should have started, should have started with the *if-we-could-then-we-woulds* and then got into the fucking *we-cannots* then we could maybe have had an actual conversation or maybe we should have just waited until the morning. But, then we'd both be tired and she'd need coffee and we'd be in a rush to finish the invoices from a week ago, having to get in earlier and earlier and earlier to catch up on what we can't finish later and later and goddammit, there's just no time for words that work! There's not a single moment to say a single solid thing!

And you could just let us know when it is that you'd want us to come on by. Could even tell us, Carl, that you really don't want anybody to come by at the moment and then we could have left it at that but the more you don't answer the phone and don't answer this door when we knock and when you very well, of course, obviously know that it's us that's doing the knocking because we don't believe for one iota of a fraction of a split second that you haven't listened to the voicemails. Left you a message saying we were going to come by, didn't we? Said it might be a touch later than usual, watched Winnie this afternoon, had to take care of errands, but that we'd still come by and we were going to bring you some stew like we did that one other time but this time we weren't going to let the potatoes overcook and go to pieces and we don't believe at all ever and forever that you didn't get that message. So here, how about this then: How about we just dial you up and then, yessir, go on and press our ear to the door, you can't skirt away from us, not after all what we've lived through as friends, damn near brothered and sistered our way through life, so you best watch it, don't mess around when it comes to family, just dial you up and press our ear to the door and yep, can hear it buzzing away on your table or something, so don't you act like you ain' home, like you don't have time for Shareese, don't you act like you don't live in the same world with the rest of us Carl, you can't just hide away and read yourself to safety, we all gotta be in this together! So, you think you're not gonna answer that? Think, see we know for a fact that you're in there now, so you can't just hide away like this, can't just, we'll call your ass again then, you stubborn old bastard. Not gonna just let you hide yourself away until you disappear, no sir, no sir, no sir, not a chance in Heaven or Hell are we letting, oh cut it off again? Squeak of your chair at that ratty old card table, just gonna sit back down and act like we ain' never done nothing for you, like we deserve to be treated like we're annoying you or, petty old bastard Carl, don't think so, no sir, no sir, no sir, we're gonna get in there if it's the last thing, we're gonna make sure you're okay, because you ain' just gonna disappear on us, boy, you don't get to just brush us away, no sir, no sir, no sir, no way in Heaven or Hell! We promise you, you're gonna open this motherfucking door!

Ow! Fuck! Goddammit, son of a bitch, Jesus-Mary-And-All-The-Godforsaken-Children, Holy Mother of, what would possess us to *punch* the fucking door? Jesus, just the worst option. Kick. Get a hammer. Pick the lock. Throw a shoulder even, but don't fucking, Goddammit! Goddammit! Goddammit! Motherfucker, just, oh great, already fucking swelling up all goddamned purple and fu-uh-uh-uh-uck! Jesus man, like why would we do that? Why? So fucking unreasonable, ridiculous. All this for what? Just asked her if she'd mind, well, no we kind of demanded, did the whole putting-our-foot-down routine, sounding like our fucking Dad or something but what we were ultimately asking for is still pretty reasonable, like Jesus fu-uh-uh-uh-uck, can't even bring our fingers into, can't even make a fucking, can't even make a goddamn even like make a fist and red and purple and Jesus did we, all we asked was that she bus down after work, that she hang out at the docks while we finished up and then like, ugh, *keep an eye on her*, shouldn't have said it like that. But that's what we meant, still, why wouldn't we, break something? Did we just fucking break our goddamned, no, no way that's what's, never a conversation, it's always just action and reaction, just everything burning itself down to uselessness and...

&&&

Nothing. Then a hazy something. The start. The beginning beginning. Fade *from* black. Amateurs always gotta make it arty in some way. Suppose it helps ease the world around them. They've got to know, though, that it's a waste of time. Got to know though that everyone watching is doing exactly the same thing. Got to know that we're all out here laid out naked and sweating and on the bursting verge, hog in hand, just looking for that one moment that'll make our own world disappear long enough to spill ourselves out. Acknowledgement of the artifice only serves to spoil the endeavor, obfuscates the goal, piles too many more precious seconds between now and then that we'll have to hopefully wipe away. Reminds us all that this is no better than the alternative, actual flesh on flesh, where *everything* is confused, objectless, and crushingly crucial. Have to come here now to this because it's simple. Quick and easy. Saccharine, innocuous, hollow.

Walls, bed. Floor out of frame and windows curtained over. Unnatural light illuminates the dimensions of a carnally unnatural life. A replacement for the sun. The sky. Everything higher than this right here on the screen. Can never forget that. Even when it's as real as it can possibly be, something like `IRL COUPLE FUCK U IN LUV4REAL` or `RE@L GRRL ORG@SMIC @N@L FUCK REAL`, can never forget that we're holding it, phone in one hand and cock limply impatient in the other. Balls climbing cold in the moldy air-conditioned air since summer's come on early with all its heaving, humid gargantuosity faster than anything could flower. Can't ever shake it out of our minds that this isn't the real thing, that this is the height of fiction. Can never forget it because it's in our hands and we're the only one still doing anything about it. Can never forget it because she said that it was, that what we had could maybe have been something real, that maybe there was room in this fifth-floor walk-up for something as crampingly pluralizing as love. But then she'd get so, so, so mad at us. So mad at us for wanting to stay where it was that we'd met in the first place. But she didn't understand because we were something happening to her, that's how she saw us, as an event imposed on her by a world bigger than the both of us. But we, we knew her and saw her and kept her as something that *had happened,* water from the wellspring, a trusted occurrence that could only be counted on to continue as long as it kept having been, so we had to keep going back to get it! What didn't she understand?

Then there's music. Soft and like air. Air since there is nothing to breathe on the screen. Unnatural light. Floor out of a frame. Curtained over and music. Space in our brain, hollowed out by this bumbling urge, now filled sudden and bloody with engorgeously encouraged anticipation. Heart like a hunter's now. It's all at attention as the faint, bottomless swell of synthesizer chords rises and slippery cascades fall from this pseudo-world's vaulted sky and rat-a-tat war drums roll for conquest and there, there, there's the bottom! A woofy ump-a-bumping bass sound as She walks in, flicking Her hip under Her hand, knees rising just above frame. Little pink band-aids on the caps, Xs to mark the spot where She'll kneel and get what She's got cumming in Her or on Her who knows we'll see won't we so long as this gets a move on and doesn't bog itself down with arty fucking nonsense. We're all here for the same reason: To forget we aren't fucking. Can't see Her face yet though, still out of frame. Was on the thumbnail, that's why we've clicked it, because of the face on the thumbnail. Devastating in all its angles, wry and portending of an appetite that would be, must be, must at least have a chance at being, diagnosed as *pathologically libidinal.* But get on with it! We're all here for the same reason: To forget why we aren't fucking! To clear our heads and curdle cluttered guts, to empty our balls and remind ourselves of our own real filth. To, goddammit! To, goddammit! To goddamn forget her jabbing for the last time her rhinestone-ringed knuckle in our lower back, saying: "No, no, no you don't Roh. You keep on walking. Don't you stop. Tell you one thing for certain tonight, Mister, I'm not about to drag your happy ass up these goddamn stairs again."

And we'd stopped just short of the second-floor landing. Grabbing onto the staircase's handrail to stop our swaying. Hand came up to our face and our shoulders began to shake and there's nothing we can do about it sometimes so it's just not right that from behind again:

"Roh, I'm not gonna stand here all night! Get your ass up these stairs so we can go to bed. I swear to God–"

She'd said that we'd gotten worse, but also that she didn't know anything different from us. She said she'd had no evidence of us ever having been better than this and that she met us crying drunk and now we're always crying and drunk again. She'd said that insofar as she could reason it was all the same, that it was the consistency of it all that was dragging her down. She'd said there's nothing wrong with having a routine, but there is certainly something supremely fucked up about *this* routine.

And we can't help it if we cry sometimes when we drink too much because sometimes that's how much you've got to drink to feel like enough life's been left behind to really, really start over. Sure, it's pathetic. Sure, sure, but didn't she for maybe a single second think that maybe that godawful slurpy sound of snot sucking back into a nose, tongue clicking through thick saliva, words mushing pasty in our mouths was driving us to the brink as well? That all this reaching out through the dark for somewhere to just, just for a minute now, just for a second, to sit down was just, "No, goddammit Rohaan. I swear to God Almighty if you don't–"

Too late. We'd found our seat on the lip of the landing. No moving us from there, not then. Turned to face her, difference in incline bringing us almost lovingly eye to eye, and leaned against the wall. Jelly quake of cheek. Shivering lip. Eyes no doubt all red and puffy. Snot glistening in our week-long mustache. Just needed to open the floodgates just a little so that we could just...

"Roh." And she leaned in. Smell of booze and smoke out from us and onto her, ruining without touching. Never-washed uniform holding the odor of every evil we'd committed since Dad left. "Roh, I need you to get the fuck up and go up these stairs or–" No fair to use ultimatums on us in a state like that, every sheet to the wind, bordering on blotto, erased from the moment, but nevertheless, "–Or I'm going to fucking leave and never come back."

And there it was suddenly then. There it all went. Face cast over in flowing glass, everything shiny and wet. God, the sounds we make when we cry. Worse than fingers and chalkboards and forks and porcelain. Arms out all grabby, trying to pull her back and, can't blame her. Can't blame her for having had enough of all our broken man-baby bullshit. Can't expect her to shift gears from lover to mother every time we get too sad to pretend we're coping...

So, the music fades out and She is centered in a frazzle of ambient space. Full-on and forward, but head and foot still out of frame. A tract of rib cage, rolling plain of tummy, and a suggestion of the sop yet to be seen. The knave begging the blades toward chops. This is maybe something they all get wrong in some way. Spit into our palm and wake the poor guy up, this is taking far too long to get anywhere. They always think it's the body we're wanting, but it's actually the face. That's where the person to be ruined lives. Eyes are the window to the whatever and we're here to have a lack replaced, so while it's nice that this dress's neckline dives all the way from Her shoulders to Her belly, just above the button where Her abdomen twitches and rolls as She sways side to side and the light from off-screen cuts shadows sharp on Her softness, miles and miles of flesh and body on the screen, while all of that's just grand it's here, this moment: When She drops to Her knees and suddenly Her face is framed just like it was promised in the thumbnail. Smiling like She shouldn't be. Wry and glossy. It's really this moment that brought us all here and that keeps us all at attention.

A look up and to the left and another shape enters the frame. An organ that our hand strokes the paltriest imitation of... Pretend, pretend, pretend that it's ours. She's looking the length of it because, the nature of form, it's still us that the look is for. Even though She's got her cunt growling for what's in front of Her, acting that way anyhow, can't ever forget that even when it looks and feels as real as this is and we were that it's all fiction of the highest order because we can't even remember her name, we're the one holding and even though it's not our cock, She's not smiling at our cock, it's still *about* and *for* us and all of us alone that She's smiling so it's, it's, it's that giggle there as well as She shellfishly slurps his testicles below the rise She'll soon endeavor to swallow. Really wish we could use our other hand as well. Prop the phone on something so we can shellfishly crack oysters along with Her. Big fucking balls in Her mouth and strands of spit. Silver, silver, glinting silver ropes of diamond-dipped white gold as they pop then back out of Her lips. What a sound. What a smile. Sound and smile and then and another one, the other one. Get the whole mess just wet and, Jesus Her hand looks so small, so dainty, wrapped like a lacy little lacy thing around his, around our, ours, supposed to be ours, analogue, around The Cock and then a voice off-screen, from up and to the left:

"Take it all, bitch! Put the whole thing in your fucking, my God!"

Red-faced and bulgy eyed, when She can open them that is. Tears flowing fast. Levee's broken. Streaming almost maybe. Red. Red. Red. Veins and cords in Her neck. He's got his, we've got our, we've got our, hand on the back of Her head, jamming and jamming and jamming and bubbles from Her lips and nose and and and, fuck, oh fucking fuck, fucking goddamn fuck, and the whole of Her heaves, gags a gutty animal sound and, on Her knees, it's like when the City used to knock the lugs from the hydrants after a heavy rain to wash the murk from the main, rust from the line. Steam from backs. Break the fever. Playing with Jawad and the neighborhood kids. Cool in the hard water. Crystal scream beating bellies burnt cherry. There it is. Thick and enmeshed with itself. Every gnawed bit a memory rinsed from our mind. Boogers of shrimp and fry fluff. Leaves of lettuce toothed translucent. Cuspid-cubed carrot and flecks of flecked stuff. All held together by an unidentifiable orange meal and mash...

IV.

Putsch: ...Yes, sure, I took some time yesterday after getting in to have a look around the grounds. Really wonderful.

Dr. Lloyd: Certainly nice this time the year if you've not got allergies or anything. That pine pollen kicks some people's ass right around the block, you know. But that's good that you managed to get down there. Have you had a chance to go over to the Museum? That's where they've put most of the actual objects and bits-and-bobs and all that. They've got her Chandelier hung up in this whole space they've got for it, as a commemorative sort of thing. It's really quite–

Putsch: Yes, you'll have to show me around while I'm in town. But, and you may not know the answers here so, that's fine if you don't, but I'm fascinated by what the whole thing was like before you and the Committee stepped in to–

Dr. Lloyd: Well, let's be clear here, Mister Putsch. I don't want to give any readers or anything the impression that all of this rests on my shoulders. The Committee was already well into the project by the time they approached me about writing up all that fluff or what have you about the Estate being granted landmark status. I think at that time even maybe you could take the bus up to the grounds and they had those hiking trails already so, I just don't want any of this to come off that I'm involved in any way with the political side of things. I just did some research and wrote some essays for some local papers, magazines, and for the city council or whatever, I was just–

Putsch: Let's get into that then. What exactly *did* they approach you for? Moreover, maybe, why? Why was an academic perspective necessary? Just so I can get a fuller picture of what it is that we're looking at. I came with all these questions prepared and–

Dr. Lloyd: I was surprised to get your call. Didn't know that anyone outside of Madiston took any interest in any of this. Read your name in the rags and all that. So, knew who you were. Actually think a few years back, when would that have been? Anyway, up north for some conference and I think myself and a few of the other Art History fellows went to see your show, what was it called? The one with the resin. What was it?

Putsch: *Mollification* was the show with the resin–

Dr. Lloyd: And gemstones. Yeah, yeah. That gallery was freezing, absolutely freezing.

Putsch: An unforeseen hiccough. Glad you got to see it. The lady that runs that place, Andrea Somethingorother, hasn't spoken to me since! Won't be given reign over a whole room like that for quite some time, I'm afraid.

Dr. Lloyd: It was a real spectacle, I have to say.

Putsch: It was a brief moment, but boy did that blip glitter. All but swallowed up by the whole pop art, commercial kitsch thing though. Cans of soup and assembly lines and, best not to be bitter about it. The world can't be spoken.

Dr. Lloyd: Indeed, indeed.

Putsch: Shame you didn't get a chance to the see it the night of, though. Have you seen any pictures or press release type stuff from the actual opening or–?

Dr. Lloyd: No, no. I wasn't familiar with your work at the time and, well, even now I suppose my familiarity is only of that one show so–

Putsch: Not a worry, not a worry. I know little of you and your research as well outside of your involvement with the Belchard Estate Preservation Project. It's probably better this way. Conversation between unfamiliars tends to dwell in the realm of their similarities more than their differences.

Dr. Lloyd: Sure, sure.

Putsch: So, you only saw the–

Dr. Lloyd: Yeah, yeah, just I think it was a week after the opening or something like that so what we saw was all the gemstones stuck to the floors and walls and the big piles of gems and resin on those pedestals with the, how would I describe it? All of it sort of looking like it was melting off the pedestals and, yeah, some of the stuff that was stuck to the floor had even had footprints in it, from shoes, as if someone had stepped in it all and–

Putsch: A week after, you said?

Dr. Lloyd: Just about, I think.

Putsch: Wow, so you just barely got to see it. They shut it all down a week and a half after the opening. Keeping the room that cold got to be expensive and, well, there was nothing really to be bought, no *pieces* as such so I can't think to blame them necessarily but... Like I said, I won't be given reign over a whole space like that again any time soon but–

Dr. Lloyd: They weren't for sale as sculptures or anything?

Putsch: No, no. If you took them out or raised the temperature they'd just melt again and–

Dr. Lloyd: Wait so, wait, they weren't made to look they were melting they were–

Putsch: Just made to melt.

Dr. Lloyd: Okay, so...

Putsch: Should have seen the opening, man. The whole thing was, the piles as you called them, the big melty piles with all the gemstones were, at the opening they were these big resin prisms and *inside* them the gemstones were arranged in the form of constellations. Real tchotchke and, you know like big lampwork paperweights.

Dr. Lloyd: So, it all what? It all melted at the opening?

Putsch: Oh yeah, God, I wish I'd had brought pictures or something. I didn't know you knew about that show. Should have seen it, man. It was something to witness. I didn't know, you know like the plastic resin, this compound, we used was pretty experimental, this company called Zyracom stumbled upon it basically by accident and didn't know what to use it for and well, whatever, that's all a story for the patent books, but we didn't know that it was going to be so runny, right? We had no idea that, I mean we thought we'd have these sort of gradually collapsing things, right? Slow decay of order. Very undergraduate. But instead they all just, I mean you should have seen these people's faces. It ruined clothes and, how I don't know, but it got in people's hair as well and just, I mean it was a scene to behold. A travesty by any metric but my own.

Dr. Lloyd: It sounds like quite the night.

Putsch: Oh, it was. I mean we of course wanted the whole 'entropy' of the thing, but we didn't bet on absolute chaos which–

Dr. Lloyd: Which is the opposite, from what I can tell.

Putsch: Sorry? What do you mean?

Dr. Lloyd: You bet on entropy and got chaos... Usually the story goes the other way around, right? Want anarchic chaos and all you get in the end is boring, old, unstoppable entropy.

Putsch: Saying something like chaos is the aesthetic shell over entropy's substance then, right? Chaos is the spectacular aspect of decay.

Dr. Lloyd: What we're terming *here* as chaos, sure, wouldn't be useful to disagree. Maybe more though that in this case chaos is the shell over entropy's substancelessness, that chaos is maybe the *shape of the lack*?

Putsch: Chaos is fire and entropy is–

Dr. Lloyd: Ash.

Putsch: Fantastic. Which might be a good solid segue back the way we came from–

Dr. Lloyd: Which would be?

Putsch: Well, I didn't come all the way out here to lecture you about *me*. I came here to pick *your* brain concerning the preservation efforts of–

Dr. Lloyd: Of course, yes. Suppose there's not much more I can do to stave off that line, so let's–

Putsch: Well, let's start with entropy then.

Dr. Lloyd: Chaos is more suited to beginnings, as the Good Book will tell you.

Putsch: Good Book also claims that the beginning started with The Word.

Dr. Lloyd: Which was what? *Order?*

Putsch: *Catastrophe?*

Dr. Lloyd: Apocalypse?

Putsch: Different thing altogether.

Dr. Lloyd: Than catastrophe?

Putsch: Perhaps they can describe the same object or event, but what they're describing about that object or event, I'll say, would be two different aspects.

Dr. Lloyd: Go on.

Putsch: Don't think you can edge me off topic. I've still got my questions for you.

Dr. Lloyd: Perhaps we can trade, tit-for-tat.

Putsch: Or perhaps we're already on topic.

Dr. Lloyd: Maybe.

Putsch: Well, let's see, then... What exactly was the condition of the Belchard Estate when you were asked to write up a defense of it being granted landmark status?

Dr. Lloyd: No, no, not just yet, Mister Putsch. I want to hear more about this distinction you're drawing between apocalypse and catastrophe.

Putsch: Well, alright, but we'll have to go back to the Greek for that.

Dr. Lloyd: Alright, all fine and good. Let's hear the etymology.

Putsch: Okay, alright. So, let's start with catastrophe then, which I'll go ahead and claim that this is what we really mean when we describe something as apocalyptic–

Dr. Lloyd: Though both can be aspects of the same object?

Putsch: Yes, but two different aspects. And I think the overlap between them is less than we're given to think.

Dr. Lloyd: Alright, alright. I'm with you so–

Putsch: So, in the Greek, catastrophe is a compound formation between κατα- and -στροφή, respectively meaning 'down' and 'turning,' more or less. And in the Greek, much like today is used to describe events or, in the terms we've surrendered this discourse to, objects which, without making any qualitative judgements, change *suddenly*. So, all that is fine and well and good and, yeah, that's how we use the word usually anyway–

Dr. Lloyd: So, it's not catastrophe that's the misused term, it's–

Putsch: Apocalypse.

Dr. Lloyd: Which is what then, exactly?

Putsch: A combination of the roots απο- and -καλύπτω–

Dr. Lloyd: Meaning?

Putsch: Well, what's the last book of the Bible?

Dr. Lloyd: The Book of Revelations. Or the Revelation to John, depending on the tent.

Putsch: Right. Well, in the koine, the Greek that 'John' wrote it in, it's **ΑΠΟΚΑΛΥΨΙΣ ΙΩΑΝΝΟΥ**, which is to say 'The Apocalypse of John' more or less, but more than less.

Dr. Lloyd: So–

Putsch: Well, that text would prove the point that both terms can be used to describe the same object, but just two different aspects. The Book of Revelations describes an apocalypse of catastrophe in which the catastrophe itself is the process of a greater apocalypse.

Dr. Lloyd: Vision of a disaster in which the disaster being envisioned serves to reveal a greater truth.

Putsch: Exactly. The text is both catastrophic and apocalyptic, and describes events which are both and the same simultaneously–

Dr. Lloyd: Got it, got it. So, catastrophe is the change and apocalypse is–

Putsch: It's messy to unpack without a specific object to attach it to.

Dr. Lloyd: Well then, let's give it an object. Let's take a look at the Belchard Estate then.

Putsch: Perfect.

Dr. Lloyd: So, Belchard Estate, apocalypse or catastrophe?

Putsch: You tell me, you're the one who–

Dr. Lloyd: Wrote an essay about it deserving landmark status because a real estate firm wanted to level the land for a shopping mall and the city had all but dissolved its parks budget. I haven't been up there to see it in years probably. Last time was to take my nephew fishing in the creek and that was–

Putsch: Well, what was it like before the declaration of its landmark status and, what I'm assuming is, an increase in parks funding? *Both* of our terms here have to do with change, one epistemological and the other material, so what was it–

Dr. Lloyd: I mean it was basically in ruins. The manor was anyway. Like I said, pretty sure you could walk the hiking trails, but I also don't think there were as many there as there are now.

Putsch: Well yesterday, when I was up there, the house up there on the hill was absolutely pristine. Looked like it had never been touched, much less lived in.

Dr. Lloyd: Yeah, they gutted the whole thing when they finally came out to clean everything up. Like I said, all the objects that were there, Chandelier and all that, are either on display at the Museum or in their holdings in the basement, I think. I could give some people a ring and maybe we can plod over there, have a look at the actual–

Putsch: Oh, my interest here has nothing to do with the actual objects that were there. Sterling does nothing for me, and I've done the gallery thing long enough for blood diamonds to leave me cold. No, I'm much more interested in the–

Dr. Lloyd: Well, I could put in a call to some of the committee members and maybe they can–

Putsch: No, not that either, Dr. Lloyd.

Dr. Lloyd: Reggie is really fine, Mister Putsch.

Putsch: Well, you're welcome to call me whatever you like as well then, Reggie.

Dr. Lloyd: Noted.

Putsch: Now that we're just two friends talking about old houses, let's not derail this line of inquiry. It strikes me as frustratingly delicate and woefully incomplete, so we'll have to handle it with care from here on out. Deal?

Dr. Lloyd: Sure, sure. Sorry. It's just best practice for academics to stay within their field, and Madiston and Regional History aren't my forte. Much more of a–

Putsch: Not to worry. Leave any question you don't feel confident in answering unanswered and I will redact it from the record of being asked at all. Deal?

Dr. Lloyd: Deal.

Putsch: Alright. So. You said that it, the house or mansion or whatever, was *gutted* when they were doing the restorations?

Dr. Lloyd: Yeah, all the objects removed and taken–

Putsch: To the Museum.

Dr. Lloyd: Yes. Just the frame left behind. That was one of the stipulations the city wanted to make. Whole argument about maintenance and all that. Honestly, when they came to me I asked why not just level the land anyway and turn it into a park wholesale? Wondered then, and still do honestly, why we need the mansion to remind us of why all of our fathers drank. Seemed sort of cruel to me and–

Putsch: Makes sense, uhm, but okay, so, City stipulates that the mansion can stand–

Dr. Lloyd: Which is what the committee wanted most of all. Gotta have something to mark the land if you're going to declare a landmark, otherwise it's just 'public property.' If it's just public holdings the city or state has a much, much, much easier time selling it to the highest bidder. Tried it with Riley and, well, Mother Nature had something to say about that so–

Putsch: She's a mean bitch when she wants to be.

Dr. Lloyd: God bless storms.

Putsch: Storms *are* God's blessings...

Dr. Lloyd: Anyway, look, so, yeah, City says fine make it a landmark but we aren't paying to keep the house in order–

Putsch: So, they gut the whole thing and just leave the walls? New coat of paint every few years or so, make sure the garden is kept looking nice and–

Dr. Lloyd: Exactly.

Putsch: So, the house is chaos.

Dr. Lloyd: What? I–

Putsch: Because earlier we concluded something like that *chaos* is the aesthetic aspect of *entropy*, and, though we said that maybe entropy *is* substancelessness I think we both know that it's more the process that operates with a tendency toward substancelessness so–

Dr. Lloyd: Yeah, alright. I'll bite. Sure. Chaos is fire, entropy is–

Putsch: Ash, yeah.

Dr. Lloyd: But that's only the case in the relationship between fire and ash, which is only metaphor for things that fit that analog, so yeah, okay, okay, okay. The house is chaos, or chaotic, sure, sure. The inside is entropy or the inert result of entropic processes which–

Putsch: Is catastrophe, or are catastrophic. So–

Dr. Lloyd: So, then, what's the apocalypse? Is that the next line of this eschatology? What or wherein all this is the apocalypse?

Putsch: Or, or, since catastrophe and apocalypse *can* describe the same object or event but don't necessarily *have to,* or there's no guarantee–

Dr. Lloyd: That they describe the same object. Squares and rectangles, sure, sure so—

Putsch: It might be a tad undergraduate, but alright so, yeah. An object or event or state of being which is chaotic is necessarily entropic. Done, easy peasy, but—

Dr. Lloyd: An object or event or state of being which is catastrophic is *not* necessarily apocalyptic.

Putsch: An object or event or state of being which is entropic can be described aesthetically as chaotic, regardless of its ovations toward order, but—

Dr. Lloyd: No, no, an apocalypse is entirely dependent on catastrophe but—

Putsch: Because of the chaotic spectacle of catastrophe, which is nothing but the aesthetic condition of entropy, there *are* catastrophes which do not prove to be apocalyptic. Which is ultimately to say, in the face of catastrophe and chaos and entropy that—

Dr. Lloyd: The best we can hope for is apocalypse...

&&&

We have to come out here now to go at all. The shower works well enough for if we've got to piss, but that bottle's really fucked up the possibility of taking shits. Water bill is going to be higher now that we're worrying. Buck'd thought he'd figured out how to get the damned thing out with a coat hanger and duct tape and a whole bunch of flushing but we think it just ended up poking enough holes in whatever it was that clogged up around it, feces and tissue and chunks of everything else, poked enough holes in it all to let the water flow through enough to make it do something like a flush but took a dump later that day, remember, and it was even a watery one and it still didn't flow all the way through before the water rose back up to kiss us on the bum before we finished wiping and well, just have to, we just have to get used to it is all. Turns out, something they never got around to telling us until we'd already learned it ourselves, that a lot of life is just getting used to the things that we'd rather not exist at all in the first place. Do even the worst of anything enough times and maybe it becomes just another normal thing and therefore, maybe that's the secret, maybe the next metamorphosis after normality is that it stops existing altogether and we're all just, the way we've got to figure out how to live through it all is to move toward the new as the world around us fades out of existence altogether and then when there's nothing new to do, that's when we'll never be able to get used to this smell here though, can't imagine ever getting used to it and would hate to meet the one of us that did. Didn't believe it could have been true the first time anyone ever told us, but now after what's it been two or so weeks of scheduling out lavatory relief as to save ourselves the trouble of having to breathe this putridity more than need be it seems obvious that such heinous measures were indeed taken. Public restrooms are of course never particularly pleasant places, but there's at least usually, even in the dirtiest ones, water in the bowl. Not in here though. Harris Park's had that shit shut off for longer than we've been around. No chance of them changing that on our account, so it's all just more stuff that we'll for now just have to get used to. Just more stuff to make normal.

The walk over's longer than we thought it would have been. He made it seem like it was just take the B down and then get off and then boom you're there, but we've found it now to be much more along the lines of get off and then, well, we should have brought headphones or something but never know, do we? Never know if that vibrating in our ears will set one off, if that's all it might take today to get a migraine roiling away, so just have never made a habit of keeping a pair on us. Which only really ends up meaning that we'll hear it every time now because the only thing more foolish perhaps than not having headphones to block the world out when we don't want to be in it is to think for a single iota of a moment that the world, all those who live here around us, is bound to will toward anything but our continued discomfort. Going to hear it again every day now as we walk from the bus stop down to the shipyards. Going to catch the same snaggle-toothed, patchy-bearded wind of something like, "Hey sugar, what you hiding up under there?" Boxy billow of our uniform jacket, which now we can't change out of now because if he sees us again tomorrow walking by the body shop in, don't know, something reasonable for the weather like shorts and a t-shirt or a completely out of character sundress or something then he'll know that he got to us the first time and then, like they always do, reason his way into thinking how he can maybe get more of us to the point of demanding all of it. So now, knowing how long the walk actually is, we're going to be stuck for the duration of the rest of all this to walk it sweating in polyester and without headphones to block out the babble just to prove to it all that it didn't get to us, that we stand separate and away from its influence, that it'd better hear every dragged footfall of ours as a foot put down for the final time. Full stop, so that we can get on with whatever it was that we were trying to get on with before he caught wind of what it was that Jess's doing to keep them afloat. Fact is, and it's something that we already should already know, is that life and the shapes it happens to take around us is and are completely and forever out of our individual control. There's only so much any one of us can be expected to hold onto. Further, that the ultimate inevitability is that at the end of it all whatever we're holding is something we're going to eventually drop.

Sickening to think that we know now how it piles. Learn something new every day of the same upon the same stacked same as the same is the same as. Can see and smell here in the bowl beneath us everything from probably since two or three days ago. That's when we started to just use the one stall every time because we came in and she was well, have to assume that she's a she because can't really see and certainly don't have it in us right now to bear trying to figure how to look to find out who or godforbidit but most likely what exactly she might be. Or was. Or was, because that's the probable whole reality of it if we could shit easy enough to let that sink in. Was more likely because it's been the same pair of shoes there untied, ankles crossed, and swelling. Yeah, maybe a trick of the light, but it's been three days at least because it's hard to forget shitting on top of our own shit. Can't fix the toilet to forget it all yet, need a couple hundred more and rent is going to be due and still need a couple hundred more for that so it'll all have to wait until next month at the earliest and that's really only if, well, just need the money and best not to bet on Buck... Probably not a trick of the light though, her ankles crossed and swelling blue to black around the collars of her shoes like the blood's fallen the length of her leg under her skin down to wonder how long it takes. Could look it up but we might then be able to deduce the truth and know that she's, probably she, but know that whatever whoever this was, definitely at this point have to assume them as a was most definitely because they haven't moved from the stall next door and our shit has already piled high enough to fill the air with, no, if they're she and was and now just not anymore then it's not only our piled shit that's smelling all the air this thick and wretched because it's also what's left of her that's started to fall away and swell her crossed ankles and eventually, right? Like on crime shows that when they find an old body, the killer's first victim or something dug up and wrapped tarpily in plastic, it's always swollen and juicy with fluids that were once separate but are now unified for a moment on their way to a new curdling difference, that eventually no matter how still she or they or whatever was in the next stall over was now is or are it'll all have to come apart in the end.

And we've got to ask, before a new pain sets in, what exactly is it that we're trying to hold together? Seems less to do with love than with fear. Because maybe love doesn't make demands like this, maybe love just shuts up sometimes. Maybe when it's right and pure like it ought to be if it's going to go around calling itself love it does less going around and calling itself anything and just sits back and asks, just asks of its object what can it, what should it, what do we need from you that we can't give ourselves and vice versa inverted stood on its head and flipped inside out? Maybe sometimes we also have spent so much time loving that we haven't had the chance to realize that there's nothing pleasant about being loved. Because he just wants us to be safe is all, and we can't fault him for that desire, that would be unfair because we want him to be safe too as well also and, but we're never going back to Mama's house so he shouldn't be worrying so much about that. We won't ever do what Jess is doing because we know, and he should trust this, because we don't want to do it and what Jess does and wants to do isn't any of our business really in the end so why, suppose, why does that mean that we have to come out here now? He said we drink a lot but so that's just how people have to drink sometimes. Sometimes drinking a lot is the only way to erase enough of our life to feel like we stand a chance at starting over because, maybe that's what he doesn't know because that's maybe something we've never said, that we still feel like even though we've got something going between us and it's something that's really good and we like it so much that we love it we still feel like in the rest of life outside of us together we don't really maybe feel like we've ever really started yet at anything at all and now with you getting so suddenly scared about what happens when things don't go perfectly, when there's a possibility of doing things that might have to be done, everything has come to an absolute standstill and we have to come all the way out here in the heat, walking down the from the B just to make you feel like you still have your hands on the wheel because you can't admit that one of them is broken.

What he'd said was that this was the chance that we'd been waiting for, that this was the horse we'd bet on, that we can't back out now, so it'd be best to just go all in as deep as possible. That he needed us to make sure that was what happened. He'd said that if this was going to be the story that we came out here with the fantasy of it being, that if we were going to rise above all of this and transcend these conditions we'd willfully fallen into, that if we still wanted to be free at the end of all of this we'd need to put it all on this now and let the bet ride. Again, though, that he needed us to make sure that was what happened. This is how, he said, the story goes if there's going to be one, that if it goes any other way then we don't have a story at all after all. But kept saying 'we' even though he said that it was us that he needed, to be clear, that we wanted this to work but he couldn't do it himself and needed us to do it without him so that we could, and kept saying that part, kept saying 'we' over and over and over all the time even though it was us that he needed and not him that was going to do anything.

And what he means is that he thinks he knows that we need him. He thinks he knows just how deep the pit we're dangling over goes so he can make for us whatever demands pop up in his mind to make. Thinks he knows and means to say as well that he loves us and that everything he's asking is for our own good because he thinks he knows just how bad everything was before he came along and swooped in to scoop us out of our mother's den, and maybe in part he's not quite exactly wrong to think he knows those things because some of it was true. Mama was hell and we needed to leave, sure, fine, absolutely, but we didn't need to leave only because Mama was hell but also because we hadn't had a chance to be anything else for ourselves. We needed to leave to be free and what he means is that he thinks he knows that we can't handle being free just yet so he needs to hold onto holding onto us until he's free enough to let us go just far enough away. But that'll never happen because we know that a lengthened leash is just a tighter grip and he barely has the intention of finding freedom for himself anyway. That he thinks he knows he means to say that it shouldn't be something that would bother us at the end of the day, that all he's asking us for is something that we're already doing because we've got rent to pay and the Museum's checks don't bounce sure, but they only splash enough to keep the overdraft fees from flying so, he means that bottom line you're doing it already so what's the harm in shaking and showing it all for someone who might have a shovel enough to do some real digging. He means to say that his arms are tired and this hole is already too deep to dig out of alone so what if we just snuck into the Gala and showed Putsch our proposition and then on the way, as detour away, what if we showed him his stuff and said that maybe could you help us? And get all pouty faced like he thinks we do on the internet for people we don't know and don't see and don't care about. That's the part he won't ever find a way around to finding out, that we can't do this stuff if we care about who it's being done to, that this only works if it's just a job and he's not the boss of us!

All he'd asked is for us to stay put. Maybe that's something they've all ultimately gotten wrong about love, that it's a verb or a state of being or something or other. Maybe it's an object and to be in love is to be trapped just as being loved is a sticky morass all its own. All he'd asked is for us to stay put, to bus down after work from now on for a little while until everything gets back to normal and he can use his hand again and Jawad stops being Jawad. A whole lot of stuff that will never get around to happening. Things are always the way they are now until they're not that way anymore, then they're that way until again they change. So, this is how it will be now:

Off the bus at the stop between the Cobbles and the industrial bottom of the Bay. Walk the shattered sidewalks and run our hand over the clatter of cyclone fence. Ignore the sound of dogs barking and men howling.

Walk all the way down. Walk all the way down until the partitions of property fall and give over to a dirt path, tire-tracked and steep. Step lightly there. Don't slip. Don't fall. Just make it all the way down to where there's wood and gravel and boats and cranes and keep close to the cinderblock-and-wire walls and watch out for falling things, watch our head and he said he told everyone that we'd be coming down so we shouldn't have to worry about everything we weren't warned about on the way down from the bus stop.

"Well, hello there, little lady!" From behind us. Always from behind. Always got to scare us to break the ice it seems.

We turn and there is a man who looks in charge. Broad-shouldered but softening steadily in the gut. An outgrowth, a tumescence, a swelling to sag.

"You must be Laura." A grease-hard hand.

Shake. "Aura actually. Just with no 'L,' but yeah..."

"Oh no!" His hand finds his face with bruising force, "Goddamn mush-mouthed Derek! Make me look the fool in front of his woman."

Hands away and, "You must be Jawad, then?"

"Indeed, sweetheart. Indeed. Glad to know he pronounces it clearly when he's bitching about us at home." Digs in his shirt pocket for a smoke. "You don't mind, do you?"

Shake our head.

"Excellent. Well, alright. I'll take you over to him." Hand now guidingly on our back. "Been grumpy the past few days. Bum hand is giving him some trouble. I been telling him a long time get new gloves but, I'm sure you know as well as I do, sometime ain' no way to get through to these young men except letting them break themselves open their own self. Been inside with paperwork. Sure he'll be glad you stopped by."

Walking now across an empty concrete plane. A cinderblock shack with a corrugated tin roof in the middle of it all. In the middle and away from the cranes and boats and warehouses. No windows. The closer we get the louder it is. Buzzing from the drippy bottomed A/C unit.

"He's in there, so just give it a knock... Lockers are in there too, so we'll all, all the other boys, have to come in and get out of our work clothes and get dressed for our own women so no funny business. Wouldn't wish you the embarrassment."

So, we approach the door, wet with the swampy air and, maybe just a peek, just to know. So, through the gap. Just the left eye. Yep. She. Yep. Dead... Slumped forward on the throne, thank God, so we can't see her face. Just the way her hair hangs. Wet because nothing stands a chance of drying in here. Arms limp in her lap, touching enough to catch something pooling and thick and brown that's dripped lazily for days down from her slack mouth. She's wearing shorts, though something clotty and exploded is leaving from the seams, blooming chunkily from beneath hems. Wonder how long before her back gives out, cracks inside her body's bagged softness and sends her plummeting to her own feet. Sack of soup. Wonder if she hadn't been wearing these shorts, if she'd died taking care of another sort of business, wonder if then she'd already be spilling out of where she's as open as the rest of us, piling like the shit we are and make in that waterless bowl. Wonder how long it takes for us to finally, fully, fall apart...

This what's coming then? This what comes for all of us? Reduced to an object in a state of reduction? What are we supposed to do then when he asks us to stay and then demands we move? Or when he makes us move but only just so far away? Everything is coming away and falling apart too fast for arguments over shrapnel. Do it to prove it won't work. Drive it home that we can't be there in a way that removes him from having to do anything. Make him aware that he doesn't want us as all around and staid as he thinks he does. Make sure it crumbles enough for them to know that they can't build out the world themselves, that they need us to be there as we are, as we will be, as is inevitable, but that the way that we have to be can't be dependent or dictated by the world they're envisioning. We can't make it all the way they want it made and they'll never make it the way we want it to be. Reality is somewhere in the rub and different for all of us and everyone's doing something to make everyone else's world. Ours is far from the only one being made by us. So, stay and go and do and destroy and love and fuck and fight and cry and laugh and eat and shit and sleep and do everything, everything now we can think of, all at once, just to prove to them that we're alive and waiting for them to prove the same to us!

&&&

Alright, fine, so then *what* is all the rest of this? Or more what then is most of everything? Chaos the shell of entropy and apocalypse the hopeful aspect of catastrophe, fine, maybe, but that doesn't just, unless it does, cover everything there is under the sun. What about us? What about all of us? Those of us who've got to live in this world that according to y'all is all just, well, what is it that y'all were even getting down to getting around to saying about the world then? That it's all just falling apart and that it's all going to be over soon or was it that it's all just already fallen apart and it's over already and the best we can hope for is that we might learn something from it? But neither of you seemed all that keen on either one of those readings of what you were saying so maybe you two weren't really even thinking all that hard about what you were trying to say in the first place.

It's hard to say. That's the key though, right. What's the way that Putsch had put it? That we can't speak the world. That hardly seems likely after everything else he'd written in that book, if there's even anything written in that book worth having read because Putsch doesn't seem to want to believe in people. No, no. That's not it and we know that. It's more maybe that Putsch doesn't seem to, whether it's wanting or having the belief it doesn't matter necessarily because we only have the words as the words are on the page to know anything about what he thinks about anything and it would have been nice maybe if we would have been the sort to talk to Reggie about all this before he went off and went away because then maybe we could have some other words off the page to lay over the ones that Putsch's put down and we could maybe then see what shines through then and get something closer to the truth because the more we think about it it's not maybe that he doesn't seem to believe in people it's that he absolutely doesn't at all believe in the person whereas, don't know, we've seen enough people maybe to know that there's a person in there somewhere...

218

But we've got to breathe deep and again remind ourselves that maybe there's no use rushing through any of it. Let it all fall as failingly as it may and if it's not revelation, apocalypse moreover, know that we know we can draw a difference, then at least find something interesting in the disappointment that Uncle Reggie didn't seem to want to, but what could we have expected? Not the strong and silent type, but definitely if memory serves, which we can only hope it still does because we can only hope that the silence we're remembering him having, the shortness of his speech moreover, the seeming choosiness of his words, that all this quiet about the memory of his face isn't just because he went off and went away and died in that car crash that didn't know we wanted to ask him a question about what's the difference or why there's a difference drawn. We only think he's silent because we can't remember anything he said off the top of our head because our head is so full of uprooting Putsch and catastrophe that the reason for all of this in the first place is just...

Breathe a bit deeper than that. Know the air is thick and muggy and already heavy with a summer that hasn't started. Days are getting longer and moving faster. We're sleeping too much and reading too slowly or too fast or maybe the answer isn't there because the reality is that this might be a bit deeper, come on, none of this squeezebox, pack a day, cardboard rib cage, shallow, phlegmy bullshit, get a big, big, big breath in our lungs because if this is, if this is just a catastrophe without any apocalypse, if this is, if all a life like this is a person among people or, worse yet and more likely maybe, people bumping into something enough to declare it a person among them or something but if this is all that without the apocalypse or the chaos even, if this is just the ugly ashen entropy left over after it all or if the chaos here is like that on the hill there on the grounds up by the water way away from all these groaning junkies here in the Park then we really should have, we really should have opened the door last time Shareese came by because maybe that was going to be the last time and now just because we didn't let her in that last few times maybe now we really are all alone and what happens now, what happens now when a person is left without any people, what happens now, what happens now?

"Hey man, you got any change?"

Too much and mostly it seems. But it's always change to something lesser so suppose that's the whole entropy thing because in a way maybe ash is less than fire, though that doesn't quite scan because that's not quite how anything works but the fact remains that it's harder for fire to open the door once the door is only ash and we really can't be mad at anybody but ourselves and the real problem isn't that, isn't that, isn't that lovely when just a touch of the sea breeze manages to make its way through all these trees and we catch just as we start in on getting it all together enough to really for once and for all and for everyone to breathe because that's the real goal right is to make it all to where everyone can breathe and everyone can sing because then if we could all just get there then maybe we could sing in harmony instead of all this discordant muddle that makes the world around us all wordy.

Should have let her in last time she knocked because then maybe we could still stand a chance at being something other than an argument between Putsch and Reggie. So much of our mind has been made of Putsch lately and Reggie came in so soft and now all we've got are questions and that's what's so maybe so great about Shareese is that even though they're mostly lies she's at least usually got a little bit of an answer somewhere in there to anything that might be making us hurt and Lord in Heaven can she cook and Lord in Heaven she cares which is enough to remind us that we are to somebody else a somebody else enough of a somebody to be and what's that? There. Pulling up at the bus stop far side of the Park. Squint and maybe, squint and maybe, squint and maybe we can see what it says. There on the side of the bus. Logo for the Museum and, and, squint and maybe:

Madiston MAM Presents:
A Contemporary Spotlights Exhibition–
MadStone:
New Works by Dermot Putsch!!
Opening June–

V.

We came to this lonely place way out here when it was only empty with tittering pine and it was during the spring if memory serves, the spring a near decade ago and the air was thick and she'd said something like we bought all this and then no, not all of it because what exactly could she have meant by all of it? How far into it all did our eyes see? The lot was clear and the road's dirt was replaced by grass growing soft out of a brush of brown needle and puffball and it was quiet and lonely though if we were to orient ourselves just so, a step or two in one direction, and to have looked out toward the horizon it would have been easy to see that all the trees lined up in neat rows, that they had been planted not all that long ago in terms of how long it takes a tree to grow which is to say we came to this lonely place that was made for us or with people like us in mind, filled to the brim and empty with tittering pine.

"Hello?"

"Hello there, Missus–"

"Miss Sherry! Miss Sherry!" And the glass door comes open, spilling Heidi into our diaper bag-laden arms. "Miss Sherry! Miss Sherry! Thank you so much for coming!"

"Oh, sugar. It's not a problem at all. Just–"

"Come in! Come in! Set your things down and I can give you the whole tour. Come in–" The place we put here in emptiness's place. That's the way we said it, just like everyone did, said at the time that we were building a house and have said since that we built the house. Story it seems like of everyone in Kenton that they all built their own houses. That's what they say anyway when they're having a home built for them. We'd been the same and suppose we still are in every similar way, just the same as the same is the same as everyone around here building their own houses. Signed the checks with our own two hands and really made it very clear that we wanted something with an open floorplan.

"So, you can set all of your bags down right here somewhere and–"

"Alright, thank you very much, Heidi. It's good to see you! Seems like that baby didn't leave nothing behind."

"Oh, one must take very good care to keep the baby off of your bones. Make sure that everything it brings in it also takes back out with it." Strikes then an angular pose. Kissy-face sharpens her cheeks.

"Nothing wrong with letting motherhood grow on you though, Missus Heidi. Can't fight it sometimes–" We can hope that we don't wear our lives on our faces, but that's all it's good for. Hope. Say it then and look at our hands even. Say that we built this house and then look down at our hands and see that the only thing marking the skin is the blue, bruising roll of nervously fiddled-with ballpoint pen. But it's only ever now the soft-handed that are building their own houses, that are interrupting these pristine and new emptinesses, tittering pine groves with puffball-pocked undergrowth, and erecting great hulking nothings in their place. An open floorplan was key, she'd insisted that we have an open floorplan because it would never go out of style is what she'd said. That's why we needed to have such a total nothing in the emptiness that surrounds us now, because nothing ever goes out of style. A blank slate can always be filled, right? There is potential in oblivion so if everything is going to be pristine and forever it's got to have as little to it as possible. The easiest state of affairs to maintain is that with the fewest affairs instated, right? Unstated affairs taken for granted as instated. The fewer elements, the fewer potential contradictions. Less friction, less chance of flame, but where there's smoke there's fire and where there *was* fire there *will be* ash left behind, which is more inert than whatever it was that burned so, back down to the booming basics–

"–We insisted on an open floorplan when we were building the house. Less risk of something going out of style that way, you know Miss Sherry?"

"Oh, certainly, sure," look up and around the big room that spills all about. An area that seems like it's made for sitting, black leather couch soft as obsidian, television ensconced in the wall, all centered dead on a rug over wood floors, shifts gradually to the morguish chrome kitchen we've set our bags down at the edge of. The room goes on for a small forever before it hits the walls that set it off from the outside where, can see it where we're standing, all the pines line up. Neat rows of still, thin, young trees all reaching up to be the first to canopy. But no, not all of it because what could she have meant by all of it. We bought, and a hand rose then to point out one of the four orange flags that marked the limits of the property, to that flag and then, turned to point at another, to that flag and we've got our own slice of the land here and all these trees are ours so we can knock them down and burn them or we could even have instead of building a house we could have dug a big old hole in the ground just in case we ever needed one. We bought from that flag to that flag to that flag to that flag and all of it just far enough away from the road so that we won't even ever have to hear what it's like for cars to drive by–

"How were your travels, Miss Sherry? Did you find the place easy enough?"

"Oh, sure, sure, hon. Not a problem one. Just took the bus down to–"

"Took the bus?" Asks while fixing her hair in the mirrored surface of a cabinet, "You surely did not *take a bus* all the way down here to Kenton, Miss Sherry, did you?"

"No, no, just took it down to the Depot south side of town and then hailed a cab from the concourse there."

Heidi turns on her heels to face us. Gapes for a moment with a look of small horror before: "Miss. Sherry." With that sort of indignation that fits so snuggly over shame's cold shoulders, "Miss Sherry you *did not* pay for a taxicab to have to come and bring you all the way out here!"

"It's no trouble, hon." Lift one of the heavy duffels from the floor. Unzip it and set to busying our hands out of this line of conversation. Hate it when they do this, always every time we take care of someone that's got money to spend they've got to act all like they're the only ones allowed to spend it. We said we'd come down here to all this, so you go on and let us figure how it is we want to get around to it. Eveyone's got to build their own house and all that, only way it seemed at the time to go about it. Whole thing was supposed to be that it was like staking our own claim on the world, right? That we would come down here to all this and from that flag to that flag and from that flag to that flag make all of this our own. And that's how we would do it, we would build here in this emptiness hollowed out for us a place and we could do anything that the homeowner's association approved of so long as we made sure to take down the Christmas lights by Valentine's Day they seemed like they were saying since because of all the trees and largeness of space between our neighboring properties that we could honestly in truth do whatever it was that we liked. And she liked whatever we wanted to like so long as it had an open floorplan because–

"No, no, no. Miss Sherry, that simply will not do! I should have had a car come to get you and–" Swings and snaps open her clutch. Graceful fingers flick past debit and credit, business and membership cards to find a flappy fold of cash. "Here, here. You shouldn't have had to have, I should have made sure that, here, no, no, no, you take all of that for the cab and for the car back and *I*, Miss Sherry, will call a car for your way back home so, so do not worry about that mistake happening again. I cannot believe you that you took the bus–"

Know that thank you would be just as gauche as refusal so we'll just take the wad without counting and, thickness, if they're all twenties then somewhere between eighty bucks and a cool one-forty but, no we shouldn't yet get to worrying about all that. Shouldn't have honestly have had to have taken the bus in the first place. Foolish going all the way out and up there to Carl's just to knock away again for who knows how long he had us waiting for him to not answer the door. Could have stayed home and called a cab from there but, no, had to go all the way northside, all the way to the Jaspers, just to make sure that he for sure doesn't answer the door for a damn thing anymore. Even left a voicemail a few days before that hey we could maybe get you your job back but nothing at all back at all. No such thing as a lost cause and we know that but it's difficult to argue with people we ought not have to argue with anymore. Should just know, should just know that we're only ever trying to help and that the nights get darker when we find ourselves alone. The lights in the other houses, those way past our trees in amongst their own trees, probably started with flags as well. Flags and a dream like everyone else's dream. Flags and a septic tank and a dream, but the lights are always off in the nighttime, just like ours, so when the dark comes it comes all the way up to our windows and presses in and the glass, if we look up into it, just shows us a darker version of ourselves. Can't hear the roadway sure, but thought for all the trees that when we moved out here and decided that we would build a house in the midst of it all that there would at least be the sound of something! The hoot of an owl or mourn of a dove at dawn. But the woods they built for us to build a house in amongst are silent, dead quiet, as nature knows better than anybody or anything else that stable states of affairs offer nothing in the way of shelter. The only sounds here are our feet on the wood floors because they'll never go out of style, the shutting of doors, humming refrigerator and washer and dryer and air-conditioning, the occasional moan of newness settling into stasis and–

"Right on cue it would seem, don't you think? Just before I could make my escape!" Heidi smiles as the bray falls from upstairs. "It's like the little troll knows his mother has things to do." That look, doesn't matter how much they think they've got or think they've lost by making something new, they all always have that look she's got now, don't they? Glassy-eyed and smiling, that exhausted grin against the reality of failure. Something they all never get right is thinking that they ever any of them stand the chance of getting it right at all. Biggest realization they've got to come to is that they're going to, guaranteed and nothing can be done to stop it, that they're going to mess it up, they're going to without a doubt get something so drastically wrong that they won't be able to do anything to recover from it, basic fact and hard one to swallow but they've got to swallow it and know it and that's why they all, no matter how much they've got or how much they think they've lost, have to at some point call on everyone like us, because they'll all realize at some point hopefully not too late that they aren't really in love. We were never really in love. We loved her, in that obsessive way that makes you want to buy heaping clods of nothing from that flag to that flag to that flag to that flag all the way down the path to the road far enough away from the road so that we won't even ever have to hear what it's like for cars to drive by but don't worry because we're far enough away that we won't hear, but she was never really in love with us maybe. Or not, who's to say, honestly? One thing we ought to have learned by now is that we'll never really know a damned thing about any other people or person at all ever. That's maybe what marriage serves to teach us the most then, that we'll never really know each other in any real or big or intimate sort of way. So, we spend a whole bunch of possible something on a promise of nothing so we can fill a place with only ourselves, right? Make the whole rest of the world go as far away as possible to where we can't even hear it anymore and then, left finally in a place built empty for us, we come to know that maybe we don't know a damned thing about what we don't know and all we've got to go on is the way things are, right, the way the world builds up around us, the way we fill the nothing with ourselves, right, fill it right up with the world that builds up around and out from ourselves so that when she says she loves us we can hold up the shape of those words against a world like this one and we can ask ourselves then how that love for us fits in with a world made out of trees planted in perfect rows around land marked out by little orange flags for decimation for the building of a foundation for the erecting of a big whole bunch of empty space to be filled with as little as possible and an open floorplan as to never go out of style while we work away until it's time until we know that the only thing we know about each other is that the other says it loves us just enough to make the possibility of another other, a smaller one, possible at all in all of this lack we've labored over the luster of because maybe then that softly bawling shape will fit into the whole in the nothing that our love has made and she certainly holds it like she thinks she loves it, so that's more than we can say for some that we've seen, Tash with her Winnie for one, held him like she hated it, like she didn't know she'd made him for quite a long time, few months if memory serves. Terrified by the delicacy of them, that's what gets so many mothers these days it seems, like no one's ever told them or they've never realized that most every one of us was held by someone so, believe us, you don't stand a chance of being the first to hold the little one the wrong way. He'll cry and tell you what he wants, you've got to listen, got to be attentive to the subtleties because they come out of people as people just as much a person as we all are–

"Isn't that right, my little one?" Against the silk on her shoulder. Little hands all grabby for what's behind the bodice. "No, no, no. *Skjerp deg, skatten min!* Must not need so much so often." And little pecking kisses all about the baby's head. "*Skjerp deg.* Let's meet Miss Sherry."

Lean in then into the dark of the nursery and coo, "Hello, my little angel."

"Look here, Anders, and say hello to Miss Sherry." The child's head moves away from mouthing the fabric moist and turns up to us. Eyes glimmer and bug in that special and spectacular way that all babies' eyes do, a toothless grin of briefly infinite joy at the arrival of something new. An honest shame that none of us ever really get to remember what it's like to feel that face right there crack across our cheeks. Everything always new and you filled with just enough something to know that. Everything pouring in to push out the emptiness inside his mind, glorious, blessings, but can't have that thought without its opposite rising, can we? Everything is either a wonder or a horror and growing up, they'll soon realize as all parents do, they'll soon realize that all this growing up they hope for their child is nothing but sandy and arid land rising out of the sea, its own brand of hopeless nothing. We can't afford to get hung up on thoughts like this, can afford all the less to not think them as they arise, always in the face of some gloriously grinning child. Can't let their innocence convince us of the world's purity. But we can try and make a world that's pure for him, that's something maybe we've both agreed on in terms of the child. She can hold it and sing to it and teach it two languages and name it and we can just, we can just, we can just stay as far away from it as she needs us to, it's not even a compromise, it's plain and simple and logical and look we get it, alright? Wouldn't want someone like us necessarily around the child either so we're just glad, honestly, honestly, we're just glad that we could in some way facilitate the establishment of the nothing and pristine emptiness that will keep the whole wide wavering failure of a world away from the child because we know that there's the risk of him getting all filled up with the worst of it all, right? It's so easy because they're so soft when they're like this all new and soft it's so easy for them to get squished or molded into some shape that wouldn't have had to have been if it weren't for the world all around him so since we couldn't just bring him out with fists all clenched and teeth sharp enough to bite back then we couldn't bring him out all until we were far enough away from the world to not even hear it anymore and but the worst part is and we see it too so she'll get no argument, she'll get no undue resistance from us on this front because it's not even that it's not a fight worth having but that more that there isn't really a fight in it to be had at all because she's right, she's right, she's a one hundred and ten million percent right that we've got too much of the world, the wrong parts of the world as well, we've got too much of the world on us to be so close to something so soft and new like this child so freshly brought into all of this so yes, we've facilitated the building of all this nothing in this impenetrable emptiness and well, now that's just fine and good and well and now it's time to maybe, who knows where it all goes from here? Tried to stay away and not get tied up in it but then that caused problems because the world still thinks it needs her and we've proven that we can't step up to take the child in our arms and prove to this mother that she's got good hands to leave it in. All the same as the same is the same as but can never tell them that. Theirs has got to be just the most precious and innocent and perfect little thing that we've ever seen every time there's a new one. Would be a better world if that's how it really worked, if every baby ever born came out more precious and innocent and perfect than every other baby born before it, would be really and honestly an endlessly amazing thing if that were the case but it just isn't because they're all the same as the same is the same as which isn't of course to say that we think that it isn't amazing that they're *all* like that, because it is, it is absolutely just wonderful that they all come out as innocent as they do, that they all come out crying and then suddenly laughing and then crying again and then laughing again and then they get for a little while all quiet like this one here now in our arms.

"Oh, he likes you. That's, that's good, Miss Sherry. He likes you. It makes me happy that he likes you, makes it easier to—" They all like us, hell, they all like everybody unless you make it so very obvious that they shouldn't. They don't know anybody else other than who y'all've shown him, so of course he likes us, sugar, of course he likes us.

"Makes me happy too, hon. Good to know he knows you'll be leaving him in good hands."

"Oh! Leaving! My goodness! Miss Sherry, I am so sorry, but I have to—"

"Not a worry, dear, not a worry one. You go on. I'll be just fine, you've got nothing—"

"Thank you, Miss Sherry, thank you." Turns toward the nursery door. Adds: "I shouldn't be too late tonight so don't you worry he will most likely probably want to be asleep before I even get home so you can just–"

"Missus Heidi, don't *you* worry."

"Okay, okay, okay. I am going, I am going now. Okay."

And she's down the hall to the stairs before, shit, better ask–"Missus Heidi! One quick question–"

"What is it?"

"Just wondering on whether I can be expecting you or Mister Benjamin home first or–"

"Benjamin will be much later than I will I believe, he is–" Listen to them. That's how we really know we've done exactly what it is that we should be doing. Know because they know us now as just another piece of the nothing all around. Not even that we've sunk into the background or anything like that but that instead we've more probably the word for our place in the world would be *dissolved* or atomized or something along those lines probably because it's not like we've taken a step back from the situation, right? It's not like we've taken a step back and said something like hey, hey, hey you just let us know whether or not we're needed for anything because we'll always be here just in case you need us for something so just let us know and we can just come on in and offer up whatever our hands can offer, no it's not like that even at all in the slightest bit whatsoever because it's more that we've just not disappeared because we're still here but that we've dissolved or atomized or something like spring pine pollen or maybe better aspirin tablets in water or iodine in the salt or fluoride in the pipes where before maybe, and this is the hope and why also we had to come out here to make our big nothing to shelter away a new soft something, the hope that we've managed to in our dissolution away from it all that we've managed to *add* something necessary to the nothing because maybe we're like where there was only lead in the pipes there's now at least fluoride as well or iodine in the salt at the same time as the sodium or maybe we really are just like pine pollen all in the air just *all* in the air and getting on everything, spreading coward yellow everywhere we float and making it harder to breathe and maybe it's only good to have dissolved if hopefully the hope is that the wind will take us far away from all this so that when we do finally land and come back down it's not to choke and smear all over everyone here that's doing so well now that we've dissolved into the atmosphere. What happens if instead of dissolving we disappear? Who would sink to the cliché of missing us then? Whether away with the wind or assimilating completely into nothing it doesn't seem that either would truly make much of a difference at all because we've done what we were needed to do in the first place, we labored away to shell everything into this void and now that it's all shelled away and safe and warm and nobody seems concerned at all for us even though we haven't spoken to a soul in a month maybe a month already couldn't have been, not quite that long, no it's just, it's nice to have something real and breathing and warm and true in our arms after all this having been squirrelled away from everyone and everything for a month not quite a month but long enough to feel like we aren't even really around anymore. Now more than ever before it's like they do their best to act like we aren't there at all anymore and look, we get it, been in it long enough to know that management will always be situated at the end of long leers and side-eyed glances of derision. Worked it long enough to know now that even when we try to be on the same wavelength as everyone else they just go and change the station on us and look that's alright and fine and well and good and it's almost over because soon the Ballroom or Contemporary Spotlights Gallery or whatever it is that they're wanting to call this lark of an idea which mind y'all per my last email we are all in full support of so but still it's basic best practice to call it what it is, a Hail Mary and all that, and we all know that we should all know that nobody knows how much time this place has left, that it's all becoming around us a different world and there's very little that we can do about it and but that's not even much of our business anymore now though is it? No longer on us to concern ourselves with everybody else so long as we maintain the institution that does that for us. None of our business or concern because our job now is to just sit down. Our job now is to sit down at that desk for at least eight hours a day and act as a node in the line of communication. Sit behind that closed door and at that desk and foster just a hum of quiet. Answer emails at a steady pace but with language imprecise enough to create the illusion to all lording parties above that the middle tier hovering over the workaday is being very, very, very deliberate in our responses, that everything is being considered with its due weight, and that yes, it will all get done when the time is right so let's not go about making rash decisions that could have deep effects on the lives of those we hold contracts of employment with. Let's not forget our duty to the citizenry of Madiston and, honestly, the surrounding towns and counties, the state even. The citizenry of the state, moreover. Public servitude and all that. We at Madiston MAM must work diligently to maintain our status as not only a cultural center of the region, but also as an educational touchstone and community forum of sorts, divorced as much as possible from the cynical marketplaces that have sprouted up along this coast, commodifying history and culture and reifying it all as somethingsomethingsomething but this here is what's real and that's what we can't ever forget and sometimes it's just nice is all it's just nice to be reminded of it all is all. Nice to hold something so new that just wants us to warm up the milk, just wants us to look at it so it can look at us and smile all toothless and true. It's just nice to see them now in the corner of our eye just as the microwave dings

we nearly leave our skin behind as we see ourselves walk into the kitchen. Christ Almighty where the hell did we come from? Thought we were alone. No, we knew we would be here just not maybe who exactly we would be when we got here. Trusted her not to make this any more difficult for us than it already is since we came all the way out here the middle of perfect damn nowhere to take care of everything for her so that she could, Christ Almighty, sorry, just didn't know that we wouldn't be just us and the child didn't know that we were also here and, well, Jesus, it's been a long minute hasn't it? What a month now maybe, no can't have been a month but probably just short of it since we last saw ourselves and, hell, well she'd said that we'd be much later than we are and where have we been? Here. We've been here. The whole time? The whole time we've been here, we've been here. Oh, what for, then why are we here if we're here also can we just look after the little one? No, afraid not because we, uhm, well, suppose we're too busy maybe to look after the child so it's up to us to do it and she says she'd prefer it like that anyway so... Said she'd prefer it like what? Said she'd prefer that we watch the child instead of us doing it because she we guess trusts us more than she trusts us and well, Hell, Christ, haven't seen us in forever-and-a-half! How've we been? How're things at the, uhm, at the Museum then? Have we been busy? Is everything coming together? Hope so because leaving us behind like that was really, well, we know, we know, some of us just can't cut it under the pressure and, oh believe us when we say *we* know. Don't know how we used to do it, and we did it for so long, as long as we've known ourselves we were in that position. Yeah, yeah, but can't forget that it's on account of us that we ever got off the floor and into an office of our own. Gotta remember that, gotta remember that it's us who lifted ourselves up and it's on account of us that we get to go any higher at all. Always at our own hands. Always looking out for ourselves and making sure that we get what's ours make sure that we don't take it for ourselves and, well we sure are glad that we seem to be doing just fine then after all this. Oh yeah, we couldn't be better. Have we seen this place? It's pretty much paradise. Well, it's quiet certainly which, if that's what we're after then we really couldn't ask for much more, now could we? No, no, we couldn't. Quiet like this just means that we get to be as loud as we want because we're so far away from ourselves. None of us can hear us so, yeah, it's pretty nice. We wouldn't want to complain without due cause and all, no, no certainly wouldn't want to do that, now would we? We came out here to be alone together, so that we could have a clean sort of slate to make sure that we could make something safely and well, but, wait, didn't we say that she won't let us even hold the, no, no, not exactly that, we can, yeah, we can hold him whenever we want, but it's more that we just, it's more like is it really our place to be holding the child and all that or is that more *our* job. We've got to make sure that all of this is maintained so there's really not all that much time to hold our child when we've got to keep the world up and disaster at bay so that's why we, that's why she, we suppose, asked us to be the one to come out here and hold it because we definitely can but maybe it's not really our place to yet so, so, we *can* hold it, then? Yeah, yeah, I can definitely, well that's fantastic because we have *got* to go to the bathroom, just barely holding on here, so here why don't I take the child and the milk in his bottle in the microwave should be done so we can even start feeding him so we'll just run to the, here, I'll just take him and support his, support his head or his whole world will roll away so, here, yeah, just I'll just take him so that we can go use the little ladies' room right quick so just

take him and, yeah, I'll, but my, just make sure his head is supported so that his world won't roll away and I'll just, wait, wait, wait, I'll just yeah okay just make sure the okay, yeah in the crook of my elbow then that should work so, yeah just and the bottle now and, oh, he already knows what do with that so don't need to worry I'll just hold it and looking down at him at and into his, uhm, his eyes all globular and glassy and clear and goddamn so big that they can see everything probably, see everything that's new and can see me holding his bottle for him and behind those eyes the whole world then coming constantly into being and now there because he's, look up and yeah, there's me, there's Daddy, there's

June

I.

Cracking across the cheeks, saccharine, innocuous, hollow, and baring teeth that would sooner cut out their tongue than stoop to honesty; at the bell, a smile:

"Welcome, y'all! Come on in. Come on, come on. Don't be shy." Waddles out from behind the register. Voice muffled beneath the face's big rubber grin. Jowls shake loose about the neck and shoulders where the body blooms back to flesh.

Shareese to my left nearly jumps out of her skin: "Lord in heaven! What in all? Scare me half to pieces popping out like that!"

Miss Rubber-Muffled: "Oh, I'm sorry ma'am, really didn't mean to, just, the greeting is important. All part of it so I'm trying to make sure that I'm–"

"No, no, no, I can't," she looks over her shoulder back at me and then over at the Director's towering, covering her mouth as tension releases to giggle, "I can't, can you just take that thing off while it's just, do you mind if," back up at the Director, "can she just–"

"Makes no difference to me, Miss Shareese," and he steps further in, onto the sales floor, into the cloying thick of it.

Turns back to the masked woman, caricature of the, memory serving, actual cashier at the candy store down the Cobbles, blue eyes bigger and pupils giving sight to the real eyes behind, same sort of chopped hair, grinning with teeth the size of playing cards, and asks her again: "Hon, would you mind just–"

"Sure, sure thing. No problem." And the dead face rises. She's cute. Very cute, in fact.

"Thank you, hon. Just dreadful that thing–"

"All for the art." Wipes her forehead, bangs sweated together. Splotches of red and pink on her skin where the rubber has raised rashes. "Gotta break a few eggs and all."

"Oh, I suppose so, I suppose–" And Shah's swept up in it, stepping behind the Director as he passes through the pastel aisles and variform displays. Plastic metropolis of dead sugar. They've really nailed *everything.* Another actor, holy shit even got his eyebrows, what was his name? Alvin or Albert or something. Eyebrows and driftwood smile. Working replica of the taffy machine. Whirring and jangling, chains clanking. Empty arms rehearsing their juggling routine.

Lean toward the young woman, how old? Twenties? Definitely, probably, and say, "This is, this is uncanny, you know?"

"Oh, it's a feat for sure." Lifts the collar up on her shirt to wipe the sweat off her nose. Slight upturn. Septum ring. Full lips and eyes like– "His masterpiece, I'd say. But, I'm partial so–"

"You know the guy?"

"Yeah, been an assistant of his for, well since grad school," reaches underneath the register and produces a bottle of water. Sips and exhales relief, "He was a like visiting artist or, I don't remember what they called his position exactly, but he ended up taking a bunch of us with him when he left. Gave us work as fabricators and PAs and stuff–"

The Director's voice booms across the gallery, the store, moreover: "Constance?"

"Yessir?" she breaks off. Constance, Constance, Constance, gotta remember that, put that one away for– "What's up?"

"Do you know where," stepping toward us now. No man, just, c'mon, we were just getting to talking– "Mr. Putsch had said that he would give us a walkthrough of the installation before doors tonight. But, it doesn't seem that he's here right now, perhaps he has–"

"No, no, no sir, nothing like that. I, uhm, I can give you the rundown of everything, uhm, he said he was going to visit an old friend and, I don't know maybe he got held up or something," takes then a big swig from the bottle and recaps it. Rolls it back into the cubby beneath the register, "But, yeah, I'll, uhm, I'll give y'all the quick tour. There's not really too much to–"

"Miss Shareese! Would you like to join us for a brief tour of the exhibition?" C'mon, dude. What the fuck? Can't I just, didn't you see we were starting to have a bit of a conversation here? I mean, Jesus Christ.

"So," turning toward us with that bright eyed tour guide condescension, "I'm sure y'all recognize what we've put here. It–" Looks nothing like before. Ballroom completely a memory, and a hazy one at that. Even seems like, definitely not even seems, they *actually* lowered the ceiling. Drop panel now. Built walls with fake windows toward the, yeah, matte painting of the Bay. I can't fucking believe it, even nailed down the smell and the labels and yeah, I mean, look at this–"Excuse me."

"What's that?" Shit. Hadn't been listening. Got kind of sucked into it too I guess and–

"If you could please just be careful with those," gesturing to the wrapped candy bar in my hand, "if you could just, we really spent a lot of time making sure they looked right and–"

"It's fake?"

"Yessir. Well, I wouldn't say *fake* necessarily. The, uhm, gosh, Dermot's much better at explaining this than I am, but, uhm, sorry," plucks one of the candy bars from the rack nearest her, "so, yeah, this isn't edible, and the wrapper wasn't manufactured by, uhm, by whoever normally they get to manufacture it, uhm, let me just... Here, okay, so the candy inside this wrapper is a sculpture, like a hyperreal sculpture but *not* chocolate and nougat and nuts and all that, even though on the inside of the sculpture are sculptures of nougat and nuts and like resin caramel or whatever. The wrapper is like hand-painted and, there's even a few I did buried in here somewhere, so there's a lot of work that went into every–"

"So," can't help it. Uncanny. "So, none of this is real?"

"None of it is *edible*. I don't want to misspeak here though, so you may have to ask Dermot when he comes back around, but it *is* all *real* in the sense that it's all, like, yeah, maybe best to just wait on Dermot to explain it all maybe, maybe best to just–"

"Grab a drink before you go?" She'd said no. Which is fine. But, I mean, no need to be cagey or say it like I'd asked her a million more times after that or already. No need to be all like, "No Buck. I've got to at least touch base with–" Like I don't understand the situation, like I'm missing the point or something. Not my problem, honestly, not my fucking problem she won't draw a line in the sand herself.

"Hey, Tanisha! Let me get one more and close out if you don't mind."

"Alright, B." Handing a stack of bills, change, to a patron at the other end of the bar. "Same glass okay?"

"Yeah, yeah, sure thing, babe. Just that's all I can have," gotta be clear headed, gotta be crystal as possible if this is going to go down like it needs to. Swift of foot and nimble of mind and all.

"You want the shot as well? Still happy hour for a few more minutes."

"Uhm, okay, sure thing, sure. Okay." Check the time and, message from Jess. Better not be pulling out, can't get cold feet. Honestly, not to be a dick or anything, but no way she gets cold feet. This is a cake walk compared to the usual routine. "Probably going to stick around until I've got to go back to the Museum."

"Oh, aces." Mug under the taps. Pulls the Belchard handle. A stream of deep amber then a foamy sputter, a bubbling spurt, and dead moist gasping. "God-fucking-dammit." Turns back to me, "Buck, the keg kicked —"

"I know, I saw. A bottle is fine, don't worry about it. Shift's almost over anyway, right?"

"As soon as Craig gets here, yeah."

"Leave it for him then," smile all shit-eating. She sets the bottle down, pops its cap off, and replaces the gold in my shot glass.

"Keep an eye. I'll be downstairs."

"Nah, nah, Tanisha, come have a drink with me–"

"I can't just leave an empty keg. I'll be right back." Rounds the sinks, rounds the corner, and disappears.

Phone rises then back to my face. Swipes and numbers and Jess's message materializes: `Hows this?` Then the image attached: Smudged mirror selfie. Red dress with the deep neck and short skirt. Looks like probably she's in heels. Necklace or just a weird hair-and-lens flare? Thought we were, `Thought we decided to go with the green dress...` Sent and descent, back to its pocket right as Tanisha returns.

"So, where is our little shining Aura? Is she not doing the event thing or whatever with you?"

"No, no, she is. So far as I know anyway." Say it with less stink. No need to get all worried and edgy just because Jess changed her mind about which dress to wear. "She's got to go like, I don't know, check on her boyfriend or something."

"Something wrong with him?"

"No more than usual insofar as I'm aware."

"So, what's the issue, then?"

"Oh, I don't know. It's none of my," phone buzzes in its pocket, Jesus Christ, "none of my business, you know?"

"No. I don't know, Buck. I don't know the guy."

"What?" Peek into the pocket to see if it's, yeah, just Jess again. Probably with some backtalking bullshit, some smartass fucking whatabout, "You've never met him?"

"No. I don't think so."

"Oh. He and his friend David hang out here whenever we're around, but–"

"I don't hang around here long after work, Buck. My off-the-clock attentions are the privilege of you and Aura." Phone again, follow up, buzzes in its pocket, "Don't even think I've met *your* little lady."

"Oh, wow. That's weird. Shit, hadn't realized–"

"Mm-hmm, I've got no allegiances to any boy that's got my Aura on a leash, if that's what all this amounts to. I'll go kick his ass right now." And she turns away. Walks back to the register to count out the drawer before the shift change.

Check the phone. Two messages: `Green one is covered in cum so…` and `Prob with this one??` Best not to engage right now, not while my nerves are up like this. Let the second whiskey settle- n before taking a dip into these waters here. Holy shit, man, just, alright, cool off, everything is going to go just fine. Just get out of the way and be cool. She said she'd do it and she's going to do it so just no use in getting antsy about it. Shot in the dark anyway, but who knows, right? But that's the thing, *who knows*, so what if it *does* end up mattering if, what if he hates the color red, what if he finds the cut of the neck to be too slutty or the hem to be, I don't know, what if he thinks he's being invited further than the plan is planned to invite him, what if? Fuck, just take a drink, man. Just take a big nerve-numbing swig of the old **'As Good As It Gets…'**

After all, best that can be hoped for is some sort of fraternal recognition. Nothing more. Not going to spill his soul or anything so, no matter how many times it plays through my head I've got to know now before going in or anything that in reality it's not going to be at all like it is in my head. Fantasy. Not going to gather me up in some sort of hug, declare himself or myself long lost godfather or godson or something like that. Best that can be hoped for, honestly, is that he remembers Reggie at all. That's really, want to take the step out of fantasy and start getting the likely hypotheticals straight? Best case scenario is that he shakes my hand and says something like, says something along the lines of, 'Oh, yes! Reginald Lloyd! A fine thinker in his own right. Saddened for a decade now at the knowledge of his passing. Taken from all of us at too young of an age, though is there really a ripe enough time to die? Very probably not, I'll have to say, but of course you already know that. See you've brought with you the book and... That right?... You don't say? His copy? The one which I, oh yes indeed that is quite splendid, now isn't it?' Higher probability of course, given the time between publication and now, that he may very well not remember Reggie at all and, or perhaps even, can't quite yet bear the thought of that though, can I? No use in thinking that he'd have anything bad to say about Reg, no reason even to think it! Sure their conversation bordered on combative, but that's how debate is bound to go between such minds, such diametrically opposed yet morally concerned minds, that of course they'll get each other's blood up, so no use thinking that he'll have anything bad to say of Uncle Reggie, more even perhaps maybe he'll be surprised, given that I get to speak with him even that long to get into the finer points as such, but maybe he'd even be surprised that the first *I'd* heard of *him* wasn't until Reggie had passed, and that it was by complete coincidence that my reading him has aligned with his rearrival here in Madiston, maybe he'd be surprised that he wasn't on the forefront of Reggie's mind either but why, why, why, come on now, don't get all heated and prepared for some sort of confrontation or something, just silly. Odds are, as with everything probably, that it'll all be much calmer than you'd possibly expect. Odds are he shakes my hand, maybe he's heard of me, maybe he knows me as Reggie's precocious nephew, maybe Reggie said things about me and it's Putsch who'll actually have the questions but, come on now, gotta finish the book, can't let the mind wander like this, just get back to the page okay? Just go on, only a few paragraphs left, finish it out, have it fresh on the mind:

12: How then are we meant to go on living? The solution of Philosophers and to a lesser extent, though let's not allow the flamboyance of their pallet to paint their hands any color other than the red of universal blood, Artists, has been largely nothing more than the invention of the very categories they comfortably occupy, to divorce the concerns of Eternity from the concerns of the Everyday, to separate the Cosmic from the Banal in an attempt (again, a generous gloss here) to create a vacuum-sealed place for the very same Cosmic and Banal to interact under close and unobstructed observation. But in this vacuum, and further *on account of* this vacuum, the categories the Object has been divided into lose all the qualities that make them separate categories in the *outer-world* that they were extracted from, that made them Objects *to begin with*. Between the covers of a book, in the lines of a poem, among the flicker of a film's frames, or in the sanctified systems of logic and reason the monstrous forces of waning reality can play themselves to their conclusions in ways that the basic forces of the *already-waned-reality* that produced their failing forms would forbid by its very nature, i.e. only here in the vacuum can the Almighty confront the Sinner, can the two lovers die to live forever, and so on. This is all very well perhaps, no aspersion is usefully cast toward these methods in and of themselves, but the critique must take place with further regard to how the products of these methods are applied to the reality they purport then to expose the facts of or *if,* moreover, they've exposed the facts of any present reality whatsoever. It seems, knowing the nature of the methods of idea extraction and understanding the impulse toward the codification of concepts, that the only realities that claims of explication may be laid on are those [realities] that are already dead and gone and passed away. *Further,* the sadness of subjectivity presses on Us: The need for these experiments, from the ethical to the aesthetic, to be conducted in the seclusion of the individual mind does little toward the application of the discoveries made therein. The discoveries are delicate; see any debate on nearly any subject between two or more persons fostering different but 'equally' rigorous conclusions. Crystalized conclusions shatter almost immediately when exposed to the forces of anything outside of the systems or arguments that produced them…

"Wait, wait, what? I thought we'd agreed that you were just going to–" Slandering creation with false esteem, making dead wood more blessed than living lips, hasn't even looked up from the stack of papers at me once. Just standing here sweating and can already feel behind the eye that driving nail, so–

"No, Derek. *You* said that I didn't need to worry about it, and *I* said I was going to–"

"Well, fuck me then, babe." Looks up now. Mouth gaping and loose, a child told no. "What am I supposed to do then? I was planning on–"

"Go hang out at St. Never's for a little while or something, D. I don't fucking know. Take some extra time and catch up on these–"

"I've been doing paperwork literally all day, babe. Aura, I can't–"

"Then don't. Hang out at the bar. Buck and I will come by after we get off and, I won't even drink, I'll drive us home! Take the night off and get hammered. Relax or something and–" stop looking at me like I'm perjured, murderous, bloody, full of blame, savage, extreme, rude, cruel, not to trust, because "I need the money, alright? A little extra cash to just–"

"Should just quit, babe. I don't understand why you won't just quit. I make enough here to hold us up and–" He's mad in pursuit and in possession so, had, having and in quest to have extreme, so–

"No, hon. I've already committed. I can't just bail on them, so, alright. Look. I'll see you later tonight. Shouldn't be much later than ten, alright?" Walk to the desk and lean over the stack of papers where his eyes have again descended, "Look at me," move the lamp out of the way, "look at me, babe. I've got to go. I'll see you tonight. I love you. We'll lay in bed all weekend, okay? Order take-out and watch movies and stuff." Kiss him and say it again, "I love you." And then, "See you later."

And then back outside to shut the door. Take a deep breath as the foot comes down. Don't mind now how thick the air is. Did it, followed through, and there's nothing that he can do. Can't keep me locked away and trapped and like, I'll do as I please, I'll work when I want. Our lives are supposed to be *together,* don't know how else to explain it other than, no. Take a deep breath because the foot has come down. Thick evening air. Summer on its weltering way. Out of the sea's greatening grey, cast in the setting sun's burning ocher, there it is, the source of this slow-churning, tummy-curdling pain. Rusty nail turned screwy behind my eye. Off there where the horizon meets the sky the stormy ambition has risen clumpy and leaden in its heft. Piling and piling and knowing of its eventual fall, but held there by the thickness of the air it climbed up through. It'll swirl and swirl and bring a hammer to my mind with its crushing salt winds and I'll be locked up in painful time, swirling and swirling, but for now, sun coming down, it's held at bay over and away from the Bay by a wall of fiery gold whose head hangs about my head and shoulders and brings all that new booze fresh out of my skin. Can't hardly hold a buzz in this weather. Nerves just come back up the minute the heat hits and, light up a smoke, feels like huffing straight from a muffler. Goddamn. Goddamn. Goddamn, this uniform. Polyester in the summer just holds all the worst parts of the sweat. White shirt run yellow in the pits and around the collar. Jacket heavy on my shoulders. No better when it's cold though. When it's cold it holds nothing. May as well be naked. One day, one day won't have to wear a uniform though, that's what all this is for right now. That's why it's got to go off exactly like it needs to, so that I'll never need to wear something like this again, never need to cocoon myself in something so slumping and lumpy, make myself the same as the same is the same as, no. After today, tonight, if everything in this heat goes off as it should, as it has to, then after all this I'll be, Jesus Christ, what's this? C'mon, all this fucking buzzing, all this goddamned–"Hey, babe. What's up?"

"What's up? What do you mean *what's up?*"

"Sorry, I don't–"

"Is the dress okay? Can you answer my, I've got a lot of getting ready to do! Just tell me if the dress is okay."

"Yeah, yeah, hon. The red one will be–"

"Have you been drinking?"

"What? No. Only a little. Killing time. Just–"

"Jesus, Buck. You know, I can't just have all of this on *my* shoulders. You've got to–"

"Oh, c'mon, Jess. I just had a few beers between shifts. Chill out. It'll all be, I'll be completely straight in like an hour, half an hour. Roll a joint and level out. I can handle my–"

"Fine, whatever. Red dress, then?"

"Yeah, babe. Yeah. Red dress is fine. Should be just–"

"You've got to answer when I text. This whole thing hinges upon you answering when I–"

"Alright, babe. I will. C'mon. This is literally *my* plan."

That's what's got me worried at all in the first place, B. All of this, Buck, has been *your* plan. From the get. *You* said best to get a start in a city like Madiston. Blooming art scene, you said. Just going to take some time, just have to get in on the hustle. All that bullshit. Haven't seen you fucking paint a goddamn, doesn't matter, this is the last shot. Fuck this up and, well, fuck, you know? Just, you know I've been here through all of it. I saw the fire in your eyes and heard the rumbling hunger in your belly, I believed it all when you would wax poetic and rant about how everything is and, well, this is just, getting to end of a rope here is all, so let's get fucking serious and get to work and make this happen otherwise, I mean, holy shit, don't know if you realize how deep this hole we've dug for ourselves is, don't know if you know, I mean, you can't just skirt the system entirely, I understand that you think you're, and you might be, I don't know, but I love you and. One thing you should know if you know anything at all after all of this is that I fucking love you, and I've proven that I'm willing to put up with quite a lot to keep you so, well, so, before a joy proposed and behind a dream I'm going to need a coffee or something, going to have to once again, always like clockwork cliché, pain always rises just when I'm about to shun the heaven that leads men to this Hell. Come on, Aura, hold it together long enough to make it back to the, Christ this heat doesn't help a damned thing. Eyes nothing like the sun, no such roses in her cheeks, breath from my mistress reeks. Thou art as tyrannous so as thou art, beauties proudly make them cruel. Squinting teary eyed and, amazing how fast it can come on. Should do more, should have done more to jump ahead of these pains. Should keep, I mean, it's basic fucking basics, should keep some pain meds in your purse or something. But they never work. I know just, thy face hath not the power to make love groan. Thy black is fairest in my judgement's place. In nothing art thou black save in thy deeds. And thence this slander, as I think, proceeds–

"So, I guess, yeah. Any questions?"

Oh, sugar, more than are useful, and that's the truth. No point in prying. Answer never does what it needs to anyhow. Ain' my first time through this. Seen it over and over again on that second floor. Always a disappointment, this art stuff. Can't get a head around it because it seems like it does everything in its power to keep your head from getting around it. Not my problem though, not my battle, glad someone enjoys it. Glad this girl here seems so excited for it and maybe that's all there is to it. Problem is though, seen it a thousand going on a million times seems like up there on that second floor though, every time a new gallery, a new rotation, a new artist, a new idea before anyone can really get their fingers dug into the last one. Glad, honestly I am, because there's nothing else useful to be I suppose, that all these people and all seem to enjoy it, to put some importance in it because, well, gives me my job, I reckon. I don't have to understand it necessarily to understand that it allows me to, well, just, it's good, it's fine, it's time to, uhm, yes, uhm, "Uhm, Mister Rohaan, I'm just going to take a step outside for some air real quick."

"Sure thing, Shah. Sure thing."

Wouldn't have noticed if I'd just disappeared, would he? Got his head so far up that little girl's ass and, no, come now, just, problem is, Shah-baby, and you know this and you've got to be the one to change it, see, but the problem is that now in this new position I am very much steward to all this alien irrelevance. Interim Assistant Director. It's a nonsense title and, if the past few weeks prove anything, a job that can be done with one's eyes closed. The Director is going to make his own decisions and the day to day staff are going to make their demands and it seems that all I'm being asked to do, all they're paying for is for me to just say yessir to the words coming down from on high and no, I'm sorry, there's nothing that I can do to everyone else on the payroll and that's, heartbreaking as it is, easy enough, so no, hon, no I don't and won't and will never again I reckon have any questions. What's that smell?

"Oh! Hi there, Miss Shareese!"

Of course, should have known, it's "Mister Buchanan! Nice to see you showing up on time."

"Yeah, uhm, Jesus, you kinda scared me–" His foot shifts to smudge a smoldering smidge on the concrete.

"Wait, wait, Mister Buchanan, don't just–"

"What's that?" Foot stops just short.

"Just, uhm, unless my nose deceives me, I don't think you'd want to let all that go to waste."

Smiles. Nods. Bends to pick up the weeviling roach. Again at his lips, a puff and, "Oh, yeah uhm... I don't know, thought you would maybe tell me to–" He rocks back on his heels, briefly perhaps losing a bit of balance.

"Oh, hon, it has been made very clear to me that the Attendant staff are no longer any concern of mine." No longer any concern of mine. Let Rohaan deal with it. Bigger fish now to ignore forgetting to fry. "Been known to have a toke myself when the occasion calls for it..."

"Oh, word? You, uhm, want a puff at all?"

"Not got any funny business in it, does it?"

"No, no, nothing like that. My guy's like all natural and all that, so no, but, I mean it's strong stuff, so maybe–"

"No sugar, ain' my first rodeo, you know. Pass it here, I'll have just one little," puff, just enough to grease the lungs and loosen the mind. If they need me to be perfectly out of the way then what better way to get there than letting myself float up above over everything? Ought to maybe just embrace the detachment and watch it all happen. Fall fully inside my soul to let it free and fly over everything and maybe then I can see what, maybe then, completely drunk on myself, maybe then I'll understand what all this is about, maybe then it'll click why they had to go and replace one lie with another. Take the damn Ballroom out, so pristine and gutted of the worst parts of its history, take the pit from the peach and replace it with what? An actual stone? Something completely inert and unchanging? Something synthetic?

"Maybe, uhm, you could give me one more little run down on what exactly all this is for again..."

Rolling the mask around in her hands, "Uhm, yeah. I don't know. It's basically like, well, other than what I already said like you'll have to ask Putsch about exactly what it means when he gets here. You know?"

"No, no, I get it but, I guess I mean to ask more what do *you* think about it?" Lean then on this little counter. Eyebrow raise would definitely be too much, she's got to get the picture by now.

"Well, I–"

"Alright everyone!" The Director. "Places, places! Doors are in under half an hour. Let's make sure we're all ready to–" C'mon dude, can't you see? It's like you aren't even paying attention to anything other than, you know what, it's fine. I'll crack this nut, I'll–

"So, are you planning, uhm, are you planning on standing by the door during the opening or–?"

"What's that?" Begging there in her eyes. Yeah, she gets it. She knows what's–

"Because, I don't know. It's going to be hard to like do the whole routine and if you're there the whole time. Kind of kills the illusion or–"

"Oh, I thought all of this was *very real*."

"No, it is, it's just, maybe it'd be better if you stand over by the uhm, by the display of," points then to somewhere in the gallery just far enough away. Playing hard to get, I see, want me to *see* you in action. Totally get it, "In fact," digs around in a cubby beneath the register, "maybe you can also hand these out." A rubber-band bound stack of program notes for **MadStone by Dermot Putsch**. "Maybe even give one a read before we open the doors, you know? I'm sure most of your questions will be answered therein."

"Alright then, sounds good. Thanks and–" Hand out for a shake and possible peck, "What was your name again?"

"*You* can call me Britney."

"Alright then *Britney*, I'll just take up my post over there and, well, maybe we can chat again once all this nonsense is over," make a show of it now. Turn and take from the pile one of the pamphlets. Open it up and:

"We're back now with some updates on the weather here, ladies and gentlemen." Feet up and crossed and, oh God that's perfect, lean the seat back. Couldn't have bought a better recliner, Benjamin, really couldn't have, "Kick it over to Tom at the doppler." A field of blue and earthily browned green, land and sea. Salt Creek, the sliver of Riley, Madiston itself, Bay like an open mouth, and something heavier, some feathery amoeba there off to the East. A slight swirl to its approach. "Thanks a lot, Cooper. So, as we can see here that low pressure system that was hovering about this morning has seemed finally to have solidified into something quite stormy. We are, of course, entering into what we all know is in fact our storm season, but this as we can see here, can we zoom in a little bit?" The digital doppler projection whips and refocuses, singling out the tempestuous mass, "Ah yes, good, good. So, as we can see here, if you all can remember where we were this morning when the system was first taken note of, a simple depression, the rate at which it is now mounting is not unheard of, but surely unusual this close to land. There's no way yet to know, of course these things are forever unpredictable, no way to know when or if it will make landfall, but perhaps we should all take this as due warning to get our emergency preparedness plans locked in place, because–"

Better becomes the grey cheeks of the east. Can feel it now on my own cheeks: A saltily fished gust, cool and sea-slimed, screaming across the Bay after breaking over Riley's soft, humped back. Breathing deep the breath of the sea as, pain rising higher and higher and higher, already set to spread and slur my speech, the fever is breaking. Breathe in, maybe even my ribs snap, and look out over it all now: Dusk casting the beast's rising shoulders in shattering gold, as those two mourning eyes become thy face. Beauty herself is black and those clouds look fit to fly to the firmament's top, fit to pour down and wash away all that is foul, because it really is all fundamentally foul, that's got to be the key to what he's trying to get at, right? No way that "There is fundamentally less than us" can mean anything else... I mean, okay, give that another gloss real quick, wait, what time is? Okay, okay, fine, fine, just got back a tad to where it says:

...shatter almost immediately when exposed to the forces of anything outside of the systems or arguments that produced them.

The temptation here to critique the systems or arguments themselves is certainly understandable, but even that critique (to be as pedantic as possible) would find itself vulnerable to the same assault. We can roll around in mud of that sort all day; already been doing it for centuries. The next impulse, and to some perhaps the final impulse, is to do away with systems and arguments entirely, to embrace the pure nonsensical chaos of the World as the only reasonable conclusion, to hold up empty hands in pleading surrender to the void. For some, this may be fine; according to the logic of many systems and arguments that purport to bring forth *different* conclusions it may also be the only actually reasonable stopping point. But, dearest readers, if we've made it all the way the twelfth step in this program, we should know by now that this can't possibly be where it ends. This still provides no answer to the principle question of: How then are we meant to go on living?

Is it not enough to torture me alone? Me from myself thy cruel eye hath taken. No hon, can't let him get to me like that. Just got to, just got to go to work and do what I promised. Fight through now and just walk the way back to the bus. Don't get sucked up and lost in these thoughts and angry fantasies, they just aren't worth it. He isn't anything like Mama, he's not gonna do what Mama did, so stop trying to push him to act like Mama, stop pressing buttons that don't need pressing. Get all riled up and salty thinking about him like that at the end it's only myself and thee I am forsaken. So no, hon, that's right, foot's been put down and don't start in on picking it back up yet, alright? He's just stressed is all, hurt himself and all and worried too about money and me and a torment thrice threefold thus to be crossed so I'll just not be a problem then and walk my way back to the bus stop and, he loves me, that's all, fine, but you can't renege on a promise, said I'd work tonight so I'm going to, just, take one more big one more deep breath of this air with the salt and cool of the ocean and forfeit myself for thou art covetous and he is kind, so him I lose through my unkind abuse and, no, he plays the whole yet I am not free and–

This still provides no answer to the principle question: How then are we meant to go on living?

So then, knowing full well the question has yet to be answered in earnest and that all systems and arguments and logics used heretofore have produced nothing but raw gasps from already asphyxiated lungs, that all conclusions are simply the death rattles of apes that forgot they were living, let's do the unthinkable (in terms of these systems we should by now be joyously rejecting) and move forward with conjecture as our lone methodology, with heresy as our orthodoxy. Let's move forward by doubling down on our unproveable claim that the World is absolutely, in its sum total, less than Us, and furthermore that without Us there is quite simply no World to be lived in. Again, as a reminder to the reader who's read this far, and as reprimand perhaps to those who have skipped ahead, I will drive home the caveat here that this central claim is in content and quality wholly different to similar claims levelled by various Phenomenologists, Mystics, Psychoanalysts, Philosophers, Clergy, Prophets, and worst of all again, Artists of the past in the primary sense that the claim recurring here is *not* existential or ontological in its nature but completely *eschatological!* It is not the nature of existence which should inform our answer to the question of how to go about living, nor is it in some naively dialectical way therefore the nature of nonexistence which should inform our answer, but instead it is the processes by which things pass *out of* existence which should draw our focus, it is the sand slipping from our hands at every tidal break being dragged back to sea forever out of our drowning reach, it is the rising water itself that we must contend with...

Christ, what a head high. Shit hits fast. Falls away just as quick as well, but Lord Almighty takes you right up to the moon before it lets you go. Brings the world into sharp relief, see through walls type of shit. Feel like I'm all squirrelled away now behind this counter. Running coat check for the event and, where's Aura? Where is, but safe, all safe and squirrelled away. Get to watch as soon everyone will be coming in for the big event and it's like a zoo but one where the animal gets to watch the people because they'll all think I'm like a squirrel in my cage but it's them, it's actually them who'll be catching the gaze, dig? It's actually them who're going to be watched by me whenever they all get here and where's Aura? Has she? Wait, check the phone and Jess's messages still flashing and nothing from Aura but maybe, who knows maybe Derek took her like a troll back to *his* cave or something or maybe she forgot or who knows but maybe, Jesus Christ, this stuff is wild, can almost see the like, the atoms that everything is made of or something, crazy because the whole world is mostly empty space you know? So much less of it than anyone would ever think that kinda makes us all the more solid for seeing it or something like that and that like maybe because there's not really that much world and there's like *so much* of us we can do like amazing things if we wanted to, like all we'd have to do is just like apply thy will. Will to boot and will in overplus. The sea, all water, yes receives rain still. So thou, being rich in will, add to thy will. One will of mine to make thy large will more and full like the moon, just hovering above it all now, Shah-baby. Just putting the tags on the hangers, just number after number after number just floating above it all, just something to do because, Heavens to Betsy, what was in that little roach? What in the name of everything holy is that crazy boy there smoking and, where is Aura? Can't go do what I've got to do, which is now to just float up above everything, be as close as far away can get me and, but where is Aura? She's got to be here or else I'm gonna have to, I'm not going to be able to, can't float away if she isn't here because I can't leave Buck down here all alone to just get swallowed up by the crowd, can't leave him here all alone to maybe drown–

...because we, once again dear reader, are the tide.

We are not only the tide, we are the sea itself. We are the whole of the waters that bring life to the planet. We are the wetted land lapped by kind currents. We are the crumble of a cliff shook finally from its hold by convergent cataclysms. We, dear reader, moreover and again are the cataclysms' very convergence. We are the rub, the atomic friction from which all heat rises. We, in our kinder moments, are the icy absolute still patience of inertia. We are supernovas and fireflies. Mass and void. Gravity and Absolute Lack. Mind and Instinct. Consciousness and Dream. Will and Bondage. Between Man and the Mirror's Image, We are *The Mirror*. The World will only ever be, can only ever be, whatever we scream back at it. So, dear reader, how then are we meant to go on living?

Simply: as gods.

"These depressions springing-up and coalescing suddenly are becoming progressively more common as the waters of the Atlantic warm. Should only need remember this time last year, remember the ceaseless barrage experienced by our neighbors to the south and along the gulf." Screen now showing quick-cut footage of grey waters flowing through city streets, foam where there should be traffic. Gonna make a whole thing of it, aren't they? Make it a whole show, a whole performance as everyone hunkers down and gets all scared and then what? Just a storm, it's always *just* a storm. Only takes what it can get to, you know? So, yeah, feet up and lay back and watch the hens cluck. "Now, the way these storms usually form, and what makes this one we're tracking and others like it so exceptional, is in the confluence of winds off the West African Coast meeting with the warm waters of the Atlantic Gulf Stream. This usually takes these storms toward the Caribbean where, if they are too weak, they break to bits over the islands or, provided they're a tad stronger, gain more mass before making final landfall on the North American continent. Now, this storm is nowhere near as massive as those that become hurricane cyclones, but it is building up quite quickly and is still an hour-and-a-half or so we're predicting away from making contact with Riley Island. That is, of course, provided that it makes landfall at all. It would be a totally different scenario, however, if it takes a turn further out to sea, a scenario, mind you, that could portend of a much larger system a few days from now, so," screen displays the hypothetical super-storm inducing route, where the mass swirls eastward to loop back upon itself, growing and growing and growing. Always tell it like a story. Almost have to root for the storm at a certain point. Take bets on when it'll make landfall, over-under on damages. Even name the big ones they were just talking about. Something perverse there, feels like, something sinister. Name the storm, but the people she drowns are all lumped together under a single growing number. "In the past, Riley has proven itself to be a fair buffer to storm winds, so perhaps we can all rest assured knowing that it's only potential flooding that we've got to worry about. Now, to talk to us briefly about flood preparedness and, maybe, make some predictions as to what we can expect should this current squall make landfall, we have here in the studio," Oh, Lord, this guy. Real schlubby sort on the screen now. Lead engineer of the newest additions to the flood-prevention systems, eldritch network of dams and levees. What's he going to say of any use? His job is on the line if anything goes awry. The corners he's no doubt cut only sharpen the blade of his personal guillotine. What's he going to say? How fine is he going to guarantee everything? How, a braying cry from upstairs and feet down, standing now, taking the staircase two at a time, get there before she does, before she can once again snap the child up before–

Alright, fine, and well enough said no doubt, but where exactly does that leave me, Putsch? Where am I, newly minted as a simple god, supposed to bring creation? See, the problem is, gotta bring this up when, if, no *when*, Carl, make the claim and stick to it. Gotta bring this up when I get in there to speak to him, bring up this usage of the word *We* so much. Problem is, and there's no way he doesn't know this already, hell, it's where they tripped up over each other the most in that interview section, the *We* versus *I* as the *a priori* of consciousness thing, that whole chicken-and-egg fight about how in a vacuum there can't possibly be an individual, that the individual is entirely a product of the collective, which was Putsch's take unless I'm totally misreading him, which is, keep in mind, wholly possible, no doubt there that he'd be easy to misread, but I know what Uncle Reggie's position would have been and noting the tone of disagreement between them it's maybe perhaps easy to build the case that Putsch was or wanted to be making, there's a distinction to be fretted over until the very end of it all, but that the case Putsch made or whatever had to in some way differ from Reggie's more complicated and holistic stance, whether the holistic nature of the stance is on account of wishing to preserve the truth as revealed by previous folly or is the product of some sinister conservatism is another, perhaps, argument to be had, but that Reggie's position in general was always something along the lines of something like individuals make the collective, the collective then creates the conditions under which individuals live, and thus changes in the paradigm can only ever come when an individual transcends the collectively generated order which is much different than what Putsch seems to be presenting as a fact that the individual is a wholly false category, that it is ultimately the product of needing to name the sensation of the feedback of the collective observed from a singular point in that collective and that once this node is removed from the mass, the molecule from the matter, the thing from the general state of affairs, it ceases to collect information and therefore, as its existence is predicated not on its singular corporeality, not on its physical substance as perhaps a stone's or coffee mug's might be, but entirely upon the *sensation* of observing and *being observed by* the collective, it too ceases to exist in any important or notable way, a cog without a machine, organ without body, an open hand out to grab whatever is given to it:

An umbrella. Another umbrella. Lots of umbrellas. Fewer coats than umbrellas. A few coats though. But mostly umbrellas so, well, there are tags on the coat hangers for coats but what am I supposed to do with the umbrellas? Is there a bucket or is there–

"Mister Buchanan? Hello. Mister Buchanan?"

Look up and there she is.

"Look alive, Mister Buchanan."

Out now into the lobby and, holy shit that's more people that I'd, fuck. "Sorry, Miss Shareese. Got a little, uhm–"

"Not a problem, young man," Smile slithering tight across my cheeks. Bite it back. His eyes are *so* red. Watery bursting tomatoes and, haha, mine can't look much better but, haha, no, no, no, don't start giggling now, just–

"What should we do with the–" Hold it out like a fucking sword because, Christ, the word has completely escaped me, hasn't it? Long-ass line here and, holy shit, where's Aura? Why is Miss Shareese the one helping me? What, wait a minute, just, "Hey, can you hold onto this for just one second?" Hand the, uhm, whatever it is, the rain-thingy, back across the counter here and, phone out to see if she–

"Mister Buchanan, can we please pay attention here?"

"What's that?" Eyes up from the phone screen, holy shit that's more people I'd, shit, fuck, "Oh, sorry. Got a little, uhm–"

"No problem, Mister Buchanan. Let's just do the umbrellas like we'd do the coats alright? Just, uhm, take the ticket from a hanger and hook the little, uhm," heavens, what's it called? The little, uhm, oh, no bite back that smile don't you start giggling now, just, "hook the little hook through the hanger and–" no, can't help it, can't help but to fall into...

A fit rises from my gut like a raw instinct, pulling tight my lips and baring my teeth to shine as a giggle fizzling belly laugh brings tears to my eyes. Sing it: "Hook the little hook through the hanger. Hook the little hook through the hanger. Hook the little hook through the hanger." Both of us now, doubling over at the sound of it. A pure joy.

If among a number one is reckoned none, then in the number let me pass untold.

In they come. It's always the same as the same is the same as with these sorts of things. Everyone to the nines, walking with that 'don't touch me' glare, led by their nose, seeming to try to seem to float. All the worse now in this little abomination of an exhibition. All hoitied and toitied they now enter one of those places that there's no way in hell they'd ever catch themselves dead in out in the real world, though, there it is, that's the line he's trying to draw isn't it? Something about how it's all real and constructed, that the real world that we all seem to think is like, I don't know, as it is or something that is real, capital, underlined, italicized is no more real in the real sense of the word the way we normally use it than this candy store here is and that in fact, and it's things like this that make the whole thing art right? It's these sort of *in facts* or *actuallys* that make it art, these insistences toward truth as something absurd, something completely other than our usual everyday and not everyday, our usual banality versus like, the how's it in the pamphlet? Banal versus Cosmic or something like that. But that the in fact here that the artist would like to insist so as to make this whole vulgar display into something so much more than a scale model to the scale of a scale model to the scale of a story no one remembers is that this whole thing in its inedibility is actually more honest than the actual real, capital underlined, italicized candy store down there on the on the Cobbles along the Bay itself because it's not lying about its, ha! Not a one of them can keep composure when she, shit, name? What was her name again? Gotta listen, Roh, can't just, anyway, that mask scares the shit out of everybody it seems like. No one quite knows how to go about it. Usually it's an open floorplan with paintings on the walls maybe some sculpturish things to get just enough in the way. Drinks and gossip and all and they can pretend to know more than what everyone else is pretending to know. But this is like, I mean, don't care much for any of this sort of stuff even when it's supposed to be really the best of whatever it is that it's supposed to be, but gotta commend him for really figuring out what buttons to push. All this crystallized kitsch and all just drown everyone in exactly what it is they've rendered for themselves.

But, Putsch's whole thing isn't, like Reggie'd have it maybe, it isn't so anti-transcendental. Just, just makes the claim that it isn't the individual that transcends the power of the collective, that the individual is maybe the byproduct or something like that of the, I guess, shit what would be the best word? He even uses byproduct in a different way than that so it's not even that exactly. The individual isn't a byproduct the same way that like, shit, I don't know, carbon dioxide emission is a byproduct of burning fossil fuels or whatever other clichéd example, it's more that the individual *isn't* in an ontological sense. Using that world right, Carl? But, maybe then in like a deontological way perhaps the individual is an ought posited by the murky mess of the collective or something. Like that because if there are many there must be one or something but Reggie's whole thing is that like, and the evidence is Shakespeare and Homer and Picasso and sort of whoever else a person could name, or moreover the very fact that there are names to be named, right? Moreover, moreover the very fact that that any individual is capable of naming these other distant individuals, not only naming them but also possibly being able to enumerate their exploits, tell their histories and all basically that Reggie would say that that there is evidence enough that individuals do in fact transcend the collective or whatever. But the counter argument of course arises that, as Putsch put it, 'they only fly so high because *we're* holding up their stilts...'

Shit, shit, shit, can't breathe, can't fucking breathe because: "Hook the little hook through the hanger!" And even *she's* crying now! Doubled over, head on the counter, heaving with hardy laughter and, it's good, it's good to laugh because fuck these people. Fuck all this fucking 'yessir' and 'yes ma'am' and, fuck you, hang up your own umbrella. Hook your own little hook on the hanger! Hook your own little hook on the hanger! Don't look at us like that, like we're some kind of, if only you could see yourselves! Could see how silly all of this is, how absolutely ridiculous it is that you think you have to care about any of this shit. You hate it, you hate the people who make this stuff, you hate people like Putsch and like, ha, ha-ha, like me maybe even one day hopefully. I know you fucking hate us now when we won't hook your little hooks on the hangers and, but here's what y'all don't get, here's what y'all don't understand, here's what y'all don't see:

Dark coming on quick, carried by the wind. Great pall from the east. The west all diabolical gold. Thou blind fool love, what does thou to mine eyes as the watery pain rises full. Fucking phone's dead and goddamn stomach is hollow and full and immaculate and sour and what beauty is, see where it lies? The best. Take the worst to be the beginning. Still mind enough to hope that it'll subside, but there behind my left eye it all falls away and, anchored to the Bay where all men rise, why of eyes falsehood hast thou forged hooks? Oh god, fuck, why? No, no, no. Fuck, alright just get to the bus before, sudden changes in weather, always, always, always, Aura. Seasons change and boom! Struck dumb and blind and whereto the judgement of my heart is tied? Or mine eyes, seeing this silvery pooling now, tongue knotted and swollen and shit, fuck, of course, of course, of fucking course, fair truth so foul a face. My heart and eyes have erred and, and, and, to the false: plague...

They flood. Crashing all against each other here. Not meant for this many people, a model of place not meant for all these folks all this, and then there's at the back the guy with the eyebrows, the old fella and his machine and he's, goddamn it's just uncanny. Rolls my belly just looking at it. Flabby faced and bushy browed, a rubber caricature and, listen,

listen, listen: "See, my daddy, Papa Brown, built this here machine with his bare hands. Can you believe it? With his own two hands. Whole thing hisself with all the machine learning he'd learned in the army. Yessir, and ma'am, come home from the big war and was gonna open himself a candy store. Said seeing what it was he'd saw'd make any man appreciative of the sweeter things in life–" No fucking kidding. Gonna tell it the same then? Gonna go through it all just like they do at the actual shop? Untouched and unaltered, surviving since field trips? Studied the 'colonial period' every year it seemed. End of the eighth day to somewhere around the second time the world fought itself, birthed all the fixins that this place and people still decorate themselves with. Bus down to the Cobbles along the Bay and get a taste of history. Carriage ride along the water. Po' boy lunch. Authentic. Real stuff recreated over upon over. Always starts with the patriarch, the Big Dad, round bellied and good natured, slow of heart but stuck around longer than anybody'd given him hope of. Krauts didn't kill him, so what the hell else was gonna try? Built the machine like he'd just said, own bare hands and all that. Sometimes even invented it himself, out of thin air and good cheer. Brief explanation of the nature of the machine, right? Gotta pull the taffy to get it aerated so that it, that's why it's all fluffy. But it's never actually fluffy, just sticky and sweet and, yeah, yeah, all the different flavors all taste the same basically as well, just nothing but corn sugar and a suggestion. 'But why saltwater when it ain' even,' said through chews by a window-toothed smartass, 'when it ain' even salty tasting? Is there saltwater in it or anything like that or,' and the answer is 'No, not at all! Nothing of the kind!' but that gets the next movement of the tale rolling, the part about the storm. Big Dad. Big War. Big Storm. Bible shit. Sounds like when you boil it down, like the parts the counselors didn't ever read from when they started in on the actual program, the pieces without forgiveness, where God acts like a god. In brief: Big storm comes through, floods everything, whole town, whole street, everything. Courthouse, library, factory. Symphony orchestra paddling out of the concert hall using the cellos and basses and kettledrums as rafts. Old fisherman in the middle of it catches something big, tries reeling it in but just drags his boat over the open water, fights the fish for days before the ebb reveals the hook was snagged on the church spire, water rose that high. Caught Christ with a dime store jig. Anyway: Big Dad. Big War. Big Storm...

Yeah, support him up under the arms there, froggy baby legs straddling the knee and: "Horsey, horsey, rider, rider!" Loves that. Little mouth stretching all grinning. Not a tooth one yet but a smile nonetheless. Comes with a giggle up from his belly, soft-nailed hands on your wrists. Holding on for dear life as the "Horsey, horsey, rider, rider!" shakes him up and down and eyes all glittery with that diamond-edged love for his father. She'll poke her head into the room every now and again, and that's just fine. She can come take him whenever she likes, I've got no problem with it. Take him away to feed him or sing to him in that language I really should have learned by now. Change him or put him back down for bed. Just as much his mother, but I'm not going to be treated like I'm not at least a little bit his father so, "Horsey, horsey, rider, rider!" She can have him, but she can't keep him from me. Smiling. Face all shiny in the television's blue light. Wonder if he can see it in my eyes, see the man come back on to tell us the news that there's definitely now, nothing to do about it, absolutely without a doubt going to be a storm tonight. Last ferry out to and back from Riley, batten down the hatches and all that. Wonder if Anders can see that I know that when they start closing the ferry service that means that I know that it might get really bad. Wonder if the little one knows because you'd never be able to tell he knows anything other than "Horsey, horsey, rider, rider," the way his cheeks are glowing and his smile is showing and a giggle up from his belly, but wonder if he knows, if he can feel the pressure changing in the air, if he can, well, wonder if he knows he'll be safe here, wonder if he knows that he is loved.

I swear it's the truth and I believe though I know it a lie that I am fine. Breathing perfectly right and if I squint this one eye, can even almost read the sign. Bus will be coming either way, so there's no need to, fucking Christ, I'm no longer an untutored youth, unlearned the world's false subtleties, I know how I seem, I know what he wants me to be so, so, he thinks me young! But, I know my days are past the best. I can only credit my false-speaking tongue: On both sides thus is simple truth suppressed. Unjust. Old. Love's best habit is trust. Therefore, I lie to him and he to me and in our faults by lies we flattered be. So:

"Yes, ma'am. I'm very sorry, ma'am... Of course, yes, I don't know what came over us just then but sometimes you've just got to," let it all go and see if the world still holds itself together. Step away and maybe the whole thing'll come down. Almost did, reckon, and that's why she's now got to keep it together. Tells you to just go by the hanger and hook the little hooks through the, see? Even just thinking it makes me almost fucking lose it again. Magic shit there Obbie, absolutely magical stuff, "Y'all have a nice time now. Enjoy the evening... Yessir. Of course, yessir. Just the?... Oh, I see, a scarf as well, okay. We'll go ahead and give you a, uhm, excuse me, Mister Buchanan?'

"Yes ma'am?"

"Would you mind making sure that the scarf here gets its own hanger and number? Separate from the umbrella." Bites her lips in against a grin. Can't hardly make eye contact without falling into it again just, oh, c'mon, who cares just...

"Of course, Miss Shareese. What, uhm," gotta hold it together just long enough to get the rest out, "what was it that, uhm, what did you want me to do with the umbrella, again?"

"Oh, you can just hook the hook through the hanger–" And it all pours out. No use in trying against it. Why would anyone deny themselves a laugh like this? Who cares about these fucking people and their art gala fucking whatever it is? Just, just, oh Christ, here, sing it again:

'They only fly so high because *we're* holding up their stilts,' which the rebuttal would obviously be, though I can't remember exactly what it was that Reggie offered, but the rebuttal seems apparent and easy enough, just 'irregardless of our holding the stilts, *they're* still the one's flying so high.' Of course now, and no doubt this is the tack that Putsch would take, the key thing here now is the presence of the stilts and the illusion of flight. However, a phrase like *illusion of flight* cheapens the achievement. Change the verb, because something is still happening, just as the rebuttal claims the stilts bring them to their heights, so the height remains. Just a difference in mechanism then, raised instead of flying which of course flies directly in the face of what maybe Reggie would claim at all in the first place, this idea of individual transcendence out from the collective. So. The breakdown then of this image here would be something more along the lines of the collective being responsible for generating the material means *by which* an individual within this particular illustration is raised up to begin with. So ultimately the transcendental mechanism isn't the will of an individual, *nor* is it somehow again in a naïvely dialectical fashion the antithesis, some sort of perverse transcendence of the collective by way of the collective's very non-transcendence or whatever, but instead that which is transcendent is the *material* which brings about the raw possibility of an individual flying. The transcendental mechanism is the pair of stilts, is the tool, is the–

Taffy machine. One like it in every store, all of them claiming to be somehow the original and all of them made by hand or at least by special order or something. It's a silly story. The whole thing is silly when you get to eat what's being made, but how much sillier it is now when the machine's arms are pulling, I mean, what is it? Watched him do it now a few times. Takes the glassy slab from the table and slumps it through the arms and, well, I mean the machine does exactly what it, I mean the whole thing is exactly like it is down the Cobbles! Takes the slab and the machine stretches it a whole bunch, color lightening and then he puts it through some sort of rolling and cutting machine and it spits out all those wax paper plugs and, hell, these people here want them! He hands them out at the end of every spiel, one-per-customer style, while she, Christ what was her, what was her name again? Goddamn Roh, boozing's got your brain sieving. But she, same greeting every time, just like when you and Shah and the Director walked in, everyone gets the exact same sort of, but still none of it is, can't eat any of it, but they, every one of them wants it. Wonder if they know something about it. Like maybe it'll be worth money, like 'I have one of the blue raspberry taffies from Dermot Putsch's Madstone' or something. Wonder if their world is just that simple, if that's what it all comes down to. Because, goddamn, if it is then, if I'm understanding this correctly, they're missing the point entirely.

Wonder if he knows that he's safe here. Knows that even maybe if things might one day be cold, if Mommy and Daddy work too much and are never really around, knows that even if that ends up being how things are that he'll be safe here. That we brought him here, brought him into this world, this big, mean, unsafe, like-to-storm-at-any-moment world, that we brought him into this world sure but that we brought him into it *here*, far away from any place that might not be safe. Wonder if he knows that or if he'll ever be able to know that because I know one day, I can almost guarantee it with the way things are bound to keep going, that he'll grow to hate this place and hate us for making him in it but I wonder if he knows that when the anchor says "Beyond a certainty at this point that the storm will make landfall" or "City officials have expressed their doubts as to how well the flood management systems will respond to what looks to be quite a sudden downpour," that when those words get said they don't apply to him, that those fears aren't something he has to be afraid of because the water will never rise high enough to wet his little feet. "Horsey, horsey, rider, rider." Wonder if he knows that, wonder if he's smiling because he knows that he'll never, so long as I'm his Daddy and his Mommy is his Mommy, that he'll never have to, never need to, that he'll never need to know that the World is what everyone ends up *making*, not themselves. That's the whole thing, I guess that's what Putsch is really getting down to getting at then, right? That's where he and Uncle Reggie couldn't quite get to where they could see eye to eye maybe is that what ultimately transcends the collective of individuals isn't the individual that steps outside of the collective, but instead the world that the collective ultimately comes together to make and that, and here's the sort of maybe like if I'm using the world correctly again it's hard to tell sometimes, but here's the real sort of blind like deontological thing that happens, in the sense that it's our oughts that render the is's we've got to know to deal with, but that eventually that world, and here's maybe where Putsch's distinction is really driven home in his whole World as Byproduct thing in the sense that the byproduct is more wholly unconscious right? That the byproduct just is always going to happen, right? That like the whole capital double-you World We're making transcends Us only because maybe We don't realize or haven't yet completely concluded that We're the ones that were making it the whole time and now the problem really is that maybe its transcendence is Our extinction, right? Like how We killed God, or in Putsch's smaller pantheon, continuously slaughter the gods, so too will our World which we've made, perhaps even unknowingly populated with minds as frustrated as Our own, the obscure souls of plastic army men, come in the end to murder Us...

So, since I am near slain, kill me outright with a look and rid my pain. Head on the window's glass and feel the road on one side and the bottomless pit of agony pounding language into soup on the other. Be wise as thou art cruel, my tongue-tied patience. Testy sick men when their deaths be near, no news but health. God. The sick is one thing, the confusion is maybe probably definitely another and it's the, it's the worst part of it for it I should despair, I should grow mad, and in my madness might speak ill. I do not love thee with mine eyes. My heart loves what thy despise. Nor are mine ears with my tongue's tied tongue-tied tune delighted, nor tender feeling to base touches prone because everything is slime and sandpaper and nor are taste or nor is smell desired to be invited or any other sensual feast, five wits nor my five senses, everything makes me want to fucking barf and goddammit I hope this is the right bus just keep one eye open and thy dear virtue hate, hate of my sin grounded on sinful loving, false bonds of a love as oft as mine–

"Mister, uhm, I'm sorry what was it again?"

"Rohaan," Goddamn blends in rather well with these folks doesn't he? Didn't even see him coming, just materialized from the crowd all big and barreling. "What can I do for you, sir?" Look over his shoulders, around his girth, play the vigilant employee.

"Uhm, do you know where Miss, gosh, you know I need to be around more, can't for the life of me remember anybody's names or–"

"Don't worry about it. Got a lot on your plate I imagine." More and more people now. They flood and flock for this shit, they really do. That's what it all comes down to, ultimately, gotta be, just getting enough of these fucking people in a room long enough for money to start changing hands or something.

"Hmmm, you'd think so, but, don't know, all this seems like it can take care of itself–"

"We're all just babysitters down here, sir."

"Ha, I'm sure." Turns away from me to look over the gathered heads.

"Looking for Miss Shareese, then?"

Back down: "Yes, I am. Do you know where she might be?"

"Oh, could be anywhere, reckon. She's definitely not one to keep her hands out of other people's business, so wouldn't be surprised if she's off–"

"Dammit." Director raises a fist to bite his thumb.

"What's that, sir?"

"Putsch is here, snuck in half an hour ago, and, well, has made it very clear that he's uninterested in talking to me. Do all this work for these artist types and, Christ, have your tie too straight and they think you're some kind of, I don't know, but I've not got the patience for it." Can see in his eyes, the shiftiness, that he believes something about the future is dependent on Putsch's approval of the evening. "Hoping maybe he'd take more kindly to Miss Whatever-Her-Name-Is."

"Oh, well, good luck there, sir. Good luck pulling her away from whoever she's convinced herself needs helping…"

"Do, do you mind, Miss Shareese, if I pop out for a smoke real quick?" Line has dwindled enough, mostly everyone is inside the gallery or perusing the grounds in general. Can hear it all on the other side of the foyer. Din of decadence and all that.

"Not a problem, sweetheart. Take your time. Give that girl Aura a call if you don't mind as well, see if she's–"

"No problem, will do." And outside to where, Christ, sudden quiet. Still. Dark. Early yet for it to be this dark though, isn't it? Look out to the West and yes, there along the trees or what I can see of the horizon is that sliver, a hard band of fiery gold light and up now those clouds are low and swingingly pregnant. Wonder if, check the phone and still nothing but those few texts from Jess, no word yet from Aura but known her long enough to know that maybe she's laid up in bed already perhaps taken full to her keening darkness, seems enough like the sort of weather than would give her a migraine so perhaps it's getting ready to really rain, getting ready to all come finally down and break the fever that's been hovering over everything the past few who-knows-how-longs, and who knows what something like that will take with it, who knows what will be left when everything changes, because it's becoming increasingly obvious to me with all this that they couldn't just fix the Ballroom, right? Couldn't just add back to it what they'd taken away from it to make it more palatable for everyone, had to take its soul away because its soul was the ugly part and maybe there, maybe that's the fear, maybe that's the terror of being forced so far away from everyone is that up here, floating up above everything, drunk off myself and hands up all surrendering, maybe way up here I might really have to see for the first time that it's the souls of everyone that make it all so ugly, that because you know up close everyone's soul shines so bright and hot and full of real honest life but maybe once you're this far away, once they make you have to be this far away maybe then I'll see what I'm already starting to see that everyone's soul is so exactly the same and brightness and heat and all of that only matters when it's different when it's special when it's something to be protected but it turns out, godblessit, that everyone's soul is just exactly the same as the same is the same as everybody else's but there's still so much darkness between everybody because the World we've made, the World rendered forth by the collective is what is actually doing the transcending, it's what actually ends up stepping outside of all of Us and making for itself, no, no, no, not for itself necessarily, no need to grant it with some sort of sentience that it has no interest in claiming, for all We know sentience itself could be one of the factors of our failure to maintain ourselves in the face all that it was we transcended ourselves, and that's maybe where it comes all apart is the fact that it's all stuck together that we can't transcend ourselves because We are Our Selves or something like that but never can we forget that we've made something bigger or maybe it's the realization that we're making something bigger than will eventually allow us to be something bigger because the whole thing Putsch has his whole thing hinged upon is that there's nothing bigger than us, but that's not it exactly either and maybe it's too much to ask for the sort of consistency I'm trying to ask for from someone as blatantly uninterested in being consistent, much less perhaps even clear in any way, as Putsch is very interested in being safe. Safe and smiling and even if you stop smiling, Anders, even if you do get just as unhappy as life makes everybody, "Horsey, horsey, rider, rider," even if when the world outside of yourself starts to end like we all know it must, even then you'll still be safe. I hope you know that now and come to continue to know that into however long the future is going to be. All will be fire and water and the air will be poison, but you, Anders, will be safe among the misery. That's all that I can promise you because I don't have any other powers other than keeping you as, yes smile all toothless because I'm going to try my hardest, my son, I'm going to try my absolute hardest to make sure you never need to use your teeth even when they come in. I can't promise you anything other than safety because well the world disappears if we get too close to each other, spend all my time in life making sure that everyone is taken full care of and the world around us is so small, only made up of everyone else and but then, hell, start thinking about everyone else all of a sudden the world gets so big, so endless in catastrophe and then reach back out to bring everyone back to my breast and, and, and as a careful housewife runs to catch one of her feathered creatures broken away, a neglected child held in chase, crying to catch whose busy arm is bent. No prize in the poor thing's discontent. It all runs away, flies away from thee! Catch thy hope, play *thy own mother's* part! Kiss and be kind, have a will even if you turn back to crying and still–

"What was it Shakespeare said of situations like this?"

"Oh, sir I haven't the faintest idea," just started talking to the man and he's already acting the artist. Director said to just stand and listen and pretend that I had something to do with how successful this all seems, so that's what I'll do. Just stand and listen and pretend and maybe he can again tell me what the hell that little lady with the bangs's name was. "I've never been one for Shakespeare."

"Ah, that's a shame." Putsch crosses his arm and looks through the crowd. "But you know, to be honest Mister Rohaan, I can't remember what it was the son of a bitch said about situations like this either."

"Ha, that so?"

"Certainly, only know that he most certainly definitely absolutely had *something* to say about situations like this. That's what reading him is for and, also, that's what the principal critique anybody could level against him is. That, I mean, that he had *something* to say about everything, and by proxy or whatever therefore had nothing really at all to say at all–"

"That so?"

"There's certainly an argument to be had, but one in that direction has been made. Don't know how much stock you could put in it either way. Some want to point pretty strictly to the multiplicity of it all and call that truth, right? Sort of say something like insist that it *all* is in the same way that *everything* is, which is fine enough, but to claim that someone like Shakespeare, or anyone for that matter, was capable of saying all of it enough to capture everything that is is, well, simple perhaps. Too much credit to give to a single person, but. But you can't deny the ease of pulling quotes, right? So much of what Shakespeare wrote applies to so much of what life is for us. This is I think relatively uncontroversial, correct? But to say that all of Shakespeare is all of life is foolish. Perhaps. Think maybe the formulation might be more along the lines of something like—" Back from commercial now and, there's the channel name and brassy fanfare and anchors giving their welcome again just like they do every fifteen minutes, and from the welcome into a slideshow. Black-and-white image of a beach that must be Riley. Above the water line those beach houses on stilts. Then more photographs. The beach wrecked and strewn with wood. Toppled trees in the sand. Houses collapsed as so many spilled matchboxes. An anchor, the weatherman, gives voiceover: "It was the late seventies the last time Riley Island was populated by anything other than the research outpost and swimmers looking to catch some waves. A time when the spark set by the developments in Cortland County to the north tried its best to catch the kindling of the old city and county seat of Madiston. The debate between developers and those interested in the preservation of the city's unique history was a heated one and much to the credit of the Municipality, it was the history that won out..." Color image now of the Belchard Mansion up on its little hill. Another again of, is that? Holy shit, wow, the Ballroom Gallery at the Museum, lit up bronze and golden and marble and, "Of course compromises were made. Swathes of the until-then pristine Riley Island were summarily divvied up between several real estate developers and, much to the chagrin of the wildlife, including the now endangered loggerhead sea-turtle, the live oak forests of the island's bayside were leveled, jetties jutted out into the surf and, seemingly overnight, the Eden of Riley Island was rendered severally into resort villas. That was, of course, until Rosalie in the summer of '78. Rosalie leveled what the developers hadn't and crumbled what they had raised. The property damage and mounting deficit was such that development projects no longer continued on the island and, within the next decade, each sold their claim back to the state at a loss. Something poetic there perhaps, destroy the natural environment and the natural environments comes right back at us, reminds one maybe perhaps of *The Tempest*, that perfectly planned squall of revenge conjured from Prospero's magical art. That's what he calls it as well, which I don't think we can ignore. That he calls it his art and Shakespeare is, mind this is the *last* play, so there's a whole lot more to say about it in regards simply to it being a late work, a deathbed piece or whathaveyou, but that he calls it his art is maybe perhaps important, though maybe not the hermeneutical line that we ought to take. All this though does bring that play to my mind. I feel that any moment now some harpy with withered wings, gnashing ragged teeth, is bound to swoop down upon us and start in with Ariel's terrifying and fierce monologue in Act 3, that all of a sudden this installation and all these people will disappear and a hateful voice will shout at us from the void: 'You two are men of sin! The never-surfeited sea hath belched you up onto this island, where men do not inhabit for you among men are unfit to live' and we'll find out that all of this has perhaps been orchestrated as a further illusion as punishment for sins unwillfully committed. You ever get that feeling, Mister Rohaan? Ever feel like–" A demanding hand, gloved in something expensive, little numbered ticket in its palm. Barely making eye contact she's so far away from me. But, ah-ha! That's what she doesn't know! That I'm just as far away from her as she is from me and that I have just as much cause and reason to stay as far away from her as I can as she has to keep away from me so, ah-ha, ah-ha, so neither the one of us can see the other's shining soul and now it's all the darkness that's gotten so close that there may as well not even be any light at all because the Nothing is bigger than Us, that Fundamentally there is only less than Us, that We are the only thing keeping the void at bay and everything we've ever made fails in the face of the very void's immutability! It is fundamentally the thing that is less than we are but, just as a hole in the ground can perhaps be said to be less than the earth it's dug in, is less enough that any one of Us could fall into it and once you're there, right, once you've fallen in and given up your godhood or lost faith perhaps in Our godhood then you're gone to that which is lesser, that which isn't at all, so maybe it's more that no individual can transcend the collective because the collective is itself the category which is transcendent from the individual, that maybe that man as monad is the basal bottom of humanity and that once We are together as a collective we make a world together or fall apart from each other singly or maybe I ought to just ask Putsch what the hell he means by any of this because maybe I could spend the next eternity and a half trying to figure it all out only to find out that maybe he doesn't even know or remember or care even at all that much about some stuff that he'd written so long ago or about a man he talked to thirty or forty something some odd years ago and maybe his mind is somewhere else maybe he's looking at other stuff maybe he's found the better angel of your eye. A man right fair stood out there in the night looking up on the worser spirit of a woman, an angel in another's hell. Those lips made by love's own hand. Straight in your heart comes mercy's chiding tongue, ever sweet giving gentle doom. Not you and save my life, my poor soul, the center of sinful earth, pin within a suffering death. Shall. Shall. Shall, shall. Shall worms inherit my excess? Eat up thy charge? Is this, is this this body's end? Feed on death that feeds on men and death once dead, there's no more dying then—

Hook the little hook on the hanger and there it all rises up again as she hands me the ticket because I'm not going to apologize any longer now for being completely free in myself because I won't let myself be blinded by the light of you someone new and different and wholly not myself shining out the world I don't really even know if there is a world at all for you to even start shining out through and that's the whole of the thing maybe now as the laughter crawls angry up my throat that the only world really is the one that's now laughing in me because you need the hook unhooked from the little hanger and so you need me so that I am now the world and whole of it for you are nothing now but a moon a moon only shining the light of the star the greater star shinning behind me the greater star illuminating me because I am of course the whole of the World comes into being by our hands, fine, as Byproduct, I'll offer no rebuttal. But, Christ Almighty Goddamn, what are we supposed to do then? How then, Mister Putsch, are We meant to go on living? As what? As what? Simply as gods? Was that where We came to rest, at the place that this is all some kind of circle then? Snake eating its own tale? Are We all really just that sort of cliché? Simply. As gods? I mean give me a break because isn't it that you said that all gods are already only ever born dying? So is that what We're meant to, is that then how We're meant to go on living is simply to just go on dying in the face of a world that's transcended Us? Is that it? Give Ourselves over then? That the real story of Christ? God finally giving Himself over to His creation? Hanging Himself up on the cross, not so much dying for Us then as giving into the torture towards murder that We'd been for Our entire existence putting Him through. We transcended the son of a bitch so now He's got no choice but to die around Us? Maybe He didn't answer Our prayers because, maybe He knocked the tower of Babel all down then because He couldn't understand a word We were saying! Maybe We were so much silence to the Almighty until finally the loneliness set in heavy enough for Him to hang Himself on the cross and just be all the more done with Us! Certainly is a Monday, ain't it then? Like just made to wash away Sunday. After every Sabbath, a new beginning. The Lord doth find himself yet again hovering over the face of the waters, a week's work washed away! Every night a flood and so on and so the God of Abraham is made a Sisyphus, His world an ouroboros, and He commits again and again the very mortal sin of Onan and on and on! Must rest every seven days! Pulled His pud raw and tunneled His carpals! And so the foam of the rising waters is seen now to crash against the modest seawall down there at and along the Cobbles. Can't see Riley for all of nothing at all, just the dark, held up as inky satin by the streetlights and in the wind they're swaying like to be or like trying to be pulled from their concrete hold as the storm comes now finally replaces with its best the failure of the land and, "Now we're clocking the windspeed at somewhere around," blusters across the man-on-the-ground's microphone obscuring the words that would have faltered to tell the truth, "and now as you can see we're just now getting the," beginning of the whole reality of the affair, the first fullness of the brunting deluge. It's the part that looks the scariest most assuredly, it's all the wind and rain and hell of a lot of wouldn't have thought that there'd be this much lightning just tearing at the night, tearing even the darkness to shreds, a thunderous argument that no one seeing it could possibly soon forget, the very difference between the two poles here, light and dark, fire and water or whatever, being and sudden deafening nonexistence blurred or perhaps better exposed as in no way opposite at all but all part of one unending cataclysm that nothing survives this is what the general thought is when the little monkey inside starts, "horsey, horsey, rider, rider," kicking up through the brain's salt and mush, easily frothed into panicking foam by something so common as the sight of a storm, every one bigger than the last and therefore heralding the inevitable encroachment of the one that will be so completely the very last to ever be anything at all the water comes down like the end the whole end the very final final until another crack of light and rumble of thunder as existence reasserts itself on the nothing but it's all so fleeting for even now, look, look, look now the water flows thick enough over the cobblestones as to no longer on its surface show the variegated variations beneath, it's covered it all and kicked open the doors of the Runaway and the everything else so desperately authentic, looks as though it will or has already also taken for its claim the graveyard's grassy peninsula, looks to have committed itself full to swallowing everything it can get within the reach of its waters and "It just didn't seem to me like there was anything at all else to make. Couldn't do better than this. Not that all this is a copy per-se of what's down there so pristine and plucked from history, that charming little part of town, what's it called the Historic District or something like that. Love that, amazing to have the gall to call it that. It's just as much of a preservation of history as all this around us now is a copy of it. Does that make sense? Because the substance has been removed from all this, it's just the forms now. But hopefully not for the purpose of being a referent, it's not simulacrum, but something totally new and eternal in its substancelessness, does that make sense? It will be forever because it's, well not to harp once again on *The Tempest* but there's another similarity between that and this that might be worth extracting and bringing into examination, right? So *The Tempest* is notoriously without plot, and therefore often criticized by those who seem to think it needs it, but often criticized along those lines. The response of course being that what it lacks in plot it makes up for in character, but even there I'll have to diverge. It's this supposed need for substance, that the meaning and depth is derived from the, I guess to be as lay as possible, the nutritional value of the food for instance, right? The thing, the essence moreover, contained in the form is the whole magic of it all, right? Well, bullshit I say. I say it's the form itself. It's not the candy, it's the store. The simple fact of the matter is–" Desire is death and past cure I am. Frantic made with evermore unrest and the rain all comes down, comes down like a madman's discourse: black as hell, darker than night. False eyes dote. The sun itself sees not till heaven clears. Shines bright and cruel and can't say I love thee not. All-tyrant, for thy sake, Love, hate on: For now I know thy mind. Those that can see thou lovest, and I am blind. Who taught thee how to make me love thee more? The more I hear and see: The more there is only storm and water and wind and darkness and sudden light and Christ and water and where has everything gone and foam and the whole of sea seems to have risen and sound the alarm and or perhaps it's already too late and it takes trees down with it and whole houses are going to sink and somebody is going to and more than somebody and a whole goddamned lot of people and people are here and now and there and then the water will rise and the water is rising and right now and the sky has fallen and the water has risen and

I do betray my nobler part to my gross body's treason and all my honest faith in thee is loose oaths of thy love thy truth thy constancy all a truth so foul and honestly that's why I had call it Madstone you see and I'm struck more than anything that no one here has thought yet to ask that suppose it's rather gauche perhaps for these people to ask something like that to beg something of clarity from an artist they've all come here to make ovations toward admiring or judging or criticizing or something like that but I had to call it Madstone because well because a Madstone is nothing but the raw and pure the indigestible leftovers of substance once the substance has been drawn out and away from it and moreover that a Madstone is supposed to be a cure for rabies an alchemical cure for the fear of water it has magical curative properties regardless of the fact or perhaps on account of the fact for the very reason of it being made of nothing useful but a whole bunch of nothing useful that it at the end of the day there rolling around all those years in a deer's belly is nothing but nothing and it cures madness because maybe it cures madness because it's nothing but pure and true and raw and powerful nothing so it can borrow from this holy fire a dateless lively heat still to endure the strange malady a sovereign cure for the little god is asleep and we are all alone now as my pen will move with only the storm in mind for its coming is all the larger or feels all the larger than these I've penned in its prior though not perhaps for the rains it brings nor the winds nor the dark not for the light or land that leaves not for the islands it sinks nor even for the lives it ends which honestly I am aware is inhumane but should I here labor over lungs filling with saltwater or bodies being crushed in their homes or the towers up over by Harris Park being toppled in the flow as Salt Creek's bursts and burbles and hell I can only hope the reader would take perhaps the conjured sight of the Belchard Mansion finally falling to ruin upon its hill as something beautiful not only perhaps as overwrought and poetic and I've even mulled over the possibility of presenting the image of as Harris Park floods that what would float in those waters wouldn't so much be bodies of the junkies I've had sort of in the background of this text but instead so many of the tattered and soaked volumes of our Carl's strange library all those half-read books floating away in the floodwater's foam but that all seems so spectacular in its attempt to strike you reading right now and though perhaps not dishonest at the very least not honest in the way that I'd like to be because to me it seems that this storm is all the larger or feels all the larger than what I've penned in its prior not for what it destroys but for what remains in the unkindness of its waking day the days after already where the sky hangs low and still pours a drizzle a drizzle a drizzle until even days after the wind carries a cleaner edge glinting with what might be now that I'm thinking about it a truer tragedy yet because trust me now I've labored and dreamt written and rewritten the shape of this storm and it all always comes out the same grey mess a dull cloud of death so perhaps since I have thus far so liberally rent the Bard from his context for the superiority of his language or perhaps even just for the gesture of his superiority or something sometimes I can't make heads or tails of it but so it is that it was rent from its context perhaps in the case of this storm that must swallow the story here I ought to do the same to old King James what I've done with Shakespeare and simply say that the waters increased the waters prevailed and increased greatly the waters prevailed exceedingly that flesh died that moved upon the earth both of fowl of cattle of beast of every creeping thing and in men whose nostrils was the breath of life of all that was on the dry land died living substance was destroyed which was upon the face of the ground both man and cattle and creeping things the fowl of heaven they were destroyed from the earth and the waters prevailed upon the earth and then as the winds pass over soon to assuage the waters the fountains of the deep the windows of heaven and rain from heaven and the waters begin to abate and that while we wait upon the mountains of Ararat as the waters decrease perhaps you could find the occasion ripe to listen to the opening bars of Schumann's Symphony No. II in C Major only the first minute minute-and-a-half two minutes or so with the soup and slow fanfare breaking in the brass just up until the allegro...

II.

–Doesn't seem possible for there to be anything fundamentally less than this, does there?–

Waking again to the sounds of everyone around him already awake. Family in the little clutter of cots nearest breaking into their sack lunch breakfasts. Smell of bodies and cheesy feet. Everyone got a pair of flipflops for the showers so that scales don't spread–Week and a half now, fewer and fewer but still so many of us. No solid word of anything–

Sound of pattering rain on the roof. Hear it on the windows, too– Better than it clobbering all dreadful on the metal or aluminum or tin or whatever it was roofing the garages. So many then at the start when they were still cruising city streets on hovercrafts and john boats and air boats with the fans, searching for whoever'd managed to swim through it all long enough to be found. Busses brought them in as well. We were all piled into the Depot garages and, sleeping bags, smell of motor oil and– Just the terminal now. All the benches have been removed and it's like one big hospital ward. People stranded trying to stay dry. Wrapped up in thin sheets or ratty crochet blankets dredged from some church's charitable basement. The Depot's concourse outside is set up like a mobile military base: trailers and tents, medical unit and mess.

Lights from above, those fluorescent tubes that give everyone headaches, make it all look frigid and sterile, but in reality it's hotter than hell, every surface is a petri dish in steady bloom. Air can't really move with all these people. Lines for the showers outside are forever long, and no one is adequately bathed.

Carl's shadow is left in sweat on the sheets as he sits up to wipe his eyes. The number of folks are dwindling day by day, all those simply blindsided by the storm having made their arrangements elsewhere and off the state's stale dime. Left behind now seems to be mostly Jasper folks, section eight. Recognizes a lot of them. A lot of them recognize each other –Such a leveling force, such monstrous implacability can't even bring us around to humble ourselves. Certainly we're less than at the least the storm was, right? Whole world wiped away and we still can't look each other in the eye long enough to–News'd come once the garages were emptied and they'd managed to fit everyone left in the purportedly air-conditioned terminal that those who were reliant on state housing may need to reach out to family and friends to secure future arrangements–Word was the Jaspers actually came down. Salt Creek had, heard anyway, heard Salt Creek had spilled up enough to rush a river's worth right down Jefferson and Murphy. Harris a lake now, Jaspers brought down in the surge, legs swept out from under them and see? Can't even make enough of something other than ourselves to weather the storm, to hold out in our absence, so, so, obviously something's bigger than us if it can so easily mount and plow down–

No one seems to know either way. All the stories are about the same. Repetitions of the repetitions they all watch through their peripherals on the news every night: Televisions hung just out of channel-changing reach along the terminal walls, utilized previously to display the timetable of the bus schedule, now play the local and national news stations. Muted and subtitled, the same images flash day after day, especially from the local outlets. Crowds with their hands up in the rain toward a gustily hovering helicopter. A rope everyone is afraid to climb. Massive walls of water rising and falling and crashing over land that very well may no longer be. Doppler map of the storm in comparison to dopplers of the last year and the year before and the year before that...

–Very well could have come down though, no doubt there. Not even an outside possibility. Happens often enough people are shown the crumble of their ruined arrogance, so wouldn't be a surprise in the slightest. Older than most of the city's other apartment complexes and never once praised for its upkeep. Lucky it didn't fall before the choppers could show up and pluck everyone from the roof. Water's rough enough. On the boat, all huddled and vomiting. Putsch looking around in the wet darkness, terror in his eyes the, well, all of us, one by one, down the main entrance's stairs until the steps disappeared beneath the slurried brack. Rescue craft there at the edge, rocking up and down, moored to the emboldened neck of one of the eagle statues, drowning flightless sentinel. Man in rubber waders and gloves, walkie-talkie screaming from his hip, leaning off the edge of the boat with his hand out and helping each on while the freshly risen sea crashed, flows already cruddy with crushed city. All of us huddled then. Tarp thrown over us, sound of the storm in harsh relief and rage. Nervous vomit pooling along the boat's bottom boards–

"G-Good morning, Mister–"

Eyes brighten at the sight of a child standing at the foot of his cot. A little girl, pulling behind her a wagon full of– "Well, hello there, sweetheart. To what do I owe the pleasure?" A regular occurrence: Churches and non-profits, student groups from further inland, charitable foundations and all have been sending their acolytes to tend to the wretched stranded by the storm. From adults it comes down as condescension, but when it's children Carl's heart always sets itself melty. They come with sashes across their chests, glittering plastic-and-rhinestone badges and, he scooches to the end of the bed and looks her in the eye. "What can I do for you today, little miss?"

Looks up at the woman trailing behind her. Chaperone, organizer, youth group leader, pastor's wife: "Go on, Virginia, tell him–"

"Oh, Virginia is a lovely name, now isn't it? Here, now what have you got here in this–?" Wagon piled haphazard with books of bargain-shelf condition. Frayed fabric on the clothbounds, creases beyond repair on the paperbacks, covers missing and no doubt whole chapters dog-eared to the end inside. "Fantastic, Miss Virginia, have you, have you brought us all some books to read?"

Little girl nods. Pulls the wagon up closer to the cot's edge.

"Well, sugar, count the stars because it must be my lucky day. You see, I seem–" Pats around for pockets even though all he's got on is a t-shirt and shorts from the clothing drive "–I seem to have misplaced all of mine. Used to, used to keep a whole library with me wherever I went, but –" Scrunched up face in a searching leer "–but, I just don't know what has happened to them all."

Virginia laughs.

"Say, sweetheart, what's your favorite book? Maybe you can help me build my library back. Here," picks one from the pile "what do you think of this one?"

Blushes and shakes her head.

"No? Well," grabs another, "what about this one then?"

Blushes and shakes her head. Smiles. Antsy little feet.

"Not this one either, huh?" A quizzical furl, "Well, Virginia, which one do you think I should read? Which one is your favorite? You know, you can tell a whole lot about a person by their favorite book–"

&&&

Until. Go on. And hands around, submerge her wrists in the water, hold them tight and cold until they disappear into the slosh that's got them both. Another: *Until. Go on.* From her lips bluing to green and a smile like she shouldn't. Water climbs her cheeks, rippling out away from her forehead. Dress wet and clinging, a finer lizarding skin. Opal, ivory hair like sea grass and fall again to where a kiss ought to catch. Nothing. Salty. Salty nothing, just enough to maybe drown in. Up again and she's still there, held down in the shallows, writhing against a body that refuses now to feel what it sees. She whispers fishy, the only warmth, *Until. Un-Until. Go on.* And grins as every thrust between her icy legs, void opened by the risen tide of her lifted skirt, falls completely dark. Misses and collides with nothing. Every thrust a failure witnessed by those gathered above this circle of soaked shoes. *Go on. Go on. Until. Go on.* A pair for each of them, laces and soles caught in the rise. Froth of waves climbing up their pant legs, up their stockings, water wetting all the candy and that great gaudy chandelier hanging, swaying in the storm, threatening at any moment to come down and, *Until*, crush this gathering, flatten and mush them all together into a putsching putty of bucking muck, sink her back to tearing salt to sop the taffy for sale. *Go on.*

"Untle Rohaan."

Jerks awake with an apneated gasp. "What the–?" Little monkey Naseer there at the edge of the bed. "Na-nah, what time? What time is, Na-nah, what do you want" Reaches to lift the pj'd child onto the mattress. Lays back, dream still sandy in the crevices of his brain.

"Untle Rohaan."

"Yes, Na-nah. What is it?" Hand over his eyes and a grimace at the shame–Same shape for the past few days, recurrent every night. Still can't quite get it all sorted–"What do you want?"

On all fours, crawling over and onto the empty side of the bed, mussing up all the sheets on his way.

"Na-nah," grabs him by the trailing left footie, "Na-nah, what do you want? Why did you wake me up?"–Almost made it that time through, almost got all the way to the part where the water rises and everyone drowns around the two of you. Get woke up at the moment you can't fuck, the moment when the water first starts to come up. Everyone watching the struggle. Never get to finish–

"Is it," whispering, "is it time to, is it breakfast yet?"

"I don't know, Nah." Grabs the alarm clock from the nightstand, "Tell me what it says." Plops it clattery down on the pillow.

Naseer rolls it around in his chubby fingers, clicks buttons which appear to do very little. Exhales a little confused breath before–They come in, the two of them, dripping and she's shivering. Carl bearing some big book pouring water from its pages. Can see all of her through the way the dress is clinging. Where her bra isn't, where her belly button ohs the whole of its little moan. Panty line along the front, rise of her *Until. Go on.–*

"What? What, Nah, what?" Eyes open again, the child this time right at his ear.

"Untle Rohaan, is it breakfast time?"

"I don't know, Nah. Go ask your Dad?" They're all in the same room, whole family sharing a double. Jawad and Angela cuddled up safe in one bed, Rohaan the other, and Naseer *should be* in the rollout cot at the foot of his parents' bed. Taken a recent liking to his Uncle though. Father figure without all the authority–Like him too, but not while she's just walking in again, this time so obviously ready and willing and intending to do what she couldn't have done in catastrophic reality. Recognize the recognition, catch the falling shame before it can completely collapse, and take you into her arms as the waters rise so that, coupled and complete, you may explode while everyone else sinks–

"I did. Daddy said to ask your Untle."

"Tell me what the clock says, Na-nah."

"I–"

"Do you know the numbers?"–Read the signs, couldn't see on my face that she'd just walked into what I'd been waiting for. Know every inch of her already, she'd be falling into the most open of arms possible if she'd just read what the mute face was so obviously saying–

"Yeah, I know them."

"Well, what are they?"

"I don't know."

"Read them out. What's the first one?"–Wouldn't need to cry anymore if she could read it. No more cords in her neck or hands across her face. Just soft touches and kind words and, would love her like she'd never been seen to be loved–

"One."

"Yeah, what's the first number there?"

"One. One."

"Okay, the second one. What's next?"–Could have drowned together and left all this ending world nonsense Putsch was ranting about. Fallen into each other's arms and just let the water take what it wanted. Wouldn't even need to swim, just give in–

"An, a zero. One and zero."

"What's that make then, Nah?"

A smile. "Ten!"

"Very good. What's the next bit?"–Wouldn't have had to have been rescued and she wouldn't, Lord, wouldn't have had to have fallen into that kid Buck's noodly arms, could have had, but, could have finally just had it all and–

"Two dots."

"No, not a, not a number. Other side of the two dots. What is it?"–Wouldn't have had to have waited for help, for Jawad, for a conversation about what next , where to go, how much money is left from the check and all that. Wouldn't have had to have done anything because then, because then it would have just been a fuck until eternity cuts everything back to black the way it was before–

"A two and a circle, but there is a line in it–"

"A what is? Here let me see."–Two and an eight so– "That's a two and an eight, Na-nah. Twenty-eight."

"No, cuz, no cuz eight is a snow man and that's a–"

Hand it back. "Wake me up, Nah, wake me up when the two and the eight turn into a four and five and then we'll get breakfast, okay?"

"Okay, Untle Rohaan."

"Alright then."–So maybe this time now, maybe this time now when she comes in you'll just leap because you know, because you know what not leaping gets you. Or maybe this time, maybe this time–

"Untle Rohaan?"

"What, Nah, what?"

"Can I have waffles when we have breakfast?"

"Ask your Dad. Now, shhh..."–She'll see it so obviously on your face. That you know her. That she could have anything she wanted, that you could make her safe, that you could die together because, maybe she'll see it on your face that you're all already, already dead and that that's all you're all gonna be soon enough, that the water's rising and it won't stop just because, that eternity is already always here, it's in the dark, that the water's rising and it won't stop just because–

&&&

"Hey, hey," thumb-and-index pinch at his flagging t-shirt hem, "grab me one of those little packets of Tylenol or something."

Slides back into the driver's seat, worry wracking about beneath his cheeks. Terror's glare brought all the more to the fore by the sunglass tan lines creamy about his eyes. "Are you, uhm, are you having one?"

"No, no, hon." Squints and shades her eyes as she shakes her head. Morning sun already white hot behind him. East always chasing. "Just still feeling it from last night is all."

Derek shuts the door, slides the keys in the ignition, and cuts the engine back to life. Radio comes blasting and the A/C starts its icy whine. Her hand follows the sound and pounds the console's power button down. "You sure it's just a hangover?" Brushes hair out of her face and palms her forehead.

She smiles and lets it ride—Fever inn't a symptom, but he's gonna be sweet so may as well—"Yeah, hon. I'm sure. Can't keep drinking that sugary gas station shit. Gets me every time."

"Alright, alright," adjusting the vents on the dashboard so that as many as possible point right at her, "just let me know if it changes at all and, uhm, okay, Tylenol and a coffee and some Gatorade and, what else? Anything else?"

"No, hon. Don't you worry."—Can't blame him, not after what he'd walked into once they'd finally let him in. All said, as well, honest to goodness miracle there hasn't been one since then. Usually anything at all'll set one off, but, shit, been up in the mountains, down in the delta, along the gulf, Ozarks, and now desert, endless and free desert, and not once other than as prelude to blissful convalescence has anything bloomed. Lucky, lucky, but the sand is always trickling—

Door shuts behind him and he enters the store. Aura reaches over to the radio console, preemptively cuts the volume down, and switches it back on. Miniscule warble of wailing guitar, the inane noodling of a decade long forgone, forever forgiven, and rotting in its resurrection. Another twist of another knob to alter the station. Skipping over talk scrunched whispery, rat-a-tat rendered rattle, un-bottomed bombast, and jangle softened jingling until she finds a static place to settle. Once the fuzz is found, up again comes the volume and she closes her eyes dark in tandem with the whiteness of the noise—Cellophane crinkling cellophane, variation piled atop its variants, source smothered, sizzle of grease in the pan, gurgle of the coffee pot, the honest amplification of silence and the obvious pitter of pattering rain. Woke up to it, rain, outside, rain and a steady beep. Felt tied down and dizzy and then, because the static comes back, the rain gets louder and faster and darker and then it's all wash, then awake again this time with someone hovering above. Some lady scrubbed and distant, scratching pen on a pad and reading the story beeping inscrutable on the screens reading you and then it, remember, back into it all, static, wash, painless aching nothing, then:

"I've just got a few questions for you, sweetheart," and pressed her fingertips to shoulder, sending the body back into the bed. "If you could just answer them best you can, no need to search, just whatever comes first, alright?'

Must have then nodded in the affirmative or said '*uh-huh*' or '*yes'm.*'

"Alright then, can you tell me what year it is, hon?"

This year.

"Okay, good-good, and who is the president?"

Who cares? Where am I?

"Alright, can you tell me your name?"

What it's always been.

And then there were more pokes and prods and, "Have you had problems like this in the past? Anyone we can call? Family? Emergency contact? Anything?" Patter then was definitely rain. On the roof. Saw then the whole thing was makeshift, none of the walls met the ceiling, everything an approximation...

"Hey, where am I?"

"Mobile hospital unit, hon. Been in and out of consciousness for a few days now, dehydrated and, well, exhausted is all probably. Best we can tell is you had a seizure during the storm, bad timing."

"A what?"

"Seizure, a *tonic* seizure to be more specific." Scribbled then on her pad. "Though, could probably be even more specific suppose. Early observation it seemed to oscillate, tonic to atonic," broke at the increasing technicality, "means you were going stiff and then relaxing, very slow spasms of the muscles. I can explain further when you've–"

"Seizure?"

"Yes ma'am. Probably focal initially, but general as it progressed. Best guess as it stands now, need to run some–"

"No, I had a migraine. Headache. Really bad one." Words still hard to carve. "Had them since I was a–"

Scratched again on the pad, "Interesting and noted. But, alright, that may very well be, had them since you were a kid, chronic episodes, probably usually in times of stress? But, okay, lay back, hon. Safe here, don't need to get worked up–"

Tension crawling about shoulders. Heart kicking cold fear.

"–Shh, shh. Look, hon, Laura is it? Aura? Yes, sorry, Aura, listen: What you've interpreted as migraines could very well be something more along the lines of epilepsy. We'll have to run some further tests to confirm it and all. Definitely not the place for it right now, but, look we'll keep you under observation and, anybody we can call? Let them know that at least you're safe here and soon enough, week at the most, really depends on what clean-up is like, whole city is underwater, in and out is hard right now, but, okay, okay, okay–"

Laid there for just shy of a week, listening through the curtains between beds to the progression of disease: complaints of injury at first, all broken bones and weeping wounds, abscesses and tears, bloody. What followed were ailments, the outer elements and conditions finally manifesting themselves on the insides of the patients. Pneumonia and pleurisy, ear and sinus infections, unshakeable colds and, for more folks than expected, tremorous withdrawals. The quality of the scream or moan is different. A shoulder being reset or shin's break perfected pulls from the patient a sound entirely animal, easily shifting between rage and submission, whimper and hiss. The warning nature of a growl becomes obvious. Bared teeth rarely bite. But, when that stomach flu was being passed around starting on that fourth wakeful day, the sounds were undeniably human. They were weak and smothered in prostration, pleas against their unseen inner malfunctions directed constantly upward to something invisible and mute. All at language's softer inland edge until, finally, the day Derek's head popped smiling through the curtain, the complaints were at the level of nuisance. Ringworm and athlete's foot. Toothaches. Ringing in the ears. Allergies. General discomfort. Lethargy. Insomnia. Loneliness in the cotted crowd.

"Hey, babe!"

Grins shattered then across cheeks as arms came up and he bent down, doing his delicate damnedest to gather up what he'd been missing without tearing it away from its baroque trappings.

"I'm so glad you're okay," both at the same time pulling away then coming together in a kiss and again back together as close as possible without breaking the tethers.

"Did they say I can go? Can you take me–"

"Yeah, yeah." Said shifting a folder higher up under his arm, "Just talked to the nurse, said you were free and–"

"What's that there?" Pointed at the folder.

"Oh, it's, uhm, some charts or something. Doctor said they'd make an appointment with a specialist to get your headaches checked out, said you came in knocked-out cold and that–"

"Where?"

"What?"

"Where's the, when? When and where and–"

"No, no, no, don't worry. They've got it sorted. Told them your mom's address and they found something close to–"

"No, no, no, we can't go back to–"

"Don't you worry about that, we won't. Jawad gave me the contact for the hotel his family is at, up in Cortland County, no kidding, babe, storm brought the creek up so high our place is straight up gone, took that much of the riverbank with it," face screwed into that bunch he gets when he's trying to organize his thoughts, "it was hell getting out here, you'll see, it's crazy out there, but, damn, company came through and gave a solid severance to those of us that needed to pull out, that couldn't yet just relocate, it's all gone, you know? Bay's like, fuck man, all ocean from what I can tell but, anyway, look got enough to hole up in Cortland county for a while so we can just–"

"No!" Came gunshot. Silence for kick, then another round. Can't. Won't. Just. Let's "Go. Let's just go and never–"

So, now it's just desert. Static and still, all forever around–Shift and sound and the volume comes back down:

"Here babe," rattle of pills in a bottle, "got a whole bunch just in case."

Eyes open and the sky comes back bright and white. Searing dry heat. "Sleeping?"

"No, hon." Opens the bottle. Frustrates her thumb through the foil. Flicks the cotton ball to the floor. "Just relaxing is all."

Pulls out of the parking lot and back on the road. "Like it out here?"

Swallows two tablets dry, chases with scalding coffee. "I do."

"It's different isn't it?" Pavement opens westward and straight. Sign recites the distance to Vegas. "No water, no ocean. Just–"

The exact opposite. Shimmers now in her peripherals are nothing but certain mirage, distance and heat. Forever has its limits here. Everything is solid. "Could get used to it, reckon." Squints at the white sky.

"Could."

Reaches to turn the knob up, fuzz rising.

"Here," Derek says, "Let me find a station that's–"

"No, no." Stays his hand. "Leave it for a bit." Closes her eyes. Reclines the seat. Breathes in deep. Clinches her teeth.

&&&

"Here, here, cut the light off," her face shines slick and moony in the harsh blue. One hand wipes the stringy glisten away from her mouth, the other reaches across to cover the screaming diode. "Just cut it off a second–"

"Nah, nah, I was almost. I was almost there, babe."

Opens her mouth and wiggles her jaw. Rolls her neck. Pins the hair that's loosed back behind her ears. "Are you still recording?" Grabs the base and stands the falling up straight.

"Yeah, yeah, but we can cut all this. Just, I was almost there. Just, yeah, yeah, action or whatever–" Takes him up again–Hard to balance all this, that's what she's got to fucking understand. Can't just pretend, can't all be make-believe. Need the pop-shot, seen the comments on the last few, talk about how it looks fake. It is fake, but suspend your own disbelief you fucking creeps, but gotta make it look, goddammit, she's good at it that's for certain, no doubt there but, all this, gotta, see it's just that like the mind wanders anyway, all the time and at this point, Christ, almost hurts. Sure she's tired, totally get it. But, can't close your eyes, team effort there. She's got to look up at the light so that her eyes shine and all those fuckers on the internet can feel like she's looking right at them and–

"Watch the screen, B." She's up again. "Here, let's just, just cut the light off, cut the recording, just–"

"Alright, alright," pauses the recording. Rolls just a bit to reach off the bed for the charger cable. Drains the juice like it's sprung a leak when filming, especially with the light on and everything. Reaches up then in the new dark for where she's disappeared. "Here, come here, come here."

Descends then to his chest, laying atop him.

Wraps his arms and says, "I'm sorry, hon."

"I'm trying, B. I'm trying–"

"No, no, I'm the one that's trying. You're doing great, just–" Taste of that on the tongue, weird moment to get all paternalistic. Pat on the sweaty back, no, no, no, hon, it's me that's got to try. You still give great head. It's me that can't seem to fucking just goddamn, it's me that's the problem, babe, see? It's me that can't fucking cum on camera–

"Anything I can do different?"

"No. Just maybe give me a few minutes." Already going soft under her belly. Spit shellac running cold and gummy. "Kinda goes numb after too long, you know?"

"Yeah, I get it. Just need to have something to post by–"

"I know."

"It's no problem if you can't, you know. Can just get some yogurt or something like last time. Splice it in–"

Room around them is collapsingly dark. The depressive mess that had previously occupied it had installed black-out curtains on the two windows and painted the walls a similar hue to the navy blue of Buck's old work uniform. The decorations were sparse, few belongings other than a stack of used occult textbooks and a small collection of records. Occupying an opportune void...

"Don't worry either way," Obbie'd assured them as he dropped Jess's purse on the pristine, empty desk near the door, "they usually stay at the clinic for six weeks or so, sometimes more and, well, I guess no rush is what I'm saying. Get situated. Get comfy. Welcome home and welcome back." Lucky for the vacancy.

The only luggage they'd brought with them was Jess's purse and a big paper shopping bag full of clothes and travel amenities, all plucked from clothing drive bins or handed to them by the charity groups that flocked to the Depot during the days after. Everything else was lost. Buck'd said that then when they'd met Obbie at the terminal exit. Obbie'd asked, "That all?"

And Buck said, "Everything else is gone."

It was true. Flood swallowed the whole of their little neighborhood there along Murphy. Drowned all of Harris Park as well–Strange watching the news with everyone laying in their cots, constantly told what everyone already knows, recap of the disaster over and over and over again but the number never changed much. Rose the first few days. Three dead. Tons missing, but that dropped quickly. Less missing but only a few more dead, ten say. Weird feeling, seeing what it looks like in numbers every night further away from the life that it ruined. They don't serve as monument enough to the actual loss of a life, loss of a future moreover, because that's what it really comes down to. Still alive but it's the future that feels like it's gone. Even then though, once they settle, once it's what it will be in the books, what? One-fifty, was it? Finally settled on one-fifty direct dead, that's the term they use, direct dead because the whole fucking town is still underwater and doesn't look like it's not, never mind, but a solid chunk of that one-fifty is just Harris and the rest of Madiston's homeless, or maybe they aren't even counted because they maybe wouldn't have even been reported missing enough to die–

"No kidding," Obbie said then pulling out from the hug. "Well, fuck," reached out toward Jess, "at least let me carry *that* for you–" At least, at least... Paid for the bus, the plane, and now offering shelter... at least, at least...

The drive back Home was quiet. Jess conked out in the back seat, using the bag of clothes as a pillow. Buck and Obbie passed a spliff back and forth before they hit the interstate, then Buck chain-smoked the rest of the way. Hadn't had a cigarette one in the shelter–Too afraid maybe to ask anybody for some of the last of something they might soon lose the whole of–

Obbie broke the silence just before the exit that led Home, "You know, bro, at least you tried. Not many can, like, you know what I mean? Gave it a shot and, fucking natural disaster isn't your fault so like–"

"Nah, I know man. I know. Just, uhm–" Tried *what* exactly? Painted like three canvases. Then like fucking destroyed them or whatever, but that's *all* that got done. And that's all gone now. Bought those canvases, no joke, bought those canvases and paints and all that shit first week after moving in. Painted it all like, what? Two weeks after. Month in Madiston and all the work that was ever going to get done there was done. She'd ask, though, she'd ask, are they finished? And they never were, right? Never, just on and on and on never finished but never changing and, what if you hung them up at the coffee shop and sold them or whatever and then held off on getting a job so there would be time for painting, but there was never any painting after that! So, try *what* exactly? She started streaming when it became apparent you weren't going to work and then, *then* you went out, got the art museum gig, thought you'd get to meet some people then, but artists don't work at museums! They make art! So, what? Tried what exactly?–

Silence was broken again finally and further when Obbie pulled the car along the curb in front of a black and purple gothic-revival style house. Big wraparound porch. A turret. Riding the line between baroque and dilapidated. "Welcome to the Tel Megiddo," as they all exited. It'd had a different name last Buck was in town. That's how these co-ops are though, change names every so often. The Iron Bitch. Phenomenologist's Hideaway. The Speak. Café de Sade. Trust Fund Bounce Haus. Our Son, Dream. The Blind Eye.

Two weeks they've been here, not a moment of silence to spare. Even now as she nuzzles into the warmth of his neck, planting a kiss where there was before only sweat, there is the constant sound of a house being lived in. Bass from speakers in someone's room rattling the floorboards of everyone else's. Dishes clinking around in the sink. Water always running, always running somewhere. Flush through the old pipes. Television, laptops, phone, all speaking, clacking, laugh-tracking. Inane conversations about whose turn it is to do what, always something about something to be brought up at the next house meeting. Sound of fucking through the thin walls. And the ever-present patter of footfalls, creaking floors, opening and closing doors–You can hear them, they can hear you. Can't even take a shit without eavesdropping–

A little summer evening light leaks through a break in between the blackouts' leaves, cutting a column of sunset down her spine. Nuzzles further and his arms rise to take her full. A kiss there in the dark, slice of light igniting the shrinking space between them. A deep breath as it all dawns.

Hand down and around. A smile shines brazened bronze. "Ready again?"

From the bottom, where the light'll never manage to reach, where the pit of it all is still being dug: a hollow surge and foundering.

&&&

–Always something sticks around. Some stuck crumb that'll only soak to smear, that'll only concede under the truth of fingernail or steel wool. Unrisen fond or a burnt bit sunk to the stew's bottom where the metal gives over to fire–

She'd let it soak since the middle of the rush round lunch–Coming later and later though, isn't it? The rush. People all finding now that there's places they've got to be instead of places they can't go back to. Drier it gets the more they cling back toward the life that washed away. Sort of operation Pastor'd set up here redonning its designation as a social shame, line out along the sidewalk, a line now, no longer the clotted mass of hungry all out in the parking lot, sat on the blacktop, leaning on the pylons, set up like a picnic some of them in the grassy islands there after the mud'd finally given up, shorter and shorter the line though. Reckon for some people maybe saying you're hungry's worse than the pangs themselves. Won't have much longer at it here though, Pastor says, soon enough, once it's all clear, get a letter from the Fed talking about permits and all and y'all'll just have to shut on down. Can't afford the charity.

Seems though, things like Harris Park and the Cobbles, hell most of Murphy and, though there's some hope they'd said on the radio this morning, Riley's damned near sunk, sand all washed away, seems though that there are some places that'll never yet manage to dry out. All glisten morning pink glint on still water where there used to be cars and bars now trees leaning and buildings crumpled from soaked parsimony. Nowhere for the water to flow except back to sea, nowhere lower than here–The bottom. Another squeeze of the bottle sputs gurgling strands into the hot brown froth. Running out–Should have mentioned it to Pastor before he left, need some other things as well. Getting honestly to hate the smell, so may try for a different brand–

Small circles. Flecked clouds of foam in the wake of silver wool scrunched to a useless pill. Shareese cuts the scalding flow and drops the pot clattering into the sink's well. Wrist up to her forehead. Wipes the bloom away and rubs where a tension has risen between her brows. Small circles and breath–Could just let it soak overnight. Have to get in extra early tomorrow though, not enough stock in the fridge for a batch even if, tomorrow's Saturday so count on the line being a bit longer than today. Everyone with work again off again–Been sweating all day. She'd come in early this morning as every morning now, picked up by Pastor just as the sky broke for the day. Stepped from sleep out into the unwavering mug, slid into the passenger's seat of his forgone Sedan, crapped A/C blowing only dusty whispers about her cheeks.

"Good Morning, Miss Shareese." He'd said then as her wrist rose to her forehead to wipe the bloom away. "Ready for another day in paradise?"

"Certainly am, Sugar. Certainly am." Leaned back in her seat, pulling the little lever to recline a touch. Seat back meeting resistance from the sack of potatoes and onions piled behind, along the floorboards. Closed her eyes.

"Like some coffee, Shah?" Motioned then to the cup holders. Two paper cups, lidded, steam rising a thick finger in the surrounding swelter.

Her stomach rolled, "Oh thank you, hon. I'll just let it cool off before I–" Pulled then from the curb to make their way to the church.

Sundays Shah used to walk the distance, an easy path over a few modest streets. Businesses of the sort going steadily extinct beside her all along: Butchers and tailors, bookstores and hardware outlets, hole-in-the-wall restaurants. A right turn at the small public library and a pleasant enough doddle down several magnolia-and-willow lined residential blocks before the church rose, flattening a welcome clearing in the mounting arboreal clutter. Now though, those roads are closed, the shops and houses slowly growing out from the stubborn ebb of glass-faced floodwater. The way to the church grounds now is winding and wide, made to meander by orange plastic and sandbag barricades, incomprehensible signage, detours into ravaged wastes and a precarious stretch of road cut through a muddy sump threatening to renege on the remittance of its flow. But, the sanctuary still stands, in part and against all, spire as ever tall, aloft against the storm its fetish of man beheld.

Took one hell of a beating, though. Caught on its flank some monster of an oak ripped root and all from the earth by the squalling wind. Whole southern side of the thing collapsed inward. Beyond repair. Structural damage demanding demolition, a costly return to the foundation, which at this point Pastor and the regional synod can only hope isn't also shattered. Thank the water that loosed the earth enough to give the wind its still-living tree, though, that the spire was spared. Thank the rain, for the tempest's thunderous hurlings did their damnedest to bring it down burning.

"Should have someone down soon to yank that sucker out. Any day now." Pastor said as he kneed a sack of potatoes higher up against his chest. "Should be a sight to see."

–Whole thing'll probably come down then, held in balance for too long, completely unable to find its own footing. Knife in the chest, right? Knife in the chest, or anywhere probably the same principles apply. You leave it in there. Take it out it tears more wound away, starts everything bleeding again. That which causes the wound keeps the wounded alive–

Luckily, the Annex, sanctuary's squatted fraternal twin, with its kitchen and 'event space,' was spared the worst of it all. Once inside they'd set about the ordeal that'd become so recently routine: Potatoes relieved of their sack, dumped into the sink. Pastor rolling up his sleeves, faucet on, knife in hand. Wash. Halve what's small. Quarter what you can palm. Lengthwise and then cube what's too big. Poke out the eyes and, Shah'd been insistent here, leave the skin on. Didn't go through all the trouble of making a brown stock just to have the potatoes empty and naked of their value. If we're going to take care of people, we ought to really take care of them. That's why he'd called her in the first place. He'd said any number of the church ladies still in town could make a soup or a stew or what have you, any number of them would have been perfectly willing to, mind, to feed the masses but only you, Miss Shareese, I know would be keen on committing to providing real *nourishment.* To that she heartily agreed, under the condition of course that he wash the potatoes and cut the onions. While he washed, Shah set about browning the meat to build the fond, bottom up, layer by layer, that sticky caramel richness that is responsible for the depth of flavor she renders out of nothing but ordinary vegetable and bone. It is this fond, however, that is ultimately responsible for making the task of cleaning the pot one of such Herculean nature.

–Damn stuff just won't come up. Can't leave to soak overnight though, gotta get a stock started first thing. Hate that that's how it'll be, can't rush a stock but, well, hard to keep track of how much ought to be made when the line is so unpredictable. Best policy now, best policy now moving forward–Drags her wash-soft fingernail along the pot's inner rim, scraping away what she can. A silvery wake and knuckling ache. Soap burning where the wash-wear has carved canyons into her fingers–Make more than enough. Stuff keeps a long time, so just make a whole bunch, right? Maybe do bigger portions if possible, serve bigger portions. Yeah? Don't know. Difficult to say. Would just be easiest to, of, who knows, would just be easiest if something didn't always stick around, be easiest if the water would do its work and just wash it all away–

"Hey! Wh–!" Pot clatters and splashes sudsy as something sudden takes her by the knees. "What the, Oh heavens! It's–!"

Little curly head pressed against her thigh and within the instant the little one is up in her arms. Not a word as the salty swell rises in her eyes and mingles with kisses over his cheeks. Belly laugh, that wonderful little belly laugh, hiccoughing chuckle of shook joy, and he settles then over her shoulder, soft hands digging at her shirt collar, squeezing out all the hug she's got to offer.

Winnie situated now and Shah wipes from her eyes the teary blur. Kitchen comes back and standing in the doorway, hair pulled tight in a bun, green scrubs, is an exhaustion-eyed but sterling-smiled Tash Jones, Winnie's mother. "Pastor said you wouldn't mind if we dropped by and–"

"No, no, hon." Quivering against the rising corner of her mouth brings then another flood of joy, "Not at all, sugar. You come here!" And Shareese's arm stretches out to guide her across the kitchen, taking Tash into her chest. "Been worried sick about you two. Tried calling I don't know how many times. Don't you ever–" Had just taken for granted that everything had been, well, that whatever was stuck to the bottom was all there was ever going to be anymore–

Away from the hug, looking up at her, Tash: "Trust me, Auntie, we would've come by sooner. He's been asking every day after you. Been telling him that we'd come see you soon, when I get off work, when I–"

"No, no, don't apologize, hon. Just–"

"Been a nightmare. They've got most of us down at the Depot still. In trailers and these mobile units, like a war zone. Shah, everyone is sick all the time. *Been* sick, this is just the first time they've had a doctor around and, it never, it never stops. Always, always there's an emergency and–"

"Never will, baby. I don't think. Whole world is sick." Resituates Winston.

"Don't I know it... Anyway, we finally, uhm, finally had some time to–"

"Well, hon, I'm awfully sorry then that we've run out of stew today or I would make you something to–"

"No. No, Miss Shareese. Don't worry over us. No, look here, we wanted to, well, I should say *Winnie* wanted to bring you something–" Holds up then a white paper bag, bottom splotched with the sort of grease stains that can only portend of something fried and sweet and necessary.

End.

MADSTONE

295

ABOUT THE AUTHOR

K Hank Jost writes fictions. He believes language is the only remaining commons, and through its meaningful deployment all lost commons may be rendered fresh. In the beginning was the Word: from a New Word, a New Beginning.

His short story collection, *Deselections*, was released by Whisk(e)y Tit in 2022. *MadStone* is his first published novel. Hank is the Editor-in-Chief of the quarterly literary journal *A Common Well Journal*.

ABOUT THE PUBLISHER

Whisk(e)y Tit is committed to restoring degradation and degeneracy to the literary arts. We work with authors who are unwilling to sacrifice intellectual rigor, unrelenting playfulness, and visual beauty in our literary pursuits, often leading to texts that would otherwise be abandoned in today's largely homogenized literary landscape. In a world governed by idiocy, our commitment to these principles is an act of civil service and civil disobedience alike.

www.ingramcontent.com/pod-product-compliance
Lightning Source LLC
Chambersburg PA
CBHW060906210726
48293CB00006B/1978